THE HARBINGER OF ELEMDALE

Southern Lore—Tales of Elemdale: Book One

BEBO FRANKLIN

A NOTE FROM THE AUTHOR

This book starts in the Llano Estacado (translated into English as the Staked Plains), a region encompassing eastern New Mexico and northwestern Texas, during July of a drought year.

Post Civil War, the United States Congress seized an opportunity to dispense with two groups it found troublesome—Indians and nominally freed African Americans. They created six Black regiments, known as the buffalo soldiers, and pitted them—one oppressed people against another—in the most direct way possible: war. During what is now solemnly referred to as the Staked Plains Horror, buffalo soldiers (and one White buffalo hunter) perished in the name of duty: guarding mail routes, protecting territory, hunting down raiders, and chasing outlaws and thieves. But it wasn't duty that killed them. It was thirst.

Elzi Dupre is my buffalo soldier.

This book may kick off in 1877, but *The Harbinger of Elemdale* is really a story that I originally saw come to life set in the 1990s, a time I enjoyed as a teen. The main character was Frankie Bowman. As I teased out his story, as well as the other characters and the history of the town of Element Dale itself, things started to blossom. It shifted and morphed forward and back in time until I realized I had a series on my hands. So the original lines I wrote will not be found in these pages. They will appear in a subsequent book.

I also never set out to write historical fiction. I still don't claim this novel to be one. I will say that I absolutely adore the research portion of this whole writing gig. (See Historical Notes included at the end.) I've learned so much about history, about humanity, about life in general—and try to slip a bit of it in here and there. But it's really fiction with a light dusting of a few real and true events and people. So don't get too caught up in dates and historical inaccuracies.

I tell you now of the Buffalo Soldier Tragedy of 1877 to get your headspace where it needs to be for this book. It's a Southern Gothic novel of suspense. Readers will leave this work metaphorically scathed by tragedy, violence, destitution and decay, oppression, corruption, tainted religion, and of course the relentless cruelty of nature. There is also a supernatural edge to it. That bit took me stretching my idea of serious writing; however, that stretch brought me to Elzi Dupre. For him alone, I have a newfound reverence for the gravitas that can be found in writing the stories of souls past. While Southern Gothic literature strives to highlight the faded elegance and facade of respectability of the Deep South, there is a beauty here—unique and powerful—a charm and charity that can be intimately understood by the Southerner. I too hope that shines through the ruins of these pages.

Bebo Franklin

A postscript in the form of an excerpt
By character Jeryl Larson

[. . . before you dive on into the pages, babydoll, first a warning: We've preserved the antiquated and offensive language of the time, along with peculiarities of spelling and punctuation. I argued this point with Lucillia, but she would only come back with, well, if Elzi and I had to live through it, the least you could do is let me write it. I can relate, I suppose. Some of these words are the words of folks who lived long ago, before some knew any better, or before some knew but held tight to their roots, as rotten as they may have been. Having left you with this assertion, let us begin, darlin'.

Warmest regards.]

This is my way of informing you that this book is for mature audiences and some may find the language, scenarios, and general crass nature of the time and characters offensive. If you struggle with violence (physical and/or sexual), racial slurs, death and suicide, religious digs, foul language, alcohol and/or drug use, etc., this may not be the book for you.

THE HARBINGER OF ELEMDALE

A PLAYLIST BY

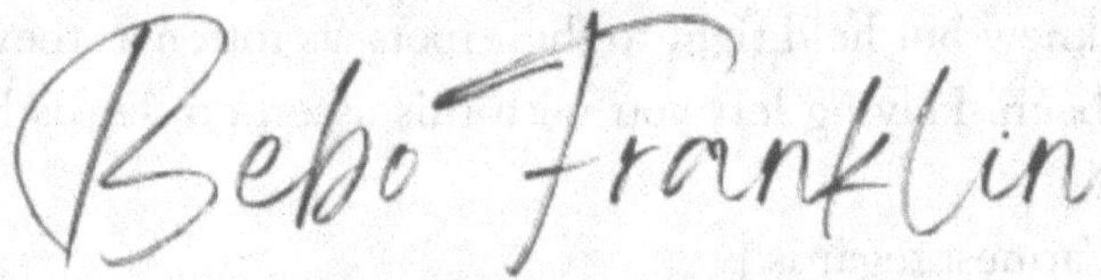

No Shoes (2:24)
John Lee Hooker

On the Run (5:06)
The Jompson Brothers

Crucify Your Mind (3:19)
Rodriguez

Blue Side of the Mountain (3:27)
The SteelDrivers

A Life to Fix (4:00)
The Record Company

Colors (6:23)
The Black Pumas

Only Prettier (3:07)
Miranda Lambert

Texas Sun (4:12)
Leon Bridges

Bringin' Home the Rain (6:36)
The Builders and the Butchers

Harvest Moon (2:39)
Bedlam

All the Time (3:55)
Bahamas

Life by the Drop (2:27)
Stevie Ray Vaughan

See That My Grave is Kept Clean (2:50)
Gatemouth Brown

THE HARBINGER OF ELEMDALE

CONTENTS

For The Fisherman

CAST OF CHARACTERS

ELEMENT DALE, TEXAS, from 2023

Jeryl Larson, editor for *The Southern Press*
Lucillia Baldwin, writer, recluse
Gregory Peters, founder and editor in chief of *The Southern Press*

THE STAKED PLAINS, TEXAS, from 1877

Elzi Dupre, private, U.S. Army Tenth Calvary buffalo soldier
Albin Banks, buffalo soldier, Elzi's best friend
The Commander, U.S. infantry commander of the African American
(buffalo soldier) regiments
The Captain, U.S. Army Tenth Cavalry captain of Troop A
Jasper, buffalo soldier
Isaac, buffalo soldier
Thomas, buffalo soldier
Luke, buffalo soldier
Henry Ossian Flipper, second lieutenant, U.S. Army
Indian of Black and Bones, rogue Hadacho Indian

Henry Hadiku (Blackbird), rogue Hadacho medicine man (conna)
Ora B. Dupre (Baroness of the Catacombs), Voodoo priestess from NOLA, Elzi's birth mother
Irving Whitewing (Baron of the Catacombs), Elzi's birth father, Hadacho medicine man (conna)

EMPIRE STATE OF THE SOUTH (GEORGIA)

Dixon (Dix) Artope, almost physician, attended defunct medical school
Dr. Eddington Locke, chair of the Anatomy Department at Southern Physio-Eclectic School of Medicine
Trent Miller, fellow medical student
Mary Lamott, cadaver
George Lamott, her husband
Caroline (Chuck) Higgs-Colley, widow of Davis Colley
Dr. Geoffrey Hamilton, psychotherapist
Thomas Higgs, father of Caroline Colley, Higgs Plantation owner
Mary Higgs, deceased wife of Thomas, mother of Caroline and Minnie
Minnie Higgs, sister of Caroline
Octavia Kassoula, Geechee refugee, house woman of Thomas Higgs
Mable, Caroline's childhood imaginary friend
Henrietta Moss-Artope, best friend of Caroline
Martha Moss, mother of Henrietta
Buford (Ford) Artope, husband of Henrietta, brother of Dixon; surveyor for Texas Railroad Commission
James and Margaret Artope, parents of Ford and Dix
Lawton and Claire Phillips, hotel proprietors
Donald Akers, Georgian hotelier, father of Claire Phillips
Dr. Josephus McNally, quack druggist and physician

THE OLD NORTH STATE (NORTH CAROLINA)

Walker Westberry, third-generation moonshiner
Sam Westberry, moonshiner, Walker's younger cousin
J.P. Westberry, blockader, Sam's older brother
Westberry Twins, lookouts
Nadene Westberry, moonshiner, Walker's cousin-wife
Waylon Westberry, moonshiner, deceased, Walker's pa
Willard Westberry, moonshiner, deceased, Walker's peepaw

SUGAR STATE/CREOLE STATE (LOUISIANA)

Byron Banks, deceased, Albin's twin brother
Hattie Mae Belgrave, Elzi's girlfriend
John and Edmee Godwin (Pa and Maymee), Elzi's adoptive parents
Pastor Grimes, Calgary Baptist Church

ELEMENT DALE, TEXAS, FROM 1880

Clifton and Paulette Nelson, owners of Nelson Inn and Nelson Post
and Shipping
Samuel Nelson, their child
Elmer Nelson, deceased child of Clifton and Paulette, entombed at
Catacombs of Hadacho Hills
Anna Olan, deceased mother of Paulette Nelson, entombed at
Catacombs of Hadacho Hills
Sterling, well-digger, mute
Reverend Nathan Forrest, former pastor of First Baptist Church of
Elemdale, deceased
Wrath, feathered hound of Hell

SOUTHERN ROOTS

Lord, help me dig into the past,
And sift the sands of time,
That I might find the roots that made
This family tree mine.
Lord, help me trace the ancient roads,
On which my fathers trod,
And led them through so many lands,
To find our present sod.
Lord, help me find an ancient book,
Or dusty manuscript,
That's safely hidden now away,
In some forgotten crypt.
Lord, let it bridge the gap that haunts
My soul, when I can't find
The missing link between some name
That ends the same as mine.
—Anonymous

JERYL LARSON

September 1, 2023
Element Dale, Texas

Lucillia Baldwin's voice quavers with the exhaustion of time. She looks straight ahead, rocking in her chair on the old porch, and answers, "My best friend is dead. And not like how you come to know a person more deeply over the years and then one day death comes a-knocking and the friendship is a mere memory. No, he was—*is* my best friend who just so happens to *be* dead. Always has been. Well, in my lifetime, anyhow."

Mmm-wait. What? I follow up for clarity. "Always has been your best friend?"

"Always has been *dead*," she replies, looking me straight in the eyes.

If you're confused so far, Dear Reader, you're not alone. I sat next to this woman on her front porch for many hours, this woman who seemed of sound mind, quick in wit, funny, articulate in her—what I'm going to call—signature Southern speak. Her weathered skin reveals long hours working outdoors. Her hair is pulled into a large, low bun. It is dark, mostly black, with streaks of wiry silver cutting through. Her eyes are bright and piercing, though interestingly two different colors: one the clearest blue, the other a dark green. Her voice shakes slightly, as one might expect of a woman in her eighties. But her surety and soundness of mind, I somehow do not question. Even though I fear I probably should.

My reason for being here, my mission, is to somehow talk this woman into fulfilling her writing contract with us. Technically, she's missed her deadline—and not by a little. Years. She owes the publication either the promised novel or the paid advance. They assigned Ms. Baldwin to me with the instruction to either get the book or the money, preferably the book as it would no doubt be profitable for *The Southern Press*. And I am to do so within the next six months. But, honey, Ms. Baldwin doesn't like to be pushed or prodded, doesn't like to do anything on anyone's terms but her own. And she's clearly lonely, so I visit with her regularly, hoping each visit builds a little more trust—and gets me closer to getting "the book."

Once when we were having drinks on her front porch, she'd lifted her glass and held it just above head high, the sunlight breaking through it, as if she knew this secret; that if one wished to look directly into the sun, he need only eye it through a prism of whiskey, which then I realized hers was a whiskey lacking ice. Today I decide to comment on as much.

"No ice for you?" I ask, trying desperately not to wrinkle up my nose. (I know my thoughts flash across my face like the lights of Broadway. It's a curse. What can I say? I'm an expressive thinker.) I am fully ready to hop up and retrieve some from her kitchen, should she so allow me the honor of entering her little cabin.

She responds with a bit of incredulity. "Ice? Nah. Comforts such as ice just intensify a person's perception of the heat, especially come Ju-ly. I'd just assume face reality. When it's damn hot, ice don't change that," she says very matter of fact. Her spotted and veined hand tips back the glass. A little belch escapes. She then places it on the small, old wooden milk crate between us. She leans over her armrest and picks up the bottle stashed behind the back leg of her chair.

Face reality, huh? I think.

She eyes my glass and declares, "You ain't big on whiskey, I see," then pours two fingers into her own. When Ms. Baldwin had offered me a "Texas Tea" upon sitting down with her, I fully expected a cocktail with a Southern twist. What I was handed was a glass of fire, no ice, certainly no tea.

I force a sip, the liquid biting my tongue. "Oh, heavens." I force the swallow. "Ms. Baldwin—"

She holds up a crooked finger. "You can just cut the Missus shit, you hear? Lu will do." She isn't exactly irritated, but certainly has no desire to beat around any bush.

I reply, "Okay, then. Lu. Lu, you're clearly a beautiful writer. We'd love to see more of it, to publish more of it. We—*I* am just curious as to your current work, how it's going."

The Southern Press has been attempting to get in touch with the elusive Lucillia Baldwin for some time, as in more than six years, since she accepted the advance for a promised book. When I was assigned as her new editor—the last had completely thrown in the towel, defeated by Lu's cynicism and disregard—I started by reviewing everything she had produced so far. Actually, since my first introduction to her gritty and compelling works, I've dreamed about meeting her. I remember, I was just out of college and absolutely ob-sessed with alumna Gregory Peters, one of this publication's founders and its first editor in chief. A former Harvard Lampoon writer myself, I tracked his career closely, applied for an internship at *The Southern Press*, and spent the last six months of that year working like a dog. And I loved every minute of it. I only saw Mr. Peters a handful of times. I was merely an intern, but he never treated me as anything less than a fellow professional. (Though I did catch him side-eyeing my wardrobe selection a time or two.) But it was when Ms. Baldwin's short story "Don't Water Down the Whiskey" came to my desk for proofreading that year that my

Cap'n took a lot with him. The five of us kept pretty well together at first. But now it be just me, Albin, Jasper, and Luke. Isaac, he disappeared in the night. I tried once to yell for him, but my voice cannot. I'd say, of the five of us, he seem the most demoralized by the whole ordeal, talkin' often about what it would feel like to take a shot to the head. What you might feel for just a bit before the lights go out. To be so thirsty, he sho seem to talk without end. Talked about his dog, talked about fishing the Big River. Which thinkin' of the river make me wanna shed tears, though I ain't got a one to lose. Then he took to talking about our hero, Flipper. He say, "Ain't never thought one of us would be no officer. But he sho is." This made me smile. But only on the inside. My lips cannot take a smile. They blistered, cracked, caked with something I do not know.

We stopped walking. We pretty much played out. Even though when we did walk, we walked like the dead, the pounding of my heart was the only thing reminding me that I weren't dead. I figured when I leaned up against this mesquite that my heart would ease up a bit, but it still thinking I'm walking—or running. Slow down, mighty heart.

I'd give anything to sweat, to feel something cool on my skin, on my tongue. I bet if Hattie was here, she'd bring me a big ole glass a cold tea. She'd let the sweat off the glass drip on my foehead and give me a gentle blow with her sweet breath to cool the drops. She'd put the glass to my lips, and I'd pull in the ice-cold drink and feel it trickle like an icy waterfall down my throat and to my stomach. Oh, I wouldn't wish Hattie here in these dunes of dirt. But I sure wouldn't mind to seeing her once more. Maybe one more kiss. She wouldn't too much take to this heat or to the tireless vulture that's followed us from lakebed to lakebed, from trail to trail. He's waitin' on death. To pluck out our eyes. Eyes too dry and dirt-filled to be worth plucking if you ax me. But he been circling, waiting.

I see you, bird.

I'm thinking it's been maybe eighty-two hours or so since we been having any water to drink. And we ain't moved from our new camp since yestahday. Albin found us a mesquite bush. Good sign—the curiosity about her began to mount. If you've not read the works of Ms. Baldwin, let me tell you, honey, she writes just as she takes her whiskey. Straight up. I was enthralled.

Sadly, each attempt to learn more about her fell short. After some time, I just had to let it go. I have a life, you know.

Then, some years later, her file landed on my desk. My new client. Lucillia Baldwin. I remember my stomach twisting with excitement and dread all at once. I was doomed to fail for certain, just as past editors had. But I cannot lie, I loved the idea of being *the one* that got the novel out of her.

I had hoped to learn a bit about her through my research, since I finally had a few more details about her from the file. That fell completely flat. The woman is virtually invisible, I tell you, as in her personal life is nonexistent to the public eye. Nothing exists aside from her past published essays, an anthology of shorts, and a book of poetry, all now decades old. Reclusive and contrary as she may be, her work did well for *The Southern Press*, so they somehow talked her into a contract for a novel. And voilà, here we are.

I'd heard she refused interviews time and time again and ignored any and all literary recognition she received. There is no phone number for her. I'm finding that, in these modern times, she may very well be the only person in this country without an email address. (Good lord, can you imagine?) My snail-mailed letters went unanswered time and time again. I had all but given up. Getting an interview with Lucillia Baldwin seemed the most difficult, impossible thing in the world. Then . . . the easiest. One glorious day, I received this in the post:

My dear editor,
I expect the sun to burn off these clouds this weekend. It's been hiding as of late, and this drab

weather is no good for the joints. Being as such, I intend to show my appreciation on my front porch in the company of my two beloveds. My afternoon will likely be devoted to a mean read, but should you wish to stop by, well, that'd be mighty fine.

I've enclosed directions. Don't come after 7 in the evening time. It's rude.

Sincerely,

Lucillia Baldwin

Guys, she called me dear.

After driving for what felt like miles out in the middle of nowhere, certain I'd gone too far, I finally spot the turnoff to her place. I ease down a long and winding dirt road, glimpsing reflections off the river from time to time in between the trees. Her entrance is just as she'd described: two shaggy cedar posts topped with one that spanned the distance between the two. Two chains hang limp where a sign had once been. Drab really. My words, not hers.

I make my way down this old dusty road and pull up to what I can only describe as something from another time—or has rather the remnants of the past scattered about, as if throwing them in a proper trash bin is just not an option. The yard—if you wish to call it that—is merely dirt with so many items that the longer I study the area, the more items come into my view: rusted-out wheelbarrows, makeshift shelters for (I'm assuming) either the chickens or goats milling about, car parts and rotted tires (though I spot no car), gardening tools, milk jugs, paint brushes submerged in coffee cans of I don't know what, two broken ladders, rusted forty-gallon drum barrels—so much more. To the east of the house sits a garden with wire fencing around it. To the west, a fence-like wall of cut wood stacked almost five feet high and spanning a good forty feet. A tree stump with an ax imbedded, just as you see in the movies, stands just ahead of the wall of stacked wood.

Ms. Baldwin rises from her chair on the porch as I park my car. I step out and am aggressively greeted by the clucking chickens I scattered as I drove through. It is shocking how their innocent curiosity ramps into an almost threatening approach. From the porch she yells out to just "Come on through, now. They'll get out your way, sure enough." She isn't smiling and has a tone as if irritated by my reluctance to step through the teeming fowl.

I tiptoe up the four steps, constructed simply of stacked cinderblocks, checking back to make sure I'm not soon to fall victim to a poultry ambush. When I reach out to shake her hand, she waves me off, focused on backing up to sit back down in her chair.

"Have a seat," she says. "Some outfit you got there."

"Um . . . *thank you?*"

"Texas Tea for ya?"

I take my position in the rusted sky-blue metal chair that sits adjacent to hers, an upturned wooden crate serving as our side table. I pull out my notebook and pen as she fills two glasses sitting atop the crate.

It is difficult for me to reconcile the woman sitting next to me with the writings I had admired for so many years. This elderly Southern recluse, now bending down to pick up a coffee can with which to spit tobacco of some sort—chew or dip I believe people call it. This woman whom, after hours and hours of visits on this very front porch, I'd learned lived in this little house on her own for as long as she could remember. She had told me, "I learned to fend for myself as a little girl with the help of two unlikely men: one homeless, one dead—both invisible to the folks of this shit town." She claimed Lucillia Baldwin was the name given to her by, quote, *the woman who did nothing but dump me from her rotten womb into this hell of a life.*

Again, Dear Reader, odd I know. Just stick with me.

Attempting to steer the conversation to something less . . . dementia-esque, I ask, "But what of the rest of your family?"

"What of 'em?"

"Your mother abandoned you. Who raised you?"

"I raised myself," she answers, again somewhat incredulously, as if I'm dense. She's mulling it over. "Well now, that ain't entirely true," she recants. "I spent my baby years with a preacher and his wife. Then, when I was about two or three, the church found me a foster family. They brought me up till I's six." She leans over, spits in the can, then wipes clean her chin with the back of her hand.

"What happened when you were six?" I ask.

"Goddammit. I thought we were here to talk about writing. I don't want to talk about kid stuff. Let's just say they were just like the rest of the folks in this . . . shit . . . town." She eyes me for a moment then says, "And you can un-purse those prissy lips anytime, Mister."

"Well."

I soften my face as best I can, but she is a challenge, to say the least. If I ask to talk about writing, she dodges and talks about life. If I ask to talk about her life, she dodges and talks about writing. Most questions land me a side eye, a scoff. And they definitely all irritate her. Sometimes she just stands up and shuffles to the door, completely dismissive. With her back to me, she'll wave me off, her hand making a large swatting motion behind her back like I'm some kind of gnat.

Today she snaps without warning, "I s'pose I'll see you next time."

The front door slams behind her. I am left to myself on the porch, save the lone goat standing aloof on the cinderblock steps, chewing a never-ending bite of whatever it is goats eat.

"Mmm-kay. Warmest regards to you too, Lu."

ELZI DUPRE

Summer 1877
The Staked Plains of the Taysha State (Texas)

*We been roaming this Great American Desert under the ruthless
Southern sun and cloudless sky from one dry lakebed to the next. I
done crawled on my hands and knees like a dog past skel'tons of
buffalo, licking drops of morning dew from what few blades of grass
they is. Now we walked so far that those blades of grass just turned
into red dirt. We was once huntin' Indians. Now . . . we huntin' water.*

*I ain't got no problem with Indians, so to speak. I mean, they ain't
done nothing to me as of late. But I couldn't no more take it back there
at post. Fat pig, the Commandah, hates Indians—and niggers alike, he
say. Two strikes for me. F'get him. The Army's one thing—I's proud to
serve, be a buffalo soldier an' all, make my thirteen dollahs a month.
But when they ax who wants to join this troop and go find these
Comanches, I wished I'd said I weren't missing no Comanche and just
kept to myself. But I's itching for a bit of adventure, I s'pose—and to get
out from unna Commandah's thumb. I think now I'd much prefer the
Commandah's wrath than to commence to falling out like the others in*

this broiling heat. We been 'bout eighty-two hours or so without water. I done watched men drink they own piss, they horse's piss. The worst of 'em went plum mad, slit they own wrist hoping for some sort of refreshment from the blood to quench the thirst.

I did like the man—the Cap'n, that is. He was very much kind, and funny. But he seemed distracted sometimes by the burden of sorrow— lost his wife earlier this year, I hear'd—and I think pride from failing this very expedition the year before. That's what some of the mens say. He was a man intent on completing his mission of finding those Indians at all costs. And cost it did.

I ain't never been as hot and thirsty as I been these past days. I believe it's been about eighty-two hours or so that we ain't had no water. And though the nights are a break from the sun, it's hard to not drink all ya got. But dem's the rules. You always fill your canteen before leaving water, and you always ration.

One night a few of the guys and the First Sergeant took to drinking brandy that the buffalo hunters brought along. Kind of a way of forgetting the worries once the sun went down and stopped beatin' on ya, but that just made things worse. They ought to have know'd better. But a man can be some kind of stupid in tough times. Next morning, the hangover caught and they took to guzzling what was left in their canteens. They's fresh outta water right from the start. When we arrived for Cedar Lake to replenish our supply, we had to dig out the mud to get for any water. Cap'n came undone in a fit of rage at the sight of a empty lake with the skel'tons of buffalo scattered about. And when the First Sergeant suggested we all turn back, Cap'n demoted him for allowing the mens to not have provisions and getting us in this mess in the first place.

Truth is, Cap'n got turned around. That's what I think. And then he made to trusting a former Comanchero, acting as a trail guide for the buffalo hunters. That Comanchero steered us every which way but wet. We walked this trail and that trail, dropping men, horses, mules, provisions, and sanity along the way. Them Comanches set out to win and I think they intended on using thirst as they weapon.

We thought drinking muddy water was bad. Then we thought the piss was bad. Yestahday morning one more a our horses fell out. We all stood there in a circle surrounding the thing, just staring down, seeming—well, just lost. It laid there on its side, big puffs of red dirt clouds billowing about its face as it panted. I's thinking we should just put it out its mis'ry. It never shoulda been here no how. Just a discard from the White reg'ment. No doubt more than ten, eleven years old. Finally, a trooper called Jasper bent down and slit its throat, the kind thing to do. But then, well . . .

I've always been part Indian, part Negro. Now I guess I'm also part vampire. I had to fight for that drink of blood. There weren't no patiently waiting your turn for a swallah neither. Jasper pulled out his canteen to try and fill it, blood running everywhere but in the opening. One of dem buffalo hunters come up and kicked him hard in the back, clear out the way. That man dropped to his knees, lapping up that thick blood straight from the cut like a wild animal. We becomin' crazed. And now we can't no more eat. Mouth too dry to chew and swallah the venison we brought along. Tongues fat and hanging. I believe we done been 'bout eighty-two hours with no water to drink. Albin, he done lost his hearing. Never knew a man needed water to hear, but sho'nuff, he can't no more. And skin so gray.

Most these mens have taken off somewheres else. Cap'n split us up, thinking we'd have a better chance of finding water. Most the bison hunters think Cap'n a joke and gonna get us all killed. They prolly right. They took off. Cap'n sent me and Albin with Jasper and two other soldiers out ahead to see if we cain't find water and report back. Cap'n say, "You find any water, you boys give off a shot. You hear?" We ain't needed no gun, though there's been talk of just taking one to the head and calling it done.

I count somewheres about eighty-two hours or so since I had any water. When we set out, we's about sixty of us, soldiers and hunters. The troop had forty-five horses and seven mules—or maybe it was forty-seven horses and five mules. Our group has none, as we had to sacrifice our last to thirst. The bison hunters took off on they own way.

mesquite bush. Only thang eats mesquite beans is the mustang. Mustangs don't venture no mo' than three miles from water. So we gots to be close. Albin throwed his saddle blanket up on the low branches for shade. Isaac done took off, I s'pose. Hattie wouldn't much like it here, but I sure would like to have a drink a her tea. I asked Albin if he been seeing the black bird. He don't pay me no mind, though. I see him slapping hisself upside the head as if to knock som'in loose. Jasper been taking a good long nap. I don't see how, in this heat. I cain't sleep till the sun go down. The saddle blanket just give us enough shade for our heads. I think it's comin' up on eighty-two hours or so since we filled our canteens.

The sun startin' to burn out for the day. And I can smell the wind. It smell foul at times, like death, old blood. This evening I smell bits of water. Maybe it gonna rain. Maybe God feelin' bad enough for letting so many perish. Or maybe he just pity us stupid soldiers. Or maybe not. Maybe that water I smell is a tease, a punishment. What'd I do? Let me think. Maybe I shoulda just said I ain't lost no Comanche when I's axed to go help find 'em. And I smell that bird. He decided to come in for a closer look, peering at me with dem beady eyes. Landed right on top of Jasper's foot. Jasper done kicked off his boots and pants during the day. That turkey vulture perched on his socked foot. Army ain't wise to give us wool to wear in the summer months. But who we to complain? Army give us thirteen dollahs a month, and medical, and food. They give me a uniform of the U-nited States Army—I wear it with pride.

My pants is stiff with horse blood and dirt. And flies—I give up shooing them off, waiting for sunset and them to trade shifts with the skeetas. I think maybe the skeetas can just make a meal of the blood on my pants and skip the biting. Though Jasper be easier to bite, his legs bare and all. I ain't got the energy to shoo that bird off his feet no more. Each time, he just makes to fly away and lands again right on Jasper's foot. I axed Albin to shoo 'em off but he too busy trying to clean out his ear with a piece a twig. We three make pitiful scarecrows.

I'm not sure where the gun went. If it was in my lap, I'd surely *shoot that beady-eyed buzzard right off Jasper's foot. He'd wake up from his nap then. Probably go to swinging at me. And I bet Albin would be happy to hear that shot, hearing som'in, anything. And Hattie would say cheers and give me a drink a her cold tea. I's thinking it's been somewheres about eighty-two hours since she gave me a drink a tea. Or was it eighty-two hours since Isaac went to go get us a glass a water? Or maybe Isaac did get some water and already brought it back but we was sleepin' and missed him. And where did Luke go? This bird must be here to send me a message from Isaac that he gone come back and refill my glass a tea. Or maybe it be from Luke.*

All this time we's really s'pose to be looking for Indians. They think we out here hunting Comanches. But we's hunters of water. Water hunters. Not Indian hunters. Comanches didn't steal my hides nor my horses, nor take my scalp or my friend's scalp. Yet here I am. Hunting Indians—no, hunting water. Tomorrow when I wake it'll be prolly about ninety-three or maybe ninety-fo' hours since I had a drink a water. I'll not care to locate no Indian. But I'd kindly take a kiss a Hattie's cold tea.

DIXON ARTOPE

Southern Physio-Eclectic College of Medicine
The Empire State of the South (Georgia)

Dix Artope spent his twenty-first birthday sweating over the grave of one Mrs. Mary Lamott. It was not how he envisioned his final weeks of medical college, digging up his seventh body. But a future doctor's got to do what a future doctor's got to do.

The Southern Physio-Eclectic Medical College was none too different from other medical colleges of the late nineteenth century. Owned by two well-meaning physicians hoping to educate the next generation of healers, its opening boasted excitement among the town's citizens, faculty, and students. Although the state made liberal appropriations to neighboring colleges during this boom of medical institution openings, it was student tuitions and outside individual grants that funded Southern Physio's various departments, filled the libraries with resources, and furnished the medical school with the supplies required for its anatomical museum. It could not be said that the school was exactly financially thriving. A boost in money to address much-needed repairs would have been nice, but it held its own, even with the shortage of legal cadavers. That is until its eleventh year.

For its ten-year anniversary, the college hosted a grand celebration—a gala—in part to commemorate its tenth birthday, in part to announce its progressive decision to increase its student population by admitting women into the program, a decision the dean and administrator felt would put the school on the map as a historical step into the future of medicine (and generate additional much-needed funds). The guest turnout was excellent. The gala featured a lavish meal of pork chops and rosemary potatoes. Guests wore their finest attire, waltzed graciously and gracefully, all with the expectation of making their donations. However, it became apparent that the town council and private investors were none too happy to hear of women entering as equals and felt the school went a step too far when the dean hopped up on the stage and introduced its first two female students without so much as a warning, much less an ask.

The whispers of leaned-in heads were only the beginning of the supporters' rejection of this announcement. Within a year, the college's decision to allow "any fee-paying student"—meaning female—entry into the school became a point of contention among the owners and faculty as it was adamantly opposed by organized medicine. Tensions grew. Students withdrew. New applicant numbers fell to an all-new low. The appeal to private benevolence fell short, and the school began scrambling to support what students remained. Supplies dwindled, and the procurement of anatomical material became a weighty challenge.

The chair of the anatomical department, Dr. Eddington Locke, had gone toe-to-toe with the dean demanding supplies and was told, "You can't squeeze blood from a turnip now, can you?" Enraged at the thought of all his hard work being pissed away by the poor decisions of the administration, Dr. Locke fashioned a plan. With the help of the local undertaker and a few students trustworthy enough to keep their mouths shut, the anatomical department would obtain their own materials from the potter's fields in the neighboring cemeteries.

What could it hurt to advance medicine with the temporary use of criminals and paupers, lessers and vagrants? What better way for them to repay society their debt owed?

So, in the dark hours of the night, when mothers and fathers, sisters and brothers, friends and coworkers of the dead and buried slept soundly in their beds, the chosen students of Dr. Locke sneaked along the edges of the boneyard looking for the corner of the property where the unwanted, unknown, and forgotten rested. This practice of procuring dissection material was not one whit different from how many of the medical schools of that day operated, but that did not mean the unsavory act was widely accepted by the public. After all, nothing so vehemently inflamed the righteous as the violation of the sanctity of the dead, pauper or not. But there were only so many vagrants and criminals and the Black folk raised too much a ruckus, brought unwanted attention to the school—they cherished their dead after all. As the legal supply of cadavers dwindled to nothing and the graves of the unwanted had all been picked over, Dr. Locke and his students found themselves faced with a most horrible and repulsive decision: to throw in the towel and admit defeat, possibly starting again at a stronger state-supported school, or become highly educated body snatchers. With little debate, they chose the latter. It was a necessary evil. Not all schools of that time required anatomical laboratory and dissection. But Southern Physio did. And therefore, the anatomical laboratory would engage in resurrecting the loved ones of the unamenable. At least until things turned around financially.

Dix's last two and a half years of study had been all he had hoped. He thrived in the structured environment of the classroom, hanging on his lecturers' every word. He had been the recipient of a generous scholarship and had spent every night poring over the pages of his coveted *The American Practice*, the only text of its kind on reformed medicine at the time. His dream was to become a respected healer, a prestigious doctor, a skilled surgeon. He was the second-to-last of eleven children, had spent his years near the bottom of a family totem pole, and wanted more from life. He'd been the tenth to bathe in the shared waters of the family washtub. He'd been the seventh boy to wear the dingy and holey trousers passed down through the years. He'd been the recipient of every hand-me-down toy, the last to be picked for a team, the first to cry as he was very sensitive, and the one child to get poked fun at for hating to be dirty. He'd always felt dirty, unclean. He hadn't known what germs were. Nobody did then. Germ theory hadn't yet been discovered, offered, nor accepted or rejected. But something innate in him led him to have such adverse reactions to the filth of others that he was often mocked. But this aversion to human filth was something that would later in life serve him well.

Growing up, he'd watched his family navigate illness and death with the expectation of help from only God above. *Surely God wanted his children to at least try to help themselves*, he often thought, in near indignity. He watched as his mom raised a herd of kids who went through serious illness like seasons; she'd handled death as expected of a mother of eleven. On his sixth birthday, instead of being celebrated with a song from his family, Dix watched his father lower his baby sister's body down into a hole dug earlier by James, the first born. Two weeks after that, James had to dig another hole. John, fourth in line, died coughing and sweating just like Elsa had. They'd both died of a continual violent cough that their parents had left solely to nature and time to cure. Time and nature had obviously failed. Prayers to God had failed. What his sister and brother hadn't had was treatment, medicine. Dix had known this in his very being, even at the young age of six, that man could and should intervene.

Dix had studied under Drs. Evans and Locke, had passed his annual tests in each subject (something he hoped would add prestige to his degree as many other schools had not yet required annual testing of its students), and had mere weeks until his completion and graduation, just before the holidays. What a gift. Although he had not participated in an actual surgery, Dix had cherished his time in the amphitheater with his fellow students watching over Dr. Evans as he lanced the boil from the face of a geriatric woman and then dressed her wound. Dr. Evans spoke of operations to remove tumors from organs, decaying limbs from bodies, toxic blood from the vascular system, but the students were never so lucky as to see such an operation. This part of medical study, to Dix, was the most captivating subject of all his learning. In the second term of his preceptorship, he was witness to and assisted with the birth of a child where he enthusiastically utilized the stethoscope to determine the veracity of the child's heartbeat, but no sound emitted from the newborn. He'd not gotten to hear a thing. The child had died and, with it, so did Dix's opportunity to listen to a brand-new heart.

He and Trent Miller both knew the potter's field was no longer a viable source for dissection material and, because of that, the undertaker had ceased giving any help. The anatomy department, deplete of funds, had no means to continue procuring their "professional" grave robber who'd upped the ante to eighty dollars a grave. And so it was unspoken that the two were looking for fresh dirt anywhere they could find it. The school had now exhumed, used, and returned six bodies on its own; however, the disturbed graves did not go unnoticed, at least by the no-longer-employed grave robber, and this would come back to bite them later.

The turnover of cadavers was high, and dissection was often hurried because of the limited time the bodies granted the students before decay took hold. On this lucky night, however, the latest autumn storm had finally passed, and a fresh grave at the far corner of the potter's field sat like a birthday surprise for Dix. The class had one last dissection project to complete and Dix and Trent, along with one resting Mary Lamott, were going to make it happen.

CAROLINE COLLEY

Just Outside the City of Melroy, Georgia

The Higgs Plantation, Caroline Colley's childhood abode, was the largest pecan plantation in Melroy County. Its impressive trees formed perfect canopied lanes running in precise perpendiculars for frolicking children, walking sweethearts, wandering deep thinkers, and a weary Caroline to escape into, allowing a break from wearing the hefty stoic mask she wore intermittently between times of pure hysteria and murky delusion.

Sleep brought about terrible hauntings. To avoid such visions of her dead husband, she often turned to sleep fasting. In the beginning, she was able to elude the 'mares of the night, until one day those inescapable dreams crossed over into the waking hours. And so Caroline, her hours now filled with nightmares and daymares alike, found herself in the presence of one Doctor Geoffrey Hamilton of Savannah, psychotherapist and proponent of the Rotary Chair. Her frightened father had fretted so over the mental fragility of his motherless and widowed daughter and, in desperation, had procured the services of Hamilton and his state-of-the-art and forward-thinking healing methods.

The white-haired doctor with the big fat rosy cheeks of a politician strapped the limp and ambivalent Caroline into a suspended chair, then spun her around at a high rate of speed. "This procedure, sir," the doctor yelled out over the spinning woman, "is proven to reset the brain. Spinning at this therapeutic velocity will evoke such a state of extreme fright and equilibrious discomfort such that the body will have no choice but to reset to its prior homeostatic state."

Fright and discomfort were achieved, as well as a voluminous outpouring of bile and what food remained within Caroline's confines. To Mr. Higgs, Hamilton had said "Daughter's Disease. It's not uncommon for a well-to-do young woman who bucks to conform to throw her household and family life into confusion with irrational buh-hav-yah." Thomas Higgs, heavy with melancholy and despair, cleaned up his green-faced daughter suffering from hysteria and left for Melroy, hopeful that by journey's end his efforts would have paid off.

A plump and heavy-faced Octavia greeted the wagon carrying the father and daughter. Thomas Higgs took no measure to hide failure and disappointment, his head hanging low and eyes sorrowful. Octavia helped Caroline down from the wagon and walked her inside where she stripped the woman of her foul dress and washed her face and hands.

"Yer tata say you sick at yer belly. Take dis, chile." She held out a glass of warm and fragrant ginger tea. Caroline took a sip. "Dem way ain't gone hep ya, Miss Caroline," pronounced [Car-ah-leen] in her Geechee tongue. "Spinning round and round like a little chile sound like some foolery a me. Lift up, now." She pulled a sleeping gown over Caroline's head. "Now lay yer head, chile." Octavia had cared for the motherless sisters since Mary Higgs had died giving birth to Minnie, and she loved Caroline dearly, but that didn't stop her from speaking matter-of-factly at all times.

Caroline ignored the demand to lie back and remained sitting, a headache mingling with the fear of sleep overcoming her.

Octavia sat down on the bed beside her. "Miss Caroline, you must let it be. Let Mr. Davis 'lone."

Caroline, in protest, said, "But Octavia, it's he who won't let me be. He's everywhere. I don't want to see him. I can't escape him."

"Him's just a memory, Miss Caroline—"

"He's not just a memory. He's here! Every day he is here!"

At this, the door creaked open and Mr. Higgs stepped in."

Octavia, let's leave her be."

Octavia looked from the weary man to his daughter, now holding her knees to her chest and rocking. The plump dark woman leaned in and whispered, her words making their way through the tangled hair and into the ears hidden beneath: "You best find yer way back, Miss Caroline, or dey's gwine find a place fer you that you won't much like."

At this, Caroline lifted her head from her knees and looked into the same eyes that had eased her as a girl through so many troubled times. She could see fear in the weary and yellowed eyes of Octavia for the first time in her life.

Octavia placed a hand carefully but firmly on the crown of Caroline's head, just as she'd done hundreds of times, and pressed down gently before she got up and walked away.

Thomas, still standing in the doorway, said, "Chuck, I don't know what else I can do. Dr. Hamilton suggests we return to take you in for extensive treatment—"

And before he could finish his words, Caroline conjured up something akin to a smile. Quietly she said, "I'll be fine, Daddy. I'll be fine tomorrow. I just need to rest."

WALKER WESTBERRY

Westberry Mountain
The Black Mountains of the Old North State (North Carolina)

Walker Westberry watched from the cover of thick trees in the mountainside. It was dark, just before 4 in the a.m. Ten revenue agents crept around the distillery below. And though it was in the dead of night, Walker had been prepared.

He'd been waiting for them to come for him, his rifle across his lap as he dozed, when his guinea fowl began aggressively *chi chi chi'ing*, screaming and clattering—watchdogs of his precious white lightning. Their alerts sent him straight up onto his feet and into the woods. And from there, he had a bird's-eye view of his place below situated in a deep hollow with heavy growths of timber giving cover to the still house. With the moonlight sneaking through branches here and there, he could even spot his tiny cabin nestled a few hundred feet below the still house.

Walker saw the ten men split as they approached from the west. He watched three of the revenuers head to the north side of the distillery, cautiously making their way around to the front. They walked low and slow, their guns held out in front of them, ready to shoot back at the government-hating moonshiner, presumably inside, who'd just weeks before shot and maimed one of their own during a failed raid to collect.

It had been another attempted midnight invasion. Walker and Cousin Sam had just sent off a wagonful of five-gallon kegs with their blockader, Cousin J.P., to sell to the taverns in the neighboring county. The blockader was intercepted about a mile or two down the road, the man beat by the revenuers after being forced to dump the liquid, and then apprehended. Witnessing the poor fate of the blockader were the Westberry twins, out fire-hunting along the creek.

Hoping to poach a deer, though willing to settle for any fur-bearing animal, one boy held up a wooden torch and quietly stalked. Rather than seeing the glow from an animal's eyes, his torch cast light on the backside of his brother, clearly distracted.

"You see one?" whispered the boy holding the torch.

"Nah. But I might could see something. Hide that away," he whispered back, swatting at the air behind him to bat away the light of the torch.

"What? Why?" hissed the boy holding the torch, clearly irritated.

His twin snatched the torch from his hands and quickly dipped it into the creek. The sizzle was quick and let off a small plume of smoke.

"They's something wrong up ahead. Look."

As the two looked toward the main trail, they could make out J.P. standing up in the back of the wagon. Men were standing out to the side, one with his Springfield rifle aimed true at the man.

"Reckon they done got a load," whispered one of the boys, who had sneaked up closer and crouched down in the bushes for a better view of the scene.

The man in the wagon, J.P., was tipping the kegs off the back, a revenuer busting each keg open and its liquid assets spilling onto the ground.

The agents then turned toward the distillery, no doubt to nab Walker. Before they could get there, the boys ran ahead, cutting through the thick woods to warn their older cousins. Walker refused to abandon his place. But Sam, never the least bit stalwart, wanted to run. Walker called Sam a fucking coward and the two bickered until they were interrupted by shouts to surrender. Sam held up his hands and an agent stepped out of the darkness, announcing his allegiance to the United States Internal Revenue Bureau, to which, without hesitation, Walker commenced shooting. The man dropped to the ground and scrambled into the woods. Shots whizzed past the cousins as they ducked for cover in the still house. Shots pinged and tinged off of the great copper cauldrons hissing and seething.

Crouched behind kegs, Sam shouted at Walker, "What the hell you thinkin'? They a-gonna kill us with you shooting like that."

A voice from the woods shouted, "You Westberrys better come out. Ain't no shame in givin' up."

Walker hollered out, "Fuck you! We ain't givin' up shit! You best get yourself ready 'cause you a-gonna leave here one way or another. You can go on and leave us about our business or we can hunt you down, tie you to one a these trees, and leave you for the hogs!"

"Mr. Westberry," the voice shouted, "the law is the law. Now come on out before we have to come in after you!"

Walker leaned around a keg and gave a shot in the direction of the voice.

"Got-dammit Walker!" shouted Sam. "Stop shootin' already! Let's just go on with them. We'll go sit at county for the twenty-seven days, eat good, and come on back after our time's up."

Another shot was fired at the house. Though Sam was ready to run, Walker had no intention of giving up his family's place. The law could go fuck itself. He had a business that supported him, his family, even the community in a way. The people wanted a product. Walker supplied it. The government could just keep out as far as he was concerned. But he was backed into a corner. He thought a moment. "What say we talk this out?" he shouted. "Make us an arrangement?"

"We ain't interested in doing business with anyone pedaling social evil," returned a voice.

"Social evil?" Walker shouted. He looked over to Sam who was by this time white in the face. Walker whispered a chuckle to him, "pedaling social evil."

Sam simply nodded his head and closed his eyes. "Walker, we might should give up."

"Nope. We ain't fixin' to give up shit. Now, don't be a pussy." He shouted over his shoulder out to the men, "How 'bout we sit crooked and talk straight? You and your boys take what you want from the wagon and we'll just get back to it."

No answer came.

Then he offered, "A little coin your way?"

"Sir, coin is what you owe the United States government. Now if you have a mind to pay what's due, we can talk."

Walker sat and thought a moment longer. Life was hard in the mountains indeed. Dealing with the revenuers, paying the Klan, buying the loyalty of neighbors with either hooch or force, it was tiresome. He could easily resolve this issue by just paying his liquor taxes. But Walker was bold. He was defiant. And as everyone in these mountains knew, he was as malicious as ever.

"Aight!" he shouted.

At this, Sam looked up. Disbelief—and relief crossed his face.

"I'll come on out," shouted Walker. "Don't be shootin' up the place no more." With a groan, Walker reached up and hooked his hand on the edge of the barrel, heaving himself up off the dirt floor. He lifted his rifle up over his head and began walking out of the still house.

"Lay that rifle on the ground!" Two men walked out from the trees and into the moonlight.

Walker bent down and placed his gun on the ground, stood up, and held his hands into the air. At this, an agent approached him, gun first. Walker eyed the man, held a smirk, leaned and spat to the side, and said, "Now, you didn't have to go beatin' on old J.P. If what you's after is less—what'd you call it?—social evils, I'd imagine beatin' a man just trying to do an honest day's work would buck that, now wouldn't it."

The agent scoffed, "Ain't a thang honest out here. You's nothing but some lazy brigands set on gettin' drunk instead of using what you got to feed yourselves."

"Brigands, huh?" Walker now stood with his hands resting on top of his dingy felt hat, his fingers laced together, elbows dangling.

"You hear that, Sam!" he shouted back to the still house. "We's a bunch of brigands! We's a bunch of no-good dirty brigands! Brigands is what we is! You hear that, Sam!"

At this, Walker began to laugh, and laugh some more, bent forward carrying on as if this were the funniest thing he'd ever heard.

"Shut your drunk mouth!" hollered the agent. Dis-ease was setting in and the man's voice betrayed him when it cracked. "Anyone else here, you come on out too!" he shouted.

Walker continued to laugh, and the agent grabbed one of his arms and spun him around. "Face away. Put your hands behind your back." The agent motioned for another man to help who then approached with a rope. "Tie this"—he drew out the word brigand—"bri-gand's hands." All the while Walker continued laughing maniacally.

More men appeared, cautiously stepping from the woods into the moonlight. Sam shuffled his way to the opening of the building, his hands high above his head, his lanky body quivering in fear.

The agent spun Walker around and he now faced Sam. He grinned and hollered out at the top of his lungs, "Sam, you fat old peckerwood! Come join us!"

Sam, clearly unsettled by the mania in his cousin's voice—and oddly being called fat—cautiously approached. Once near, three of the men grabbed him, a bit of an overkill as Sam barely weighed much over "a buck o' five" as his daddy had liked to say.

Walker continued to yell, "You old fat fuck, come join us!" The agents sat silent, eyeing one another. Sam, being tugged this way and that, stared a hole in Walker, confused as well. Walker yelled out once more, this time irritation overtaking his sarcastic jocular tone, "Peckerwood, you motherfucker!"

At this, a loud crash thundered from the woods, ripping through brush, snapping across fallen limbs. And then the roar came.

"Pigs!" yelled one of the agents. "Run!"

Thirty or more feral swine burst into the opening from the bushes and tromped toward the men, squealing and snorting, the ground rumbling under their feet. Instinctively the agents began backing up and shooting. The blast of gunshots and thumps of bullets hitting the oncoming animals and their screams added to the roar of the sounder fast approaching. Walker, laughing wildly, spun around to see the men retreating into the dark. He shook off the half-tied rope and picked up his gun. He began shooting, hitting a man square in the left butt cheek. The man fell face first and the sounder of hogs trampled over him, one after another after another. Within seconds, the quiet returned and all that remained were the heaving wheezes from Sam's lungs.

Once the pigs had gone, Walker and Sam loaded the agent's limp body into a wheelbarrow. The man's head was caved in like a bowl and pooled with blood and bits, probably the contents of what once were his facial features. They passed him off to the twins. "Go dump 'em."

The boys eyed the mass, its legs and arms hanging about. One grabbed a stick to try and fling an arm up and inside the wheelbarrow to avoid catching on briars and such along the way. They rock-paper-scissored over who had to take the heavy end.

"Nah, best two outta three!" shouted the loser.

"Nope, I won fair and square. Now grab them handles and let's git."

The loser, also the smaller of the two, grabbed the wooden handles while the other gathered up the man's legs. He turned away, snugged each of the man's boots up at his hips, and marched ahead, pulling him along. They carted him off to the edge of the creek where they were to dump him.

"Good thing we come up on them pigs, huh, Peckerwood?" teased the boy pulling at the feet.

"Shut up, you fat fuck," the other had grunted as he struggled to dump the load. "Clearly Walker weren't a-talkin' to me!" At that, the wheelbarrow wobbled and ultimately tipped to the side, the man landing face first on the ground.

"Well shit. Hep me roll 'em."

The two rolled the man like a log until he reached the edge where he dropped down into the rushing waters.

Walker wasn't willing to lean on luck anymore after being saved by the twins and the sounder of hogs during the last raid. This time, as Walker watched from the hills, he was ready. Prepared. His birds had earned their keep. He could see two other men were crouched down at the south of the building, hiding. *Pussies*, he thought.

The birds were relentless, screaming at the men coming around the north side, disturbing the night and wilderness that attempted sleep. He watched as a few of the guineas set about attacking one man who kicked and swung his gun at the birds to no avail. The birds retreated and then set about after him again, holding their ground. This was their job, to protect their home and ward off intruders. Last time, the Westberrys made it out by the skin of their teeth, luck being on their side when the boys came upon a sounder of pigs rooting around the creek's edge. They drove those pigs right to the agents. But that was just dumb luck that night. They couldn't risk another raid. So the Westberrys stole a bunch of guinea fowl, who took to the place nicely—and therefore their jobs seriously.

At the third bird attack, the man reached down and snatched one of the guineas by the neck, slung it like a whip, and then chucked its limp body back at its own flock. The birds went wild screaming in protest. Up in the mountainside, Walker sat uneasy knowing that left one man unaccounted for.

Walker had come by moonshining honestly. His daddy and his daddy's daddy had always produced. It was a way of life. What small bit of land they owned produced a decent amount of corn. Yes, they could get about twenty or so bushels of corn in a wagon and make a good ten dollars or so. Or, they could cook down forty bushels of corn into white whiskey, fit it in that same wagon, and earn up to a hundred and fifty bucks. It was common-sense economics, an easy financial fix to an otherwise destitute situation living in the rural Mountain South. That is until the government took to taxing hooch to cover the costs of the battle of the North and South.

The Westberrys had manufactured and sold moonshine for generations, had survived the Whiskey Rebellion, skirted taxation during the War of 1812, and then entered into a business arrangement with the Klansmen, who used intimidation tactics to quiet down any rural neighbors intending to take legal action against the distiller, or was rumored to act as an informer for the revenuers. All the Klansmen required for their service were a few jugs of mountain dew and a small cut of the profits. Walker placed nothing above getting his money, not the judgment of others, the safety of others, not the law, not the government, not his family, not even his wife.

ELZI DUPRE

River City in the Creole State (Louisiana)

Elzi Dupre and Albin Banks had been best friends not long after Elzi punched Byron, Albin's twin brother, square in the nose under the bald cypress tree at the Calgary Baptist Church.

Elzi lived off Zepper Marsh Road in River City. He'd lived there most of his life and knew the rivers, swamps, and marshes like the back of his hand. He spent most days helping Edmee and John Godwin—Maymee and Pa, he called them—around the place when he wasn't attending the local school for coloreds. Anytime he had free time, he'd sneak off into the marsh to hunt frogs, snakes, mess with the gators, or to the river to fish. Sometimes he would sit and read, though there wasn't much reading material other than his pa's bridge book—*Fences, Gates, and Bridges: And How to Make Them*—that was mostly pictures; the Bible, which he didn't much care to read on account that he didn't understand it; and Ora B. Dupre's book, the journal of his natural mother.

That book was his favorite. He loved to run his finger along her handwriting, imagining her holding the quill. He loved to sit and think about her drawings coming to life. He most loved dreaming about her magic, envisioning her over a fire creating healing potions for her loved ones. She had been a spiritual priestess after all, according to his blood uncle Oliver Dupre. Though Pa Godwin told Elzi that magic and spells and potions weren't real, that they were the uneducated beliefs of the Indians and those that lived by folklore and the like, Elzi chose to believe anyhow. He *wanted* to believe his real parents were special. And though it gave him the slightest pain in his tummy when the Godwins dismissed the tenets of his birth parents' belief and practice of Voodacho, Elzi was grateful and respectful enough to never challenge their stance on the matter. He just nodded his head and read Ora's book in private. The Godwins held no hesitation when they chose to take on Elzi as a young child, but that didn't mean they didn't hold him to a higher standard than that of a White child; and as difficult as it was for a White couple raising a Black boy in the old squalid South, the last thing they needed was the extra scrutiny that would come from a boy yapping his mouth about his magic mother and medicine man father. Fortunately, Elzi gathered this early on and kept his heritage to himself.

The summer Elzi turned fourteen, he took to redfishing in the mornings before the sun heated up the shallows. He'd been walking up the road not long after dawn. Three redfish dangled from a string slung over his shoulder. His morning had been a success and the family would be grateful. As he approached the turnoff from the dirt road that led him back to home, he was met by two boys. They were the Banks boys and Elzi knew them from church. They'd joined some months back after a fiasco of sorts at their own house of worship landed them without a church home. The Bankses were a family of freed people living at the edge of the Sugar Coast, day laborers consisting of a father, mother, and four children. Although emancipation gave these good and faithful laborers a taste of freedom and wages, sugaring allowed no time for such freedom or education.

The work never ceased, and their hard work on the plantation never seemed to pay off. But the parents tried. They tried to give their children a better life, a chance.

Albin and Byron were twins and the oldest of the four siblings, which locals often teased that, had the Bankses known the twins were going to be so much trouble, they'd bet "they would'a thought twice before having mo' children." The twins were rowdy and raucous and often caused trouble for the Banks family. It was inconvenient, not to mention slightly humiliating, for the family to travel past their local church all the way to Calgary Baptist to attend. This was the church Elzi's family called home. Calgary was unique, however, in that it accepted Whites and Blacks alike. Mr. and Mrs. Banks, if they'd had their druthers, would have liked not to attend a mixed church as it was just easier, but Albin and Byron had been chased out of their last church in front of God and everyone by none less than the sweating pastor himself yelling in unadulterated fury. After the door slammed shut following the twins' exit, the remaining four Bankses had gathered themselves and quietly sidestepped down the pew to leave. Not a sound was heard but the heaving of the pastor's chest, the wave of fans cooling the ladies' glistening faces, and a cough from the crowd here and there. Once the Bankses were gone and the doors pulled to, the pastor turned and said with full conviction to the stupefied crowd, "Clean out the old leaven so that ya may be a new lump of leaven." And the people sat silent as he made his way back up to the pulpit where he wiped his brow and remarked under his breath, "Hallelujah, by an' by."

Elzi had only seen Albin and Byron once at the Free Mission Baptist school. The school had a whopping twenty-two students ranging from six years of age to sixty-three. People were eager to learn at any age now that they could. Class was held in an old church with one room, dirt floors, and four rows of desks. The Banks boys managed to get expelled from there as well. It was their first day of kindergarten. The teacher didn't much care for being called Madame

Cracker, nor did she like the boys poking fun at the elderly man who attended. Her first attempt at discipline was to have them each outstretch their arms and hold books in each hand, a fight against gravity. The boys stood at the back of the room holding up the books, at first smirking, then quavering at the burn in their scrawny arms, until finally their big brown mischievous eyes met. The boys simultaneously snorted up and spit out a wad of mucus onto the dirt floor and then slammed the books down into the snot before being escorted out by the tips of their ears. So after some time and a few more expulsions, the Banks family gave up on the idea of their boys learning to read, write, and figure. They could just tend to the sugar plantation and hopefully their reputation would not precede that of the girls when it was their time to take a stab at an education.

The official meeting of the twins and Elzi took place after church on a sweltering August day. A group of the adults were visiting under the massive bald cypress out front as they always did following a service. Although the church accepted all men, women, and children regardless of their color or income status—"a true Christian church" the White congregates often prided themselves with saying—from afar, one could still see the divide. Light skins congregated just off the steps and into the shade, staying close to the building; dark skins gathered at the farthest points where the shade came to an end. The children, however, ran and jumped and played all together around the tree, over the branches, under the branches, around and around. And though they did so willingly, that didn't mean their playmates' skin color, or that of their families, went unnoticed.

On this day, it was Albin that first gave off an insult, calling Elzi a cracker. "Hey Crackah, get away from our sistah!"

Elzi had been pushing the youngest of the Banks siblings in the swing tied from the cypress. Albin and Byron stood off to the side, never far from one another, watching. They were known to drum up trouble and so this was no surprise to most of the kids. Elzi continued pushing the girl, unaware that it was him whom the boys chided.

"I said you, Crackah, stop pushing our sistah."

Elzi grabbed the swing to stop its momentum and turned to the boys. The little girl in the swing tilted her head of three big puffy braids and plainly stated to her brothers, "But he ain't White." She leaned back kicking her legs, signaling her desire to swing again. The other kids near enough to hear laughed and Elzi's face began to burn.

The twins were identical and often operated as if they shared one mind, one boy finishing the other's sentence, or the other boy laughing before something had even been said. Jokes and shared insults surged invisibly between the two, making all others feel out of cahoots, always, when they were around.

Elzi began pushing the swing again.

This time Albin kicked at the dirt toward Elzi and insulted him once more. "Crackah, crackah, you a crackah!"

His sister, confused, objected again. "Albie, he *ain't* White."

Albin started to reply, "Yeah, bu—"

His twin cut him off: "But his ma and pa sho is!"

They pointed and laughed and held their bellies as if it were the funniest thing they'd ever heard or said, and the burn of tears threatening to leak from Elzi's eyes. But he wouldn't, couldn't let nobody see him cry. So, he reacted in a way completely unlike anything he'd ever done before. He let go of the swing, walked up, and punched Byron square in the nose. Byron instantly covered his face and bent forward, this time hollering instead of laughing: "You done broke my nose! You crackah! You done broke my nose!"

The other kids, in shock, all abandoned the scene and retreated to where their respective families stood. Under the bald cypress stood Elzi, Albin, Byron, and an empty dangling swing. Remorse instantly fell upon Elzi. Hitting—hurting was not in his nature. So he cautiously drew closer to Byron who was still holding his nose with tears streaming down his cheeks.

"I'm real sorry. I don't know—"

Byron cut him off with a hard shove to the chest and then bolted. The sudden push caught Elzi off guard and he came off his feet, landing flat on his back in the dirt. When he looked up, only Albin remained. The two locked eyes and Elzi wondered if Albin might jump on top of him, beat him down. But he did not. Instead he outstretched his hand. Elzi thought twice before accepting it. This boy had after all just minutes before started all this mess by calling him a cracker. As Elzi eyed the hand, and then the boy's face, and then back to the hand, he made the decision to accept it. Albin yanked Elzi up onto his feet. Elzi began dusting off the rear of his trousers and backing up some. He still wasn't sure whether Albin was going to retaliate on Byron's behalf or not—or if Byron himself might come blazing back.

About that time Edmee Godwin approached. "What's going on here, ya two?" she asked with legitimate concern on her face.

Both boys froze, not quite sure what to say. Elzi looked Albin in the eyes, hoping for a truce. Any fight, no matter who started it, always ended in punishment for all involved.

"Well?" she asked again, this time with a bit more expectation and authority in her voice.

Elzi noticed a trickle of blood from Albin's nose. Albin wiped it quickly and then said she'd nothing to worry with, that they were just getting to know each other. Edmee looked at them both suspiciously for a moment then smiled.

"Well, Elzi, clean ya-self up. You're covered in dirt. And you, son," she smiled broadly at Albin, "you just made ya-self the best friend a boy could ask for. He's the kindest and would love to have someone for wandering the marsh with, I'm sure. Pass on by anytime." She patted Elzi atop his head and then turned back to the front steps where her husband stood shaking hands goodbye with Pastor Grimes. She hollered over her shoulder, "Elzi, come on now. We got to get lunch going. Tell ya friend you'll be seeing him."

Elzi turned back to Albin. He looked him over quickly and spotted the smear of blood on the cuff of Albin's shirt.

"I ain't hit you," Elzi said, his statement also a question.

"Might as well have," replied Albin. He snorted up the remaining blood and hawked it out on the ground. A red-tinged loogie floated atop the dirt. "Don't seem so *kind* to me," he said mocking Edmee's compliment of Elzi.

Elzi replied, "You called my folks crackers."

"No, I called *you* a crackah. Byron the one said ya folks is a crackah, not me."

"Well, either way, ain't no one gone call my folks names, you hear?"

Albin replied, "I don't see how's them ya folks no how. So what do ya care?"

Elzi answered, tilting his head from one side to the other with each phrase, "And I don't much see how what I do to ya brother makes you a differ'nce. Yet here you's the one to bleed."

The two boys stood, getting closer with each comeback, until finally they just stood in silence, forehead to forehead. Then, just as the anger had washed over Elzi like a wave of fire, it left him. Something about Albin interested him. Something about Albin he liked, he was drawn to. But he didn't quite know what that was. He reluctantly said, "I gots to go. See ya 'round." And he turned to walk away.

Albin stood there for a moment watching Elzi as he walked after his parents up ahead. He finally shouted, "Ya maymee say I can pass by anytime. So you better watch ya back."

Elzi kept walking and waved him off. After a few more steps he turned back to see the boy still standing. Albin's mouth turned up into the faintest smile. Elzi smiled back and then saw Byron run up to Albin. He watched as one brother said something to the other that was answered with a small shove. Elzi turned back and half ran to meet up with his parents.

Albin too felt drawn to Elzi. He wanted to hate him. He had hit his brother after all. But he couldn't. As he and Byron ran to catch up with the rest of their family, he wondered what it would be like to have White folks as parents. Wondered if it'd feel like you were White too, or just living real close with people you got to watch out for.

That next morning the boys happened to cross paths on the old dirt road leading to the river. The twins were headed back home from town, back to the shanty their family lived in. Elzi was returning from the river. He had three fish slung over his shoulder. The three boys stopped just about the point of crossing one another. No one said a word at first. Just stood and stared. Byron shuffled his foot back and forth in the dirt, uneasy. Then he could no longer resist the standoff. They had been standing still as if waiting for the starting pistol.

"Ya busted my nose," Byron finally said.

Elzi could see Byron's eyes both slightly purpled and his stomach sank. He felt bad for hurting Byron, even if he had deserved it. Elzi said quietly and cautiously, "Ya know, fightin' you boys is like killing two birds with one stone."

Albin wiped his nose at the thought of it bleeding in response to his brother taking the actual blow.

"Don't seem fair no how," Elzi said as he thought on it some.

The three stood, pondering what they all knew to be true, that when Elzi hit Byron, Albin's nose bled just the same. Everybody knew twins were different, special, and possibly sometimes had abilities that other *regular* siblings did not. But those were just stories. Everyone had a story about something someone had once told them about the twins that their friend's cousin's neighbor knew. But no one actually had their own story of these connections. Now Elzi did.

"How's about I give you this here fish and you 'cept my sorry?" Elzi proffered.

The twins stood as Elzi held out the three handsome redfish dangling off his line, their copper skin glistening in the morning sun. They looked at each other for a moment, as if holding a secret conference, and then together reached out to accept the fish—and with it, the armistice silently offered by Elzi Dupre.

John was disappointed when Elzi returned home with no fish. The few copper scales John spotted stuck to the back of Elzi's shirt signaled that the Banks boys had something to do with Elzi turning up short for food. John had once told Elzi, "You keep away from dem

Banks boys. They got a monstrous bad name for meanery and shecoonery of all sorts." But Elzi had liked Albin and was enamored at how the boys had some sort of connection others didn't seem to have, not even other siblings he had seen. Their twin-ism was like magic to him, and he had always liked the idea of magic.

DIXON ARTOPE

Southern Physio-Eclectic College of Medicine
The Empire State of the South (Georgia)

Mary Lamott died at the state insane asylum. Upon notice of her death, her husband loaded up and began his long journey to claim her body. But Mother Nature was not on his side and an autumn storm had left the roads treacherous with deep ruts of mud. The asylum staff, growing impatient, gave up waiting on him and contacted the undertaker to haul the body away. The asylum was a hospital after all, not a storage facility for the dead. For reasons quite objectionable, Mrs. Lamott—the wife of George Lamott who very much claimed her existence—was laid to rest in the potter's field. A false representation of insufficient grief.

It was an unfortunate happenstance for the Lamott family but a lucky twist of fate for Dix and Trent, the unofficial resurrectionists of the Department of Anatomy. The unsettled earth upon her grave easily fell away and digging her out took but a little over an hour with their quiet wooden spades. Beside Mrs. Lamott's resting hole was a tarpaulin spread out to avoid disturbing the nearby grounds. The men started at the head of the grave and dug down until one of their spades contacted the coffin, emitting a wooden thud. At this, Travis took a crowbar to the body box, wrenching it open at the head. Then came the disturbing part. The dragging. Rather than exhume the entire coffin, the time-conscientious approach was to merely wrap a rope under the shoulders of the corpse and drag it out. This, to Dix, was the most indelicate and disrespectful aspect of the ordeal. But science was not always respectful. And it certainly didn't have feelings. This callus act, at least in Dix's mind, was offset by the benefits Mrs. Lamott's body would provide to modern medicine.

The woman he dragged out was pretty but extremely thin and emaciated—again, a lucky happenstance for the men as this would save the students time from having to scrape away any fat. She looked to be in her early thirties, blonde, with her pale arms grooved with fresh and healed marks as if having been attacked by a cat every day for the past ten years. Once out of the grave, Dix and Trent wrapped the body in a sheet and rolled her over to the side. They hastily returned the dirt to its original site, loaded up their tarpaulin and spades, and carted Mrs. Lamott to the wagon they had inconspicuously placed in the neighboring woods.

The fellow future doctors never asked any details about where the bodies came from, how they were obtained. They simply got right down to business as there was no time to spare when it came to dissection. They raced against time, against rot. They cut and drilled, peeled and prodded. And it was on this second day, just as the students were lowering the brain of Mary Lamott into a vat of brine, that the janitor flung open the lab room door in a tizzy.

"The law's here," he hissed. "Dr. Locke's talking to them now!"

At first, the students froze. The tone of the man insinuating they'd done something wrong rattled them. But they hadn't been doing anything wrong. They were in medical college, performing medical research. "Dr. Locke can deal with the law," said one student with great arrogance. "We'll be here furthering science." At that, he turned back to the table where Mrs. Lamott's mutilated body lay.

Dix and Trent locked eyes. Knowing they'd robbed this woman from the earth like a sneak thief in the night plucking a neighbor's long-awaited peach harvest, their hearts dropped. They were surely busted. That had to be what this was about.

Trent spoke first: "Grab her legs!" He ran to her head and began shoving his arms up underneath her. Her head bobbed back, liquid dripping from the empty bowl that was her sawn-off skull. "Grab her legs!" he yelled again.

The orders gave Dix a start, his glasses slipping down his nose. He quickly shoved them back in place and ran down to the foot of the table. The other students stood in stupor, confused by the haste and panic. The two lifted the woman and dragged her off the side of the table, her body sagging low at the hips. They began sidestepping toward the door.

"To the lecture hall," instructed Dix.

Moments later, Dr. Locke, the sheriff, the undertaker, and a man with the look of great fear and rage entered the lab. Dr. Locke was profusely sweating, but the sight of an empty table clearly brought relief upon him. He gestured into the room.

"This is our anatomy lab, as you can see," he huffed, winded from adrenaline.

The students all stood around a few feet back from the table, aprons donned, tools in hand.

The intruders regarded the room. "What is it they's supposed to be working on?" asked the sheriff.

The empty table was left a mess, covered in fluids and bits. But nothing substantial remained. No one had a response. At this, the tall man that accompanied the group shoved Dr. Locke aside and bolted from the room. The sheriff looked the room over once more. His eyes stalled at the brain floating in amber-colored liquid. He looked up at the students remaining stock-still for a moment longer and then turned to catch up with Mr. Lamott.

Dix and Trent could hear Mary's husband rushing through the halls, his boots clomping, doors flinging open and slamming against the walls. He was looking for them, looking for her. "We need to get rid of her," whispered Trent. But there was no way of doing so. They were being hunted. And Dix was sure their hunter was grieving the un-named woman who lay a crumpled mess between them in the floor.

"Can we get back to the lab?" asked Dix. "They've already looked there once. They'll not need to look again. And they'll be here soon enough."

The two sat staring at one another, their breaths quick and shallow, their brows beading with sweat. They decided to try.

Dix and Trent bent low, peering around the doorway of the lecture hall. Dix pushed his glasses back up over the bridge of his nose, the sweat burdensome. They could hear the slamming of doors, the overturning of carts, equipment crashing to the ground. They could hear Dr. Locke yelling and pleading for the man to stop with this *mad destruction of great property*. The man was furious and out of his head. They could hear his threats echo down the hall and back to their cowardly ears: "My fury knows no bounds, you retched thieves! And what I've learned about your debauched school from your indignant populace . . . well, I'll bring hell upon you all!"

Once the man was seen entering the office of the dean, Dix and Trent acted fast. They scooped up Mrs. Lamott's naked body once more and scrambled back to the lab. It was empty. The debacle had frightened the students. All had fled. The two men flopped her body back on the table, quickly draped a sheet over her, and followed suit. They too fled, leaving Dr. Locke to fend off the madman for himself. He did have the sheriff there, they thought, so there was that.

Apparently, that night, Dr. Locke was held in the jail until things could be sorted. The following morning, he was returned to his precious lab, only to be met by somewhat of a resurrection riot out front of the college. The dean suspended him until further investigation to appease the mob. The anatomy lab closed its doors "until further notice." Within the month, the Southern Physio-Eclectic Medical College locked its doors for the last time, sending its students away with an elaborate certificate in lieu of a legitimate diploma.

Thanksgiving came and went. Christmas came and went. Dix could not bring himself to attend either, the shame overcoming him. His closest brother and best friend, Buford, had written letters begging Dix to come on home, that whatever mistakes that misguided school had made, they'd work through it. Ford brainstormed when Dix finally had said there was nothing to be done, that he was all washed up. He wrote to Dix:

> I could try to get you some work alongside me for the railroad. I know it wouldn't be as sophisticated as the elite healer you once envisioned yourself to be, but you'd be supporting yourself and any wife you took with a good and stable wage. Dix, I have no doubt your indomitable nature will prevail, but please don't let whatever has happened smolder your provocation. You're one of The Lucky Sevens and don't you forget it.

Dix couldn't bear to tell Ford the sins he'd done, especially since it seemed it was all for nothing, but he did take him up on his offer to come home. He was exhausted and defeated. Yes, he felt remorse for what George Lamott had suffered. That poor man had come to town thinking the big blunder was his wife being buried somewhere other than her family resting place. What he found was not only was she buried as an *unknown* in the forlorn potter's field, but she'd been stolen from it as well and used like a biology class frog. She'd spent her last years in turmoil, trapped in her own personal hell. He'd had no choice but to take her to the asylum. What else was he to do?

When she'd succumbed to the ultimate self-annihilation, he'd told himself that at least now she could finally rest. And then this. So yes, Dix felt remorse for Mr. Lamott, but more so, Dix felt it for himself. He'd been robbed too, Lucky Seven or not.

Just Outside the City of Melroy, Georgia

In the hours that Octavia Kassoula's people refer to as day clean, when the remnants of night clouds are being punctured and swept away by the morning's first rays of light, Caroline's ears tuned in to a slow and ever-so-slight *squeak, creak, squeak, creak, squeak, creak,* a high then low revolving pinch of sound at the foot of her bed. She had lain there some time, unsure if her eyes had already been fixed on the light sneaking into her room from the window beside her bed, or if the sound opened her eyes with one of its many repetitions. So many mornings began this way—with Caroline unable to discern her waking thoughts from those still lingering from sleep. She rolled from her side and reluctantly stole her gaze from the beautiful morning sky to where she was certain her husband was slowly spinning, suspended by a noose above the foot of her bed.

As he spun, his hands bound behind his back came into view, then the front of his trousers, wet with guilt, then his hands again. The man slowly turned until at last he limply and gently, with only the slightest *squeak* and *creak,* swung from side to side. His hooded head tilted down and to the right in what was once the condescending head tilt that Davis Colley fashioned when speaking to those of whom lacked his intelligence and wit—let alone deserved to be in his presence.

The first, second, third, or even the eleventh time of waking to her hanging husband was no easier to bear for the petrified and trembling Caroline Colley. Just as she'd done time and time before, she jumped up and scrambled as far back against the grand headboard of her childhood bed and drew in her legs as if to serve as one final barrier between the murderous mirage before her and the pounding heart behind her knees. She tucked her head and rocked, rocked, rocked, desperate for the world around her to simply disappear.

A voice of distress and suffocation called out to her: "My dear, why do you avert those pretty eyes so from your beloved husband?"

She continued to rock and tremble, hiding her face in her knees, waiting for the moment that he would be gone.

"Caaaaroliiiine?" His voice was devious, nasty to her ears.

She rocked.

"Caroline!" he hissed. "It was for us—for you!"

"It was not for me," she whimpered into her knees. "It had nothing to do with me. Leave me be," she pleaded. Her voice began bubbling up in a rage of trembling, bursting whispers. "Leave me alone. Please!"

"Oh, my bride. You don't mean that, now do you? Come now. Be a dear and let's see about pulling this maddening hood from—"

"No!" she interrupted. Caroline rocked and squeezed her eyes tight. "Leave me be, Davis. I don't want you coming 'round here no more."

"Oh, but you need me. You *all* need me."

"No one needs you," she wept.

Forcing a thick Georgian drawl, the hanging body croaked, "Of course y'all do."

She imagined a devious smile spreading across his face under that black hood. She could hear it in his voice, the way she used to hear it just before he delivered his husbandly backhand. She peeked up from her knees, and through gritted teeth she quietly ordered, "Go."

"I'll go when I'm good and ready, Mrs. Davis Colley!" he screamed through strained vocal cords. The forceful outburst was delivered with a great buck of his hanging body. Caroline flinched at the body swinging about.

"Get out!" she screamed. "Get out, get out, get out!" Caroline began rocking and digging her fingers up into her hair, grabbing thick wads and pulling hard.

The door swung open, bouncing off the wall behind, making way for Octavia who, without a word, hitched up her apron and skirt and climbed onto the bed, took hold of the rocking woman, and pulled her into her heavy bosom. "Chile, you safe. Hear now? You safe. Dis day new. Dat day gone. Dis day clean, chile, a new day fer you. You safe."

"But I'm not safe, Octavia! I'm not! None of us are!" Her anguish was palpable as her words burst forth like a flood. Octavia rocked and quietly shushed her as she had done many a morning. Caroline said, "He's going to get us. He's said so himself." Her voice muffled between her knees, but Octavia knew the words all too well. These nightmares were becoming more frequent and merging into the day, enough to make a Geechee woman say her daily prayer to send the evil spirits that planted these nightmares away—just in case.

She rocked with Caroline and stroked her hair. "Ain't no one gwine get us, Miss Caroline. Ain't no one here. You fine, chile. Just leave him be. Leave thought of him be."

Caroline looked up and pushed herself away, matted red hair stuck to her face in wet rivulets of tears and snot. Pointing to Davis's hanging body she cried, "He said death would visit soon, Octavia. That Mother Nature would wield her poison upon one of us. Octavia, he's going to kill me, just like he—"

Octavia pulled Caroline back into her arms. "Hush, chile."

At first, Caroline resisted. But the weariness was weighty and the bosom of Octavia seemed the only escape that Caroline would ever find. She reached around the plump waist of the closest thing to a mother she'd had since she was five years old. The two rocked slowly in a tangle of arms and tears, rocked in a rhythm with the *squeak* and *creak* of Davis Colley's rope until at last it faded into the sound of Octavia's low hum of one of her old Geechee songs from a time and place long lost.

WALKER WESTBERRY

Westberry Mountain
The Black Mountains of the Old North State (North Carolina)

Willard Westberry, whom Walker and his cousins called PeePaw Westberry, was a kind and generous man, even though he had little to give other than his towhead blue-eyed genes. On his property, wedged between the creek and the hillside in the Black Mountains, he grew corn. At first, he grounded the corn. Fed his family the corn. Sold the meal for cash as he barely scraped by. Later he found a more fruitful method of corn transformation: he culled it, grounded it, soaked it, and shined it. He shared his moonshine with all except the relatives who'd found Jesus. Not that he had anything against the folks. It just seemed most of the Bible thumpers frowned upon his craft publicly, while rejoicing in it privately. He was a man of integrity. He liked to exclaim, "I practice the ree-li-gee-on of civility. Ain't no sellout, for Christ's sake. And don't be a-forgetting what old Lemuel done say anyhow: *Let him drink and forget his poverty. And remember his misery no more.*"

It was a solitary business at first, and a hard one. Then when the laws changed, it became a taxed one, therefore a secret one. Willard had to hide his stills. He made the decision to move his operation up into what he later took to calling his Honey Hole, a cave a few hundred feet above his homestead. He entrusted his sons and his sons' sons with the heavy lifting, requiring the hauling of enormous copper tubs, copper tubing, lumber, bushel after bushel of corn, and giant bags of sugar through the woods and up the mountain to the cave above, all the while leaving ne'er a trace. He used the emptied-out still house situated near his cabin for corn storage. But the hooch, it was safely tucked away in his Honey Hole. He had no intentions of paying the government this obnoxious tax, whether it was to financially back a war or not.

Years of the illegal business garnered moonshiners a bad rap as simply tax evaders. But PeePaw Westberry had a deep and abiding love for the craft. He loved his family. He loved his land. And he loved the art of the shine. He just didn't see how the government had any business interfering with the goings-on of his own land. He hated that the craft carried no respectability. And so he tried to infuse his sons and daughters, nieces and nephews, and grandchildren with the pride that came from crafting his signature corn sweetness.

PeePaw Westberry was proud of his product and took the crafting of it seriously. Walker could remember his peepaw talking him through every intricate step of the process. He remembered him admonishing him should he not carry out each step carefully: "Getting blind drunk is one thing. But you forget to toss the foreshot, why you'll wind up blind dead." Walker had listened carefully, taken in every word, and taken many a tasting. He could remember his first. As soon as he held the liquid to his lips, the vapors tingled his nostrils. But that was nothing compared to the fierce burn that followed, slapping his senses awake and leaving his body shivering in recoil. Or was it delight?

Walker too experienced the pride, but it held no candle to the flame that burned within him for the thrill of it all. Walker lived for adventure, trouble. He thrived on taking over this illicit business simply for its high-risk nature, and the prospect of legal cooperation was never a thought in his mind. No fuckin' way, he would say.

They say the apple doesn't fall far from the tree. The Westberry tree seemed to have turned somewhere after PeePaw's reign, its roots infected by ignorance and greed, its fruit spoiled and sullied. After PeePaw's time of pride providing for the family and others with this craft, the family tree produced Waylon Westberry, an apple as rotten as they come. Where Willard Westberry was kind and generous, prepared and cautious, a man who loved to teach and share, his son was vitriolic and full of spite, a man whose stubbornness and impatience, combined with a mean bout of alcoholism, left him a *drunk gimp* as PeePaw would say. He'd taken to sampling during the distilling process often, despite the many admonitions. Once Walker found his father at the entrance of the cave, face down and convulsing. "Foreshot poisoning!" PeePaw had exclaimed. A week or so later, blind in one eye and unable to walk without help, he began his insistent campaign to move the distillery back to its original location. He wanted those stills moved back down the mountain to the old still house where he could get to it. PeePaw was getting old and his authority waned. And Waylon, despite his weakness and gait of a badly strung marionette, was not taking no for an answer.

PeePaw all but cried at the sight of his family hauling his distillery piece by piece back down into conspicuous territory. But what was he to do? His son Waylon had threatened his life many a time. To cut him in his sleep. And the more time went by, the meaner and more physical he got. The others kept their heads down and avoided crossing him at all costs. He was hated. Somehow, even with his high, sloppy knees, his kick-like steps, his heels slamming the ground, him digging in hard with homemade canes to support his weight while he catapulted over his planted foot, he was feared. And feared by all. Particularly by his son, Walker. And it was this deep abiding fear and hatred that led to his demise.

Walker had taken to Nadene Westberry, daughter of his uncle.

That'd made them first cousins. Waylon liked to chide his son any chance he got, and when he caught him and Nadene behind the outhouse exchanging peeks at their personal bits, he made Walker bend forward and hold his ankles, bare ass to the sky. He belted Walker's backside, making contact with his buttocks and genitals. And when Walker cried, he called him a sissy.

"How you a-gonna be a man and cry in front of this here girl? Huh?"

Walker stood back up with tears in his blues eyes and a fire in his belly. At this, his pa challenged, "You ain't got the grit to take no swing at a real man." And Walker's head dropped in shame.

Waylon took to calling the two children kissin' cousins from then on. *Walker, go tell your kissin' cousin it's time to clean the sty. Walker, go get your kissin' cousin and y'all go help J.P. load the wagon.*

Walker had always denied any care for Nadene. In fact, the harassment from his father was so intense that he eventually came to see Nadene as a point of pain rather than a fellow victim of Waylon's abuse. And so he either ignored her or treated her poorly.

One day, when Walker was well into his teenage years, Nadene still prepubescent, she had had enough of his mouth and slapped him. Walker punched Nadene square in the eye like a man. Told her she ought not make a swing unless she's willing to take one back. She fell to the ground, and after scolding her from above, he bent down to help her up. She swatted his hand away and hid her face. He tried to push her hair away to see her eye and she swatted at him again. At this he grabbed both her wrists and pushed her straight back to the ground, his body landing on top of hers, her wrists pinned above her head. The two laid there, breathing heavily, nose to nose. He kissed her and she squeezed her lips tight. He smirked, then bit her on the chin. Hard. She cried out through gritted teeth. He shifted to gather both her wrists into his left hand, pressing them hard into the ground above her head. With his right hand he pulled his pants down just low enough to grab himself. He stroked and grinned. She did not squirm. She stared him straight in the eyes, her attempt to show no fear, but a tear slipped out and defied her. His face was so close to hers, their breath was one. Within seconds his eyes reddened with pressure, a vein protruding from his forehead, his mouth gaping. She thought he might be hurt. Before she knew what was happening, her wrists bound and throbbing from his grip, he quickly scrambled up her tiny body, hiking his right knee up and pinning her left arm to the ground. He swung his left knee up pinning her right arm and mounted her flat chest, the bits she once giggled at now engorged and in her face. She saw his hand grab hold and stroke violently. She squeezed her eyes closed, clamped her mouth shut despite the palm of his hand wrenching her jaw down toward her chest. Within seconds, his warmth trickled from her lips and down into her ear. With it he exhaled and rolled off of her, still panting. They both lay in the leaves, his chest heaving, her lying stock-still.

When she opened her eyes, he was gone. She had heard him rustling. Heard him get up. Heard him mumble something about *such a fuckin' waste*. But she did not move. Not until he was well enough gone and she could wipe the fluid from her face without witness and cry in private.

As the years went by and Nadene matured, the two became lovers in the most functional sense, first exchanging hand jobs in the woods. Occasionally during chores, with a few minutes of privacy, he'd shove her against a tree, hike up her dress, and force himself inside her from behind. It always took him less than twelve thrusts. She'd counted. He often pressed her face into the tree with the back of his forearm while steadying himself by grabbing onto her hip, sometimes leaving scrapes on her cheek from grinding into the bark. "Not so damn hard!" she'd lament. Sometimes, after he was done, he'd give a "sorry" while tucking his shirt back in. But most times he'd just spat and walked off. The lovemaking was never to her benefit, but it was all she had known.

ELZI DUPRE

River City in the Creole State (Louisiana)

Three redfish served as Elzi's olive branch to Byron and Albin Banks. They also served as a sign—albeit a false one—to Mr. and Mrs. Banks that the twins were finally starting to shape up, take some responsibility. Mr. Banks had given up whipping the boys as it did no good and only caused great discord for the whole family. He gave them plenty of work, as it was never ending at the sugar fields, to try and keep them out of trouble. It was really all he could think to do since school was out of the question. But when the boys showed up with the fish claiming they'd caught them for dinner, his heart filled with pride, something Mr. Banks rarely got to experience when it came to the twins.

When the first baby was forced out of his momma's body screaming into this new world, the thought of having a boy brought Mr. Banks great pride. He'd been thinking bringing a female into this world would just result in great heartache, the things she'd likely endure. Even so, deep down he really wanted a son.

Mr. Banks was a superstitious man. Placed a lot of weight on the myths and folklore of his people, and part of that included lucky charms. He'd had a special coin in his pocket the day he was emancipated. The coin had been an auspicious find on the ship, the only thing to cling to upon his forced voyage from the West African coast while being transported as "black cargo." He had survived the coasting period while awaiting the ship to fill which took months. He watched many of his brethren and sistren perish in such hideous fashion. During the voyage across the thunderous and crashing ocean from his home to his new hell, he kept the coin safe. It survived his trade in Alabama, the years of loneliness, hell, horror he spent there, and finally his emancipation where he left the state and headed to the Sugar Coast. He'd held the coin between his fingers, secure in his pocket the day he married his wife. And again for the birth of his child. He gave all the glory to that lucky coin—and of course to God.

When he awaited the birth, he'd held that coin between his fingers, rubbing it feverishly. Its luck had come through. It was a boy. As soon as he got word, he told himself he'd pass that coin on to his son. He'd been daydreaming and imagining life as the father of a boy, ignoring the inevitable truths, and beaming with pride when the midwife came back to him to disrupt his moment.

"Mr. Banks, dey's another baby. It's a boy too. You's now got two boys."

After the initial shock wore off, he considered the luck of the coin. Because there were two boys, it didn't seem right passing just one down. But it was all he had. He gave the subject great thought and decided to pierce the one coin for the first born, whom the couple named Byron. He would, after all, grow up to be head of the house, and he would need luck on his side. And so baby Byron wore the pierced and threaded charm around his tiny neck.

Not long after the twins' truce and newfound friendship with Elzi Dupre, Byron suffered a tragic accident down at the sugar plantation. Horseplay among the twins had resulted in his arm becoming tangled up in the grinding rollers. Before discovering just how dire Byron's situation was, Albin would have taken a severe beating *fit for a slave* the foreman had shouted, a White man disagreeable to all things, it seemed, who did not respect nor abide the laws of emancipation. The accident would cost him serious time and wages, and he certainly took it out of the backside of Albin Banks. It was not until he made to whip Byron that he realized the child was harmed in ways no beating could match.

Despite all lamentations to the Bankses' God above and the limited medical attention they had access to, Byron lost that arm. Elzi had made it his mission to visit the boys daily, often only allowed to see Albin, but he did not miss a day of trying. This gruesome and painful mishap inflicted Albin all the same, and he had lain in bed for days with chills and an unyielding fever as if his life were also on the line. One morning, Albin woke without the chills and fever. They had left him in the night. And with them, so had his brother.

Albin had never known a life without his brother alongside his every move, every thought, every shenanigan. Without him, Albin was completely lost. He took to Elzi, needing the constant company. Thus began the lifelong friendship of the two boys. And though Elzi remained a respectful, studious, and obedient boy, Albin stayed true to his mischievous ways.

It was Albin who first noticed Hattie Mae Belgrave, a girl about their age with a broad smile, broad nose, tight-curled lashes, and beads adorning her many braids that hit just below her sharp shoulders. They had been standing under the giant cypress in front of the church as usual following a service, though now they were too old to want to run about or push the swing. Hattie had hopped on the swing and was flying high through the air, her dress whipping in the wind. Albin, in his immature attempt to garner attention, threw a ball and hit her square in the back of the head.

"What the heck?" Elzi rebuked.

The girl immediately dug her feet into the ruts of dirt below, dragging the swing to a stop. A frown crossed her face, and she hopped off the swing. "Jerks!" she yelled to the boys.

"Not me," replied Elzi. "I ain't throwed nut'in at you."

"Sissy," hissed Albin.

"I ain't no coward, Albie. But dang."

Elzi stood up straighter as the girl approached the boys.

"Which one a y'all hit me?" she asked with her hand upon her hip. Elzi could see the sass all over her and was ready for a good brow beating.

Albin raised his hand, proud to claim the act, and snorted out a laugh. Before he could say a word, Hattie Mae Belgrave reared back her tiny hand that had rested upon her hip and landed a tight fist to Albin's left eye. For a girl no more than seventy-five pounds, she punched with the conviction and skill of someone who'd knocked out a man a thousand times.

At first, Elzi stood in disbelief. Albin, flat on his back, lay limp and knocked out cold. When Elzi looked back to Hattie, he could see tears in her eyes and she was holding her hand tight to her stomach. She obviously was in pain, but when she noticed Elzi looking at her, she straightened up, dropped her hand to her side, and asked pointedly, "Ya need one too?"

Elzi took a step back. The girl was clearly in no mood to take nothing from no one. "I's good," he replied. "You okay?" he asked, gesturing to her hand.

"Don't you worry wit' me," Hattie Mae responded. Her lip curled in disdain. She turned and left the boys, one standing dumbfounded, the other slowly trying to get up off the ground.

A hand reached up to snag Elzi's pant leg. Albin was pulling himself up, his eye already starting to puff up. Elzi looked down at the sad state of Albin and let out a long *woo-wee* and chuckled. He stood, bent at the hips and belly laughed through his fist. "That Hattie Mae done clocked you, boy!" Laughter overcame the scrawny teen and he took to skipping around Albin, making fun and pointing. "You done got CLOCKED! Ha-ha!" His voice got louder and louder. Elzi became so tickled he finally fell to the ground, holding his stomach with one hand and pointing at Albin with the other. Although Albin was quite embarrassed, he couldn't help but finally join in. Elzi's laughter was contagious, and Albin hadn't had a good long laugh since Byron had left him. It felt good to laugh, even with the pulsing pain it brought to his swelling eye.

When Elzi and Albin turned eighteen, they concocted a plan to join the Army. They'd heard of the great Flipper, the first Black student to graduate West Point, who became second lieutenant and then the first Black officer to command regular troops. They'd experienced the same wave of inspiration many young Black men had at learning of his accomplishments. The inspiration was what caught their attention, but it certainly didn't hurt that service with the buffalo soldiers garnered thirteen dollars a month, that the Army provided all meals, equipment, and medical care with their agreement of five years. It seemed not too bad a living, better than working the mills at the Sugar Coast or loading and unloading steamboats for hours on end back at River City. All was backbreaking, tireless work that reaped little wages. The Army seemed a good way to see a bit of the country they might not otherwise get to.

John and Edmee Godwin were none too happy to see their young man join. They feared a life where they couldn't be there to shelter and protect their son from the evils of ignorance, power, and oppression, from the White men who sensed a difference in Elzi and looked at him with visceral hate, calling him an *uppity nigger*. If they ever found out he also was Indian, he'd be a walking target for vitriol. Elzi would be left to his own devices to battle the shame of his Blackness and it put his parents on edge.

Mr. and Mrs. Banks had different views on the matter. They were relieved. Albin had been quite difficult as a child, as one-half of a mischievous pair. When his brother died, he became just one-half of what had once been, and altogether unmanageable. He became a downright pain in the ass. He was angry and bitter, and Mrs. Banks had spent many nights crying as she helplessly watched her husband and son come to blows, her son always ending up on the ground, crying, bleeding, and then disappearing into the night. She had lain awake many nights, praying that he wouldn't find himself caught in the night by White men yearning to teach a lesson.

The young men grew closer while serving in the Tenth Calvary and enjoyed much of it. That life had taken them from the swamps of River City and west to the Texas hills and was, for the most part, somewhat even keeled. That is until word got round that Flipper, their inspiration, had been court-martialed, accused of stealing funds by the Colonel, "Pecos Bill." The accusation had been the center of great debate even though Pecos Bill had a trail of harassment and misconduct charges. As he took lead time and time again of the African American buffalo soldiers, it became no secret that he didn't much like them. Within just a few months of taking command of the fort, he had excused Flipper from his duty and filed criminal charges against him. And any racial tensions that had been quietly smoldering were once again rekindled.

Captain, however, had always been good to the young men, never seemed to mind their Blackness. But Commander had taken to chiding the soldiers, using Flipper's circumstances as a fine example of why *no Negro should ever hold rank 'cause this what you always gone get.* He ignorantly viewed them all as slaves lucky to be there. In fact, they hadn't all been slaves. Many had been, formerly—and were illiterate—but were hardworking and dedicated to their country. Commander saw this dedication as his entitlement, what the Black community owed him. The sentiment took hold amongst the other officers and the contentment of the days dwindled as they set up camp, doing what infantries do while not at battle. Life became incredibly difficult serving under the Commander. And so when presented with the proposition to join the Comanche hunters, Elzi and Albin jumped. Albin packed up his gear. Elzi grabbed Ora B.'s book which held the secret of his heritage, his history, as well as his photograph of Hattie Mae. He and Hattie had shared everything, and bringing her picture along was a way he could share his experience of service to their country with her.

———————

Elzi Dupre and Hattie Mae Belgrave had fallen into what they thought was love quickly and easily. Once they acknowledged their mutual feelings, the two began sharing everything with one another. Elzi shared with her his upbringing, how he came to live with the Godwins in the first place—or what he'd been told anyhow—his desire to one day become a bridge builder like his Pa Godwin. He shared his curiosities surrounding the words written by Ora B. and the secret grief he had, knowing all he'd ever know of his true father and mother, of his brother who hadn't survived, were within the pages of Ora B.'s book.

Hattie shared her love of drawing, her dreams of becoming a schoolteacher one day, and her heart. In the blink of an eye she lost her heart to Elzi Dupre—and with it, her virginity.

Following that raw and unforeseen act, she and Elzi had lain side by side in the grass near the old foot bridge that traversed the creek, staring up into the sky as the colors slowly drained from the day. They hadn't known what to say following their lovemaking, so they dressed quietly and then returned to their respective spots in the grass. As dark approached, Elzi referred to the sky as the Sea of Night. Hattie thought it lovely, to see the stars as islands in the sea. She loved it when he spoke so poetically, though she hadn't known that most of it he got from Ora B.'s writings. She hadn't known that the Sea of Night was not the sky full of stars, but rather the world belonging to the peacefully dead according to the Voodacho religion.

The two could have lain there for hours. She was already going to be in a heap with her pa, coming home late like this, but it was their last night together before Elzi was to leave for the post. They might have stayed until the sun burned its way back into the sky were it not for the sounding of the whip-poor-will calling out its ominous chants over and over and over, its chants that Ora B. had regarded in her writings as *admonitions of death to come*. Elzi tried to ignore it, then tossed rocks at it, but it wouldn't be shooed. It simply took flight, circled the trees, and landed time and time again on the bridge. Something in Elzi stirred strongly at its calls and so he proposed they'd best be getting back. He helped Hattie up, promised her he'd be seeing her again just as soon as he could, and walked her as far as to the end of her road where he watched her sprint the rest of the way home, her dress swishing side to side and her bare feet kicking up clouds of dirt behind her.

At night, when the other men took to drinking and swapping tall tales of their "accomplishments" from back home, Elzi and Albin liked to sit and dream of their futures once out of the Army. They liked to call themselves The Devisers, "architects of our own damn futures." Elzi saw himself as a successful bridge builder. He had dreams of one day building the first bridge to span the 'ssippi at River City. Albin saw himself moving north, far from "this ole Negro-hating South. Maybe to New York". He didn't have much of a plan. Just to get away. Get a job. Anything other than the backbreaking work at the sugar plantations. Elzi supported this dream in theory. Talked about how he and Hattie Mae could come visit him in the big city. But Albin was illiterate, having never spent more than a few weeks in school. Elzi made offers to teach him, even pressured him to learn. "Ya ain't gone make it very easy if ya can't read and write," he would say.

Albin never showed an harterest. "You can just read to me if'n I need to know something."

Elzi would shake his head. "Albin, if I'm building that bridge 'cross the Big River, how I'm gone be reading to you in Gotham?"

Albin would just chuckle. "I'll be aight. I'm a Devisah. I'll devise me a plan and *make* it work."

"What you should do is join *this* Devisah and build that bridge with me. We could be famous."

"Or," replied Ablin, "you could come with me to New York and help them guys building the Brooklyn Bridge. Now that be a famous bridge."

Elzi smiled his gentle smile, for Albin meant well. "No," replied Elzi. "I ain't wanting to just be a workhorse alongside hundreds of other men on a bridge. I want a bridge built from my design, have my name to it."

Albin laughed. "The Dupre Bridge. Don't really have a ring, do it?"

"I don't mean for it to be having my name on it. Just that my name would be in the history books to say I'm someone who did more than break his back to build it. That it required my thinking and ingenuity to get it started to begin with."

Occasionally Albin would give in and let Elzi try to teach him to read and write. They hadn't books available at the fort, only what Elzi brought along. So they used Elzi's *Fences, Gates, and Bridges* book for reading material and some of the blank pages in Ora B's journal to practice writing.

Elzi drew out the letters of Albin's name and handed the book and pencil over. "Here. That's you. Write this down here." He pointed to a line below, drawn for Albin's benefit.

"I know my name, fool." He tossed the book back.

"Fine. Try dis then." Elzi sketched out *New York* and handed the book back.

"What it say?"

"New York," replied Elzi.

A grin spread across Albin's face. He gladly took the pencil and book. Elzi watched Albin's tongue slide side to side as if in sync with the pencil strokes.

"There. What next?"

Elzi sketched out his own name, then Albin's parents' names, his sisters' names. Each time Albin returned the book, he did so with pride.

Elzi sketched the name Byron and handed it over. "It says—"

"I know what it say." Albin clapped the book shut and tossed it over onto the ground beside where Elzi sat. It landed open, face down, a leather-bound tent. "I'm good f' now," he mumbled, and picked up a stick and began stabbing at the logs, enkindling the embers. Albin had never liked to talk about Byron, not the Byron of the tragedy or the Byron before the tragedy. Over the years, he went to great lengths to sever the ties to the memory of the boy whom he had once been the counterpart to, genetically and transcendentally connected to. Byron was a visceral amputation, no less painful than if someone were to cut out half of his beating heart and ask him to live on.

The two sat in silence. Words floated in the ether around them but nothing was said. Elzi picked up the book of his natural mother, brushed the dirt from it, and smoothed out the pages.

"I'm sorry, man," Albin said.

Elzi did not respond but just nodded his head and slowly flipped through the pages, skimming as he went. He finally settled on one. He scooted closer to Albin and read aloud:

Love is an ever-growing mystery. Once you think you have it all figured out, it changes form, moves and shifts, like an apparition hiding once it's been spotted. I once thought my greatest love was my mother. She taught me to love the earth. The earth taught me to love its laws, revealed to me its ways. Then Voodoo. Then when I met Irving Whitewing, I knew he was what love was. And our love grew and intertwined like vines until it was so enmeshed it became one in all ways. It became Voodacho. But it wasn't until my Elzi and Abe were born that I truly knew love.

Elzi closed the pages. He caressed the soft leather cover as if he were carefully caressing her skin. When he looked up, Albin was looking right at him, the fire's reflection dancing in his eyes.

"Elzi," he said with deep concern in his voice, "you gots a brother?"

"I did," he replied.

The two sat in silence for another moment, the information seeping in for Albin to work over.

"You did? You don't no mo'?"

Elzi continued to caress the book, his head tilted in deep thought. He didn't have a suitable answer for Albin.

"You mean he didn't get to go with Mr. and Mrs. Godwin wit' you?"

"I don't know. I mean . . . no."

"Who'd he go wit', then?"

Elzi sighed. "He didn't get to go nowhere. They say they think he died."

This information was all too new for Albin. Here these two had been best friends for the past four years, sharing meals, swapping tall tales, fishing together, becoming The Devisers, becoming men and joining the Calvary together to fight for a county that no more cherished them than the mules in its fields, and Elzi never once mentioned that he had had a brother.

It had always seemed to Elzi like it'd be a slap in Albin's face to try to empathize in the way of revealing that he too once had a brother. Albin and Byron had been inseparable for all of fourteen years, fifteen if you included the time in utero where the preternatural bond was established. Two boys sharing one bloodstream then entering the world seemingly sharing one mind, heart, and soul. Elzi had no recollection of his brother in the slightest. How could it compare? To even try to do so brought upon Elzi the heaviest sense of shame. He couldn't quite pinpoint its nascency, but he had always felt it coalescing with the shame he carried from being a Black boy brought up by White folks, a Black boy *and* an Indian boy brought up by White folks, though no one knew or cared enough to thumb their nose at him for his Hadacho heritage. His black skin was plenty reason enough.

Albin, with all genuineness quietly said, "I'm real sorry f'dat."

Elzi nodded solemnly. "I appreciate it," he replied. He opened Ora B's book and flipped back to the blank pages they had been using. He neatly sketched out the letters T-H-E D-E-V-I-S-E-R-S and handed it over to Albin calling out the words *The Devisers* with a gentle smile. Albin took the pencil and worked through each letter. It took some time, his grip tight on the pencil and the tip digging into the page. He handed the book back to Elzi, stood up, and said he was headed to bed.

"We leave out first thing in the morning, Elzi. Gone hunt us some Comanches and get the hell outta dis fort!"

Elzi, grimaced at the volume of his voice. The two scanned the camp, assuring the words hadn't reached any officer's ears. The men were too engrossed in their drink. Not a worry crossed their minds. Not even that of the hangover to come, the genesis of a thirst they had never and would never experience the likes of again.

Albin clapped and rubbed his hands together rocking forward and back. Once he thought the coast was clear, he bent down and cupped one hand over his mouth to whisper, "and far 'nough out where Commander's whip don't reach, ha-ha!" He straightened back up, grinning ear to ear and unnecessarily brushing and smoothing his shirt. He turned on his heels and left.

Elzi looked down to see Albin's handywork. He had written the words *Albin, Elzi, Byron, Ab*, and underneath, *The Devisers*. He had tried on his own to spell Abe's name, leaving off the E, and the gesture had muddled Elzi's heart in a way that felt both like the kinship and penance of brotherly love.

DIXON ARTOPE

Melroy, Georgia

Dix's family home was in the city limits of Melroy, Georgia, in a small budding neighborhood. It once was a farmhouse on a vast swath of land, but hard times forced Mr. Artope to sell off the majority of it, never anticipating the buyer would section off small plots and construct streets of small Queen Anne style cottages. Their home stood out, an eyesore sandwiched between two brightly colored one-and-a-half story homes. *Living on a damned street of doll houses*, Mr. Artope would grumble.

Dix stayed with his parents for the first few weeks after the shocking and demoralizing shutdown of the school, but he could not find reputable work. His certificate—not diploma—left him dead in the water the moment he handed it over to any hospital administrator or private practitioner. No one wanted to have any association with the now-infamous medical college. No one except Dr. Josephus McNally. It mattered none to him. A quack druggist and acting physician, McNally was skilled in bloodletting to relieve evil humors, blister healing, calomel dosing which was predominately a tincture of mercury and a base, and other antiquated and ludicrous methods. Dix had once referred to these so-called doctors as murderers who attacked patients with instruments of death—namely, poison and the lancet—and now he worked alongside one.

Dix was a calculated man. The closest he ever got to spontaneity happened before the sun even rose. He woke before the sunlight, lit his bedside lantern, and grabbed his Bible. Like a game of chance, he'd close his eyes and thumb the edges of the pages and open at random. With his eyes still closed, he'd run his finger along the page until he got the sense he should stop. Upon opening his eyes, he'd find his finger pointing at the exact message God meant him to receive that day. With the message fresh on his mind and a slight thrill from this daily practice of fate, he'd next hop out of bed and throw on his trousers and a thin shirt, then make his way outside where he performed his daily movements and ruminated on God's word.

Mr. Artope, sitting at the kitchen table, greeted him as he came in from his morning routine. It was Dix's first wake-up at his parents' home since having to return.

"Well my word, Dix. What, are you just coming home from the night?"

"No, Papa," Dix replied. "Just wanted to get in my daily gymnastics."

His father questioned the notion of daily gymnastics, to which Dix replied, "I strongly believe that man should begin his day taking in the bounty of fresh air provided by God and moving his body in such a way that promotes movement of blood. An hour a day, or as the individual constitution allows, is ideal to render the body light and agile, keep the joints pliant, fortify the senses, and make for a restful night's sleep. Physical Culture, Papa."

Mr. Artope nodded and sipped his coffee but didn't dare reply, lest he endure a lecture on the emorals of maintaining one's bendability and stature. It was awfully early for such nonsense.

Often, when Dix finished his shift for the quack doctor, he

headed over to his brother Ford's place in Central City. It was actually further away than his parents' home, but not by much as it sat right on the dividing line of Melroy and Central City, and he didn't mind the extra walk to clear his head. Ford's home was so much . . . cleaner than that of his parents. The filth, he struggled with. Ford's little abode was a clean respite from the anxiety his parents' place induced. Respite or not, once he arrived, looks of pity greeted him. Obviously, he could not hide his misery and his brother and brand-new sister-in-law tried in every way to cheer him up, to bolster his spirits.

Henrietta, just days before, had moved into the short-term rental not far from Terminal Station where Ford worked. Conveniently, it was within walking distance of the Liberty College for Females where Henrietta attended. Only a few days from receiving her diploma, and feeling accomplished enough to call herself a professional schoolteacher, she had to keep her excitement to a minimum as to not rub it in Dix's face. But there was no doubt she was buzzing with excitement.

She answered the door with an oolong tea in hand to greet Dix. "How was your day?" she asked.

Dix dropped his borrowed Gladstone at the door. He had dreamed of the day he would walk into his own home, plop down his own personal prestigious doctor's bag in the foyer, and be greeted by his own adoring wife. Borrowing a used bag from Dr. McNally was just another slap in the face.

He sighed, "Oh, Henri, you know, it was just another day."

Henrietta gave a polite smile and handed over his tea. Dix nodded and took the cup with both hands. A pleasant greeting after an unpalatable day working alongside the opium- and ratsbane-wielding quack. He took a sip and closed his eyes.

Ford said, "You know, just to impart a little blunt human truth, if you're really wanting to get right pert after a day with Dr. Dreadful, you might exchange that cup of yellow peril for an ice-cold honorary libation." Ford held up his glass of Chatham Artillery Punch then took a sip.

Dix snickered. "Yes, if were of the constitutionally sanguine and excitable, I might oblige. But common sense clearly indicates otherwise. I think I shall stick with my tea, brother. You can have your horse-bucket libation and I'll sip my herbal refreshment."

The two clicked their respective beverages and took a sip. Ford was the only person who could tease out what little bantering abilities Dix possessed in his otherwise staid disposition.

Henrietta waved off Ford, as if swiping his words from the room. "Dix, I'm proud of you. A man who sticks to his personal principles even though life pays him in hard-times tokens is a good man in my book."

"Much obliged, Henri," replied Dix.

"Well aren't we the little lickspittle."

Henrietta laughed. "Oh hush up, Ford. I'm not meaning to flatter. I'm speaking from the heart. Dix has had a rough go. We all know this. And many a man might conduct themselves otherwise under the same conditions. Dix has remained true to his morals. He just needs a good break is all."

Ford nodded. "I know, dahlin'." He walked over and kissed her on the cheek. "Aren't I one lucky scoundrel."

Dix agreed. "Scoundrel, indeed."

Ford said, "Say, I know work is work. And I know you feel you must work for Dr. McNally as he's the only—"

Henrietta cleared her throat.

Ford started again, "Work is work, and it's good you can help out Papa and Mother with your wages from Dr. McNally. But Dix, you're not happy. You're not happy with the work. You're certainly not happy back at Papa and Mother's. And if you ain't happy, well . . . neither are we." He pulled Henrietta in close to his side. "Listen, I've been meaning to talk to you." He paused and looked to his wife. She nodded, offering quiet support. "Dix, Henri and I are going to be moving soon after we return from our trip."

"Oh?" asked Dix. "Did you find a more suitable marital home?"

Ford replied, "Not exactly."

Dix knitted his brows.

Ford continued, "I've been offered a position as chief engineer."

Dix's face lit up. "Ford, that's wonderful."

"Thank you, brother. It is wonderful."

Henrietta reached up and gently stroked the back of Ford's neck. Dix could see how much she adored his brother. He loved that for him, for them both. He was happy for the couple, both on their planned paths of becoming professionals and then a family. The professional part, they had in the bag. Now they just needed to purchase their own home, then start on a family.

Ford said, "But it calls for a move. A big move."

Henrietta nodded along, a look of concern creeping across her face.

He continued, "To Texas."

Dix sat his cup of tea down next to him on the console. "Texas?"

Ford nodded. "They're finally gearing up to expand the tracks west of Fort Worth. And I'll be surveying for the best route. The Commission cut a deal with some big-time hotelier here in Georgia. He purchased a hotel to fix up and says we can stay, room and board free, for six months. From there, I'm uncertain as to what we'll do. The project will rightly take years. So I imagine Henri and I will look for a bit of land to homestead. I hear there's plenty of it. And dirt cheap for the taking. Well, until the tracks are done, I suppose."

Henrietta added, "And the hotel too."

Dix said, "You don't say."

Ford said, "Yes, and the hotel too. Seems Mr. Akers has big plans for it. Gonna turn it into some kind of attraction. Make it a draw for the town and try to cultivate a real economy there. It was an old Indian stead at one point. I believe there's a few families there, one or two businesses."

Dix asked, "And it has a hotel?"

Ford said, "Apparently so."

Dix said, "Odd."

Henrietta said, "They say the hotel hasn't been in operation in some time. A failed venture a few times over, we hear. Mr. Akers is looking for help on the revitalization. We've met with his daughter and her husband. They seem like a dream."

Ford added, "Pretty nice folks, really. I think you'd like Lawton. Buttoned-up fella."

"And Claire, why she's an absolute doll. Isn't she, Ford?" Henrietta beamed with excitement.

Dix inquired, "And Henri, what of your plans? I thought you were looking to teach nearby."

Henrietta's smile fell momentarily and then she perked up. "I was, yes. And I still can. I'll just have to do so in Texas."

"Is there a position for you?"

Henrietta's smile fell once more. "Um, not at the moment."

Ford interjected. "There's not a proper school in Element Dale just yet."

"Element Dale?" asked Dix.

"Yes, the town. I don't believe it has a schoolhouse. As I was saying, I believe it's currently just a few homesteads and a few trades along a main road."

"And the hotel," Henrietta said.

"And the hotel," agreed Ford.

"Once Ford gets going and the hotel is up and running and we've got our place, well, we might can look at establishing a schoolhouse there." Henrietta's innate enthusiasm returned, her optimism palpable. While Dix loved she was always positive, he feared she would struggle to withstand the matters of course any amount of failure would certainly bring. The idea of opening a schoolhouse for a handful of families in a town in the middle of nowhere seemed, to him, doomed to fail.

"Sounds nice, Henri," Dix said.

Ford said, "Which brings us to you." He and Henrietta looked at one another, grinning like schoolchildren. "Dix, why don't you come along?"

Dix immediately began shaking his head.

"Hear me out, brother. There's nothing here that—"

"And sounds like there's nothing there either, Ford."

Henrietta said, "Dix, please. Just let Ford finish." Ford shot her a look and she bowed her head, allowing the men to continue uninterrupted.

Ford said, "There's nothing there now. But Element Dale is going to be something someday. And that day is looking to be within just a matter of years. Maybe even just months if the hotel draws the folks Mr. Akers is banking it will."

"Months? Years? And what am I to do in the meantime, brother? Live off the backs of you and your bride here?" He began shaking his head again. "I'll have nothing of it. I didn't work this hard to just—"

Ford held up his hand. "Brother, please. For one time in your damn life, please, just listen. I've not steered you wrong yet, have I?"

Dix huffed and shook his head. "I imagine that's accurate."

Ford smiled. "Yes, brother, that is accurate. Grown men or not, we are brothers. And I'm your big brother. And I will always look after you. This ain't forever, what I'm proposing. God above knows you're a smart and capable man. But God also charges brothers with serving one another." He recited, "But if any provide not for his own, and specially for those of his own house, he hath denied the faith, and is worse than an infidel. So please, shut your trap and listen."

Dix couldn't help but interject. "But that's just it, Ford, I am not of your house. I should not be of anyone's house. I am a grown, highly educated, God-fearing man who should be able to provide his own roof, his own means, and not live under the wing of his big brother."

Ford quieted his voice. "Brother, under my wing you'll always be. Right at my breast, my heart. This is no handout for a sluggard. This is simply another path for you, a faithful servant of God, offered by your flesh and blood. Please, Dix, do not be proud. Try to see this as an opportunity."

"But an opportunity for what? Is there a hospital in Element Dale? A clinic? Whom will I treat? The three residents and you two? I'm not being proud, Ford. I'm being practical. I am grateful for your generosity. Truly. But I'll not hear another word on the matter." Dix picked up his cup and handed it to Henrietta who now stood discouraged, her enthusiasm having finally succumbed.

"Thank you," she said.

Dix picked up the busted and discarded medical bag of Dr. Josephus McNally, the Gladstone a materialized euphemism of his dream of being a respected physician.

"Dix, you don't need to run off."

Dix replied, "But I do, brother. You two have got a train to pack for, yes? I'll be certain to look in on the house while you're gone. Safe travels."

Dix shut the door behind him, the sky now fast darkening. It started to rain while he was inside turning down his brother and sister-in-law, and while he normally would have jogged home, using the drizzle as further motivation to move his body with intention, he did not. Rather he slogged along, letting the rain blend in with the despair that fell from his eyes.

CAROLINE COLLEY

The Higgs Plantation

Caroline Colley wore misery like a veil. Even so, in the immediate days that followed the death of Davis Colley, she had no shortage of support, the most welcomed being that of Henrietta, her longtime best friend. Just as she had been in the tender days when Mary Higgs lost her life giving Caroline a sibling, little Henrietta was at her side. Almost two years after Davis's death, Henrietta remained loyal to her friend, though others about town were comfortable enough to call Caroline "crazy as a Bessie bug" within earshot.

"At what point are you planning to run a comb through that red heap on your head, Chuck? I know you're still widowing and all, but the sight of your hair is hurtin' me something fierce."

Caroline looked up from *The Adventures of Huck Finn* and a broad smile spread across her face at the sight of Henrietta. "Henri! I didn't know you were back!" Caroline dropped the book on the porch and bound down the stairs. The two embraced and spun where they stood under the shade of the mimosa. Caroline grabbed Henrietta's hands and took a step back, taking her in. "Henri, you look wonderful. Did you guys just return? How was your bridal tour?"

"We got back a few hours ago." Henrietta sighed dreamily. "Oh, Chuck, the honeymoon was splendid. And the coast, the water—in all my life, I've never seen such beauty. Chuck, when I think about us splashing around the Ocheese as little girls as if it were some vast ocean . . . we just had no idea. And of course Ford's aunt and uncle were a delight. They took to me right away."

Caroline smiled. "Of course they did, Henri."

"But the best moment was opening a letter to Mr. and Mrs. Buford Artope. It was a card from Ford's boss and his wife. Ford had been hanging on to it, waiting to present it to me at the perfect moment. Chuck, we sat in the sand listening to the waves. We had wine. We had strawberries. And he handed me the card. It had a generous monetary gift inside, but it was seeing *Mrs. Henrietta Artope* in print that really got me. Can you believe it? I'm a Missus!" The two embraced again.

"Well hello, Mrs. Artope," called a deep voice through the screen door.

"Mr. Higgs!" replied Henrietta. She pushed from Caroline and sprinted up the steps and onto the porch where Thomas Higgs stood holding the screen door open with arms wide, ready for her embrace. "It's so good to see you," she said as she gave him a tight hug around the waist.

"Why of course it is, Henri. It's always good for folks to see me. I'm the light of everyone's day. Ain't that right, Chuck?"

Caroline picked up her book and followed Henrietta into the grand plantation home. "Oh, yes," she replied flatly then shot her father a grin as she passed through the door.

The door slammed shut behind the three.

"Henri, you've no bags?"

"No, sir. I stopped by Momma and Daddy's first thing. You know Momma'd be madder'n a wet hen if she found out I come knocking here before seeing her."

Mr. Higgs, stuffing tobacco into a pipe, turned to Henrietta. "I know that's right. It's never wise to cross Martha Moss. And certainly not on my account."

"Daddy," Caroline sighed. "It wouldn't be on your account. She's here to see me."

Mr. Higgs winked at Henrietta. "Um-hum," he replied and went back to working his pipe.

"So Chuck," asked Henrietta, "how are things? How have you been?"

Caroline replied with her standard knee-jerk response she tells anyone who asks. "I'm real good. Peachy. Busy."

"Oh yeah?"

"Yeah. The garden's coming along real nice. Octavia and I work on it just about every day. And we've got quite the cookbook we're coming up with together."

"Like meals for the modern family and such?" inquired Henrietta. "I could use that, being as I'ma need some good ideas for keeping Ford fed and happy." It was plain to see that Henrietta beamed with joy at the idea of carrying out her wifely duties for Ford. She pictured Ford coming home from a long day's work from the railroad, bursting through the front door and snatching her up for an impassioned kiss. He would have missed her terribly. She could see herself suspended in his arms, her feet dangling, and then him breaking the kiss to say, *something sure smells deeee-licious in here, Henri.* He would gently lower her back down and she would give him a spoonful, a glimpse of his meal to come.

"No, not that kind a cookbook, Henri. It's more of a preventions and remedies collection of sorts. Salves and elixirs to help you keep your health or heal your body if it's sick or injured."

At this Henrietta covered her grin with a dainty hand and reached out to Caroline with the other. She leaned forward and placed it on Caroline's knee.

"Henri? What is it?" asked Caroline.

Henrietta pulled her hand from Caroline's knee. She clasped her hands together in front of her mouth. She held them there and turned completely sideways on the sofa to get a solid face-to-face with Caroline. "Chuck, hear me out.

"Oh no," bemoaned Caroline. "What is it?" She adjusted herself slightly askew, now uncomfortable facing Henrietta straight on.

"So about Dix—"

Caroline shot up from the couch in retreat. "Nope. Nope. Henri, I have no interest—"

Henrietta stood and interrupted her. "Chuck, you don't even know what I was about to say."

"Sure I do." Caroline walked over to the bookcase at the far side of the great room. It held books floor to ceiling, a rarity to come by. She paced back and forth as if searching for a particular book, but her mind raced with irritation rendering her search but a ruse. "You think I need to move on. You think I'm off my rocker and a *man* would do me good. And worse, you seem to think I need a doctor man who can love me *and* treat me with his quack medicines and skills. Well, I ain't about to—"

Henrietta caught up to her from behind and rested a hand on the back of her shoulder. Caroline stopped her pacing as to not reject the comfort of her best friend, but she could not hide her trembling.

"Chuck?" Henrietta gave a gentle pull to spin her around.

Caroline turned but could not make eye contact. Her eyes had filled with tears, something that infuriated her, and so to avoid any further emotional nudge, she looked up to the ceiling.

"What, Henri?"

She quickly wiped at a rogue tear and then faced Henrietta straight on. She anticipated seeing Henrietta's face painted with great concern or pity or, like many other people who'd tried to help her and fell short, simple resolve. But that is not what she saw. Instead, Henrietta had wiped any possibility of pity from her expression. She now held a face of simple contentment. Caroline took a deep breath, crossed her arms, and switched her weight to her left. The urge to release any more tears was easing, the burn subsiding.

Henrietta, all too unwilling to push her anywhere near the edge replied, "I was hoping to see the garden, Chuck. Think we can take a pass at it before I have to head out?"

At this, the heavy sensation of shame and fear lifted. She perked up, uncrossing her arms. She gave a single clap. "Why yes!" she exclaimed. "And I imagine Octavia is out there now, so you can say hello to her and hug her neck."

Though Thomas Higgs owned the largest pecan plantation in Melroy County, the peach orchard was his pride as it was the doings of his lovely bride before she left his world. It sat in the far east corner of the immediate property, nearest the creek. Rough cedar fencing, overgrown with honeysuckle, hedged it in. Once inside, whichever angle you took to scan the layout, the result was always the same. Crisscrossing rows of beautiful and fragrant fruit trees with groomed paths connecting them all like a giant grid. As girls, Caroline and Henrietta loved to play chase in the orchard. No matter how close one might get to her target, the other could easily circle a tree and dodge being tagged. And when playtime was over, sweet treats dangled above for the picking.

Caroline could remember walking the grounds with her mother. Mary, grand with child, with a sack slung across her shoulder would walk the orchard daily. *To help the baby along,* she would say. Octavia joined to keep an eye on her and would attempt to walk a few steps ahead and collect the fallen fruits before Mrs. Higgs got to them. If ever Mrs. Higgs would change her course and manage to find one before Octavia could get to it, Caroline would hear Octavia clicking her tongue and scolding her mother. "No reason you 'ought be having ta bend and squat, Missus. Now let me."

Caroline delighted in helping the women. She'd skip with the bounding energy of a young child, picking up fallen peaches and dropping them into her mother's bag which she insisted on carrying against Octavia's admonitions. Many times Caroline would weave in and out between the trees, catching their trunks and spinning this way with her right hand, catching the next and spinning that way with her left. The women would get lost in conversation and Caroline would get lost in her imagination. The orchard had become her home, she its fairy. The peaches, her magical fruit. Its honeysuckle was magical too. And alive. And her helpers. She'd carry her doll and a book to the orchard and set up "class." She'd spend hours playing and reading to the doll, and when the little thing would have a booboo or tummy ache, Caroline would approach the vines and curtsy. "Excuse me," she would say, "my child has fallen ill. Would you be so kind as to offer up your magic medicine?" The little girl would curtsy again and give a hearty "why thank you!" She'd reach into a single honeysuckle blossom, pinch its long slender style, and gently slide out the "sliver of power." She'd hold the blossom's sliver to the doll's lips making sucking sounds and comforting the doll. "Now, now. That's better now, ain't it?" Then she'd slip the sliver into her own mouth and slide it out, sucking all its sweetness.

When she grew a few years older—and out of the doll phase— she'd still go out and teach. With no doll to address, she came to imagine her own students, her favorite being Mable. Mable was a little toe-headed girl, five or six, with "sparkly eyes." Until Henrietta came along, she had been her best friend—sometimes her scapegoat. Sweets missing from the kitchen? "No ma'am, Miss Octavia, I ain't seen no sweets. But Mable, maybe she snagged 'em." Tools missing from the gardening shed? "No, Daddy, but Mable can be a little sneak thief. Maybe she done took it." Mable became a common name around the plantation, in the house among family and friends, in the fields among the help. Everyone knew Mable and knew she was the mischievous one, not little Caroline.

The many trips and hours in the orchard with her mother and Octavia left her much time to explore. She'd guard the perimeter from "those union sneak thieves," lest they come to "pillage this magical fruit to win the Great Pitched Battle." She and Mable would make their hedge examinations, looking for signs of a breach. A low and thinned area revealed itself by way of small animal tracks. "Ah-ha! I knew you scoundrels would find a way in." She'd lowered herself onto her hands and knees, crawling through what she imagined being a portal in time, coming out into a raw area of the property. She lost interest within the confines of the orchard and took to crawling daily through the small space. It opened up to an area no bigger than fifty by fifty covered in brambles and briars with a few trees and abutted the Ocheese Creek. As the years passed, this became her secret garden to play in. As she grew more and more interested in plants and nature, it became her experimental garden— and a place where she came to consult Mable or, as she'd say, just gather her thoughts.

She'd taken steps to clean it up some during her prepubescent years, hence the missing gardening tools. Dreaming of having a real magic garden, she'd planted some seeds here and there with the unwittingly given guidance of Octavia. And then when her mother passed, Caroline lost her zest for magic and the garden fell back into ruins, its briars and thorny vines growing up and choking out any sign of bloom or burgeon.

Caroline and Henrietta made their way slowly to the peach orchard. Henrietta filled Caroline in on her final days at Liberty, life living at Ford's short-term rental, their trip to the coast, and what Ford's folks were like. "He grew up real poor, you know, Chuck. And they work hard. All of 'em. We stop by his momma and daddy's often. Ford takes them money when he can. But we're not gonna be around much longer. That's really what I come to talk to you about, Chuck." The two walked side by side, hand in hand, along the dirt path that led to the orchard. The sky above was clear, a baby blue. The sun was hot, but not sweltering under the shade of the oaks that canopied above the path. Their leaves allowing bits of sunshine to stipple the path here and there. There was a nice breeze, and for that, all were grateful.

The two approached the entrance to the orchard—an arched arbor covered in azaleas. Entering was like leaving one world and stepping into another. One from the past from when they were just girls and Mary could be found at one of the trees, delicately plucking her rewards from her hard work and patience. The air seemed slightly cooler, slightly sweeter. A bench sat just right of the main walking path once inside, a place where one could sit and admire Mary Higgs' creation, remember her laughter, her loving embrace. *With Sweet Remembrance, Mary, 1839 to 1863* was etched into its top wooden slat. Caroline never passed by the bench without allowing her hand to graze its words for a moment.

As they walked and weaved among the peach trees, Henrietta made her case. "Chuck, Ford's doing real nice with the railroad. And they are expanding. They need him to go out and start the surveying to the west. He got promoted to chief engineer." The look on Henrietta's face was something Caroline couldn't quite make out. She was excited, she could see. But she also was clearly not getting to the heart of the matter.

Caroline stopped walking and turned to face Henrietta. "Henri, quit yer hem-hawin' and just say it."

"Okay, fine. We got to move, Chuck."

"And?"

"Like to Texas."

Caroline replied, "Okay? So what's the big deal?"

Henrietta knew to give Caroline time. Her initial response was never one of authenticity but of self-preservation. This time, to preserve her sense of stability with those she surrounded herself with, she feigned indifference that her very best friend would soon be gone miles and miles away.

"Well, I can come visit you anytime." Caroline picked a peach and hurled it into the wall of honeysuckle.

"Sure you can," replied Henrietta, fighting off the burn of tears.

"When they get the railroad all done, and you've got a mind to, you can pop on over anytime you get a free week or two." She contrived hope, but it was a lost cause. The tears were starting to stream. She took a handkerchief and blotted her cheeks. Up ahead, she watched as Caroline squatted down, ducked into the vines, and disappeared.

Begrudgingly, she followed. Henrietta crawled into the opening of the secret garden, dusting herself and patting her hair, slightly annoyed at this little hide-and-seek Caroline was insisting upon. What once were brambles and briars were now lush rows of fragrant herbs. No more thorny vines remained. In their stead were beautiful trellises of tiny trumpets. Awe quickly washed away any annoyance and flooded Henrietta's senses. She could easily detect the sweet fragrance of gardenia, the clean smell of lemon balm, and the woodsy scent of mulberry bushes. As she made her way further into the garden, hints of mint and basil tickled her nose.

"My word, Chuck," she gasped.

Caroline held back the urge to grin from ear to ear. "It's been something else, for sure."

A voice from behind agreed, "Yes, chile."

Henrietta spun around and squealed, "Octavia!" She ran and wrapped her wiry arms around the plump woman and kissed her cheeks. "Octavia, it's so good to see you."

Octavia gave a crooked grin, "An' you. Now let meh arms loose." Octavia held a basket of cut herbs in one hand, in the other a set of shears.

"Sorry, Miss Octavia. I'm just real happy to see you."

Octavia, now free from the bear hug of Henrietta, bent forward with a grunt to set down the basket. She braced her back with a fist to stand back up. "An' you," she repeated, sounding full of exhaustion.

"Octavia, you really ought not be bending that-a-way. Kills your back every time," scolded Caroline.

"Hush, chile. Mind yer own," replied the woman. She doddered over to the corner and lifted up a small stool. She carried it over to a patch of plants, tossed the stool down, and plopped down upon it.

She dragged the basked up under the plants, and with her legs spread wide, she began pruning.

"Is that stinging nettles?" asked Henrietta. She turned for assurance from Caroline, assurance that Octavia hadn't lost her mind.

Caroline smiled.

"'Tis," replied the woman with a hint of disdain in her voice. "Nettles is mo' than just fer stepping on in the brush. You have a mind to heal, you can heal wit' even the nettles."

Henrietta lifted an eyebrow. "You don't say?"

Octavia raised a brow and clicked her tongue at her. "I *do* say."

Caroline interjected. "I've studied up a bunch on the essences of plants, their natural properties and how to use them. We've mixed 'em up this-a-way and that, and I think we've crafted us a nice little salve for gout."

"Huh," was all Henrietta replied. Even though Caroline had told her this garden was for producing the ingredients for salves and potions and whatnot, she still envisioned a vegetable garden of sorts. Thought she might make out nice today with a few carrots and tomatoes, even some fresh spinach leaves. "Well, who you testing all this on?"

"At first, just myself. Octavia showed me some ways her people used to treat this and that, and with her Geechee knowledge and the books I got, we come up with some enhancements. But I just use myself to make sure they ain't gonna cause no undesirable reactions and such. Our help out there come in contact a lot with irritants, come down with illness right easy. Octavia talked to them, and they obliged to take and use our medicinal potions. Been having positive responses. Real nice results, Henri. So we just been making adjustments here and there, recording what we find, and once we feel right nice about things, we write out the recipe in our cookbook. We now to—what, Octavia?—about seventy-five or so recipes."

"Umm-hmm." Octavia did not look up. She just kept pruning and dropping nettle heads into the basket below.

Henrietta's face lit up. "So that's why I wanted you to meet up with Dix. Dix would—"

"Dix who?" Caroline asked, as if she'd had already forgotten *the man.*

Henrietta huffed and propped her fist upon her hip. "You know Dix who. So Ford's little brother went to medical school, learned all about healing and whatnot. You two might have a ton to talk about, Chuck. Not like romantic talk. Just—I don't know, Chuck. Just *something* to talk about."

"Henri, I know you all think a doctor knows it all. Lord knows doctors think doctors know it all. But they ain't all-knowin'. They ain't God. And they damn sure ain't healers. They cut you and slice you not knowing what the hell might be the outcome. Drain you of your blood to rid *the evil.*" She held up air quotes. "Pump you full of toxins when God done made all this here to help us. Doctors, from what I've seen—and you know Daddy done made me see a bunch of 'em—is all quacks. Chair-spinning, bloodletting, lance-and-we'll-see-what-comes-of-it quacks. No. Thank. You. Ma'am."

Octavia gave a little snort. Henrietta frowned in her direction.

"Look, Henri, I appreciate you wanting me to not be lonely and all that. But I ain't lonely one bit. I got Octavia here. I got my garden. I got Daddy—"

Octavia mumbled under her breath, "She got Miss Mable."

"Whatever," sighed Caroline. "Point is, I don't need no man to keep me, love me, or heal me. I'm fine. And when you get all settled in Texas and whatnot and you're ready for a visit, I'll come calling. Until then, I'll be right here, right fine." She dusted her hands, signaling the end of her monologue.

"Okay," Henrietta resolved. "Well, you never did let me get to the real point. Just know, if you decide you're done with Melroy and these folks here, you got a place in Texas. You can start fresh." She paused, knowing this next line, she needed to tread easy. "And no one there'll know nothing about . . . " She hesitated and then mustered up what she needed to spit it out. "Well, no one there'll know a thang about Davis and your troubles. That's all."

Octavia, still bent forward over her basket, took a quick glance out of the corner of her eye, watching the two women standing toe-to-toe, staring the other down. Finally Henrietta broke the silence. "Chuck, I'm going to teach there. Ford'll be working with the railroad, surveying for the next stretch of track. Dix could start up a clinic of sorts. You could do something too. We all have an opportunity to start fresh." She paused a moment, letting the idea of a fresh start hang in the air. She took a deep breath, smoothed the front of her skirt and said, "Chuck, Mr. Higgs did tell me about you still thinking Davis is going to kill you—"

"No, I didn't say—he said someone's gonna—rather, he knows someone's gonna—he talked about Mother Nature—I didn't say—oh, whatever, Henri," she huffed and flung her hand. "I'm not crazy. This ain't no Mable situation. I ain't making him up. He ain't my friend." She began to tremble. Henrietta could see Caroline's neck and cheeks flushing. Octavia stood. Caroline continued, "I don't need no doctor man. I don't need a fresh start. These people here can just go to hell if they think I'm crazy. And so can you!"

Henrietta covered her mouth to conceal her gasp. Caroline paused a moment, wishing to snatch back the ugly words she'd flung at her best friend, but she could not. Instead, she set her jaw, made an about-face, and stomped off to the small opening in the hedge.

Henrietta watched as Caroline crouched down to scramble through the opening, a vine snagging her hat and ripping it from her head. A moment later, Henrietta saw a hand reach back through, grab the hat, and disappear. She turned to Octavia, now standing just beside her, also watching, her face twisted up.

"Octavia, is she okay?"

Octavia took a deep breath. "Can' no one say, fer certain, Miss Henrietta. But she done see Mistah Colley clear as I see you. She don't no more say so, but he here wit' she. All day. 'Er day. I sees she glance and she body shuttah. And when I look, don't nobody I see.

But she see. And she hear. And he warn she, she say. Somebody gwine die of the poison from the nature's mama."

Henrietta sighed. "Well maybe you two ought be more careful with the potions, you think?"

Octavia clicked her tongue. "Don' go tinkin I gwine kill someone. I know what I know. Geechee woman don't kill less she must. I don't have a must." She tossed the shears into the basket and grunted as she bent down to pick it up. "Let's head back to da house, Miss Henrietta. It's getting 'bout time fer me to make Mista Higgs he supper."

The two women crawled through the opening and back into the orchard, Octavia grunting and grumbling about the state of the exit way. "All dis crawling. Nonsense."

———

Laughter boomed from the old plantation home as Octavia and Henrietta approached. At the sound of her husband's voice, Henrietta broke away and sprinted up the steps and into the house. Inside stood Ford and Mr. Higgs. The two were standing in the great room, exchanging stories, catching up.

"Now there's my lovely bride." Ford beamed with pride when Henrietta walked through the door. She sprinted up and into his arms and he wrapped her in a bear hug. "Mmm-mm," he cooed and kissed her on the forehead. "Ain't never gonna tire of looking into these sweet molasses eyes." Henrietta giggled with delight and gave him a quick kiss on the cheek.

"You two looking forward to Texas? Where abouts y'all gonna be?" asked Mr. Higgs.

Ford and Henrietta parted, now simply holding hands. Ford answered, "Yes, sir. We'ah very much looking forward to going. The ride there's going to be quite the run. They say a little over a month, a little rough at times. But we'ah going to have a few families come alongside us. Should be just fine."

"And where abouts in Texas did you say?"

"Little place a bit west of Fort Worth. Railroad is expected to lay tracks out that-a-way. Well, actually even west of there. They's looking to link up the GH&SA tracks with Central Pacific out near a place called Pecos. It'll be a challenge for certain. We'll get it all surveyed and then make the call whether to dig and tunnel or bridge across some trouble spots. It'll be good steady work."

Henrietta jumped in. "And the little town we intend to start our family in is called Element Dale. Ford says it's practically brand new. Just a handful of folks just yet. So we can set it all up how we like."

Ford chuckled at Henrietta's enthusiasm. "There's a few homes and businesses along a main thoroughfare," he said. "It used to be an old Hadacho dwelling until a few families settled it. Supposed to be a real interesting location. I hear there's still the sacred Indian mounds alongside a creek nearby. Silas Creek, I think it is. Off the Barron River. I expect it'll be mighty nice. A great place for us to start life anew and build us a family. And Henri here can get her a little classroom going."

Mr. Higgs said, "Well that sounds real nice, you two. Once the tracks are down, I can come and see the place sometime."

Henrietta quickly clapped her hands with delight. "Oh, Mr. Higgs, that would be lovely!" She cleared her throat and smoothed her dress. "I told Chuck the same. That she should come. Not to visit, I mean. That she should come with us." She lowered her voice. "Mr. Higgs, I think it would do her some good to get out of Melroy. Start fresh."

Thomas Higgs tilted his head and pulled the pipe from his mouth. "Now, I don't know about all that. I think Chuck might not be quite"—he scratched his chin—"fit for that. Life on her own, that is. She's still a bit"—he paused, choosing his words carefully—"delicate."

"Ain't a damn thing delicate about me." Caroline flung her hat onto the side table, startling the others.

"Oh! Well, there's my number-one redhead." Mr. Higgs held out an arm, inviting Caroline into the room. She was standing in the doorway, a carrot in her fist. She took a big bite and crunched loudly.

"Yes, here I am," she said with slight sarcasm. "Look, I don't need you guys deciding when and where I'm gonna visit or live or whatever is it you're all planning here. I'm a grown woman. I can take care of myself. Make my own choices. I finally got my garden going. The book is coming along nicely. My sketches are in place. And I got in touch with the publishers out in Atlanta. Once I finish up these last few tests and recipes, I'll have it all organized and sent off."

"Chuck, you writing a book?" asked Ford.

"Octavia and I here are crafting a remedies cookbook of sorts. A book on healing aliments and such with plants."

"Oh! Then you should meet my baby brother. He's a doctor. I'm sure he'd love to read what you've got. He could give you a few pointers."

Caroline smirked. "I bet he could."

Henrietta tilted her head and gave Caroline a stern stare. The *please don't be rude to my new husband with your anti-doctor semantics* stare.

Caroline returned Henrietta's look with a quick flash of her best false smile.

Ford said, "He'd be honored to. I just know it. He finished up medical school last fall. Been working for a druggist of sorts until he establishes his own practice."

"Oh yeah?" Chuck feigned interest.

"You two'd have lots to talk about, Caroline," replied Ford.

Mr. Higgs jumped in. "You should invite him over, Ford. In fact, we should invite a whole host of folks over, being as y'all 'bout to skip town. How's about we have us a going-away gathering?"

Ford said, "Oh, Mr. Higgs, you don't—"

Mr. Higgs gave one loud clap and rubbed his hands together, startling Caroline. He walked over to her and wrapped an arm around her shoulder. Holding his pipe up in the air, he boasted, "Yes, that's what we'll do. This Saturday. Out back. Tell your folks, Ford, to come on out. Henri, Love, you do the same. Tell your momma and daddy we gonna have us a proper sendoff here at the plantation.

Chuck and I'll send word to the neighbors, some friends. How's that sound?"

Mr. Higgs beamed at the idea of hosting a gathering. His last had been over two years ago, in honor of Davis's political running, a campaign kickoff. The tragedy that followed soured any notion of celebration among what was left of his family—or Caroline's for some time. Caroline certainly hadn't been well enough to endure a crowd. Her father understood that, understood why. But maybe she just needed to get back up on that horse. Face the folks of Melroy again. She was a bright and strong woman who'd swung from traumatized and terrified to haunted, suspicious, and outright cynical. But now he thought a house full of laughter and friendly faces might do her some good, might remind her how lovely her small community could be if she'd just look past the whispers here and there. Any town would always have its fair share of whispers. It all just depended on which ones you let tickle your ears. Mr. Higgs thought of the possibility of Caroline enjoying herself once again among company, the possibility of even finding love again. He also knew she'd never outright agree to it. So against his better judgment, he threw in one last remark.

"And bring your brother too, Ford. I'd love to meet the great new doctor. Shake his hand."

At this, Caroline rolled her eyes and left the room. She found Octavia in the kitchen, peeling potatoes. "Well, Octavia, looks like we's having a party this weekend." Her voice dripped with sarcasm.

Octavia continued peeling, unfazed. "Not we. Y'all. Dis just means work fa me."

"I'll help," offered Caroline. She patted Octavia on the back and then reached across and grabbed the potatoes that Octavia had peeled and dunked them in the tub of water to rinse the grit. She grabbed a knife and began cubing them up. Octavia set down the potato peeler and looked at the woman beside her with a sense of pride only a mother knows. She reached out and placed her hand on top of Chuck's head and gave her a gentle press.

"Good chile," she said softly. "You's a good chile. You hear me?"

WALKER WESTBERRY

Westberry Mountain
The Black Mountains of North Carolina

In the North Carolina moonlight, a few hundred feet up the southern slope of Westberry Mountain, the hillside levels out into a wide, grassy bench before climbing again to the summit where sits the entrance to a small cave. Inside, a passageway leads down fifty feet or so along a rock ledge to a dead end where water trickles from a crack in the sandstone wall. A second passageway extends another fifty feet or so to the left to a tiny stream. This natural rock formation served as the Westberry family's fresh water source, its refrigerator—electricity not even a thought until the mid-1930s—and a hiding place for its moonshine for years. The Honey Hole. Willard Westberry always viewed it as Mother Nature's gift to his craft. Now it was an abandoned cave that simply served as a hideout for youngins to come together to kiss, to have relations of the body and heart. Occasionally a squatter would make use of it until being discovered, but it never regained its former glory once Waylon took over the business.

If you stood at the summit and stared down through the trees long enough, you could make out the rusted rooftop of the old still house down below and, a few hundred feet downhill from that, the tiny Westberry cabin. From Walker's view across the way in the red spruces, as he hid from the agents below, he could see how all could have been different. How the Honey Hole could have protected this family and its cloistered assets for years and years to come. Generations' worth of work, craft, memory, money—all lost because of the unfortunate and lazy move begot by Waylon, and then stupidly upheld by Walker out of sheer laziness.

Down below, shouts echoed from all around. Nadene, huge with child, stood on her tiptoes to gain ground while being yanked around by the platinum blonde hair of her head. The agent holding her shouted up into the trees, "Walker, you a-gonna leave your old lady here to take all yer heat?"

Nadene gave the man an elbow and in return he yanked her hair, causing her to lose her footing and stumble. She screamed, "Get off me, you sonofabitch!"

Walker felt but an inkling of concern for his cousin, his wife. He considered what he could do to help her. However, it was her own fault she couldn't get out of bed in time. The birds had done their job. Her fat ass had not. *Take her*, he thought.

He watched through the trees as Nadene struggled to free herself from the man. She held onto his wrists above and whimpered. Finally she spun and gave him a knee to the groin. The response was swift. The man, having never lost his grip on her long white hair, slung her to the ground. She landed belly first. Hard. She didn't scramble to run away as Walker thought she might. Instead, she rolled onto her side, curled into a fetal position, and held her stomach. The man stood bent forward, his hands on his knees like a spent athlete, saying something to her Walker could barely hear. Then Nadene let out a roar.

Two other agents ran to the man and Nadene. Walker could see one crouched down, the others keeping their distance. He couldn't make out what was going on. But he could hear her cries of pain. The crouched man stood. The three of them encircling her, staring down and occasionally looking around.

One hollered out, "Now's your chance, Walker. Might should come on out!"

Walker sat silent, keeping his location concealed, guarding his freedom. He could see the man talking to the other two, his arms gesturing orders. The two men bent down and pulled Nadene up from under her arms. She howled, sending birds bursting from the trees. Yet Walker sat immovable. He watched as the two dragged her off, her hands clenched at her belly, her heels rutting the ground in a trail. She no longer fought but simply cried.

The agent cupped his hands to his mouth and shouted, "One last time! Now's your chance. Old girl here ain't a-looking too good. You best just man up and come tend to her!" A few seconds passed. "We'll make you up a cell right next to her!" The agent waited certain this would do the trick.

Nothing.

He punted a rusted bucket and cursed. Walker watched as he left the clearing and headed toward Nadene and the others. Eventually all voices faded away. The trampling of leaves stopped. All fell silent. *Not this time either assholes*, he thought and chuckled under his breath. He turned and sat on the ground, resting his back against the tree. It had been a long night. But a fun one. The revenuers managed to nab J.P., Sam, and Nadene. It'd be about a month or so before he figured he see them again. He lit a smoke, leaned his head back, and closed his eyes. He'd have to run shit on his own in the meantime. *Not that I ain't been doing most the damn work anyhows. Them twins a-gonna have to get their shit together and pick up the slack.*

He tried to enjoy his cigarette, but all he could imagine was his peepaw shaking his head in disappointment and righteousness. He could hear him saying, *Well Walker, I ain't above saying I tode ya so.*

Your daddy was a drunk gimp. His excuses are his own. You's just damn-right stubborn. Maybe not right in the head neither. These raids wouldn't have happened if it weren't for his dad having the operation moved from the Honey Hole back down the mountain. That, he was certain. He knew he himself could have moved it back once Waylon was dead and gone. His choice—the wrong choice—was to keep it where it was. *Fuck the government*, he had replied to those that tried to talk sense into him. *Let 'em come.* He was too bold for his own good. Too selfish.

He took his last drag and scratched it out on the ground. Like a slapped dog, he sat for a minute longer, leery to return lest it be too soon. He caught a whiff of smoke. And not tobacco smoke. Wood smoke. He grunted and pushed his back off the tree, hopping up, and turned to face his fate.

Flames had climbed up the walls of that old still house and made the grand leap into the trees above. Smoke billowed as the flaming liquid shine below rolled down the hill scorching a path to his little log house. Through the crackling of wood and the hissing bursts of erupting cauldrons, Walker heard the whoops and hollers of the revenuers in the distance. He had no choice but to sit and watch, lest he be discovered. Within minutes, the still house exploded, the fire unable to contain its fury a second longer—with his tiny cabin's demise well on its way.

He had evaded them, humiliated them, and ultimately murdered one of their own. The agents' dogged pursuit of the Westberry operation's unpaid revenue had been a failure. But they did not hang their heads in defeat. They did not feel that sense of total loss. Because where they could not collect their revenue, they had taken revenge. Walker might not have been physically caught, but he was trapped. He had nothing left, nowhere to go. No still house. No liquid assets. No wife. No home. The Black Mountains offered nothing more to him now than sorrow and loss and defeat. Which he could not abide.

He turned his back to the flames and slid back down the tree to sit. He lit another cigarette and took a deep drag. He tilted his head back and watched the smoke above him swirl and spin with the rivulets of wind that cut through the treetops. He thought, *fuck it all. Fuck them assholes. And fuck this place.*

ELZI DUPRE

The Staked Plains, Texas

Under the night sky, black with twinkles of light dotting the void, leaned up against the mesquite bush with Albin and Jasper, Elzi dreamed of water. The mesquite rustled in the night's hot breeze. Each breath he took raked against his dry throat. A black vulture perched upon Jasper's right foot. It eyed the three men sitting hip to hip and shoulder to shoulder. Elzi rested his head on Albin's shoulder. Jasper rested his head on the other. Elzi dreamed that as the three men sat under the bush, their legs straight out in front of them, he saw a man walking toward them in the distance. As the man got closer, Elzi was able to make out a walking stick, and then feathers, feathers fluttering at the end of the stick. In his other hand swung a human head, held by the hair. He walked steadily toward the trio of troopers. Before each step the man struck the ground with his stick. *Shwack.* Something clattered along the way, creating a rhythm, a beat, like a wind chime with a conductor far more structured than the breeze. *Clatter, clink.* The feathers at the end of the stick fluttered with each swing. *Shwack.* Smalls plumes of red dirt hung in the air, trailing each foot like a ghost—*clatter, clink*—until the plumes scattered with the sigh of the wind. Three plumes of dirt as he walked, one from each foot—*clatter, clink*—one from the feathered stick—*Shwack. Clatter, clink. Shwack.*

Elzi wished he could stand, but his body betrayed him. He wished he could run. All he could do was watch the man as he came into view.

The man walked without caution. He stood strong and erect, his skin painted a glistening black, adorned with painted bones of stark white as if to display his skeleton on the outside with nothing to hide. Sweat ran down his body, streaking the paint. The moon reflected from his slick head and he rattled and jingled with necklaces of many. When he finally reached the men, he towered over them, stopping inches from their feet. Scents of charred wood, black earth, and buffalo tallow wafted in the air. Elzi could not look up to meet his eyes. His body would not move. His neck betrayed him. But his eyes did not. Before him were moccasin'd feet, slim legs slicked in black and white, and the face of a dead man dangling from a tight grip. The head, buzzing with flies, hung right at Elzi's eye level. It was that of a White man's, old and grayed with eyebrows that had grown this way and that. His face, once shaven, was now prickly gray and sun worn with deep lines. His sunken eyes had been sewn shut. Strands of thick coarse horsehair stitched his mouth closed. Elzi wanted to jump back, get up and run, but he could not—his body rooted to the ground as solid as the tree he leaned upon.

The knees before him slowly bent, and the dangling bones and baubles bounced and clanked as he lowered himself into a squat. The head hit the ground with a thud beside Elzi's legs, rocking back and forth a few times before settling in against his ankle. It rested face down. For this, Elzi felt great relief, to not have to stare into the eyes. Its long gray hair splayed about the ground across Elzi's foot and from it a stench invaded his senses. The man, squatted down before him, grabbed a canteen slung around his shoulder. He tossed it into Elzi's lap. Elzi wanted badly to pick it up and have a drink. But he could not make his hands move. He sat slumped, his head dangling. If not for the nape of his neck, he feared it too might fall to the ground and join the White man's. Elzi's cracked lips hung limp and heavy. He sat staring at his own hands, clasped in his lap. *Move*, he thought. But the hands would not. *Grab it.* They betrayed him.

Elzi wanted badly for this man, this Indian to pick the canteen up and place it to his lips. He could not even summon his head to lift and look up into the Indian's eyes to yearn. He could only see the White man's head, the Indian's knees, and his feet planted in the dirt before him. The painted man straightened back to standing. He stepped toward Albin, sandwiched in the middle. He kicked Albin's foot and Albin gave a groan but nothing more.

Wake up, Albie! Wake up! The words rushed just to the edge of Elzi's lips, never making it through. His mouth failing him as his hands had done.

Next Elzi watched as the feet stepped over further to where Jasper's legs lay exposed. The bird still perched on his foot. One moccasin lifted to bump Jasper's foot. Jasper did not yell out or groan. He did not stir or seem to wake. The foot kicked a little harder. Jasper's leg slid to the side. The bird did not take flight. It did not caw. It did not take its beady gaze from Elzi. Jasper's body sat quiet. Still. All was quiet and still, save the soft bouncing of bones and beads and the dancing of the mesquite tree in the wind.

Wind chimes of the wicked, Elzi thought.

A voice deep and disembodied replied, "No, amulets of the abandoned."

The wind burst against Elzi's face. In his mind, he could see the pages of Ora B.'s book. The breeze flipping them one at a time, three at a time. Its gusts finally easing and the pages settling on her words of thanksgiving to Mother Nature for the trees. Elzi felt grateful for this lone mesquite upon which he, Jasper, and Albin gave over their exhausted bodies.

Why do trees whisper? Ora had written. *They speak, yet what do they say? Is it hello? Have a seat. On me, under me. Allow me to offer* you shade from the fire above. Is this what they whisper? No. Maybe once, before they knew best. Not any longer.

God dismissed man from Paradise. "You're on your own," he told him.

Man looked around at this great earth and said, "I must build a roof to put over my head. A chair to rest upon. Wood to burn to cook my food. Where shall I gather such elements?" He looked to the ground, the plants, the trees. He spotted a beautiful cedar. He reared back his ax and swung.

"No," it cried, "can you not see my tears?" Man looked and could indeed see sticky tears dripping from the cut. He reared back the ax once more. "If you strike me again, I shall bring you bad luck," warned the tree. Not wishing to start this life under the spell of bad luck, the man moved on, leaving the trees to exchange their wails of warning.

Next he spotted a grouping of bald cypress trees. He peeled back some its long fibrous ridges to reveal a solid wood beneath. As he did, the tree shrieked, "Please do not tear me down." The man ignored its plea and picked up his ax. He swung and the ax sank deep into its center. "Swing once more, and you shall stumble and fall the rest of you days." The man yanked his ax from the trunk. As he stepped back, the trees began to cry, their feathering needles whispering their high-pitched admonitions.

He next approached a strong imposing white oak, thinking of how much one tree could provide. He swung and buried his ax into the trunk. It cried out, course-grained and throaty, "Do not cut me down. You will grow tired trying and I will rain my stones upon you as you rest."

He pulled his ax from the tree and swung into it once more. Its leaves flapped like many flags in the wind and hundreds of acorns rained down. He dropped his ax, ducked and covered his head with his hands, waiting for it to cease. But the moment he reached to retrieve the ax again, the flapping returned and with it the high-pitched whispers of the cedars. He ran until he came upon a clearing and tossed his ax and shook his fists up at the heavens. He shouted, "How *am I to survive without shelter and fire? Each tree I try to cut begs and pleads."*

God took pity upon this man. "Go back into the forests. No tree shall rebuke you again." The man returned. He cut a tree, parceled it, built a fire and a small shelter. No tree spoke to him.

The trees felt hapless, damned, but they dare not complain to God. Instead, they exchanged whispers anytime man entered their domain. When you see the sways of great trees, hear the beautiful sounds of gently flapping leaves, rustling whispers, do not be fooled. They do not dance for your benefit. Know that the trees are lamenting of how wretchedly man has always treated them. To avoid them dropping their sticky sap, their sharp cones, their stonelike acorns upon your head, one must express gratitude for their magnificence, their offering, even though it is us who take without permission, rather than they who give willingly.

The hand that once held the severed head by its hair extended out and firmly cupped Elzi's chin. He lifted Elzi's head, tilted it this way. Tilted it that way. Elzi met his eyes, finally, black as night. Peering back into his own. Studying, judging. Elzi's heart thumped inside the cavernous cage that was his ribs. It thumped hard, and it did so with the deep abiding shame that had followed him all of his days. He felt sorrow. Longing. But not fear. What must he long for in this dark hour? Water? That was not it. His lust for water had vanished. Comfort? Comfort of what? Home? John and Edmee? Albin? Whatever this feeling was, he could not decipher.

The breeze gusted again, grains of sand peppering Elzi's skin, settling into his nose and the crevices of his lips. The trooper and the Indian remained, eyes locked, Elzi's heart thumping hard and fast, its rhythmic whooshing covering up all sound. The Indian's mouth moved. *Whoosh-whoosh, whoosh-whoosh, whoosh-whoosh.* He yanked Elzi's head up higher and he spoke again, but his words were swept away by the *whoosh* of Elzi's blood pumping in his ears.

A blast of sand and wind stung Elzi's face and in the distance a crack of lightning revealed the coming of relief. Another gust. The smell of moisture. Granules of sand scratched at his eyes. Feathers dangling from the man's ears wildly rustled in the wind.

Boom. Thunder. Another crack of lightning. The earth lit up in all directions.

The whooshing in Elzi's ears grew into a pulsing ring. Another burst of wind swept up dirt and debris, filing his eyes with each gust, blotting out the world and the man before him, grain by grain.

Lightning struck once more. *Crack!*

The bald vulture now sat atop the Indian's shoulder, both their eyes burning through Elzi. He desperately wanted to look away, but now his eyes too betrayed him. Light filled the sky in flashes. Elzi could no longer make out the man's features, could no longer see his eyes.

Flash. An outline of a bald head, long neck, broad shoulders, arms strong and trim.

Flash. The bird, perched atop his shoulder, ragged wings open wide, resisting the wind.

Flash. Teeth, a smile somehow like his own, yet somehow like that of the devil.

A thought—no, a voice within, loud and daunting, befell him: *Wicked and weak brother, righteousness is not learned from favor.*

A blast of wind. Grains of sand and dirt spotted the earth, the sky, the light, the man's face, the bird. Until all became black.

Wicked and weak brother, forgiveness is not giving to any man who does not grieve his parted heart, his shared blood, his split soul. You shall wander the land as half a man, searching for all of eternity.

The sky rumbled. Before it was complete, a sharp crack cut its rumblings short. The black bird soared, circling. Its wings beat upon the wind. Silence fell upon the land. A crack of lightning blazed across the night sky revealing three men below, propped up under the tattered mesquite, their heads laying on the shoulders of their fellow buffalo soldier, their bodies accumulating sand like the dunes of the desert.

CAROLINE COLLEY

The Higgs Plantation, Georgia

The night of the party was exceptionally mild as far as August heat goes in Georgia. The day had brought temperatures close to one hundred degrees. Tonight, the breeze brought it down to a bearable but sticky seventy-eight. Caroline and Octavia had taken the lead on setting up for the soiree. The grand plantation home sat nestled in a grouping of massive oaks and boasted a great porch that wrapped around the entire structure, each side with steps leading down onto the lawn. To the east, lanterns dangled from branches, twinkling low-hanging fruit. Tables both high and low and covered with soft cotton cloths stood sprinkled about the lush green grass. Each had been arranged with a bouquet of flowers and herbs, all from Caroline's secret garden, votive candles for when the sun made its final exit, and tableware for the guests. What was to be a small gathering of close family and friends turned into a typical Melroy event. Everybody who was anybody and those thought to be nobody made an appearance at the largest plantation in the county. Particularly since election season was right around the corner.

Guests arrived two by two, some with children in tow to run and chase one another through the crowd of minglers. A band set up under the stately mimosa and occasionally a couple would sway or bounce along to its beat. Really, without the inhibition of booze to knock the edge off, dancing took a back seat at this party. Melroy's citizens, with their mixed fervor for Temperance, were primed to vote. The restrictive liquor legislation had recently granted voters the right to impose prohibition in the county where they lived. The guest list tonight threatened to be an easily riled one with its eclectic mix of teetotaling Good Templars, a few alumni of the True Reformers for Blacks, and the longstanding Wets.

"Chuck, I'm sorry, but I am not okay with serving your wine tonight. It's too big a crowd," warned Mr. Higgs. "How 'bout we just leave it in the keep."

Caroline stood on a ladder in the pantry and continued to pull down her bottles, two by two, handing each to Thomas. "Daddy, if they don't wanna drink it, so be it. But they ain't no law as we speak that says we can't. So why do I and these folks got to suffer the outrage of others?" retorted Caroline.

"It's just not the time and place."

"But it *is* the time and place. We are here to celebrate Henri, my very best friend, and I would like to celebrate her with a toast of my long-awaited efforts."

Summer in a glass, she had called her dandelion wine. Studying the little blossoms sprinkled about, she had waited for the perfect time to harvest. According to her, the little yellow flowers can only be picked during full sun, when the blossoms are open. The noon hour is the perfect time. Each warm, sun-bathed blossom gave off its unique scent, slightly acrid, a little bitter. Caroline had taken great care to rid each flower of every speck of greenery to avoid the sticky sap inside. "The yellah's where all the sweetness lives," she would say to anyone who had stumbled upon her nitpicking the blossoms, their nectar-rich flowers sweeter even than apple blossoms. Because of this, she took care to limit where the dandelions grew, always made sure of their removal from the orchards during pollination time, lest the bees ignore the fruit blossoms to make a beeline for her dandelions.

Thomas Higgs was no stranger to the stubborn qualities of his oldest. When Caroline went to dig her heels in, arguing with her just seemed to plant them further into her stance. But it would be a tragedy to spoil Henri and Ford's party with political debates over the sins or liberties of partaking, so in light of what he thought was best, he put his foot down. "Chuck, I said no." He handed back the bottles in hand and turned an about-face from Caroline and Octavia standing in the pantry room. Caroline could hear his boot heels booming across the planked floor, a bit heavier than normal.

"Well, dere ya are, Miss Caroline," Octavia said as she returned the bottles to their space in waiting. Octavia was not one to get involved in the back-and-forth between Thomas and Caroline. She had watched over the years, particularly after Mary passed, the two go toe-to-toe over everything from food choices to her extensive time spent with Mable to Caroline's insistence on wearing trousers.

"Chuck," he would say, "please. Your mother had two girls. And the way it looks around here, one a you decided to go on about like a man. For the love of God . . . and your old man here, please fetch you a dress before comp'ny gets here."

She would balk and fuss, claiming that until he tried to pull weeds in a dress or climb a tree in a skirt, he shouldn't be so quick to "follow the likes of everyone else's druthers."

"It's just the way it is, Chuck. You having to go rifle through men's wear should speak plenty loud enough for you. Proper ladies wear dresses, not britches. Now go get dressed."

When being courted by Davis Colley, she had given in, dressed the part. She had stood at her future husband's side on many stages making him and her father proud, looking exactly the way a budding politician's wife should look. But it didn't take long after gaining her title of widow and moving back to the plantation for her to dig out her old pants and button-downs. Her consistent disheveled look only added to the whispers about town, fueled the gossip and tales of

Caroline losing her mind and becoming *a proper lunatic*. That the *only reason she's avoided being committed is on account of her daddy.* The stares and whispers did not faze Caroline. Until they did. A few times, while in town to pick up items such as bottles to store her crafted remedies, she'd had enough of it all and shot the trifling gaggle the bird, giving the ladies even more ammunition.

Caroline pried a cork from one of the bottles and turned it up. It was undoubtedly her best batch to date. "This party's going to miss out." She turned the bottle up for a second swig, wiped her mouth with the sleeve of her shirt, and extended it out to Octavia.

Octavia clicked her tongue and scoffed. "C'mon now. Quit yer acting a fool. Put that back an' less go. We got food to carry out." She hitched up her apron and skirt and grunted, swinging her leg over the stepstool in the doorway.

Caroline watched as she padded off, her feet never rising too far from the ground, giving her a stiff-leg waddle. Caroline turned back into the pantry and took one more swig. "Mm-mmm. Mable, we done good."

"You pulling my leg?" came a voice from behind. "Don't tell me I'm still in competition for best friend status with some made-up girl," teased Henrietta.

Caroline grinned and offered her a drink. Henrietta gently turned up the bottle and took a sip. "Goodness Chuck. You've definitely outdone yourself on this batch. It's delicious." She took one more drink. "Now sit that down and let's go. There's someone I'd like you to meet." Each grabbed a platter of hors d'oeuvres and headed back out to the guests.

"And *there's* my beautiful bride." Buford Artope stood proud among his family and Thomas Higgs. He was dressed as elegantly as the heat would allow and wore his soft felt oatmeal-colored Trilby hat. Caroline and Henrietta sat the trays down. Caroline hung back to arrange the magnificent table of food. Henrietta gave Ford a kiss on the cheek and then hugged the couple to his right, obviously his parents. His father stood tall, taller than he, wearing a bowler hat, worn and dirty, though his best. His hands rested on the back of an invalid rolling wicker chair that held his wife, frail and bent. Henrietta's embrace went unnoticed by the woman. She remained stooped, her head slightly hanging, a trail of wet tobacco spit highlighting the deep line grooved from the corner of her mouth and down the side of her chin. Her hair was long and gray, wiry, parted down the middle and platted into a loose braid. She stared off into some other place and time. Ford gave her a gentle pat on the shoulder.

Henrietta turned and called out to Caroline, waving her over. "Chuck, this is my lovely mother-in-law, Margaret Artope"—she placed a hand atop the woman's hand resting in her lap—"and my father-in-law, James Artope."

The man took hold the top of his hat, lifted it briefly, and gave Caroline a slight nod. "Glad to meet ya, Caroline," he said. "Henrietta here's had a lot to say about ya."

Caroline turned to glance at Henrietta, her very best friend. Henrietta stood beaming at Ford, not holding back her broad smile. They were so in love. Henrietta was so happy. And for that, Caroline was grateful.

"Nice to meet you, sir," replied Caroline. "Glad y'all could make it out."

James Artope replied, "I's just telling ya daddy here how nice a place he got."

Thomas Higgs said, "Yes, it's been in our family some time now. We certainly love it."

A burst of laughter caught their attention. Caroline saw a group of men standing huddled around someone, all very attentive, eager to laugh and smile. *Undoubtedly someone who's somebody*, she thought and gave a dismissive huff.

Henrietta drew her attention back. "And this is one of my brothers-in-law."

A man, tall, a few inches over six feet, stepped through, parting the group to extend a hand to Caroline. Dixon Artope was rail slender, with deep brown eyes behind wire-rim glasses and groomed black hair. She noticed his features were much like Ford's, although Ford wore a beard and Dix's face was smooth, clean shaven. Caroline offered her hand. She watched as Dix Artope's eyes dropped to her hand, quickly inspecting. She saw the slightest twinge at the corner of his mouth, some thought or reaction he struggled to hold back. When his eyes returned to hers, he was met with impatience. She grabbed hold of his hand and gave it one firm shake.

"Glad to meet ya," she said flatly.

"Dixon Artope," he replied.

Henrietta quickly caught the vibe. She sensed it was off already. "So yes, Dix here is a doctor." She gave a little half curtsy in his direction. Caroline screwed up her face at her. Henrietta noticed and cleared her throat. She straightened up and smoothed the front of her dress. "He's a fine doctor. Working out in a little apothecary other side of Melroy right now, but he's looking to start his own practice."

"That so?" Caroline's feigned interest was painfully obvious.

Thomas Higgs interjected, "Doctor, we folks 'round here could use a good practitioner in town. I for one look forward to the day you get settled and squared away." He gave Dix a hearty couple of pats on his shoulder and shot Caroline a look of warning. *Behave yourself*, it said. "It was so nice to meet you folks. I've got to make my rounds. Guests are piling in. You all enjoy your evening."

Caroline nodded. "Nice to meet y'all," she parroted. She gave a little wave and departed. As she walked away, she glanced down at her hands, turning them over to inspect. Her nails were quite telling, each outlined in dirt from digging in the garden every day. "So what of it?" she scoffed under her breath and tucked them into her pants pockets.

As the evening carried on, the crowd grew and Caroline found herself making the rounds as expected, a good Southern daughter. Ladies wore flowing summer dresses and fanned their powdered faces. They held their green teas and lemonades in gloved hands and gave their best shots at relating to Caroline. "Such pretty red hair," one would say. "Has her momma's eyes," another would respond. But as soon as she'd walk away, inevitably, if she were to turn and give a quick look, she'd find the two ass-kissers leaned in. Maybe one would hold her fan up to secret their lips, hide the words of judgment. Caroline knew what the people said. Out of pity. Some out of sheer Southern meanness.

She entered the kitchen to find Octavia stacking dishes, her hair wrapped in her best cloth. She wore her cleanest apron and stood with her weight hitched to the left, her right leg kicked out. Caroline stepped in beside her. "Let me get it," she offered.

"No chile, you go on wit' yer guests. I be fine."

Caroline spun around and leaned back onto the counter. "Octavia, I think I'd be fine to not speak to another soul again. People's just awful."

Octavia chuckled. "Oh chile. Don't tink you might miss Miss Mable?"

Caroline pulled the towel from Octavia's shoulder and gave her a swat. "Shush your mouth." She grinned. "You know what I mean. People's just something else. Out there all just a-whispering ugly nothings about one another. And just a-smiling and blessing your heart all the while."

"You just werry 'bout you, Miss Caroline. You hear? Don' no-ting no man nor woman say mean a ting. Not a matter. Ah-kay?"

"I hear you," replied Caroline with a sigh. Octavia had been attempting to drive home this notion ever since Davis Colley made his untimely exit from this world. The circumstances around his death had been more than Caroline could handle. It was more than any person could, really. And the fuel that it brought to the gossip fire around Melroy was unmatched.

DIXON ARTOPE

Melroy, Georgia

It had taken much convincing for Dix to agree to attend Ford and Henrietta's party. Southern Physio-Eclectic School of Medicine was the topic of great gossip last fall, even in neighboring counties. The arrest of Dr. Locke, the closings of its doors, the rumors that weren't too much worse than the truth—Dix tried desperately to distance himself from it all. He had revealed bits and pieces of the debacle to Ford, but never could he admit to his part in the shameful act of disturbing the dead, using people's loved ones for his personal gain. And so he didn't. He told white lies. Made omissions. Let lapses and gaps in his story color the truth ever so slightly as to lessen the sin of it all. Ford and Henrietta took hold of the proverbial paint brush and colored alongside for his sake. Ford had written him once: *It's awful what that devilish Dr. Locke did. You were a victim, no less than that woman's poor husband. You were working in the name of bettering this world, brother. And don't you forget that. The Lord certainly won't.*

Forgetting was all he wanted to do, all he wanted anyone to do. But who forgets something so horrific, so public? Certainly not small-town Southerners. He was best to just lay low, avoid any details regarding his education. Lying did not come naturally for Dix, but to salvage any bit of a chance to become a doctor, he'd have to at least bend his truth.

Thomas Higgs made his rounds, laughed it up with old friends, welcomed new acquaintances to his home, mingled and introduced folks to one another. He took hosting seriously and enjoyed bringing people together. People of all walks of life. One thing losing Mary had taught him is that tomorrow is not promised, and for that, he made it his personal mantra to make every moment count. And he did his best to make it count for those around him as well.

Dix watched the man move from clique to clique, sliding into crowds with ease, making small talk, making people feel welcomed and important. He watched him pull from one crowd and insert into another, making unlikely introductions, busting up cliques in his grand mission to unite them all. Then Dix watched as he guided a plump little white-haired man his way, his eyes locked onto Dix. Dix's stomach turned.

"Dr. Dixon Artope, meet Dr. Geoffrey Hamilton." Thomas beamed with pride. Dix extended his hand and the man shook it, his great wiry eyebrows furrowed and unruly.

"Pleased to meet you Dr.—Artope, did you say?"

"I didn't, sir, but yes. Pleased to meet you as well." The temperature in Dix's face started to rise.

"Can't say I've heard your name. You practice in Melroy?"

Thomas jumped in. "Dr. Hamilton here has been a great help to my Caroline. And we are happy to travel to see him, though I can't imagine why he wouldn't want to set up shop here in Melroy. It's a fine community. And Savannah's got a wealth of doctors. No doubt they'd miss him, but like I say, we could use a good practitioner here in town. Folks can't always get out to Savannah. I feel I've done my due diligence in trying to persuade the good doctor." Thomas gave a chuckle. "Even offered him my best space in town when the last tenant packed up. Be perfect for him. Don't know what a good man's gotta do shy of bribing him." He took hold of Dr. Hamilton's shoulder and gave it a shake. "I might just offer it here to Dr. Artope."

Dix and Dr. Hamilton both forced a half laugh to appease Thomas and avoided eye contact with one another.

"Daddy!" called a voice from afar.

Thomas raised his eyebrows in delight. "Gentlemen, if you'll kindly excuse me, that is the sound of my baby girl." Thomas patted each man on the shoulder, leaving them standing face to face in awkward silence. Dr. Hamilton was the first to break it.

"So, you're not practicing in Melroy, I take it. Where abouts are ya?"

Dix squirmed under the pressure. "Just outside of town. It's a modest practice."

Dr. Hamilton continued, "And are you practicing in general or are you one of these great many specialists?" The sarcasm in his voice was palpable.

"I'm an eclectic." The moment he said as much, he knew he should not have. Anything to lead the conversation to the events of the eclectic school he attended was certain potential for discovery, which was akin to reputation suicide. His words did not come out with any inkling of confidence. While standing almost a foot higher than the round-cheeked portly man, Dix felt hot with intimidation. Stumbling and fumbling his words, he managed to relay vague terms of his employment. *Working alongside a druggist. Doubtful you'd know of him. Didn't go to school locally. A modest institution. And how about you?* He desperately wanted to remove his jacket, but it concealed his pits drenching his shirt in shame and secrecy. More earnestly, he wanted to escape. It had taken a great deal of coaxing from Ford and Henrietta to get him to attend, and this was precisely why he hadn't wanted to.

As the old doctor went on and on about his practice, his accomplishments, his theories and judgments about the various approaches in modern medicine, Dix searched the crowd for an out. Ford and Henrietta were tied up at every turn, being the guests of honor. And his parents had made their exit shortly after arriving, his mother unfit for parties, really. He was on his own. Somehow he had to either carry on with this conversation while dodging the mystery of his personal doctorly details, which surely this well-educated prominent man was soon to solve, or elope the conversation altogether. Which was his preference. He spotted Caroline approaching guests with a tray of drinks.

" . . . which the Hamilton Rotary Chair has tackled with fine results," Dr. Hamilton boasted.

"Of course it has," replied Dix, completely unaware of how long the doctor had been droning on at this point. As soon as Caroline turned in their direction, Dix reached his hand into the air. She nodded in acknowledgment and turned back to her guests, handing out tall slender glasses.

"And what do you find most effective for it?" asked Dr. Hamilton.

Dix wavered, lost. "I'm sorry?" he asked.

Dr. Hamilton frowned. "I said," he replied, giving each word its own heft, "what has been your experience in treating such a person?"

"Such a person as?" Dix's heart pounded out each second that passed after asking. He was failing here, and he could see it plainly across Dr. Geoffrey Hamilton's face. He was failing at this conversation. He failed at becoming a doctor. He failed at admitting as much. And now he was failing at hiding his failure.

"The unfit of mind!" yelled Dr. Hamilton. He had lost all patience. "How do you tend to treat the unfit of mind!" he demanded again. Conversations nearby ceased and Dix grew white hot as guests turned to face the two doctors, eager to take in any juicy misunderstanding or disagreement they may be so lucky to witness.

"Well, I—I—I—"

"Like a drink?"

He turned to see Caroline, a life raft in this conversation he was drowning in. She was offering a glass. He thought he could make out the slightest smirk across her face, that she took some kind of delight in his discomfort. He accepted the glass and took a drink.

Immediately he spewed the beverage from his mouth, the blast hitting the doctor square in the chest.

"Good God!" yelled Dr. Hamilton.

Caroline quickly turned and tossed the tray onto the neighboring table. She pulled a handkerchief from her pocket and began dabbing at his shirt and jacket.

The white-hot embarrassment Dix had once suffered now escalated to searing mortification. He snatched the handkerchief from Caroline and took over tending to the mess. "Sir, I am truly so very sorry. I had no idea—"

Dix stopped and whirled around to face Caroline head on. She was holding back laughter and it enraged him. He slammed the glass down on the table beside them. "What in God's name are you serving here?" he insisted. "What kind of knavish manipulation is this? Giving a man the devil's drink of choice without so much a warning!"

At this, Caroline burst into laughter. "Devil's drink of choice? Seriously?"

Dix frantically scrubbed at Dr. Hamilton's chest, his bright white shirt now stained a nectar yellow. The doctor yanked the cloth from Dix.

"Get off me," he hissed. He gave a few swipes and then slapped the cloth to the ground. "Ruined, I am certain," he exclaimed and stomped off.

Dix turned to see Caroline bouncing in silent laughter, covering her face with both hands. He had had enough. Enough of this party. Enough of dancing around his failures. And certainly enough of Caroline Colley.

"I should have known as much," he hissed.

"That so?" she mocked. "What is it you should have known"—she took a beat—"Doc-tor?" She bent down to pick up the tray of drinks.

Dix gestured to her tray. "I should have known someone so foolish to think they could heal a man with weeds and berries would be equally ignorant as to the sins of alcohol on the body and mind."

She raised her left brow and leaned in slightly. "Ignorant?"

She looked him up and down, taking in the tall and lanky man. He was quite handsome, she hated to admit. His dark hair and deep brown eyes were striking, no doubt.

"It's the man that's so weak that he must claim the devil's amok in a simple summer's delight that's the ignorant one. I imagine you've got your political agenda to consider. Can't be much of a doctor 'round these parts without one. And my guess is you're hoping for some backing by the Templers. Like every weak man in these parts, a sellout too weak to make personal choices lest you miss out on the blessings of the elite and wealthy."

Dix scoffed at the audacity of the mouthy redhead that stood toe-to-toe with him. She now held the tray atop her hip, the way a woman holds a toddler, her chin jutted out at him. He could see something like hate boiling up, her cheeks reddening to match her locks of hair.

"You, not unlike many women," he retorted, "are the unfortunate product of a society who wishes to keep you foolish, uneducated. For that, I apologize. But your childish reactions all but prove women's inability to sever their rolling emotions from logic. And *that's* what is needed in science, in medicine. Digging in the dirt and concocting booze from your finds, my lady, isn't the standards my medical community recognizes. Nor should any citizen who wishes to keep about them a sense of health or reverence for their maker." He lifted his chin at this, his full arrogance realized.

Caroline's stare bore a hole straight through Dix. She rose onto her toes, trying to level the playing field, but it was impossible as he stood so much taller than she.

"It's my understanding—granted I'm just a lowly dumb woman and fear I could have this all mixed up in my little ole head—but seems to me, your precious medical community isn't the most perceptive when it comes to spotting the likes of those that uphold their"—she screwed up her face and banged her forehead with the heel of her hand—"oh, what's the word?"

She was taking great pride in mocking this arrogant man that loomed above her. The same as all weak men did, men with some sort of shame to cover up. She'd seen it all her life. Her daddy being one of the wealthier men in the county, politicians and up-and-coming professionals flocked to him. They sucked up to the wealthy to get what they needed and then turned around and looked down upon anyone else, especially anyone who couldn't endow their agenda, basically anyone who wasn't a rich White man. She could see this man here was no different. Though something was off. He possessed the arrogance of someone accomplished but couldn't be forced to discuss as much. She'd noticed him all evening dodge opportunities to talk up his esteemed newfound place in life as a doctor. It wasn't humility that held him back. She could feel it in her bones. He was, after all, like them all. A pompous ass like them all. It was something quite different than humility, she was certain.

She finished her insult—"standards, as you say. Yes, those highly educated men of yours seem to be missing something about ole Dr. Dixon Artope, don't they?"

At this, Dix broke the invisible tie that bound their eyes and looked away. He took a step back and cleared his throat.

Caroline sensed she was on to something, that she had struck a nerve. The small win surged through her body. She saw a narrow window of opportunity to show this arrogant ass just how *uneducated* she was.

"You know, ya might consider taking a second drink there, Doctor." She picked up his glass and offered it back, her signature look of *I dare you* now settled in across her face. "Like many slick doctors who have killed countless innocent people in the name of science, you just might be missing something right under your nose." She held the drink in his face. "The ancient wisdom of consuming the blossoms of these fine plants has saved many lives and could save more, if doctors such as yourself didn't hold themselves above Mother Nature, burying their failures, those succumbing to deficiencies—think scurvy, Doctor—under the very ground that coulda saved them. The so-called medicine they needed was right there in the grass, green for the picking. But that's not quite fancy enough for an educated man such as yourself, now is it?"

Dix stepped back in. "Look, what you call medicine is but a mere lawn nuisance. And your blowball wine there will help a body about as much as it does a yard. One drink too many and you're basically scattering the devil's seeds, trashing the good green lawn that is the human body."

"May I get a glass?" a voice interrupted. Caroline and Dix turned to see a beautiful woman in the lightest pink gown. Her hair piled in perfect auburn curls atop her head. Her skin clear and pale as if the Georgian sun had never the pleasure of kissing it. "Not for me, of course," she amended with a gentle smile.

"Of course it's not for you." Caroline replied flatly. "Minnie, this is"—she paused a moment and took a breath to calm the rage that had been building—"Doctor Dix Artope, Henri's new brother-in-law." His name was bitter on her tongue. She turned to Dix, gesturing toward her sister. "And this is Minnie Higgs, my baby sister."

Dix held his frown but took Minnie's hand. She had gracefully replaced the drink atop Caroline's tray and extended her hand to him, high and curved, expecting a gentleman's kiss. One did not come. Rather Dix grabbed her hand and gave it a stern shake. "Nice to meet you," he grumbled and looked away, scanning the crowd for another escape as this last one was failing him.

Caroline said, "Take your drink, Minnie. I got other people to serve."

Minnie took a glass and smiled politely at Dix who was now glowering. She watched as Caroline whirled the tray from her hip and back up high, disappearing into the crowd. She turned to face the tall and beautiful gentleman before her. He stood tense, riled almost. She cautiously spoke. "Chuck has a way."

Dix did not turn to even acknowledge her words; rather he continued searching the crowd, his eyes bouncing from head to head.

She tried again. "Not sure what my sister may have said, but she does certainly have a way of getting under one's skin." She paused. "And seems to take great pride in doing so," she followed up.

"So it seems," he replied flatly, disinterested.

"You're not from Melroy, I take it?"

He replied, "I am," and continued to scan the crowd.

"Oh. Seems I'd remember seeing you, certainly."

Dix did not reply, still searching for an out.

"Where is it that you practice, Doctor?" she asked.

Irritated and distracted he replied, "I don't. But don't let me keep you from your drink. Now if you'll excuse me, I must say my goodbyes to my brother."

"Oh, heavens no." She held out her glass. "This is for my Auntie Pat." She gave a little laugh. "But I'll leave you be, Doctor. It was a pleasure."

Dix finally turned to look at her. When he did, she was smiling at him with the warmth and gentility of a true Southern belle. She gave a slight nod of the head, her eyes never leaving his, and turned away. As she walked, her dress trailed behind her airily bouncing across the lush lawn with each step. He noticed the angry pounding of his heart had subsided, the knot in his stomach loosened. He watched her approach a table. Seated around it were a few older couples, all who turned and smiled at the woman with pride and delight. As she spoke, each laughed and took her in. No doubt her beauty was unmatched. Though the way he had behaved, you'd never know Dix thought as much.

Minnie walked around to the back of the table, now facing in his direction. She bent down and placed the glass of her sister's dandelion wine before an elderly woman. She whispered and gave her a sweet kiss on the cheek. Dix watched as the woman grinned with delight and gave her a pat on the hand in gratitude. She picked up the glass and took a taste. The old woman closed her eyes, shutting out the crowd and summoning her senses. And there, before his eyes, Dix thought he could see the very moment the spirit of the devil tickled the woman's tongue with the temptation of tipple delight.

A high-pitched clinking of metal on glass broke through the laughter and rumblings of the crowd. Each person turned to face the great porch. Atop stood Thomas Higgs, front and center. He held a glass of tea in one hand and his pocketknife in the other.

"Just a moment of your time, dear folks," he hollered out over the crowd below as he tapped his pocketknife to the side of his glass once more. "Buford, Henrietta, won't you two make your way up here, please."

At that, the people in the crowd turned this way and that, looking to place eyes on the couple of the hour. Henrietta was cradling someone's baby, trying motherhood on for size and gazing into her husband's eyes.

"It suits you just fine," Ford complimented with a loving smile. "Now let that one be for now so we can make our way up to our most generous host."

She gingerly handed the baby back to its mother.

Dix watched on as his brother led his bride up the steps. When they reached the top, he kissed her and took her hand. Together they turned and gazed over the crowd.

People from all over the county—even some outside the county— had come here to celebrate them, their marriage, Ford's accomplishments, their next chapter to come. Or possibly they just jumped at the idea of being present at the Higgs Plantation for any event. Whatever the motives of the people of Melroy County, Ford and Henrietta really seemed to be doing it right, Dix thought. And people took notice.

The tiniest bit of jealousy fluttered in his stomach. Ford deserved all the good that came his way. This is what Dix had always said about his brother and best friend. He had not really been all that close with his other siblings. Once Elsa passed, Dix became once again the family baby. And while he was the youngest and naturally the child requiring the most help and care, being the tenth left him but an afterthought. By that point, babies were no longer a thing of wonder, something fragile to dote on. In a family so big, a baby became yet another responsibility, another chore to all. Except to Ford. Ford had always loved Dix deeply. From the moment Dix was old enough to toddle out of the house, the two were inseparable. Until Dix went away to pursue his dream of becoming a doctor.

He had had a plan. A solid plan. He had worked hard, studied hard. Maintained excellent grades all the while continuing to keep up his Bible studies. If anything would solidify his skills as a physician and healer, it was his devotion to the Lord Almighty. Of course it was. He volunteered at the local infirmary for the indigent. Kept up on local politics. Kept up his daily routine of walking to move the blood about the body. Avoided all drink, all tobacco, all sin of any kind—the digging of bodies was an act he struggled to identify as anything but a sin, but for his pride, and sanity, he forced himself to view the unearthing of resting bodies as acts to further the greater good in the name of science. For he envisioned one day being the doctor that turned the people of Melroy County into folks who truly understood the meaning of cleanliness being next to godliness.

He had watched as people lay vulnerable and ill, watched doctors who could not see that they themselves seemed to worsen the trouble. He believed strongly that the medical community, while bold with theory and good intentions, caused illness to grow and spread like mold overtaking a loaf of bread. He had gone to his professors, to his practicing mentors about his theory that cleanliness could be the cure. After all, he'd grown up in a house of filth and seen clearly how it invaded the body like a parasite. They always met him with incredulity and laughter, sometimes a bit of mockery.

"Son, you go on and wash up. While you spend your time at the sink like a woman at her dishes, I'll be here practicing medicine." A doctor had once said this to him just before setting a cigarette down to free up his hand that sewed shut a great laceration across the neck of a child. The child being no match for the single strand of barbed wire that clotheslined him while fleeing the chase of his playmates.

Yes, Dix had had great plans. Graduate. Set up practice. Marry.

Have children, but not too many. Become mayor maybe. How that possibly could happen now, he did not know. For the first step in his plan had become a great blunder. He had failed before barely getting started and not for any fault of his own. Thinking about it all made his blood boil. He really wanted to get the hell out of that crowd.

Thomas Higgs stood above the people gathered at his great plantation and went on and on about his pride for Henrietta and her husband. Henrietta had been like another daughter to him, after all, and it brought him great joy to see her so happy and with such a fine young man. A man who did well working at the hub of the future of transportation. "I imagine Central City will certainly miss you. These folks here in Melroy will surely. And the state of Texas will be lucky to have you." He raised his glass and the crowd raised theirs in response. "As soon as they lay those tracks, I'll be the first to hop aboard and come see the wonderful life I know you'll have established. Little Henri, Ford, here's to you and your bright futures."

"Hear, hear!" shouted the crowd.

"And to y'all fine folks, please feel free to stay and dance and enjoy this nice breeze the good Lord blessed us with on this night." Thomas lifted his glass once more to the crowd, gave a nod, a hearty pat on Ford's back, and then descended the porch stairs.

Ford and Henrietta grinned with pride and a touch of shyness. The two kissed and hugged and then made their ways back down onto the lawn where people flocked to give handshakes and hugs and well wishes, as if they'd not already spent the last hour chatting them up. Dix looked to make his way to them, to give his personal sentiments, though Ford and Henrietta knew them all too well, being as Dix had spent much time with them the past few months. Really, he just wanted to bolt. To do so, he needed to tell them goodbye.

As he wended his way and pushed through the crowd of partygoers, a crash followed by a scream stole the attention of all. He turned to see a huddle of people in the back, all fixed on someone clearly on the ground below them.

"He just fell out!" shouted a woman.

Dix shoved his way through to find Dr. Geoffrey Hamilton belly up on the lawn, panting and holding his chest, a table overturned at his side. Dix threw off his hat and jacket and squatted down to get a better look. The doctor was sweating profusely, his cheeks beet red and his dandelion wine-stained shirt tight in his grip.

"My heart," he croaked.

Dix reached across and placed his fingers to the doctor's neck. As he did so, he searched the ground nearby. "Where's his bag?" he asked of the onlookers. "Doctor, did you bring your bag?" he asked the panting man.

A woman nearby grasped the leather strap peeking out from under the collapsed table and dragged out the worn leather bag of Dr. Geoffrey Hamilton. "Here," she offered.

Dix pried it open and frantically dug, lifting out tools and bottles. "Sir, do you have amyl nitrate on you?"

The doctor forced out a grunt, "My chest." His mouth gaped wide and a large vein in his forehead menaced to burst.

Dix could sense the great crowd now hovering over them. One seasoned doctor on the ground at the mercy of this failed wannabe. He pushed his glasses back up the bridge of his nose. He rummaged once more through the bag, this time tossing pointless bottles aside. "Doctor!" he shouted. "Do you or do you not have amyl nitrate?"

The doctor's clinched eyes opened to look into Dix's. "What? No." He moaned in pain. "Morphine and strychnine." The fallen doctor reached his hand blindly into his bag, wildly searching.

Dix's heart sank. "Strychnine?" he asked. "Sir, amyl nitrate, do you have it?" He yanked the bag from the doctor's flailing hand. Dix's heart pounded as he sensed the people closing in. Occasionally a woman would scream, the drama of it all. Dix could not, in good conscience, inject this man with strychnine, *vermin killer* as his professor had chided. It had been the drug of choice for years for many physicians, with the mortality risk of Russian roulette. Dix, in his modern education, had learned to treat angina pectoris with amyl nitrate, followed up by a prescription for rest. The old ways of using arsenic and strychnine were, to Dix, an abomination, a fool's remedy. He was the product of modern medicine and felt strongly regarding treatment of the ailments of the heart, and concerning nitrates, that *in few maladies are the improvements in our therapeutical resources more conspicuous.*

He could see from the panic in the doctor's face, as well as that of the onlookers, that all were beginning to doubt his abilities to conjure any such modern practices. He had not a medical bag of his own to tote, which he undoubtedly would have stocked with respectable remedies for any such emergency, as he had not any upstanding ability to practice medicine. He had attended a failure of a medical school and from it emerged a failure of a student—technically a certificate holder, but not a full-fledged doctor. He was someone who did not hold any such legitimate diploma. He was a fraud. And his failure was shining bright in this horrible moment.

A woman broke his ruminations and shoved in his face a handful of small glass bottles. "Here!"

Dix accepted the bottles. He turned them over: morphia, strychnine, phenacetin. He couldn't believe this man, this so-called doctor still used the likes of morphia, a mixture of sherry and morphine.

The man let out a long moan. He had stopped his side-to-side rocking and had loosened his grip on his shirt. Dix grabbed the man's shirt and ripped it open.

"Pull that off," he ordered. "Get me his arm."

An extraordinary spectacle was revealed. The entire surface of the doctor's stomach was blotched, leopard spotted with various colors and extravagating streaks, the marks of excessive injections. Dix gasped. His mind reeled. These were the blissful punctures of a morphinist. The doctor's left arm was red and swollen, covered in abscesses extending from the elbow to the wrist. Dix looked up to see nothing shy of horror and freak fascination on the faces of the fancy-dressed folks.

"Please, give us space."

Dix took hold of the giant Fergusson syringe that lay about the bottom of the bag, a metal tube with a plunger extending. Dix was accustomed to a glass model, one allowing him to visualize its contents, using its markings to be more precise in his dispensations. He opted to forego the strychnine altogether—*do no harm*—and drew up a bit of morphia and phenacetin. The instant the drug entered the man's system, he calmed. His breathing slowed and the intense redness of his cheeks subsided.

"Someone get me a cool cloth, please," Dix called out. "And let's get this man inside."

He had saved the doctor's life, it seemed. Or simply just calmed the fit of an addiction. Either way, Dix had had enough of this night and was ready to retreat to—not home. He had no home but was a man trapped in the house of his childhood, running away every other day after work to the home of his brother. He was ready to just retreat, to remove himself from any ties to this county, the school, these people who were bound to discover his secret. He desperately wanted to be a healer. More importantly, he wanted to be respected. He did not see that in his future, should he choose to remain anywhere in this locality.

Dix accepted the pats on the back from his brother, from Mr. Higgs, from every other person witness to the terrible incident. He made his way from the sofa where the doctor rested in the great white oak study and back out into the yard to retrieve his hat and jacket. As he lumbered through the crowd, buzzing with excitement, he heard the whispers from folks already aggrandizing and recreating the scene that was but a few minutes in the past. He was certain the night would only prompt more and more interest in his education and training. And that, he could not abide. He could not practice medicine rightly in Georgia as all his hard work had not actually resulted in a diploma, but he could also not abide the likes of these folks using him as their latest topic in the gossip mill. He needed to get the hell out of town.

He found his hat on the ground not far from where he'd helped the doctor. Next to it sat the doctor's Gladstone bag, open wide with its contents strewn about. He kneeled down to pack it up. Not too far away he could hear a woman deep in her story, a tale of sorts.

"You don't say?" a man urged her on.

"I do say. I like to simmer the golden flowers with a bit of orange zest, a little sugar, and let it do its thing for a couple of weeks. You know, used-to-be, folks used dandelion wine to cure winter troubles like colds and coughs. Some even say it'd wipe out the winter blues."

"Really?" the man asked.

"Mm-hmm," she answered. "Ever heard it called piss-a-bed?" Caroline chuckled at her own words. "It's a diuretic, can clear the body of toxins right through the bladder. It's a very pleasant medicine, if that's what you'd like to call it. I just think of it as my blossom champagne, since it's got a natural bit of sparkle to it."

Dix grabbed his jacket and stood to leave. As he headed out, he couldn't help but make a quick stop where Caroline and the man stood.

"Excuse me," he interrupted the two.

Caroline turned to see that of course it was the pompous young doctor so rudely intruding.

"Yes," she replied coldly.

"I just wanted to say nice to meet you and thank you for your hospitality." It was the gentlemanly thing to do, Dix knew, to thank the hosts before skipping out.

The man standing with Caroline piped up. "Well, nice to meet you!" He turned to Caroline. "Caroline, this man deserves a drink! Why don't you grab him one."

"That's quite all right," interjected Dix. "I'm on my way."

"Just one. If anything you deserve a toast!" the man insisted.

Dix made to decline again, but the man had already left to retrieve a glass. Dix and Caroline stood awkwardly alone.

Caroline said, "I don't imagine you'll stoop so low as us ingrates to accept a toast from this kind man looking to praise you for your heroic deed?"

Dix now fully regretted stopping by to give this ungrateful and bullheaded hostess his gratitude and farewell. He was exhausted. His heart had pounded and raced the likes of a rabbit bolting from a coyote when he was on the ground with Dr. Hamilton. Now he was spent.

He replied, the exhaustion clear in his voice, "Ma'am, with the exception of true medical choices such as anesthetics, if the likes of morphia and your blowball wine no less could be sunk to the bottom of the sea, it would be all the better for mankind—and all the worse for the fishes. I can't for the life of me understand why the public insists on being poisoned and then exerts immense pressure on the physician, tending to force him to active treatment of some kind. It's purely the way of the devil. I would hope that examples such as tonight would allow you to see my cause."

"The physician?" Caroline questioned. She raised her eyebrow and gave a sarcastic laugh.

Dix nodded and touched his hat to his forehead. "Good night to you, Mrs. Colley," replied Dix.

Caroline watched as he lumbered away, his long legs covering great distance with each step, a grand arrogant giraffe moving gracefully among the busybody baboons below.

TRAVELLER

I couldn't tell you honey, I don't know
Where I'm goin' but I've got to go
'Cause every turn reveals some other road
And I'm a traveller, oh, I'm a traveller
—Chris Stapleton

JERYL LARSON

September 8, 2023
Element Dale, Texas

I notice every time she talks much of the town of Element Dale, the wrinkle between her eyes deepens and she taps her fingers lightly on the chair. But not your ordinary consecutive, repetitive tapping; she taps each time a pattern: thumb, pinky, index, middle; then rapidly the index and middle together twice, *tap tap*. Thumb, pinky, index, middle; index and middle twice, *tap tap. Tap, tap, tap, tap—tap tap*.

"The fatuous fucks from this town call me Old Lady Lu—when I was little they all called me Trashy Lu. Had one teacher call me Luci. You can just call me Lu. I'm a woman toiling in her eighties, ready to meet her maker—or join her ancestors in the Sea of Night as Elzi says. I don't give a rat's ass which, long as I can just be done with it. I'm tired. Tired of this world. Tired of fighting to just be. Tired of being a part of this place, a part of these ignorant and uncompassionate citizens of this damned town.

"This town—overrun by folks who wouldn't know intelligence if it slapped them upside the head. They've poked fun at me my whole life, littluns and grownups alike. And now, even though my stories and poetry have been published, even though I've managed to make my own way in the world without the help of loving parents, or unloving parents for that matter, still they taunt me and tease me. What a lot of good my writing did for me. Nothing."

Her tapping quickened.

"And these folks—that's what ignorance, unfulfillment, and boredom often produce. Plain old meanness. I've witnessed the lot of them, usually boys—standing at the tree line there—make a dash for the house. The first time it happened, my heart leapt up into my throat. I watched out the winder and thought they might were going to rush me, grab me, and—oh, I don't know what I thought. I had visions of them busting down my front door, tying me to a post, encircling me, spitting on me, setting me ablaze." She lowered her head in sadness. "Poor Dovie."

I wonder who in the world Dovie is and what she has to do with these boys—and who came up with that fabulous name. I'm struggling to follow and want to ask, but I've learned to just keep these lips shut and let Lucillia get lost in her thoughts, in her stories, and she'll let the hinges on her personal Pandora's box fly wide open eventually.

"All but one boy had bailed before reaching my porch steps. That one *brave* boy slapped my front door and do you know a roar of cheers emerged from the woods. And off he went. Little shits. These people don't care no mind for others. They only care about themselves. Which is the way of the simple-minded. They tend to be selfish, focused within. Well, I have one last story to write to fulfill my obligations, and then I'm done. Done with this thankless existence."

I can't believe it. There it is, the closest thing she's said so far to give me hope. I want so badly to jump on her words, to talk about the book. But I know better. I keep quiet, though I'm squealing on the inside like a little girl. (And beating myself up for it. I mean, she is contemplating some heavy shit.)

"Besides," she grins, "I wouldn't mind seeing what Elzi's world is all about. I know it by heart, heard the stories since I was ye high. I have a feeling that Ora B. and I would make out nicely as friends—or, truth be told, I've always imagined her in a maternal light."

That was the first time I ever saw Lucillia Baldwin smile. I quickly jot down the names Dovie and Ora B. beside the notes I have for Elzi. I mark Ora's name with a star.

ELZI

Summer, 1877
The Staked Plains, Texas

Rare summer rain drizzled down, light and humid. Elzi sat under the mesquite, cloaked in darkness save the occasional flash of lightning. He no longer thirsted. The heavens had finally given them reprieve. Had his body been quenched by the surrounding moisture? He sat quiet, dreaming—or maybe thinking. His awareness of his surroundings endured in the smells, the sounds. He could feel the hard ground where he sat, but he was not too uncomfortable. He could smell the beautiful rain, feel it trickle down his cheeks. Almost like tears. He hadn't cried tears in forever. Except for the one tear that escaped the day he told Hattie Mae goodbye. She hadn't seen the tear. He'd turned his head, a quick swipe on the shoulder of his shirt. But that tear had burned. These tears from the heavens cooled. Tears of kindness.

His eyes were not yet ready to open, though he no longer felt the sheer exhaustion that had plagued him for the last days. How many days had it been since his last drink of water? he wondered again. No matter. He wasn't too thirsty. In a moment he might tilt his head back and open his mouth, let the sky drizzle in drop by drop.

He sat and thought. His mind wandered from here to there, from here on the ground under the mesquite tree to there, up in the heavens. The Sea of Night was what Ora B. had written in the journal. The eternal resting place of his ancestors, the place where one becomes a speck of fire in the heavens, eternally filled with joy and light, surrounded by others, family in splendid light form. His mind soared, the breeze whooshing in his face. The darkness opened with each burst of air, revealing a star. He continued to soar, birdlike, zipping around the great bits of light, love growing stronger in his heart as he passed each one in a flash.

In the distance of the eternal darkness, two great beings pulsed, drawing him in. His heart swelled, filled with a great reverence and tenderness he'd never experienced before. Not with Maymee and Pa Godwin. Not with Hattie Mae even. He encircled the two orbs again and again, his body charged with energy. His heart filled with sensations of love, of missing, of comfort, of assurance. His mind filled with voices, words that at first he could not decipher. Then came a sort of clarity: *we've missed you, fear not, son, love, remain.* The words came softly in echoes and layered upon one another. *My son, love.* The words were gentle but firm, reassuring. A woman's voice: *you are but half of my broken heart.* A man's voice echoed around her words: *must stay, son, the Watchman.* Elzi's soul and mind soared and swooped, turning and spinning around the orbs, like a baby bird showing its mother its newfound strength and agility. He felt free. For the first time in his existence, he felt free, and this freedom filled his heart so completely that he thought it might burst.

WALKER

North Carolina

Walker Westberry could not remember the last time he actually full-out ran, but he was willing to run as hard as he ever had. Crouched in the trees, he watched and waited as the ground's shaking and rumbling grew more intense and, with it, his heartbeat. Finally he spotted it. A plume of smoke above the treetops in the distance. It was coming. His ticket out of here. He grabbed his bindle, slung it over his shoulder, and tucked the bulk of it under his arm. It was heavy to be running, but light considering it was now the entirety of his belongings, his unearthed stashed cash and a few provisions.

As the train approached, he remembered the words of his hoboing uncle. They'd been shooting the shit around a fire—Walker was but a young teen. He recalled this uncle showing up to stay at Westberry Mountain for a few days. He'd come in off the rails. The Westberrys gave him hot meals, plenty of hooch, and a place to lay his head that wasn't the hard floor of a rail car. Walker sat around the fire with the men and boys, listening to this uncle tell his stories of running the rails. He'd crisscrossed the country, riding as far as the rails had been built. Walker remembered his uncle talking about running hard to catch a train, grabbing hold and hanging on for dear life. About not-so-lucky travelers who'd lost limbs, lives.

PeePaw Westberry had asked, "How ya know if you can even catch one?"

An all-knowing grin spread across the uncle's face. "Well, there's a trick, see. Ya just gotta be able to spot them bolts on them spinning wheels. Cain't make 'em out? Too fast to catch. Best wait for the next one." He'd taken pride in being a train hobo, not a tramp. "A hobo gots standards," he'd said. "He'll work and wander. A tramp, why he's just a freeloading wanderer. A hobo knows it's a hard-scrambling way a life, but they's something to look forward to on down the line with folks willing to hep ya out. Long as you're willing too. They's signs here and there if you a-looking.

"Say you see a circled cross on someone's front stoop, they's telling you it's okay to approach and they's prolly a-gonna feed you a meal. But the best thing to do when you seeing a sign like that? Ask him, do you need a little hep around the place. That-a-way, you ain't just a tramping."

The men had sat enthralled as the uncle told story after story and heeded warning after warning.

"And always be on the lookout for the bulls and the 'bo chasers. Bulls a-gonna get you if you're wandering the train yard, looking for a new line. A 'bo chaser, well, consider the 'bo chaser the hunter and a hobo its prey. Steer clear at all costs, for he'll a-shoot you dead if he gets the chance—and be happy for it."

Walker saw the train's cow guard come into view around the bend. The metal-on-metal *clickety-clack* growing louder. Before long, it was right across from where he crouched. Walker spotted the bolts. They passed quickly, but he was still able to make them out clearly. He looked up and down the train. No 'bo chasers that he could see. He took one last drag and flicked his cigarette. Like a track star bolting from his starting block, he shoved off the tree and began running, kicking up dirt, pumping his arms and legs. The *clickety-clack* was shockingly loud. He ran alongside as the train passed him, one car at a time. He searched for a sure spot to jump on, but no car seemed open and available. Fearing his chance might pass him by, he ran harder, his lungs burning. The cars continued to pass faster and faster. He had to get on. With no other options, he finally grabbed hold of a truss rod underneath a car.

It was a four-foot length of plank situated along the rods and functioned as a support to keep the car from sagging in the middle. For the hobo, it served as a last-resort option for riding the rails. As he caught hold, the train yanked him hard and for a moment he feared it might drag him, his feet scrambling to keep up. He pumped his legs to keep up and finally swung one over, flinging himself facedown onto the plank spanning the truss under the edge of the car. The ground below him raced by, metal shavings popping up like shrapnel. The sound louder than anything he'd ever heard. The plank supported his body, but he was up too far. There was nothing between his face and the racing tracks but the rushing air and flying debris.

Carefully, he held onto the rods with one arm and grabbed his bag with the other, pulling it into his side. Gripping the rods with his boots, he scooched down the truss then carefully spun his body and bindle until he finally turned face up. He rested his head on the plank between two rods and thought to himself, *this shit is for the fucking hobos.*

Walker laid on that support truss clutching his bag as the train trundled along, leaving the stark majesty of the Black Mountains behind. He laid on his back, bumping along, watching the pine-covered mountains and towering crags pass by. He spotted whitetail, bobcats, and wild turkey milling amongst the trees as they blurred past. The rails rolled along from the thick trees to alongside the river valley and eventually a rushing gorge.

Dusk approached and Walker held tight as the rail line clung to the narrowing edge. The green and purple hues slowly melted into a gray, and within the failing light he spotted a family of black bears, the momma standing hip deep in the water while her babies wrestled at the edge, oblivious to their surroundings, to any possible danger. The bear looked up for only a moment to catch the train as it passed by. Walker wasn't exactly sure where he was headed but he suspected he'd go on west from Ashville.

The crashing metal on metal slowed and was soon accompanied by a great hissing and groaning. The train was stopping. He had to get off, lest he be spotted by a bull up ahead. Though slowing, the ground still slipped by at an alarming pace. He needed to jump. The adrenaline surged through his body, but he loved it. He'd always loved the threat of danger.

He took a few beats and then tossed his bindle, spun off the plank, and slammed to the ground tumbling down the edge of the gravel. Sore but unharmed, he stood and brushed himself off as the train continued groaning on. He turned back to find his pack. It was night and he was exhausted.

Once the train settled, he was left with a ringing so loud in his ears he felt vulnerable, unable to hear much else. He ducked into the woods to regroup. Once the coast was clear, he might see about finding a car to climb into. Truss riding had been an adventure and it had shaded him from the sun, but it beat and bounced him half senseless and exposed him to the harsh wind and dust and noise. He really just wanted a moment of stillness. He thought of the Honey Hole and its quiet still, all but the soft trickling of water and it sounded real nice.

Walker waited and watched from the cover of darkness, expecting officials of some sort to walk the cars, but none came. He let out a scoff and mumbled under his breath, "Hit the ground like a sack of corn for nothing." The train sat, resting and heavy. He walked from car to car until he found an empty one. He tossed his bag up and into the car and clambered aboard. Once inside, he pulled the great door shut, laid his head upon his bag, and wished for a big swig of white lightning, something to finish his day off. He thought of his moonshine operation gone, his land, the fire, and before he knew it, his thoughts had melded into dreams and then nothingness as he slept like the dead on the wooden floor.

CAROLINE

Melroy, Georgia

Caroline woke to a pounding headache, the smell of coffee and bacon, and yelling coming from the kitchen. It was her father and some other man, a voice she did not recognize. She hurriedly slipped on her robe and made her way down the stairs. She reached the bottom stair just in time to see the man disappear from the great entryway and through the front door. He had flung the screen door open so hard that it bounced against the exterior wall and slammed back shut. She hurried to the kitchen and found her father seated at the table, his head in his hands.

"Daddy?" she called. Thomas Higgs did not look up; rather he gripped the hair that sprouted between his fingers. She walked cautiously toward her father and placed a hand on the back of his neck. "Daddy? What's going on?"

Octavia stepped out of the great pantry. Who knew how long she'd been in there, always a fly on the wall. "Chile, go on back up. Brush that hair on yer head and get on yer clothes."

Caroline ignored her. "Daddy, what is the matter? You're scaring me."

Thomas raised his head, complete reticence across his face, staring straight ahead in a daze. "Please, for once, Caroline, just do as you're told."

Caroline lifted her hand as if the very skin on the back of her father's neck burned her. She crossed her arms and took a few steps around the table, leaning in as to be face-on should he decide to look up. "I'm a grown-ass woman, so very tired of being *told* what to do. I cain't in all my days think of another twenty-two-year-old that still must take orders from her old nanny."

Octavia's eyes widened and her head tilted with an *Oh is that so?* look across it.

Caroline continued, "You two go 'bout telling me what I should wear, what I should think, how I should feel. *Don't say that, Chuck; it's not ladylike. Don't wear that, Chuck, you'll never find a proper suiter. Don't drink that, Chuck, someone might get their damn knickers in a wad!* I mean, who even gives a shit what I drink or don't drink or why I drink at all!"

Thomas, having heard plenty, broke from his trance. "Chuck, people do give a shit. I give a shit. It's you that doesn't seem to care." He took a deep breath and checked himself, lowering his voice. "Chuck, I am fine. Everything is fine. Now go on and get yourself ready if you want to walk to church with me."

Caroline stood there, a child in the dark, dismissed from adult matters. She said, "I think I'll stay home this morning if that's okay."

"And if it's not?" retorted her father.

She let out a sigh, turned, and left the kitchen. Octavia returned to cooking breakfast, shaking her head.

The house was quiet, everyone having dressed in their Sunday best and gone to their respective churches. Thomas had poked his head in her room and offered her once more to join him, but she declined. When Octavia invited her to ride with her to Bethel Baptist, the

Black church out south of town, she also declined. She had grown up in both churches, sometimes walking with her daddy, sometimes riding with Octavia and a few of the hands in the plantation wagon. But she never felt at home at her daddy's church.

The First Baptist Church of Melroy was grand and beautiful, a structure worthy of God's grace, full of busybody Christians with big opinions and big mouths. Bethel Baptist was a converted barn, run down and oppressively hot, full of boisterous singing and dancing and folks who clicked their tongues at a gossip. And they never minded little Caroline Higgs tagging along. When Caroline's mother died, women from First Baptist flocked to the home bringing casseroles and stews and sweet breads and pies. After the first few weeks, most fell away. Some lingered, vying to win the position of lady of the plantation, though it was not open for the filling. After months of Thomas' polite dismissals, and Caroline's raucous outbursts, the few stragglers fell away with the rest of them. Years later, when First Baptist ate up the news of Caroline's tragedy—and her husband's shameful departure—Octavia's church took Caroline in and allowed her a place in the pew to sit. She sat unbothered, a zombie in a crowd of worship. To call the two houses of fellowship disparate would have been an understatement.

Caroline wasn't in the mood for the word of God this morning. Wasn't in the mood to see folks who had enjoyed the hospitality of the Higgs last night today sit in judgment of the sinner—sinners being any folks other than themselves, of course. She was tired of all the judgment all the time, of all the opinions and the praying. Her grief was real, and it haunted her in ways no person could seem to grasp. And no amount of lifting her up in prayer was going to cure it. If anything, it was quite the opposite.

She had made the mistake only once of walking down to the pulpit when prodded by her desperate father. The preacher had hollered out to the congregation, "Anyone who feels the powerful pull of the devil, just know you are not alone. For it is the believer— the strong in faith—whom the devil feels most threatened. And therefore the one whom Satan himself pulls out all the stops to work his evil ways, to niggle into your thoughts and dreams. Do not fear. The Lord is with you. But also, do not fight alone. For the Body sits here with you as well. And it would be a sin to cast off this Body of Christ, here and ready to come to your aid. Children of God, believers in the Almighty Christ, if you find yourself struggling, do not sit in silence. For it would be a sin to reject these brothers and sisters in Christ. Come down before the church and let us anoint you, lift you up, and show the devil that you are not weak and alone but armored with the Body of Jesus Christ himself!"

She had felt her daddy's arm wrap around her, squeeze tight, and lift her as he stood from the pew. She wanted to resist but had not an ounce of energy to do so. The two walked down to the pastor, the pianist playing the same hymn on repeat while the pastor placed one hand on her shoulder and bowed his head, raised his other hand high above, and began to shout his prayers. Once it was all said and done, Caroline had dozens of hands upon her. She felt seen. Loved. Cared for. And she was right, partly. She had been seen. Her daddy did love and care for her and feared for her sanity and soul. But the rest, they lapped up the juicy moment gifted by this broken widow. And it further fueled the gossip mill of Melroy.

"The oldest Higgs girl has been seeing the devil in her room."

"That Caroline Colley, she feels such guilt over the tragedy that she wishes herself dead, and that's why we had to pray over her."

"She's thinking of takin her own life; wouldn't be surprised if that poor man found his girl hanging from a bedsheet one day."

"You know, I heard she was a part of her husband's plan, and at the last minute she turned on him. The Lord won't abide such an act from a wife, to reject her subservient duty, no matter the circumstance, and that's how she got in this mix-up in the first place."

The rumors that had spread like wildfire after the execution of Davis Colley had been rekindled at this anointing, and Caroline never forgot it. So when she woke to her husband dangling above the foot of her bed, when she turned from the shelves in the cellar to find him swinging from the rafter, when she stood up from her garden to find his body hanging from the old oak at the entrance, her only choice was to try to ignore him. Going to the church was a reputation death sentence. And besides, pretty much anytime someone got a religion, it seemed to Caroline they received a ticket, a pass for all thinking, and became sheep in the worse possible sense.

She spent the morning in her garden, keeping clear of the house until everyone returned from church. She would have liked to have prepared Sunday lunch, have it ready for when they walked in. Daddy had certainly been upset about something. It would make him happy to see her take some initiative—and Octavia too—but today she could not. Once they left, she went downstairs to grab a cup of coffee. After she poured a cup, she turned to find Davis there, suspended from the chandelier. The cup slipped from her hands, shattered onto the kitchen floor, splattering the cabinets, the chairs. No matter how many times she turned to find him, it never was any less jolting.

Octavia was the first to greet her in the garden. She approached cautiously. "Miss Caroline?" she called quietly. She stood at the entrance holding Caroline's straw hat, concerned. Octavia had seen the hat at the house and figured Caroline had forgotten it. As she stood watching the woman kneeling down, pruning at a rosemary bush barefoot wearing only her nightgown, it seemed her hat wasn't all she'd forgotten.

Caroline looked up from where she worked. She swiped an arm across her sweaty forehead and then held a hand high, blocking the harsh noon sun from her eyes.

"Ya doing ah-kay?" asked Octavia.

"I'm fine. I 'bout waited too long to harvest the rosemary. Found a few blooms this morning, so I figured if I want the best oils, I best get to cutting." She snipped at the plant.

Octavia stood, her eyes locked onto Caroline. Her hands slowly turned the hat dangling by its brim. Her fingers nervously picked along the hairy bristles that sprung from the edges. She still had on her Sunday dress. The air was stagnant in the garden, stifling with no breeze. Quiet save the buzzing whine of the dog-day cicadas above in full chorus.

Caroline said, "Sorry for the kitchen. I just—"

"I know," interrupted Octavia. Her face was covered in beads of sweat and concern. "I did tek care of it."

Caroline dropped her hand from blocking the sun and tossed the shears to the ground. She walked over to her mother's bench and plopped down. Octavia stood in place until Caroline looked up, meeting her eyes. How she hated the sting of tears. She had cried so many times in the last months, tears of tragic sorrow and grief, and then more recently tears of fear. Fear that she was never going to be okay again.

Octavia sat beside her and placed a hand upon Caroline's thigh. "'Tis time, Miss Caroline, dat you look deep inside. Find what been keeping Mista Colley in yer head and be rid a it. Be rid a he. He no more here than me tata and momma . . . or yer momma." She paused. The mention of Mary Higgs always brought about a moment of somber silence. "Dey gone. But he, he live too much in here." She gently touched Caroline's temple then tucked a rogue lock of sweaty hair behind her ear. "Mista Higgs, he at he wits' end, Miss Caroline. Doctors telling he to bring you in fer long time."

Caroline started to protest but Octavia held up a hand. "Miss Caroline, don' none us want dat, you hear?"

"Chuck?" a soft voice called out. The two women sitting at the bench turned to see Henrietta and Thomas standing at the garden's entrance.

Octavia stood and handed Caroline's hat over to her. "Lunch be ready soon." She placed a hand atop Caroline's head and gave it a gentle press. "See you, chile."

"I thought I'd see you at church today," called out Henrietta. She kept a bit of distance. Thomas patted her on the shoulder, bowed his head, and left the two to talk.

"Nah, I think I 'bout had my fill there. Besides, I'm coming to see real clear that crisis just makes a person defenseless to cultish ways."

"Chuck, you don't mean that." Henrietta eased her way into the heart of the garden, touching flowers, frivolously inspecting leaves. She had no clue about gardens or plants. None whatsoever. For a moment, she found herself in a panic. Would she need these skills in Texas? A good wife surely can tend to a garden.

Caroline interrupted. "I do mean that, Henri."

From the look on her face, Henrietta could tell that she meant it. It saddened her. "Well, you know you always are welcome. The Lord will always keep you."

Caroline scoffed, stood from the bench, and waved the words from the air. She wore her history on her sleeve, her thoughts on her face. There was never any doubt as to what Caroline Higgs-Colley was feeling at any point in time. She hadn't the grace nor reticence nor desire even to appear any way other than the way it really was.

"I'm headed over to the seed house. You coming?"

"Sure," replied Henrietta.

The Higgs Plantation was ahead of its time when it came to pecans. Other farmers were relatively hesitant at the notion of the nuts having much benefit, but Thomas dove right in. With over 6,500 acres, various barns and outbuildings, and its own shipping wharf at the river, to say it was expansive was an understatement. Fortunately for Caroline, her garden and seed house were all within walking distance.

The two approached the outbuilding, a small but tall barn painted a dusty green with white trim. It sat nestled in the shade of a great oak tree. Two windows flanked the white door on the front of the building and small square windows placed high were spread about the other three walls. She had had this building built especially for her—to dry, process, and store her herbs and seeds. Surrounding it was a flower garden and twin rose bushes on each side of the door.

Caroline had her hands full with bundles of rosemary sprigs and tools. She gave a nod toward the door, gesturing for Henrietta to open it. Henrietta pried on the lever. It wouldn't budge. She tried again. In defeat, she turned to Caroline. Caroline gave a laugh and handed over her load.

"Here." With one shove, she had the lever dislodged and the door open. She turned back to Henrietta. "You ought to toughen up a bit, get your hands dirty more often."

Henrietta, slightly embarrassed, agreed. She had been thinking about how different it most likely would be living in Texas. She wasn't really even sure what to expect. All she was told was that the town was fairly new with little in the way of commercial development. She envisioned a pioneer town with no shopping and dirt roads. She also envisioned a dead garden and a starving Ford and children. She had no clue how they were going to get by, but she dared not mention this to Ford. Plus, Ford was adamant that they were not to worry about anything, that they had six months once there to find a place and get settled. The railroad had contracted with a hotelier out of Georgia who apparently was expanding to Texas alongside the railway. He'd purchased a grand hotel oddly situated in this infant community and promised it for use as temporary housing for select railroad employees and their families. Ford qualified as he was the surveyor mapping out the route from Fort Worth traveling west.

Caroline dragged the great door open and walked into the shadowy space. Henrietta followed close behind. As Caroline made to turn and reach for a lantern hanging high, she screamed and jumped back, dodging Davis's dangling legs and slamming into Henrietta, knocking her to the ground.

Henrietta woke that evening in Caroline's room to Octavia dabbing her forehead with a cool washcloth. She laid in Caroline's bed. Ford sat next to her in a chair butted up against it. Caroline sat in a chair across the room. Confused, Henrietta immediately went to sit up, but Ford gently pressed her back down.

"Just rest, my love," he quietly instructed.

"What—why am I here?" she asked.

Octavia replied, "Hit yer head, Miss Henri-eTTah." Octavia's Ts were always the punch of any word, far different from the Southerner's omission, replacing the T with the D sound. As a child, Henrietta struggled to even understand Octavia, her Geechee dialect nearly unintelligible at the time. But she'd always loved how she said her name, the emphasis she placed on her two Ts.

Ford tried to brush back her hair, but Henrietta could feel its resistance. She reached up to touch her head and discovered a hardened blood-dried mass of hair. "I don't even remember hitting my head. What happened?"

"I'm so sorry." Caroline stood up and walked over to the bed. "I just got startled and when I turned—well, I didn't think you'd be right on my heels. Anyways, I guess I tripped you up. When you went down, you hit your head on the rock I use to prop open the door. Then lights out, I guess."

Henrietta closed her eyes and nodded. Her head pounded.

Ford leaned in and kissed her gently on the forehead. "I'm going to fetch you some water and a new washcloth." He stood and left.

Caroline took his place in the chair. As she sat, she could sense Octavia's eyes burrowing straight through her, beckoning her to look up and meet her own for an unspoken exchange. But Caroline would not. She did not wish to see any such look of pity, or worry, or worse . . . *you've got to do something about this.*

Pressure squeezed at Caroline's chest. Reddened welts covered her neck and collarbone. Ringing built in her ears, a symphonic battle with the katydids pulsing out their chorus into the night. She needed air.

She stepped out onto the front porch to find her father seated in a rocking chair. He smoked a pipe and gently tipped his chair back and forth. His rocking did not stop as Caroline approached. The air had cooled slightly, a much-needed break from the sweltering humidity. Caroline took the chair beside him and synced her rocking with his. The two rocked in silence listening to the katydids that pulsed high then low, drowning out all other sounds of the night.

Caroline knew she was not well. She also knew she was not crazy. In the beginning, when the visits from Davis first began, she thought she might be. Because of the nature surrounding the circumstances of his death, the sheer trauma of the events leading up to it and resulting from it, no one blamed her for being disturbed. But as with the grief of anyone who loses a loved one, the casseroles and visitors eventually peter out. Life goes on. And the mourner is expected to conduct their mourning in private, out of respect for the public who wish to not be exposed to the uncomfortable nature of grief any longer than necessary. To move on as well. But that rarely happens. What does happen is the mourner is left alone in their grief. All is forgotten and, if not, it's at least not mentioned.

With Davis Colley's death, things weren't so cut and dry. Her mourning morphed. He haunted her. No one understood. He didn't haunt just her dreams. He haunted her very being. At first, she had to avoid the town square, where he spent his last moments alive on this earth. Then she had to avoid the courthouse, the post office, places he frequented in his daily life. Her father and Octavia had to become her runners, making purchases, sending letters. She just could not do it. She'd come back from a trip to town in hysterics that lasted for hours. Then exhaustion would set in and she'd sleep for days.

Davis was always there. For a bit, avoiding his old stomping grounds helped, but then he appeared in her room, her garden. He haunted the kitchen, the root cellar. The more time went by, the more the haunting limited Caroline to where she could go. Considering him to be all in her head was of no help for that meant she was crazy. And she believed she was in the beginning—crazy. But when no treatment helped, she started to wonder if maybe she was not in fact crazy but that Davis was real and unwilling to move on until he accomplished something. It wasn't unheard of after all. Everyone had some ghost story where the spirit had this last act to fulfill before they could move on: a good deed, an act of revenge, simply just having their remains laid to rest in the proper location. The story varied depending upon what sounded most riveting to the listener. The stories twisted and turned and grew into elaborate ghost tales over the years enjoyed by curious and thrill-seeking minds of the adolescent. If this were true, however, if Davis were not all in her head but a spirit left behind until he completed some last deed, what needed to happen?

Caroline had considered this before, but she usually could not bear thinking on it too long before panic sat in. For she came to the same conclusion—Davis wanted her dead. He'd said as much many times while hanging. "Death will soon pay you a visit. And he'll bring Mother Nature along to wield her poison."

Caroline shuttered.

"You okay, hon?" asked Thomas. He stopped rocking and turned to face his daughter.

Caroline sighed. "I am not, Daddy."

She thought a moment. She considered her life and how dysfunctional she'd become. Davis would never leave her alone. Not here. And now her fear had caused harm to her very best friend.

"Daddy?" she said.

"Um-hum."

"I think, if it's okay with you, I may go with Henri to Texas."

DIX

Melroy, Georgia

While some partygoers woke late suffering the echoes of last night's dandelion wine, Dix rose before the sun, feeling the same he did each and every day. He swung his legs out from under the covers and placed his feet on the floor just so. He lit the lantern and pulled his Bible from the drawer in the nightstand. The session of chance landed him at Matthew 6:24: *No man can serve two masters: for either he will hate the one and love the other, or else he will hold to the one and despise the other. Ye cannot serve God and mammon.*

He dressed in his usual thin shirt, trousers, and soft shoes, his morning uniform. He stepped outside, the morning warm, humid like a dog's breath. The night had brought no relief, no breeze to speak of. As he moved and bent his body, he repeated the lines he had just read. Worshiping money wasn't really something he struggled with. He wanted to be a successful doctor and help others, but he placed nothing above or equal to God.

He reached high into sky, stretching his arms straight up and bending his torso left and then right. He bent forward, folding near in half, and wrapped his long fingers around his narrow ankles. The pull on the back of his legs felt nice. He stood and set out on his walk, at first at a nice even pace. He pumped his arms and felt his heart beat, which these days he always seemed acutely aware of. He picked up the pace. His breath quickened with each step.

As the verse ran through his mind, Dix ran through the streets of Melroy. He had no plan of where he was going. Not this morning, not tomorrow, not ever. He had been robbed of his dream. The very thought was like throwing coal in the engine, his body the train barreling through the town. He ran hard, his steps loud as they beat the earth, his breath audible as it stole gulps of humid air. His mind raced and finally his heart and body converged, the nagging drumming now warranted. Since the night of Mrs. Lamott, the horrible debacle and subsequent closure of the school, all the looks and whispers, this moment was the first time Dix felt the pounding of his heart was a legitimate rhythm that he controlled rather than an anxious thump deep within a sluggish and depressed body. Ruminating on the Word of the day really seemed to help Dix. Or was it the gymnastics and run? He no longer knew—anything. What was he going to do?

Dix ended up at the steps of Ford and Henrietta's home where Ford sat smoking a cigarette and drinking a cup of coffee, taking in the rising sun. When he saw Dix running toward him, he immediately shot up, startled.

"Dix?" Fear crossed his face. "What is it? Is Mother okay? Is it Papa?"

Dix stopped at the foot of the steps, bent forward, hands on his knees. He reached a hand high, gesturing the need for a moment while sucking in air. He shook his head and waved. "Nothing like that, Ford." He stood and laced his hands behind his head. His lungs burned. He managed to huff out, "I'm sorry I startled you."

Ford, relieved, offered Dix a cup of coffee, which Dix declined.

"What is it you're doing, Dix? I can't think of one good reason to be up this early—and running?" He chuckled. "What are you running from, the moon?" He sipped the coffee.

Dix gave a halfhearted laugh. "I'm not running from anything, Ford. It's good to tax the body in healthy ways. And might I say, you're up as well."

Ford grinned. "Touché. Well, you look like you've taxed the body a tad much this morning. Some water maybe?"

Dix nodded and Ford disappeared into the house. A dove landed at the feeder hanging from the porch. Dix watched as it pecked and picked its favorite bits, dropping the unwanted parts to the ground. He thought about his career, now just discarded bits of his life.

Ford returned and Dix accepted the water, gulped down the glass in one go, and handed it back over. He wiped his forehead on the shoulder of his shirt and turned to make his way back to his parents' place. The verse crossed his mind once more. Had he been secretly dreaming of the wealth that accompanied the life of a doctor and that's why God pulled the plug on his career? Or maybe in his situation, longing to be revered by the public was his sin. Whatever it was, God was most definitely picking bits of his dream and tossing them aside.

He turned back to Ford and yelled out, "Thank you, brother."

Ford yelled back, "As long as you're willing to accept my olive branch, you'll always have help from me. A home, a glass of water, you name it. We're The Lucky Sevens, brother. Everything eventually works out for a Lucky Seven!"

Dix jogged a few more feet and then stopped. An olive branch, the dove—all signs from God. And then it hit him. God was telling him to turn away from the dream of being a prestigious doctor in a big city like Savannah or Melroy and to instead focus on serving. That's where he'd gone wrong. He'd lost sight of God's *true* will. He'd been so focused on his own will, God had had no choice but to derail him in the most profound way. In a fashion completely at odds with his nature, a moment of spontaneity took hold and he turned back. Ford still stood on the porch. He had been watching him.

Dix shouted, "If you're sure you and Henri don't mind, I'd gladly like to accompany you to Texas. Nothing here promising any longer. I'll find work. Pay my own way with any means I can find. Won't burden you two a bit. If you'll have me."

A grin spread across Ford's face, the same grin he'd flashed Dix as a child when silently agreeing to plunge into mischief together. For the first time in months, Dix felt the tiniest twinge of excitement. He knew this truly was what God intended. He wasn't altogether certain he was to go to Element Dale, but he felt sure he was being pulled from Melroy. He just needed to stop all the resisting.

He held up his hand and hollered back, "Tell Henri I'll see you two at church in a bit."

ELZI

The Staked Plains, Texas

A great high-pitched screech split through the darkness. Elzi startled awake to wings beating and flapping, bodies thumping and clawing, diving and retreating and diving again. The black bird and an owl. The vulture retreated from the owl then descended upon Elzi, claws first, wings wide, beak open and hissing. Elzi could see the owl trailing it. Frightened and disoriented, he scrambled backward on his butt, his boots shoving and kicking the ground for traction. At the last second, he covered his head with his arms and ducked. He squeezed his eyes shut. The percussion of the wings blasted his neck and ear and then passed. He opened his eyes in time to see the screech owl swooping down and sinking its claws into the black bird's back. The vulture cracked out a roaring squawk unknown to anything Elzi had ever before experienced. Adrenaline surged all around, a sort of electricity passing back and forth from the fighting birds to the man on the ground. He watched on, terrified, stupefied. The birds squawked and hissed and bounced from the ground to the sky in tandem, clawing and pecking until finally the vulture retreated into the dawning sky. The small owl landed before him. Elzi could see its chest heaving, its piercing yellow eyes darting this way and that, its gray-brown feathers wet with blood. The two locked eyes for a moment. A soft trill emanated from its tiny body. Suddenly, the bird burst from the ground, stirring up a small plume of dust, and flittered away.

The sun was just starting to peek through the clouds. In the distance he saw glimmers, beautiful and inviting. He picked himself up from the ground and dusted off his backside. After some time he reached the glimmers. They were no mirage as he'd feared, but actual puddles. He knelt down and splashed his face to rinse away the filth, the grit and grime between his fingers. He dropped down, rolling over onto his back. He gazed at the sky, the oranges and pinks burning across the lavender clouds, the sun deceiving the world with its beauty. But Elzi was not deceived. The great ball of fire was just revving up to char the earth within hours.

His mind raced through the last days, bouncing between memories, between reality, between dreams. Dreams of the Indian of Black and Bones, of the vulture, of the dangling head. He dreamed of Hattie Mae and her soft hand cupping his chin. Her smile. Her October eyes. He dreamed of camp, of the men dropping one by one, succumbing to the elements. Of coyotes bounding across seas of grass. Of Albin. He dreamed of the sound of a running stream, of singing. He dreamed of the voices, of the orbs, and the sweetest, saddest words he'd ever heard: *you are but half of my broken heart.*

Now go.

He shuttered awake. The morning sun was no longer. In fact the sun was no longer. In its stead, a full moon illuminated the land. Elzi thought hard, scrambling to grasp time. Each time he tried, tried to track the days, the hours, it escaped him. When he strained to recollect the passing days, trying even harder to focus his mind, time wiggled and writhed, pulling free from his grasp, like the armadillo Albin once bet him to catch.

"It's just inside dis here hole," Albin had said. "Grab its tail and pull 'em out."

Elzi had accepted the bet. The winnings would be a half dime. He'd rolled up his sleeves and crouched down onto one knee.

Albin piped up, "Elzi, don't let dat little thang fool ya. Ya best be putting your back into it."

Elzi had laughed him off, but as soon as he finally got the nerve to reach in and grab it, the animal's strength became shockingly and abundantly clear. He immediately switched up his stance for better leverage. He'd held onto its tail with two hands, fully gripping, but the animal wouldn't budge. It was a game of tug-of-war. The animal dug in, gaining ground inch by inch until finally Elzi gave up. Winded and laughing, he'd been outdone by the armadillo. The boys fell to their backs belting out deep belly laughs.

When it came time to pay up, Albin had said, "Ain't no man can drag a dilla out its hole. Cain't be done. Just like I said."

Elzi had handed over the half dime.

Elzi gave up trying to drag back his recollections of the past days and decided to walk back and check on his fellow soldiers, see how they were faring. *Maybe Albin's hearing come back*, he thought. He walked for what seemed like hours in the dark, guided by the moon, until the early morning hours of daybreak. For some time, he feared he was lost. Lost in this flat sea of sameness on his own. It was the moment this fearful thought entered his mind that he saw the makeshift cover in the distance. The horse blanket draped over the mesquite bush. Relief.

He spotted Albin, upright and walking. As he got closer, he realized Albin was walking away—and carrying a pack. Elzi hollered out, but Albin did not turn to him, did not stop walking. Was it possible he did not hear his voice over the wails of the hot wind? Elzi hollered out again. No response. Each step Elzi took, it seemed Albin took three, and the distance grew between the two of them. When Elzi finally reached the mesquite, Albin had disappeared over the bluff. Only Jasper remained. He still sat below the bush, legs still naked, but his eyes had been plucked from his head. His tongue, swollen and protruding, bulged from his hanging lower jaw. Flies bounced and buzzed around his lips, crawling in and out of his nose and the voids where once his polite eyes had been.

Elzi swallowed down the knot of sadness and fear and exhaustion and grief he'd been holding in his throat. He took a moment, feeling compelled to pray. *Pray to who?* he wondered. Where had God been? For he certainly didn't reside in the Staked Plains. Elzi thought about the Commander and his evil words, how the White men had followed suit, insulted his Blackness and that of the other buffalo soldiers who gave their lives to service. The Staked Plains was no place God could be found. Rather it was an earthly hell where Lucifer disguised himself as the sun. Elzi looked down at Jasper and thought of a great divine devil bursting from the ball of fire above, transforming into a tattered vulture and descending upon his friend, stealing his eyes, removing all means to admire the earth God created.

He looked up and still Albin was gone, out of sight. He bent down to pick up the pack thrown haphazardly to the side of Jasper. It was Jasper's and empty save for a tin cup, plate, utensils, and his neckerchief. His kepi hat lay crushed and dirt-filled beside his hip, no longer black but a reddish-brown. His Brogans still sat where he'd placed them after pulling them off his feet. Elzi saw no canteen anywhere. Elzi's haversack lay off and back a bit, almost behind Jasper. He scrambled over to it, desperate to lay hands on his belongings. He yanked out the tin cup, the small pouch of coffee. His heart once again raced like that of a jackrabbit. He reached in and felt around. Flipping the haversack on its end, he grabbed the bottom corners and shook out the remaining items into the dirt: a fork, a spoon, a knife. Next he reached for his pack and turned it up, shaking it violently. A deck of playing cards, a pair of socks, a pocketknife. No hardtack. No salted pork. And most importantly, no journal.

Panicked, he crawled over to Jasper and slid his hand back behind where he sat. He dragged out a limp pack. He rummaged through quickly and shook the pack only to discover nothing but a pair of socks. Everything was gone. He looked up in the direction of Albin. No matter how hard he tried, he saw nothing but vast openness. Dirt and dunes for as far as he could see. He looked back at Jasper. Still very dead. It was all too much. Panic turned to energy and at once he burst onto his feet. He ran hard. He would catch up to Albin. His feet beat the earth like that of a buffalo, each step kicking up dirt. He pumped his arms and ran. And ran. And ran. He ran until the panic shifted into thoughts of awareness. Awareness that he was moving away from the bush and into the maze of sameness, that he hadn't a clue where he was out in this damned hell and finally, with great sadness, that his best friend had abandoned him. His steps slowed until he was walking.

Just then, a figure came into view ahead. A man lying on the ground. *Albin,* he thought. As he got closer and the scene became clearer, his stomach dropped. "Albin!" he shouted. He rushed over and kicked the vultures from his body. They hissed and grunted as they hopped but a few feet away, eyeing him. He squatted down and grabbed his face. It was not Albin, but in fact Luke, milky gray, covered in dirt and flies, his innards mostly picked away, his pack to his side with its contents strewn about.

Elzi ripped off his hat, tossed it aside, and screamed into the desert. He crouched down and tucked his head into his hands. He stared down at his Brogans. Not a speck of black could be seen. His hat too was completely covered. *Filthy hell on earth,* he thought. He panted, rubbing his head back and forth, back and forth, until finally the worst thought of all surfaced in his exhausted mind. Not only had so many perished, not only had this Indian hunt been for naught, not only had his best friend abandoned him and left him to die, but he'd stolen his most beloved possession: the book of Ora B. Dupre.

He grabbed his hat and stood, gave it a slap against his thigh, knocking off the red dirt, and returned it atop his head. He looked out at the land. A panorama, flat until it reached the horizon, as if it'd all just been swallowed up by the sea. The sun was gaining ground and would soon be high. He thought about everything he no longer had. Not even an empty canteen. A rush of anger surged and he began to walk. Thoughts consumed him. *Betrayed* was the word that most came to mind. He picked up the pace. When fearful thoughts tried to creep in, thoughts of dying in the desert, he shoved them down and conjured up instead thoughts of revenge. He full-on sprinted, the thirst forgotten. He was broken and hurt and enraged and running wildly, kicking up dirt, headed where, he did not know.

He woke to the sound of splashing. His eyes opened. The moon above shone round and white. Confusion struck him first. He hadn't knowledge of bedding down—or passing out for that matter. He rolled onto his stomach. When he looked ahead, the same moon danced before him, ripples distorting its roundness. He pulled up onto his hands and knees. Across the way, a buffalo, dragging waves with each step, climbed out of the water and onto the earth, the water crashing into the bank. After a few steps, the great beast dropped to its knees and then onto its side in the dirt and began its glorious wallow.

Elzi was at a playa. When or how he got there, he did not know. He collapsed to his side and rolled, returning to his back, his arms spread out wide. He stared up at the moon for a moment then closed his eyes, fear no longer plaguing him. After he rested, he'd make his way back to camp, back to Albin, the deserter.

WALKER

Georgia

Walker managed to ride the rails from Ashville to Murphy, then from Murphy to Gem City undetected and unscathed. He'd met a fellow rider while hopping off in Gem City who directed him to a hobo-friendly house on the corner of Lemon and Church Streets, the homeowners a couple who owned the local drug and mercantile store. To Walker's eyes, the house was a mansion, standing two stories, white, and boasting many rooms. The couple offered him a night's stay and meals in exchange for work. They needed a pit dug in the backyard. He worked dutifully, quietly, asking no questions. Just grateful at the idea of a warm meal, a chance to clean up, and sleep indoors on a bed. When the job was complete, he stepped into the home where he was shown his way upstairs by the house woman. She directed him to a private room containing a bed, a chamber pot in the corner, a table with a basin for washing, a sitting chair, and shelving with books on the wall.

He bent down and peered at himself in the mirror. His eyes were even more striking as their icy blueness radiated from his filthy grime-covered face. He quickly washed his face and hands, already feeling refreshed. As he dried off, he noticed the walls were covered in a colorful, cheery floral paper matching the bedding and curtains. Walker imagined the room fit for a young girl, though he'd not seen anyone at the house aside from the owners and their house woman.

At supper, he sat across from the couple, trying his best to pace his eating. He was starving, had grown hungrier each mile on the rails, his provisions rarely providing any real sustenance. The fork and knife had helped avoid the appearance of a famished grizzly, but really he could have eaten the entire plate of ham, red cabbage, and greens in a matter of seconds and then done it all over again. The couple interrupted his bites with many questions, and he found himself uneasy under their quizzical gaze, though unable to pinpoint exactly why.

Walker had two areas of which he considered himself a veteran: crafting moonshine and manufacturing lies. While they fed him the best meal he'd had in days, he fed them fabrications of his origin and desired destination, his means and goals. All of which he came up with on the fly. He had been not a moonshiner but a grain miller. He had not shot and killed a federal agent but rather had been a significant asset to the Army, helping them locate and eradicate the local Klan. He had not had his illegal operation burned to the ground and been forced to flee but had decided to take his abilities and travel the South, offering up consulting services to local governments not yet able to effectively address its Klan problem.

When supper was done, he stood and thanked them. "I certainly 'preciate your hospitality. I'm telling you, I's so hungry I think my stomach was starting to rub a blister aginst my backbone."

The couple laughed and nodded. "Always happy to help our fellow man. We hope you rest easy this night. Sula will have your clothes washed and ready for you come sunup."

"I 'preciate that too. I'm sure I stink so bad I could scare a buzzard off a shit wagon."

At this, the woman politely smiled and looked away. The man

responded with deep phony laughter, holding his belly and slapping his thigh. Walker huffed out a little laugh and eyed the man. He was glad for them, for this house, for the meal, but something was odd about this couple. He'd be glad to be on his way first thing in the morning.

It was quiet in the room. Hot. The window stood open ready for a breeze, but the curtains hung heavy and still. Walker laid in the bed, smoking a cigarette and eyeing the flowers crawling across the walls. A very busy type of beauty. While he missed the tranquility of the Black Mountains, he found he was drawn to and curious about the city. Its potential allured him and caused feelings of aspiration to well up inside. What he could be, the money he could make if only he found the right town, the right deal. His mind took him to visions of being a business owner, someone people listened to, someone with money. Maybe he'd become an official with power. Money and power, that would suit him well. Before he knew it, his thoughts had lulled him to sleep.

Metal scraped dirt followed by a sprinkled thud. Metal scraped dirt. A sprinkled thud. *Scrape. Thud. Scrape. Thud.* Walker woke with a start, his cigarette having dropped from his hand and onto the mattress. He furiously beat the bed, swiping the burning butt onto the floor. He hopped up and quickly stomped it out with his bare heel. Engulfed in the strange room's pitch blackness, he walked over to the open window and flicked the butt onto the ground below. The moon hid somewhere with the stars for he couldn't see a thing. The scrape and thud continued like a metronome below where he stood. Someone was filling in his handiwork.

Earlier he had voiced his curiosity about the hole. He had been digging for hours when the man had stepped out to check on him. "A privy fault" had been his response.

This would be Walker's first tick on the cons list to city living. Maneuvering and handling your own shit—your whole family's shit— did not fit in with his view of the fast and alluring city. In the mountains, with such a small population, shit did not become a problem, wasn't such an assault on the human senses, and you certainly didn't bury it right outside your back door.

Scrape. Thud. Scrape. Thud. All his digging was being undone by someone under the cover of night. It made little sense. Yet it wasn't his problem. He worked. He got a place to lay his head and a warm meal in his belly. They could do as they pleased with their hole. He climbed back into bed.

The next morning he woke early and refreshed. His clothes sat in a neatly folded pile just outside his door. He shaved and combed his hair, no longer looking gray and dull but back to its cotton white. He dressed, gathered up his belongings, and headed downstairs. The Mister sat at the kitchen table reading a newspaper and drinking coffee. He offered Walker a cup. Walker accepted. The man thanked him again for helping out, stating the city was soon to implement a system of pipes that would carry wastewater and sewage away, that until then, they had to rely on night soil collection which meant digging cesspool holes for the house woman to fill nightly.

Walker thought about it a moment. Pictured a web of underground rivers of shit all leading to—where? He walked over and peered out the large kitchen window that overlooked the vast back lawn. It had grass with a few great towering red maples shading most of the yard. Those maples, he'd been grateful for yesterday. Beds of flowers and bushes bordered the area, a nice but almost artificially forced touch, he thought. He scanned the area. There was no hole.

The Mister droned on about the sewer systems installed in places such as New York and Paris. Walker continued to sip his coffee, looking intently out of the window.

The Mister went on, "A great city is the most mighty of dung-makers. If our gold is manure, our manure, on the other hand, is gold. That's Hugo. Do you read him by chance?"

A preoccupied Walker said, "Never heard of the man." His brows furrowed. He'd spotted it. The hole he'd spent the whole of a day digging was filled in, the dirt spread nicely, with a bench positioned atop it. Two pots of flowers bookended the bench. He sensed the man's eyes on him and the hairs on the back of his neck stood. Whatever the hole was meant for, it certainly had not been as a privy vault. He imagined something being tossed in and covered up during the night. He turned to face the man, who surprisingly was just inches behind him, making to look over his shoulder into the yard as well.

"I believe it's going to be a gloriously beautiful day. Don't you?" the Mister asked.

Walker took a step back, his boot heel striking the wall. "Looks to be that-a-way," he replied.

The man smiled hard, his eyes fixed on Walker's. Walker had the urge to look away, but he wouldn't allow it. He took a step forward, the men now standing close enough to feel one another's breath. The man continued to smile. Walker frowned.

"Pardon me," he said, and stepped to the side. He leaned, stretched out and placed his coffee cup on the table. He picked up his bag and walked out of the kitchen.

As he reached the door, he heard the man yell out, "Nothing more honorable than an honest day's work."

Walker stopped, pondered the words. A few witticisms came to mind, but he thought better of them. Something was off here in this house, and he wanted nothing more to do with it. He stepped out of the house and onto the front porch. Its screen door bounced closed behind him. He stepped down off the porch and turned right. Birds chirped and flittered in the trees above. He needed to get moving, back to the trains. He walked across the street and into a great park where children played and squealed and laughed. He watched as a boy tagged another, *You're it!* At the far end of the park, two girls stood, each holding a pair of sticks. One girl placed a hoop wrapped in ribbons of blues, pinks, reds, and yellows onto her sticks. She crossed the sticks, allowing the hoop to slide down. Once it reached near the bottom, she quickly pulled them apart, the hoop shooting up in the air in a great arc where the receiving child gracefully extended her stick, ringing the hoop successfully. The two cheered and danced with delight.

He crossed the next street and walked in between buildings and into the woods until he reached the tracks. Following them, keeping concealed in the trees, he reached the train. He hopped up and onto the platform of the last car and climbed, this time deciding to deck a car until it was clear of the town. He figured he'd be less likely found up on top of a car than to take his chances walking from car to car looking for an empty one. He'd ride up top until the coast was clear. Then he could make his way down and "ride the blinds" as his uncle would say; namely, to ride in between cars concealed by the canvas cover. It'd be the best way to keep out of sight of the bulls, though the easiest way to get crushed.

He laid face down on top of the train while it slowly screeched to life, the metal groaning as the couplings one by one took up slack. And then he was off again. Headed west. Where it stopped next, he did not know. One thing he was certain of, he was over hoboing, and trains, and hiding from rail yard bulls. Wherever this locomotive stopped this time, that's where he'd part ways with the metal beast. He would leave his destiny to chance.

Chance took the form of Fort Worth, Texas.

CAROLINE

Georgia

By the time Caroline was sorting and packing the things she wished to take along, her spirits had shifted from the resignation of a last-ditch effort to the excitement of a new start. She carefully perused through the books in the parlor, selecting ones she could not bear to part with. The parlor had always been her favorite room in the house because of the books. Even as a child, if she could not be in her secret garden playing with or reading to her imaginary Mable, then she'd do so in the parlor. The room brought her great comfort—well, the books really. As of late, if she could get lost in a book, she couldn't very well spot a hanging Davis Colley. Of course, there was also that books took her on adventures and to places she'd never dreamed of and opened her eyes to a world beyond what she was presented in Melroy.

The first book she recalled ever reading—or rather having read to her by her mother, Mary—was *Old Mother Mitten and Her Funny Kitten*. As a child, she'd loved the silly nonsensical rhyming tale and would hold the book up and recite its words to Mable, pretending to read from the pages. As she got older, it was Little Eva that had opened her eyes to the disgraceful and dishonorable flaw of mankind. She'd been raised in a loving home. Both her parents were kind people, to both White and Black folks alike. But there still existed this very deep chasm in every interaction she witnessed at home and around town, whether it be with the pretense of kindliness or outright hatred.

Caroline was introduced to Little Eva once she became a sound reader and no longer required the help of her mother. The book was authored by Philip J. Cozans. He wrote of a girl, Eva, who lived in the South and was the daughter of a wealthy planter. Throughout the book, Little Eva showed nothing but kindness toward her family's slaves. She read the Bible to them, sharing the Word, and then went on to teach the little ones how to read for themselves. On her birthday, she is saved from nearly drowning by one of her father's slaves. To show his deep gratitude for saving his daughter's life, the father frees the slave. The slave in turn shows his appreciation for being given his freedom by choosing to remain with the child and family—for he loved them so.

Little Eva: The Flower of the South had inspired Caroline as a young girl, had forced her to consider the hands around her own father's plantation. They were freed people. Slavery had *technically* been abolished for some years now; however, as much as the country might speak the words of equality, it did not exist in reality. After reading the book, she'd been inspired to teach Octavia to read. At first, Octavia laughed it off. "Go play, chile." It is true that Caroline Higgs-Colley did not just gain her stubborn persistent nature in adulthood. The family often teased that she'd been born stubborn, had exited the womb on her own terms, a trait they all liked to attribute to her fiery red hair. Once she got it in her head that Octavia must learn to read, she persisted, demanding her nanny sing along with the ABCs. Octavia already knew the ABCs, could even read and write a few things, but in time, the child's stubbornness won and the two began their Sunday lessons reading from the Bible together, sounding out the words. Caroline would read and Octavia would read—and then Octavia would explain the stories to the child. It was only fair, she thought, that the child at least know what she was teaching and preaching.

As Caroline got older, she entered a phase of questioning. She questioned and challenged everything. The book she once loved, that had once inspired her, Little Eva herself, came under fire too. Caroline distrusted and questioned everything and everyone. She wondered why anyone, particularly an enslaved person, would ever stick around once given the freedom to leave, especially after years of harsh treatment. The book hadn't mentioned any such harsh realities, but she'd seen signs of them with her own eyes: avoiding eye contact, meek demeanors, scars. It didn't make sense to her, and she grew to believe that Little Eva was simply propaganda created to confuse little ones like she'd once been, to feed them the lies that slavery hadn't been all that bad. Couldn't have been if a freed man willingly chose to remain with the people who'd once treated him as a mere commodity, right?

She had many conversations with her father about these thoughts and broad-minded opinions, of which he replied with messages of acting and speaking with grace, how a lady conducts herself, limiting her words as to not cause discord where none exists. She didn't abide by as much, and as the child of one of the wealthiest men in the county, she became a point of contention for Thomas. His opinionated first born often resulted in him having to smooth over misunderstandings and unruffle the feathers of local people of position: businessmen, politicians, doctors, you name it. Thomas Higgs possessed the ability to defuse conflict, could calm a cornered rattlesnake if necessary, and for it, he spent much of his dealings putting out the little fires his head-strong child ignited in many a citizen of Melroy County. And while it was at times exhausting, it brought him great pride to know his daughter possessed a mind of her own.

Caroline ran her fingers along the tops of the books, hooking her finger at the spine, tipping her choices back, and pulling them down.

She turned to see a generous stack. *This might be too many*, she thought to herself. *But could one really have too many books?* She answered aloud, "No, one cannot," and pulled two more.

She loaded up her selection and carried them to the trunk situated at the foot of the stairs. The group would travel by train, but the bulk of their belongings would arrive sometime later via wagon. She dropped the books in and then thought better of it. She reached in and grabbed *The Haunted Hotel: A Mystery of Modern Venice* by Wilkie Collins. It would make for a thrilling read to break up the journey that was slated to take a few days. She hesitated and then grabbed a second book. She knew she needed to pack light for the train, but she could devour a book in no time, especially given nothing else to do, no garden to tend to. She pulled out *The Lifted Vail* by George Elliot, a recommendation from which she might glean some insight. It seemed the main character was a man incapacitated by visions of the future and a cacophony of overheard thoughts, yet who couldn't help but try to subvert his vividly glimpsed destiny. Terribly relatable, she knew, but potentially helpful, nonetheless.

While she curated her personal library, hushed voices grew louder from the next room over and caught her attention. She settled on the final books and then made her way to the kitchen. Standing in the doorway, it became clear that her father and Octavia were struggling to settle something. Which Caroline found odd as Octavia was never one to voice any such disagreement when it came to Thomas Higgs.

Octavia asked, "Where we gwine stay dere, huh? Where I gwine werk? Fa who? Ima just stay here, Mista Higgs. No." She shook her head feverishly.

Thomas said, "Octavia, I've already answered these questions. Look, I'm not saying you absolutely have to go and stay. But I am *strongly* suggesting you at least go and try. For Chuck's sake."

"For my sake what?" Caroline interrupted.

The two, caught in a secret negotiation, turned to Caroline. Thomas glanced at Octavia and then back to Caroline.

"I'm proposing an arrangement I believe would be beneficial for Octavia here—"

Octavia cut him off with a headshake and held her hand up at him. She sucked her teeth. At this, Caroline's eyes widened. This was serious.

He held up a hand in Octavia's direction, halting any words she prepared to say, and continued speaking to Caroline. "Beneficial for Octavia and the lot of you, I was saying."

"Oh yeah?" asked Caroline. She crossed her arms. She could easily sense the dis-ease from Octavia, her anxiety palpable.

Thomas stood erect, chin up. He answered firmly, "Yes."

Caroline shifted her weight to one side, her hip cocked. "Octavia, what manner of constructive use is my father offering here that you find undesirable?"

Octavia's eyes darted from Caroline's to Thomas's and down to her feet. Standing between two White folks engaged in a standoff was not a place she ever wished to find herself. She simply wanted to show up to work each day, carry out her duties, and return to the quiet retreat of her single-room home, the closest in the row of houses situated at the south end of the fields. She'd lived there for years, alone, never having to share the space with any of the other hands, nor ever getting to share the space with any of the other hands. Her life had been simple after meeting Thomas Higgs. Had become consistent, safe, and predictable, all days of harsh treatment and heartbreak behind her. Packing up and moving to some camp of a town out west of here without the security of the Higgs Plantation and without the safety afforded by Mr. Higgs struck terror in her, of which she'd had the luxury of avoiding since the days before her final ones on Sapelo Island.

"Well?" pressed Caroline.

"I am proposing Octavia accompany you—and the group of course—to Element Dale."

Octavia interrupted, "Mista Higgs, please, sah. If you dig a pit fa me, you dig one fa y'self."

"No such thing, Octavia. It will be fine. I will be fine. You will be fine."

Caroline interjected, "If she doesn't want to go, Daddy . . . "

Thomas massaged his temples as if teasing out the solution, the perfect words. "I'm trying to be as diplomatic here as possible, but you both are making this troublesome for me." He paused, gathering his words carefully, and then dropped his hands. He turned to face Octavia straight on. "Octavia, I will send you with your wages. Six months. At its terminus, should you find Element Dale unpalatable, you will have your post here made available once again."

"Wait a minute. If she doesn't want to go—and why would she?" Caroline paused. "Actually, *why* is she? She lives here, Daddy. This is her home, her employment. And not to be insolent, but I never asked her to accompany me."

He turned and faced his daughter straight on. "Because I am saying so."

Caroline raised an eyebrow in incredulity. "Because you're saying so?"

"I am," he replied calmly.

He turned back to Octavia. "Octavia, please pack what you will need for the journey and six months. I'll send you with your wages in full. If you make the decision to not go, that is of course your choice. But please know, these are the terms of your continued employment at the Higgs Plantation—"

"Daddy!"

"Not another word, Caroline. I am not asking."

"You can't *make* her go."

"This is true. I cannot."

He turned to Octavia and reached for her hands and took them into his own. "I cannot. I cannot make you go anywhere you do not choose; it is true. But I can ask that you please consider my terms and know that they come from a place of affinity—and concern." His eyes searched Octavia's, became once again the desperate and lost eyes he'd shown her when Mary had died. His eyes begged, *please go with my daughter, watch over her.*

Octavia slowly pulled her hands from his. "Six months," she agreed with tears in her eyes. She turned and walked away.

Thomas and Caroline now stood alone. It was clear he had no trust that Caroline was well enough to be on her own. No matter how much she reassured him she was fine, the countless days and nights of terror claiming to see a dead husband wasn't something he could shake. He glanced at her and gave a small nod before leaving her to stand in the kitchen alone.

Her excitement was wiped clear, replaced by sinking shame.

DIX

Georgia

Dix was the last of the group to arrive at the train station. He'd spent his last morning in deep thought, journaling his reflections of hope for the upcoming move and a fresh start. Bible roulette had been good to him this morning, landing at Isaiah 65:17: *For, behold, I create new heavens and a new earth: and the former shall not be remembered, nor come into mind.* These words energized his morning gymnastics. He stretched and moved with great enthusiasm for he was now seeing that this had been the plan all along. *Never question Him,* he thought. Excitement sparked and he spoke aloud with a smile beaming across his face as he shut his parents' door behind him: "In all your ways acknowledge Him, and He shall direct your paths."

Dix carried his carpet bag with a change of clothes, his Bible, and a few essentials. His newly purchased Gladstone bag was packed safely in his steamer trunk, filled with the tools of the trade to practice once he was established in Element Dale. He'd dedicated an entire steamer trunk to his future practice, collecting instruments, tools, medicines, and of course his beloved medical reference books:

The American Practice, Joseph Maclise's *Surgical Anatomy*, and the four-volume *Cyclopaedia of Practical Medicine*.

His dream of becoming a doctor had once soured and become an embarrassing cross to bear. With the potential for a new and unassuming community, he could lay down that cross and finally put his knowledge and skills to use. The townspeople of Element Dale had no inkling of the controversial debauchery surrounding his once-esteemed medical school. All they would see is a man of confidence carrying his well-oiled leather Gladstone, prepared to save lives should it come to such matters.

At the station, Dix eyed a newspaper: *Texas lands are yet good, plenty, and cheap—and plenty of room for Georgia's sons and daughters.* He nodded in satisfaction and picked up the paper for closer inspection. He read on. It was a back-and-forth, pros and cons for abandoning one's home state for the greener pastures of another. It spoke of a man who'd traveled to Texas the year prior and concluded: *The old red hills of the Empire State of the South are good enough for me. I'd rather be a quack doctor and live in Cedar Hill than to own half of east Texas.* For a moment, the message threatened to shake Dix's newfound enthusiasm and confidence. But then he shook it off, reciting the words he knew God wanted him to hear this day, the true message, the only message that mattered.

He considered that possibly these folks that abandoned their dreams in Texas and returned to Georgia were simply homesick. A reasonable conclusion. Then he read the next line: *Crops fail in Texas.* It said: *Not Jackson County. Land is cheap in Georgia. There is not a better state than Georgia nor county than Jackson.*

"They sure are proud of Jackson County," he mumbled and tossed the paper back. He looked up to spot his group all gathered together, Caroline's hands waving in great exaggerated gestures. As he got closer, it became clear she was entangled in a heated quarrel with someone. He sighed.

Dix heard a man say, "Regarding riding *this* locomotive, ma'am, the Texas State Gov'nor stated without stutter or ambiguity, the policy of separating the races on the trains will not be questioned and we've got no colored cars available. So you'll have to leave your Negress behind, ma'am. We aren't in the business of bucking the Preamble."

Caroline shouted back, "That woman belongs to no one, you ignorant pig. And this ain't Texas!"

"No, it ain't," he said, "but that's where this here train's headed. And that's what the Preamble states. Clear as day, ma'am."

"You can stop with all the ma'ams," she scoffed.

Henrietta placed her hand on Caroline's shoulder. "Come on, Chuck. We'll figure something out."

"Asinine," Caroline hissed. She yanked her bag from the man working the train and stormed off. Octavia had distanced herself from the commotion, fearful of becoming the target of onlookers. She wanted nothing to do with any fight with a White man regarding her rights. She hadn't wanted to go in the first place. Now Caroline's outrage was stirring the attention of every passenger in sight.

Caroline found her standing at the far end of the station. "Octavia, don't you worry. I'll be talking to the station master. This is absolutely asinine. Ridiculous."

"Miss Caroline, please." Octavia slightly lifted her hand and spoke quietly. "I'm gwine go on back to de plantation. You go on ahead."

Dix felt the group's excitement fizzle. The passenger director was the prick that had burst their bubble, but Caroline was the true source of the conflict, he knew. His frustration with Caroline built. She could not be trusted to act like any type of lady in any type of situation, he thought. Thinking of building a new life in Element Dale had invigorated him, but seeing Caroline's face anywhere in that new life caused him great irritation. They hadn't even left the state and already she was a menace to his senses. He closed his eyes and took a deep breath. Lawton and Claire eased past him and onto the train. Lawton tilted his hat as he walked by. Dix picked up his carpet bag and stepped up onto the train behind them.

"Dix?" questioned Henrietta. "What are you doing?"

He turned to face his brother's wife. "I'm boarding our train, which is soon to leave."

Henrietta whipped her attention to Ford and nudged his arm. Ford cleared his throat. "I suppose we'll take the necessary steps to line out another means for travel."

"For what reason?" Dix questioned. "Our means of travel is currently boarding, and none too interested in waiting while we shilly-shally I might add."

Henrietta nudged Ford once more.

"You go on ahead, brother. We'll figure something out."

Dix stood for a moment, incredulity all over his face as he looked down at the two. Ford faced him straight on, bearing a look of apology. Dix could detect a slight bit of agitation as well. He could read his brother like a book, and at that moment, Ford's face held hints. Dix imagined Henrietta had placed him in a tight spot. Being newly married, well, he possibly could understand bending to his wife's whims, but this was a bit extreme.

Henrietta stood holding her bag and eyeing her shoes, unwilling to make eye contact with Dix. Dix spotted Octavia and Caroline in the distance, both waiting. He paused for a moment, looked back to Ford, tipped his hat, and disappeared onto the train.

A steward guided him to his seat in the coach. He watched as passengers filed into the car, all dressed for the occasion. He stopped another steward and inquired, "Excuse me. Is there not a car for coloreds on this locomotive?"

The steward eyed him with a bit of confusion, "Sir, we have the means for a colored coach up ahead. But it seems that coach is needed for alternate demands."

Dix nodded his understanding. He removed his hat and leaned his head back against the seat for a moment as the final passengers filed aboard. He closed his eyes. But the nagging vision of his brother and wife remaining behind at the platform ate at him. *Damned woman*, he thought.

Dix stood, slightly deflated, next to his bags as the train popped and hissed slowly by, his vessel to a new life departing without him.

He spotted an advertisement for a wagon outfitter named X.J. Myers. Myers managed various wagon brigades leaving the state. The outfitter mandated Heartland wagons, sometimes utilizing upwards of a hundred wagons in a train. It guaranteed that a Heartland wagon mechanic with tools and parts in tow would accompany every brigade along with a scout for Indians. After some back-and-forth with the Myers operator, Dix learned that the wagon train was run like a military operation with inspections to ensure a sound wagon and manifest for ample and appropriate supplies. Wagons unable to pass inspection were not allowed departure with the Myers brigade. Each bit of information checked off a box for Dix and seemed a plausible alternative means for getting them all to Element Dale. A much longer, dirtier, and rougher means, but plausible nonetheless.

Dix secured a place with the wagon brigade headed for Fort Worth, Texas, in two days. Surely this act of solidarity would satisfy the group and entice them to pardon his moment of dereliction.

ELZI

Texas

On the long trek back to camp, Elzi thought long and hard about how he would be received. He'd left Jasper and Luke's bodies. He'd had to, having no means to handle them. So many of the men had been in a bad way. Certainly it would be understood just how arduous and desperate the days had been. Maybe he could lead them to the locations to retrieve the bodies. And of Albin—he could barely think of the look on Albin's face, what excuse Albin might have for abandoning him and taking his provisions, his possessions. He ached thinking about that lifelong friendship ending, but he was sure as hell going to get Ora B.'s book back along with Hattie's photo, and he'd do so by any means necessary.

The camp, once a bustling tent community nestled in the trees, was now a ghost town all but packed up. Debris littered the grounds and the final tent was being taken down, its contents already loaded up into a wagon. As Elzi made his way through the trees, he spotted the First Lieutenant approaching the soldiers tending to the tent deconstruction.

"You seen any more stragglers come in?" asked the First Lieutenant.

Elzi paused and concealed himself behind a tree.

"Word is they all dead—perished for water and such. Few men came back, said they done seen rations, supplies, even weapons scattered across some twenty-five miles or so. And of course a few downed soldiers." He lowered his head.

The First Lieutenant said, "The Tenth Calvary ain't much known for desertion."

A soldier replied, "True. But they's some awful circumstances, I hear, sir."

The First Lieutenant counted several who had walked away from his command. Secretly, he could not rightly blame them. Their suffering must have been terrible. However, any deserter was subject to arrest and court-martial unless charges were dropped, and he said as much. The officer walked away, leaving the men to resume their story of the horrors they'd heard from those who'd survived the Staked Plains.

"All but one, and he left out this morning. Said he's headed home, had enough. Though he didn't look too good. More gray than black, I'd say."

"Home where?" the other soldier inquired.

"Didn't say. Sounded like a Louisiana boy to me. I told him he's deserting and needs to turn in his gun. He didn't refuse. He didn't stop walking neither."

"You didn't stop him?"

"Nah, looks a him, he'd be lucky to make it to Tahoka, much less to Louisiana. Say, you gonna go to the shindig on Saturday? Seems the local cowboys and hidesmen are throwing a ball or whatnot to celebrate the return of the dead. Got some sweet-smelling gals coming down. Gonna be some fiddle music and dancing." He stomped his foot and slapped his thigh to the beat of an imaginary song.

The man spit a stream of tobacco to the ground. "Unless those sweet-smellin' gals outnumber the rank-stinkin' hides, I'll be steering clear of any such ball at the dancehall. Its proximity to the hide yard is much to be desired. Pass."

"Suit yourself."

Elzi couldn't imagine Albin just deserting like that. But Albin was the only other buffalo soldier he knew of that hailed from the Creole State. Of course, he couldn't imagine he'd leave him for dead nor steal from him. His head spun. Nothing made sense. He'd never experienced such abandonment and loneliness as he did in this moment, and those feelings were hard to tolerate. The sting was more than he could bear. Tears threatened to surface and it enraged him. He squashed down the hurt and summoned up a ball of anger in its stead, something to fuel his long journey ahead. His journey to retrieve his book, his photo, and his dignity. A journey to avenge.

WALKER

Cow Town (Fort Worth), Texas

Walker Westberry arrived in Fort Worth just before noon. Riding the blinds had been the way to go. It had provided shelter and some sense of security and concealment. He had slept in fits much of the time, wishing for the quiet of the mountains. But the mountains were far behind him, with the revenuers, with Nadene, with the baby. For all these things, he was relieved.

He hopped off the train before it came to a complete stop and slipped into the trees. His ears rang. They'd rang for days. Once he was certain no train bull was onto him, he stepped out into the opening. Adjacent to the tracks was a building so magnificent, so out of place for this city known to many as Cowtown. The art nouveau-style building was painted a dark bronze-green and stood two stories tall, surrounded by arched doorways and Pagoda-like towers with balconies, each with flags atop its spire. The center of the main building crowned a grand dome that featured the forty-two-star American flag. It was impressive, a fantastic palace with a mission to display all Texas had to offer. Though fully constructed, the palace was still crawling with craftsman carrying out the painstaking task of ornamentation. Walker learned from a passerby that the builders planned to adorn every inch of the palace with contributions from each county in Texas, allowing for the representation of their region with the harvest of raw materials. Everything from cacti, wheat, cornstalks, pelts, hides, seashells, cattle horns, skulls, gravel, and oats would be somehow affixed somewhere on its surface. Walker couldn't even imagine.

The town was in fact a city. Once a thriving military fort, the abandoned buildings were converted into schools, stores, and churches. Its main street, hard-paved and edged with electric lampposts and sidewalks for pedestrians, bustled with life, with actual streetcars. Walker spotted various areas of landscaping in front of shops, a church, a grain center with an elevator, a fire station, a bank. Cowboys trotted their horses through the streets, clad in cowboy hats and spurs. He walked and took in the town until the landscape took a turn. The variety of retails shops and service stores became a stretch of nothing but saloons, gambling houses, and dance halls—a wood tick that sucked dry the drunks that brought their earnings to Cowtown. If the booze didn't empty their pockets, there were plenty of women of easy virtue to separate a man from his money. He watched as one man rode his horse right into a saloon. He chuckled under his breath and stepped in behind him.

Walker's white hair and blue eyes were a stark contrast to his copper sun-damaged skin, and it drew him unwanted attention. As he entered the saloon, eyes took note of him. He pulled his hat down further and mounted a stool at the bar. A whiskey sounded nice. He took a sip. The rotgut swill in his glass burned from his throat to his stomach, and instantly he missed his shine. He tossed it back and lit a cigarette. As he sat smoking, he took in the patrons. Men tossed dice, laughing and yelling, money sliding from one to the next.

"Fucking tinhorn!" a man in the back corner shouted out, only to be met with a swift fist to the mouth. The punched man quickly shot up to his feet, his pistol trained on the other.

"Take yer shit outside," hollered the barkeep.

The man fired his pistol, shooting the other square in the stomach. The place grew quiet, but only for a moment.

"Well hell," grumbled the barkeep. He sighed and flung his towel onto the bar. He hollered out, "Get 'em outta here, I guess." A few men grabbed the gun-downed man by the boots and drug him out and onto the wooden sidewalk. The music resumed and the barkeep mumbled, "I s'pose the law'll have something to say about that." He looked up at Walker. "It's because of jackoffs like these that we now have to answer to a permanent police force around here."

Walker nodded, pulling his hat down a touch more.

"Ain't seen you 'round," the barkeep inquired. He plopped down a plate of ham and beans where Walker sat.

"Yeah, just come to town," Walker replied. "Thank you much." He took up the fork and stabbed a hunk of ham and shoved it into his mouth.

"Where abouts?"

Walker thought about it a moment while he chewed. He couldn't imagine anyone here would ever come in contact with the revenuers after him, but he was most likely being pursued, being a tax evader *and* a killer now. And Cowtown had its own police force. So he needed to be careful.

"Georgia," he mumbled with a mouthful.

The man seated to his left joined in. "Lots a people making their way from there, I hear."

Walker nodded.

The barkeep added, "Yeah, seems if you cain't make it there, might as well come take up our land. Folks coming down from up north too. Trying to bring with them their ways. This ain't the north. They best be getting that through them thick skulls right fast."

"Ain't that the fucking truth," said the man to the left. He popped Walker on the back a few times. "But this here is a fella Southerner. Who'd you kill to have to run on over to our neck a the woods?"

Walker froze for a moment, unable to answer the eerily apt

question. For a moment he felt unnerved. The man and the barkeep waited for an answer.

"Uh . . ."

The two looked at one another. The man to the left said, "You simple?"

Walker turned and stared him dead in the eyes. "I killed a slimy revenuer, sent by the gov'ment to steal my earnings. Shot him right in the ass."

The barkeep looked at the man and then eyed Walker. "Don't suppose a shot in the ass is all too much life threatening." He pulled his towel from his shoulder and began wiping the bar.

Walker thought a moment. "No, I don't s'pose it is."

"But we all would like to shoot a revenuer or two," replied the barkeep. "Fucking legal thieves if ever I seen one."

Walker thought back to the sound of the pigs rushing past him, the agent's screaming stomped out within seconds. *Truth be told*, he thought, *it was the pigs got 'em in the end. I just facilitated.* "Yeah," he said.

The man next to him asked, "What? You some kind of someone, owing the gov'ment big money?"

Walker scooped up a bite of beans, shoved it in his mouth, and replied, "Naw, just pulling your chain." He chewed. "I'm here for work. Work for the train." He gestured toward the front door. The barkeep frowned at him.

The man said, "Oh yeah! You guys laying tracks eva'where. I suppose you gonna be on the crew laying to the west?"

Walker agreed.

"To the west is still some good untouched soil. Anyone having land out that-a-ways, before the train comes, is gonna get rich. Train'll bring folks right to ya before too long. I got a brother out that-a-ways, 'bout forty miles or so west and a touch south from here. He gots him some land along the river there. Bunch a folks just abandoned their place after the Great Die-up a few years back. He jumped on the opportunity and settled right in. Other side from where he at, a town's starting up. He says they's about 800 folks there or so now. They call it Element Dale. Gonna be something big one day, he says. Even gots a hotel for the rich and famous, fourteen floors high—"

The barkeep cut in. "Go on now. Ain't nobody, rich nor famous, interested in some dirt town off the river. And fourteen floors? I call bullshit."

The man frowned. "Now you can go fuck yourself. I ain't no liar." He popped up from his stool.

"Course you ain't," replied the barkeep. "Just like this man here ain't no liar." He gestured to Walker with the flick of his towel and walked to the other end of the bar.

Under his breath the man mumbled "fucking cocksucker" and threw down a coin. He slammed the rest of his beer and walked out. Walker took a quick scan of the room. The barkeep was tending down at the other end. He leaned over and slid the man's coin over and in front of his own empty plate and stood. The barkeep looked over. Walker tipped his hat to him and left.

He stepped out of the dark building and into the bright daylight. He looked up and down the street and decided to head back to the main street. After a block or two, he looked back to see the barkeep and the man in the street. The barkeep was on top of the man, punching him until at last the man had gone limp. Afterwards, he reached into the man's breast pocket and retrieved what Walker imagined was payment for his beer. Walker tipped his hat to the beaten man. "Thank you much," he said under his breath and headed back to the west.

On his walk, he spotted a drugstore with a sign in the window: DR PEPPER—KING OF BEVERAGES. The lofty slogan caught Walker's attention. His white lightning was king. In what ways could this drink be superior? he wondered. He stepped inside to find out. The store was lined with shelves containing various items and sundries. Along the back wall was a long counter. Above it hung another sign for the drink.

"Can I help you, sir?" asked the merchant.

Walker replied, "Real moonshine comes in two flavors: legal and illegal. Where abouts does this King of Beverages fall?"

The merchant chuckled. "I don't know about moonshine, sir. Here. Have a taste. It aids digestion and restores vim, vigor, and vitality." He poured Walker a sample from the soda fountain. Walker flinched at its sticky sweetness, its fizz. He nodded, not sure how to comment.

Another patron approached the bar. "You ever try Coca-Cola?"

Walker shook his head.

"Well, this Dr Pepper here ripped off Coca-Cola." He gestured to the merchant as he spoke.

The merchant replied, "Sir, I am not Dr Pepper. Nor have I ripped off any such thing. I simply sell a product, one that I might add came *before* Coca-Cola."

The patron replied, "That's a load of crap if ever I did hear it. I'm from Atlanta. I was there the day it came out. And folks been ripping off our beverage ev-ah since."

The merchant scoffed. "I am certain Atlanta would be proud should you decide to return. I know I've certainly had my fill of migrants coming to this state, bringing with them their ideas and notions. You want Coca-Cola? Might I suggest you head back to Atlanta."

The two continued with the back-and-forth. Walker chuckled. It seemed no matter your brand, no matter whether your brew was legal or illegal, taxed or not, it always somehow brought about a war. He left the two men to debate their kings.

He found himself back at the depot and stopped at the ticket counter. The tracks remained nonexistent west of there, not that he really wanted back on a train, but he needed to land somewhere and fast. He was tired of being on the move. He considered his options. He could head north toward Oklahoma. Maybe make his way on to Nebraska. He'd heard the Magic City was booming. The city was interesting but if he was being honest with himself, it did not suit him. He thought about the man at the saloon, the one who'd involuntarily sacrificed a tooth or two to cover Walker's tab. *A new town with land for grabs about forty or so miles from here. A town set off the river a bit.* It sounded a bit more to his liking. He greeted the ticket man. He did not purchase a train ticket but did come to a decision. He would head west and a touch south to a small bit of nowhere, to a budding town called Element Dale.

DIX

Georgia

The morning the brigade was to leave, Dix, Ford, Henrietta, Caroline, and Octavia arrived fresh and prepared for what they knew was going to be an arduous journey. Mr. Higgs had provided a great Conestoga wagon, pulled by six horses, to haul all of their belongings to the depot. Upon arrival, however, Dix was met with unfortunate news. The Conestoga did not pass the X.J. Myers wagon inspection. Worse yet, there was not an available Heartland wagon to accept their belongings. Because of this, they were not allowed entry into nor protection or services by the brigade. They were offered, however, the allowance to follow behind. The group agreed with the understanding that they were to bring along spare axles. Ruts were an inevitable nuisance on the trails. Any wagon broken down, not under the supervision of the outfit, would be abandoned.

Rules of the brigade were shouted out to the travelers as follows:

"One! Allow five days for each one hundred miles. Bad days, what you can make, or stay in camp if agreed on by all. Real good days, and ground, makes it easy pulling twenty-five to thirty miles per day, if camp sites come right.

"Two! Take plenty of guns and ammunition.

"Three! It is recommended you shave your heads—Indians have no interest in bald heads."

At this, Henrietta worriedly touched her hair. Ford gave her a smile and subtlety shook his head as if the man were making an unsuitable joke.

"Four! Abstain from drinking whiskey or alcohol in freezing weather lest you find yourself freezing to death.

"Five! Do not fire rifles. And if you must, may it be absolutely essential to your survival.

"Six! Do not stay up late. Get plenty of sleep when the time for sleep comes. Guards stand duty all night.

"Seven! Refrain from smoking strong pipes and cigars in close places where women and children are.

"Eight! Keep your politics and preachin's to yourself. Come Sabbath, should we encounter a preacher, he'll do the preachin'."

At this, Dix nodded.

"Nine! In case of a runaway, get down and try to ride it out. Do not jump from your wagon as you are most liable to be killed or hurt badly. The team will slow up not too far off and the horsemen will handle reintroduction into the brigade.

"Ten! All people—young, married, or not—are advised to stay within the circle of wagons while in Indian country. You are liable to lose your scalps."

Henrietta turned to Ford. "I really would much like to ensure that we are guaranteed a place within the brigade, not following close behind as the man stated."

Ford held up a hand and nodded. He whispered, "Not to worry, my love."

Henrietta turned to Caroline who watched as the man shouted out at the crowd. She appeared completely undaunted by the warnings, almost to the point of boredom.

"Eleven! The wagon master will try to pick spots so men and women and children can bathe, clean up, and wash clothes when possible. Mind you, we are headed into the cold months.

"Twelve! Be courteous and help others.

"Thirteen!—"

Caroline turned to Dix and loudly whispered in his direction, "Good God. Are we traveling or entering boarding school. These rules!"

Dix turned to her, sniffed and pushed his glasses back up his nose, and then returned his attention to the wagon master with an air of disdain. Caroline rolled her eyes.

"Do not be noisy, even with your musical instruments—only at such times when it is pronounced safe.

"Fourteen! When pronounced safe, we will have recreation and dances."

Henrietta and Caroline grinned at one another.

"And finally, do your part by all means. It'll be a race to be settled before winter."

Dix had done his research over the last hours and days. He'd learned hot weather could also become a problem as more frequent water sources were required for both traveler and livestock, though the animals required sufficient water and grass in all weather when the wagon train stopped for the night. He'd learned of means for water crossing, the plausibility of various ailments and injuries one could sustain. He'd felt confident in his securing of the outfit. And Ford's approval and praise for his quick thinking to get the group a suitable and safe means of travel brought him a sense of pride he'd been desperate for as of late.

They were soon to leave. Their provisions were packed, their wagons secured. He'd his reading materials for the journey, his medical books and his Holy Bible. At first blush, the shift from train travel to wagon had seemed like an awful consequence for saddling up with anything to do with Caroline Higgs-Colley. But after a night of consulting the Word, he'd come to think of it in a different light.

He would use the time to plan for his new life, his practice, his future in a town where no one could hold over him the shameful fate of his medical training that had died on the vine.

CAROLINE

Georgia

The long wagon train moved west. It consisted of horse wagons, carryalls, and carriages—and a pair of dairy cows—supplied with good tents and bedrolls, trailed by the group's Conestoga goods wagon. The trail east and west crawled with lines of families traveling under canvas. Octavia had baked quantities of hardtack for the journey and packed salt meat, cornmeal, bacon, eggs, potatoes, rice, beans, yeast, dried peaches, and a large barrel of water each tied to the side of their two carriages.

A new life was promised in the weeks ahead. A new beginning was waiting for Caroline in a small dale nestled between the Wallace Mountains and the Barron River. A community that was soon to become a city that attracted people from all over the country. She was to be a part of its revival. The town was officially but a few years old. Its only attraction being a great hotel to offer entertainment at its center. But unfortunate times had left the hotel, and consequently the town, to flounder.

Lawton and Claire Phillips, the new hotel owner's son-in-law and daughter, were on a train to kick off the revival project within a few days. The rest of the group would arrive in the weeks to follow. Not as timely as they had planned, but the bent nature of the South had intruded. Dix had mentioned God's plan and something to do with His good timing. Caroline wasn't so sure the wrench thrown in their works wasn't that of the devil, but she opted to keep this thought to herself . . . this time.

CONVERGENCE

Take the two extremes confronting us at this moment, the Atheist and the Christian, each a convinced believer in his own particular doctrine, but each, we must suppose, fundamentally inspired with an equal faith in Man. No doubt each in his own fashion, following his separate path, believes that he has once and for all solved the riddle of the world's future. But the divergence between them is in reality neither complete nor final . . . followed to their conclusion the two paths must certainly end by coming together: for in the nature of things everything that is faith must rise, and everything that rises must converge.

—Pierre Teilhard de Chardin

JERYL LARSON

September 14, 2023
Element Dale, Texas

My goal today is to get some concrete answers on the story Lucillia is supposed to be working on. Her deadline—our deadline I should say—is fast approaching, and I still have no clue if the work has even been started. I fear that she has not, nor has much intention to anytime soon. We've talked all about these four people from Georgia, Louisiana, and North Carolina. I've compiled pages and pages of notes. And I'm finding myself antsy to get to the meat of things, to get to Element Dale.

When I say as much, she replies, "Y'all have asked for years for me to write about my small town—it's never been the sleepy little town one might imagine it to be. I never wanted to give it any more of my attention than absolutely necessary. These goddamned assholes aren't worth writing about."

It's a sentiment she holds fast to, the whole shit-town assholes bit.

I ask, "So what do you intend to write about, then? Or have you already something in the works?" I hold my breath.

She takes a moment to gather her thoughts and responds, "Well, I'd like to write another collection of poetry that digs deep into the con-flicts of the natural world. How the sun can burn the very life it illuminates. How water can drown the bodies it once quenched."

"Mmm. Love that journey for you. I hadn't really thought of our world in that way before." I'm trying my best here, but inside I'm wilting. The deal was a novel, not a collection of poetry.

She snickers, "Oh, Mother Nature is a tricky bitch, not unlike the Southern belle. One minute she's as warm and welcomin' as a cup of coffee. You relax, come in real close to feel the subtle warmth on your lips, take in the comforting aroma. The next she's apathetic, neutral, tending to her duties. All is copasetic. You feel safe. Then she sticks it to your unassuming ass. The carnal bitch."

I chuckle. "That's one way to look at it." Hesitantly I ask, "To get back to the writing, what about putting that theme into a novel? You've shared so many stories with me in our times together on this porch. You easily have enough material for a few novels—though you only need one."

Lucillia's face lights up with unmistakable joy, and I am utterly confused. I was certain my nudge at novel writing would piss her off, so this smile is a pleasant surprise.

She says, "Well, no, 'cause these stories I tell you, most ain't mine to tell and sell. I may myself have seen a thing or two in my years, but most of what I know is what Elzi told me. He's a beautiful storyteller." She beams just speaking Elzi's name.

Elzi. Another fantastic name.

Dear Reader, just to make sure you're on the same page here, Elzi Dupre is Ms. Baldwin's best friend, the one she claims is deceased. I myself have had friends that I've lost over the years that I often think of, now serving as one-sided relationships and distant memories that I dredge up to lessen the unforgiving passing of time. But having questioned Ms. Baldwin enough—but not too much as to upset her and shut me out—I am of the understanding that Elzi Dupre and Ms. Baldwin share a friendship *currently,* a two-way friendship: she from our world and he from his . . . in death.

Wait. Please don't tap out now, babydoll. Hear me out.

This, I struggle with. Not gonna lie. But regardless of how this lonely woman views her relationships or whether or not her perception of memories is akin to looking into the sun through a prism of whiskey, what comes of it all are volumes and volumes of stories. And for that, I'm sticking around to listen. And, honey, you should too. Now where were we?

ELZI

Waterly, Texas (Unsettled land)

One thing walking offers a man is time. Time to think. Thinking offers either clarity or looped perseveration. When thinking is fueled by hurt, what loops in the mind over and over are visions of either despair or revenge. One cannot subsist on desperation. But revenge . . . revenge invigorates.

Elzi watched the history of his friendship with Albin like a moving picture in his mind. The twins with bloody noses. His peace offering of the redfish. The grief that overtook the Banks family. Albin offering a pierced coin to consecrate the official induction of The Devisers. Albin being approached by an Army scout, impressed with his size and work ethic. Albin agreeing to join, so long as his buddy could as well. The all-too-late realization that thirteen dollars a month amounted to next to nothing once the government took its share for the assigned field blues, once you had to pay for the laundress to maintain said blues, once you paid for ammunition as none was provided for the Black troops for training. Rarely had a trooper even shot a gun prior to being issued his rifle. And they were to practice shooting with empty guns, a pointless endeavor. He thought of Albin singing when all the other troopers were complaining of the awful terrain and the heat and the terrible way in which Mother Nature had so very obviously conspired with the Indians to keep the water hidden.

The recap brought him as far as to the mesquite bush out on the Staked Plains. From there, his history muddled. Where it muddled, he had to concoct a notion of what must have occurred. Albin must have found that Jasper had perished. Must have suffered extreme sadness. Must have thought Jasper had no more use for his provisions and collected what he could himself use. But what of Elzi? He pictured a frail and desperate Albin rifling through his haversack while Elzi was away in pursuit of water for the men. That when Elzi had returned, words of water mattered none and Albin had picked through and stolen what he wanted. Stolen Hattie. Stolen the words of his blood mother. The thought of Albin staring at the pages in ignorant illiteracy boiled Elzi's blood even more.

The grim fantasy continued on, following Albin all the way back to the Sugar Coast. Elzi imagined him being greeted by family, by Hattie Mae. He envisioned Albin hugging Hattie Mae, the two sharing grief for poor Elzi. For Elzi knew Albin meant to leave him for dead. Leave him to the vultures so he could have his Hattie Mae all to himself. His mind watched Albin comfort Hattie. And while Hattie cried, Albin held her close and tender. In time, he would become sweet on her.

Elzi screamed his rage into the heat, a bevy of quail bursting up before him and flittering every which direction as they were flushed from cover. The birds startled him and brought him back to the trail he followed. His anger momentarily disbanded into deep regret. He acutely regretted his decision to join the Army. One that hadn't led to anything but trouble and aimless wandering. He wandered under the misguided direction of the Captain. Now he wandered under the focused direction of fury. He spit in disgust. There had been no Indians to capture. He had seen hair nor hide of an Indian save the

Indian of Black and Bones from his nightmare out in the dunes. The Army had acquired Black men to do their fruitless dirty deeds, and should they perish? No matter. Army cared more for the horses than them. Even was told as much on his first night at camp: "First you tend to the horses, then you feed. Can't no man get nowheres without his horse. So horse comes first, you got me, boy?" *What nonsense*, he thought. He'd brushed those damned horses day in and day out. If he wasn't digging a ditch for a future latrine or running pointless drills of formation, he was brushing a damned horse. "I want 'em shining, you hear me, boy!" The Army had wasted his time and the lives of many good men. For what? A wild goose chase disguised as Indian governance. His fury grew. His mind played tricks on him, thinking he heard the sounds of nickering, the soft snorts of a pleased horse. *The horses in my head even mock me,* he thought. Then, as if his fury had any sort of ability to move heaven and earth, it conjured a horse before his very eyes. He froze.

Time and contemplation had carried him far. He realized he was no longer in the wide-open range of the grasslands under the devilish sun, but in the rough and rugged patches of broken, hilly land with sandy gray and black soil that shimmered under the moonlight. Night fell and the air was still. A grouping of cedar and live oaks followed along a line of barbed wire, something Elzi hadn't come across before. Just to the north of the trees, he spotted the silhouette of a horse standing on its own. He approached slowly, cautiously. He needed a horse in a bad way. And here one stood. He wondered if his mind hoaxed him, if the days of torturesome walking without water and means had finally gotten the best of him and this was some dream. As he got closer, the horse stomped and snorted, but it did not retreat from its place. Elzi made out no saddle but rather a robe of animal hide thrown across its back, and a bridle of hair-rope. Closer inspection revealed a series of feathers weaved into the horse's mane and tail, streaks of white paint like lightning bolts on its hindquarters. *Indians.*

To the other side of the trees, he could see the glow of a fire. He dropped to his stomach, uncertain of what else to do. The horse stomped once more. He heard a voice singing, chanting. He bear-crawled through the grass, keeping low to the ground. As he got closer, the horse took a few steps and stomped in place.

Elzi froze once more. His heart pounded. Could he possibly mount the horse and flee without pursuit? And how many Indians were there? He lowered his head onto the ground and waited, his eyes scanning in all directions. The chanting continued. One voice. He waited for what felt like hours. Waited for the sound of other men. But there were none. Only the lone voice of the one who sang.

He lifted his head and resumed his cautious crawl toward the horse. The seeded grass ripped and crackled under him as each knee advanced. The horse stomped and began to pace, letting out a series of blows. Then the chanting stopped. And so did Elzi's breath. Elzi froze and dropped flush with the ground squeezing his eyes shut tight. Footsteps crushed the grass and leaves ahead of him. They grew louder, closer. The Indian was coming. Elzi's heart pounded hard against the earth. Should he stand and run, he had no cover in the direction of his retreat. He would be certain to take an arrow to the back. Should he remain, he could be spotted, scalped. Like a deer alerted to the sound of its approaching predator, Elzi stilled himself in wait, taking stock of the approach.

Elzi's blood pulsed in his ears louder than ever. So loud he feared the Indian's approaching steps were being drowned out. With great trepidation, he slowly opened his eyes. This movement so subtle as to avoid detection allowed him a ground-level view through the grass and weeds. He kept his eyes small, fearing the Indian would sense his gaze. Ahead, just a matter of feet, stood the Indian of Black and Bones taking survey of the surrounding land. He looked far and wide, right over where Elzi lay. The Indian, now satisfied, turned to his horse, calming the beast with soft words of which Elzi could not understand. He stroked the brown horse along its neck from jaw to shoulder. The horse let out a breath, fluttering its nose. The Indian turned and made his way back to the fire, the horse pursuing him.

Elzi let out a breath he'd not known he'd been holding. His ears rang and his mind swirled. He'd never in his life endured such terror as in those previous moments. He wanted badly to be gone from where he laid, anywhere but there. He needed to get up and disappear, but his body refused.

The chanting resumed and then grew louder. The wind picked up as if on command. The chant called out and the sky answered with a burst of air. And then another. Then it hit him in the face, rich and earthy. Musky and wet. A scent that transported him to his fifteen-year-old self. A river was close.

Laden with the boldness of a young Elzi, the smell lifted him onto all fours. He lifted his nose into the air and stood. Crouching made him feel smaller, and so he crept slowly, changing his trek slightly southerly as to avoid entering the thicket from which the glow emitted. Within a few feet, he heard the whispering of water and followed its call.

At the water, he lowered himself to the ground, resting his butt on the rocks of the riverbank. Slowly he eased in and followed its gentle current. He waded slowly, quietly, and then sank down until he felt the sandy bottom with his hands. He crawled and bobbed along the shallow waters that took him past the glow in the woods, his head the only part of him that breached the surface, like an alligator. As he rounded the bend, the trees cleared offering him a direct line of sight. The horse stood to the other side of the fire, only its face and shoulders illuminated. The rest of its body disappeared into the dark woods. To its right, the Indian of Black and Bones chanted and danced, his feather and beads bouncing and whipping in the gusts of wind. He held his hands high into the air. He pranced and hopped, beads and bones clanking. He chanted and sang. The wind wailed. Elzi watched in amazement and wondered if the Indian were about to break open the heavens and bring down the rain. The wind whipped again sending sparks and embers swirling into the trees. Elzi kept his eyes trained on the Indian but did not stop following the river's gentle push. He was mesmerized yet eager to put as much distance between himself and the painted man as possible.

Another gust of wind. Then another. The wind howled, blowing the river's surface into Elzi's face, blowing the flames of the fire this way and that around the Indian until the flying embers swirled, suspended just above the fire, forming a tornado of sparks and smoke. It spun and whirled as he chanted and bounced around it. The wind whistled in Elzi's ears and then retreated, leaving the world quiet save for a soft beating sound. Drums? No. Wings.

Wings beat the air. They beat the air and soared past Elzi just above his head and toward the fire. The great black bird circled the clearing where the Indian danced then circled once more. It flew swift and tight circles inside the clearing until it merged with the swirling embers. Thick smoke twisted above the fire. Thunder clapped loud and close. The water's current pushed into Elzi's chest. He had stopped moving, enthralled by the sight before his eyes. Then the vulture vanished. Might've flown on, he thought. The winds settled. The ceremonial blaze subdued. And the smoke cleared.

The horse stood stoic and steadfast. The Indian stilled himself too, panting in recovery. Across the fire from him stood another Indian, one much older, tall and lanky with a black feathered headdress. He was greased black as well, though Elzi did not see any markings on his body like the Indian of Black and Bones. Elzi was uncertain when the old Indian had arrived. It seemed he'd just appeared. The thought of more Indians unnerved him and Elzi resumed his escape, making his way to the far side of the river. When he looked back, both Indians stood staring over the fire and to the river, their eyes like arrows shooting into Elzi's soul. He met the gaze of the old Indian, his nose crooked, his eyes beady and evil. Elzi shifted his gaze to the other. Every feature on the face of the Indian of Black and Bones spoke disdain for Elzi. The wind howled once more and Elzi scrambled out of the water and onto the opposite riverbank where he fled somewhere in the direction he prayed was east.

WALKER

Waterly, Texas (Unsettled land)

Walker had watched the mountains flatten, the trees shrink, and the rivers slow along his trek from the Old North State to Texas. Where once he walked alongside a bear foraging for berries or pinning trout against the river rocks, here he spotted thick black snakes sunning themselves on fallen branches peeking from the water's almost still surface. Where laurel lined the banks there, briars and threatening weeds choked out the grass here. He had been told to just follow along the river, but this river seemed to twist and turn. Parts of it Walker couldn't even think of as a river. More like a ribbon of murky water, as if somewhere along the way Mother Nature had pinched it tight.

He noticed how different the world sounded and smelled here. The water did not rush nor narrow into falls. The trees did not rustle quite so loudly. The ground crunched underfoot. The blazing heat had started to retreat, but still there seemed to always be a thickness in the air that suspended the swarms of gnats and mosquitoes. Though he was no stranger to mosquitoes.

Each step kicked up a spray of grasshoppers dull in color. Bugs and horned lizards that once blended in with the earth scurried underbrush when disturbed by his steps. He had walked for miles and was beginning to think he'd lost his way, gotten off the path of the river and mistakenly followed a sad offshoot.

He rounded a bend to find a series of great rust-colored boulders suspended over the water's edge, creating a small cove some ten feet below. Clothes laid strewn atop the rocks. Walker suddenly heard the river's surface break and the resultant splash and trickle of falling water. He stepped closer to the edge and peered over. Below stood a man facing away, his head tilted back, face pointed up toward the sun, naked and submerged to his hips. His back glistened with water rivulets flowing down along a few raised scars that mapped his body, a story whipped into his very flesh. He wiped the water from his eyes and then tipped back, kicked up his feet, and floated.

Walker stepped back from the edge, keeping out of sight. The blue clothes laid damp, drying in the sun. A uniform of sorts. He checked the pockets. He pulled out a necklace. Laced onto a thread of cotton hung a pierced coin. Off to the side he spotted a bag—military, he thought—three canteens, and a Model 1873 Springfield. He crouched down and peered into the haversack. Inside were hardtack bread, a few pieces of dried meat, and a leather-bound book of sorts with a tree scratched into its cover. He flipped it over. ORA B. DUPRE was scratched into the leather. He leaned forward and peeked over the edge. The man continued to float. *Ora B. Dupre*, he guessed.

He unwound the leather ribbon that held the pages closed. It was filled with writings and sketches. He dropped the necklace into its pages and closed the book. He tossed the book with the necklace into his own bag and swiped the gun. He was hungry but decided it wasn't worth chancing, eating after a colored, and left the few bits of provisions and the canteens. He stood and continued on around the bend, the floating man none the wiser.

When the shadows on the ground began to grow long, he thought it best to start looking for a place to camp for the night. His stomach growled and he'd regretted not taking the hardtack from the floating soldier. He'd come across a rabbit a few hours before and found out the hard way that the gun held no ammunition. He tossed it. Which he felt was probably best as he thought it likely was government issued and wanted no reason to draw any more attention to himself than necessary once he did arrive to Element Dale. By his calculations, based on what the man at the depot had told him, he should come upon the town sometime tomorrow. His stomach would have to be patient and settle for the handful of dewberries he snagged here and there along the way.

Walker piled the kindling he'd gathered in a small stone-encircled clearing he'd formed. As the sun dipped, the winds changed, blowing soft cool gusts. Aside from the soldier, he'd not come across any sign of human existence, yet he'd felt watched during the last hours of his walk. Being outdoors was natural for him. Living in the Black Mountains, he was accustomed to the idea of sharing the woods with tiny eyes hidden in trees and under bush. But this felt different. Being observed kept him on edge, the hair on the back of his neck tingling from time to time. He missed his moonshine: that first sip of fire, followed by sweetness and then the final shiver. He missed Westberry Mountain. And Sam. He did not miss Nadene. He wondered what may have come of his place, his family members. Guilt fluttered in the pit of his stomach, but only for a moment. For just as quickly as he abandoned the mother of his unborn child, he rejected the notion of guilt. *Fuck 'em.*

Fire would not come easily. Sparks burst from the flint strikes against his firesteel, but the char cloth he'd stored in his tender box would not ignite. The wind picked up and, with it, his frustration. He rummaged through his bindle. He pulled out the book and opened it. He grabbed the pierced coin and held it up. He'd never seen such a coin. It was crudely struck, foreign, silver, worn and dented, and had a round woven fan of grass on its face. It was laced on a raw cotton thread. He flipped it over. A crude looped T cross—the ankh symbol, he'd later learn—was stamped on its backside. He dropped it back into his bindle. He grabbed the book and opened it up again. Its pages were thick and rough and filled with beautiful roundhand flowing script with its intricate letters, flares and flourishes. He flipped partway through to find a page of sketched symbols, dark and foreign, a page containing a map, also with tiny symbols. He flipped to the back and ripped out a page to crumple up as kindling.

Suddenly, a great screech ripped through the trees, startling him. A bird of sorts. He wadded up the page and shoved it under his arranged sticks. He struck his flint rock against the firesteel once more, this time held to the crumpled page. Its sparks bit into the paper, its tiny orange flecks forming smoke. He cupped his hands around it and gave it a gentle blow. A small flame emerged. He ripped a second page from the book. Once more, a high-pitched screech ripped through the sky. He crumpled up the page and added it to his tiny smoldering fire. Just as it began to build, the screech echoed and a gust of wind whipped through the trees blowing the burning bits and dust into his face, sending him into a coughing fit. He wiped his eyes and nose.

Frustration built. The twigs he'd stacked had scattered about. He reassembled his tinder and tried once more. The wind howled sending his twigs and pages flying about. An owl let out a screech once more, but this time it was close. Very close. He looked up to find the sharply hooked talons of a bird descending upon him, its wings open wide, its beak agape. Instantly he blocked his face in defense. The owl hit him in the arms and bounded back into the air, circling and returning, this time its talons ripping across his eyebrow and cheek. He grabbed a stick and began swinging fiercely, wildly, but the small relentless owl returned time and time again. Walker's stick finally made contact, batting the owl to the ground. The momentum of the swing sent him stumbling back before losing his balance and tripping over the ring of stones. He landed hard on his right hip and elbow. "Fuck!" he shouted. Across the way, on the ground, the owl flapped wildly and squawked until it finally scrambled its way to its feet. Walker sat on the ground, his legs splayed out in a V before him. He panted. His face stung. He touched it and brought away a bloody hand. Filled with fury, he took up the stick once more and shifted over to his hands and knees to get up off the ground. When he stood, he found the tiny owl perched atop the book. He slowly advanced, stick in hand, ready to bash the bird to its death.

Footsteps caught his attention and he froze, stick held high. The owl hopped from the book and lifted, flapping until it reached a nearby tree where it settled on a branch. He heard the steps again. He quickly scooped up the book and his bag and deserted the fire pit, finding a thicket to duck behind. He crouched and waited, pulling back a branch hoping to catch a glimpse of whomever approached. He could see little but the circle of rocks and a sad bit of smoke. The steps grew louder until finally a man emerged from the trees.

The man walked right up to the stones, stopped, and scanned the area. He wore nothing but a cloth over his groin and moccasins. His body was painted a greasy black with rudimentary depictions of a skeleton in white—white, thick streaks along his arms and legs forming the body's long bones, curved horizontal stripes across his torso for the ribs. His face was painted white with circles of black around his eyes and nose. Walker's heart pounded. The Indian leaned over and picked through the failed attempt at fire, pulling out a crumpled page. Beads and bones bobbed and clanked around his neck as he moved. He smoothed out the page and held it up. Then he pressed the page to his chest and lifted his face up to the treetops. Without warning, a roar emitted from the Indian filled with such fury that it took all of Walker's courage to not bolt into a full-on run. The owl burst from the branch above and flew away. The Indian beat his chest and let out a singular whoop, crushed the page back into a small wad, and then to Walker's bewilderment, shoved it into his mouth and devoured it.

CAROLINE

Waterly, Texas (Unsettled land)

The weeks brought the wagon brigade west and the summer to an end. The trail was rough and riding in the wagons became unbearable at times. People alternated between riding, walking, and sitting atop horses or mules to break up the physical beating of the trail. The race was against winter, and the closer they came to their destination, the more unpredictable the weather seemed.

A string of covered wagons was for some early entrepreneurs a gold mine. The trails were not free of treacherous terrain, rivers, and bridges. At one point, when needing to traverse the Big River in Louisiana, the group was charged five dollars per wagon to be guided to a little-known low point in a town called Waterproof.

"Highway robbery at its finest," scoffed Caroline.

Now they waited in line for their turn to navigate the crossing of the Barron River in Texas. Caroline and Octavia watched the wagon ahead of them with trepidation. Octavia sensed Caroline's anxiety and pulled her in close. She caressed her red hair.

"How you feel, Miss Caroline?"

Caroline sighed. Her body was tired. The weeks had been hot and rough, and she was grateful for the cooler days of late. She thought about how, had they been able to ride the train, this could have been over with weeks ago. She looked at Octavia, whose eyes were full of concern. Octavia had always loved Caroline, and Caroline had always felt it.

"I'm doing just fine, Octavia." She thought for a moment. "I've been thinking 'bout what Davis says—"

Octavia cut her off. She said softly, "Miss Caroline." Her eyebrows furrowed and she gently shook her head no.

"It's okay, Octavia. I haven't seen him since we left."

Octavia nodded, feigning relief, but she was used to Caroline withholding Davis sightings. The more Caroline revealed her hauntings, the more people worried and fussed over her and threatened intervention. Octavia knew Caroline had learned to keep most of it to herself, and it saddened her to think of this woman she cared so deeply for suffering her delusions in solitude. She caressed Caroline's hair.

Caroline said, "Remember after the party, after everyone left, how sick I got?"

Octavia nodded and sucked her teeth. "Too much drink conjure up evil—spirits waiting to pounce on de weakened soul. You need to let go that dandelion wine, Miss Caroline."

Caroline nodded, slightly embarrassed. "I know. It's just an escape sometimes." She paused. "But this last time, I got so sick I thought I'd die. And as I prayed to God the vomiting would stop, a part of me almost hoped that was it. That the effects of the alcohol would take me and make Davis an honest man for once. That I'd be done with this world and his prediction of death by poison would have come to fruition and I could stop worrying my head with when, where, and how it'd happen."

Octavia listened and nodded.

"But it didn't happen. And it's not going to. The further away we get from Melroy, the better I feel, Octavia. I can't explain it"—her chin quivered and she took a deep breath to fend off any tears—"but I just know Element Dale is going to be great for me, for us."

A man guided their wagon forward toward the water and the women's apprehension mounted as they grew closer.

Octavia turned to Caroline with a forced smile and offered, "How 'bout de story of de chile called Babe?"

Caroline had heard this story a thousand times. From as early as she could remember, anytime she was hurt, mad, and particularly when her heart ached for her mother, Octavia would recite an old Geechee story, one of her people's animal trickster tales. And though it didn't always make a whole lot of sense to Caroline, it soothed her every single time, no matter the circumstance. It brought to her a sense of home and protection. With the river to cross ahead of them, she felt the story fitting now more than ever. She took another deep breath, sucking in the earthy air, and nodded.

"Please," she replied.

"One time dere was a little girl called Babe, and Babe was living with she godmother, Mama Crocodile. One day Babe did want to see she mama and she tata, so she asked she godmother to let she go to see them. Now, on the way dere was a very deep river, and dis day dere was a big shower of rain and de whole place was covered over wit' water. When Babe reached de river and couldn't get over, she begin cry. Den Mama Crocodile came up and asked Babe what she was cry fa? Babe tell she that she want to go over and see she mama and she tata, but she couldn't get over de river. It too full. De Mama Crocodile tell she, 'I will take you over de river, but you mustn't let nobody know how you get over.' So Mama Crocodile carry Babe over de river."

The wagon eased into the water, and Caroline squeezed Octavia's hand.

Octavia smiled and continued in her thick Geechee-Gullah dialect. "Now, you know Mista Hummingbird got very good hearing. Mama Crocodile call Mista Hummingbird and send he to listen to hear if Babe would tell anybody how she got over de river. Babe reached de house, and everybody was surprise; and dey want to find out how she got over, because dey all did know dat de river did wash away de whole place. Babe keep on telling dem dat she cross it herself. But dey wouldn't believe she. Den in a easy way she tell dem, 'Mama Crocodile tote me across.'

"Mista Hummingbird was very far, but he hear Babe, and begin sing like Babe, 'Mama Crocodile tote she across.' Mista Hummingbird come right up to de house, sing de same, 'Mama Crocodile tote she across.'

"Now, when Babe was goin' back, she mama and she tata know dat if Mista Hummingbird reach Mama Crocodile first and tell she that Babe give out de secret, Mama Crocodile would kill Babe, so dey pick a lot of flowers and scatter dem in de road.

"Mista Hummingbird come down, sing, 'Mama Crocodile tote she across.' But he was so greedy, he had to stop to suck these flowers.

So Babe reach de river before Mista Hummingbird, and she tell Mama Crocodile dat she didn't tell anybody how she get over. So Mama Crocodile cross she over again.

"Now, Mista Hummingbird come down, sing, 'Mama Crocodile tote she across.'

"So Mama Crocodile says to Mista Hummingbird, 'Get on me right shoulder and sing dat song.'

"He sing it on de right shoulder.

"She say, 'Get on me left shoulder.'

"He sing, 'Mama Crocodile tote she across.'

"She say, 'Get on me right ear.'

"Mista Hummingbird, he sing, 'Mama Crocodile tote she across.'

"She say, 'Get on me left ear.'

"'Mama Crocodile tote she across.'

"Den she say, 'Get in de palm of me left hand.' And after Mista Hummingbird get through sing, Mama Crocodile give he one chomp and grind he up. And de foam you see on de river whenever de rain fall is from Mista Hummingbird."

The tale brought Caroline back to her childhood. Her anxiety had gone, and the wagon eased across the river. The two sat on edge as the water rose. The other wagons stood in wait across the way. Caroline could see Henrietta waving and it quieted her nerves. She smiled.

"I'm sure proud of her. Life seems to really be just coming together for her."

Octavia could sense the envy in her voice. No malice or jealousy. Still, she knew Caroline was playing the dangerous game of comparison. She replied, "It rains, and every man feel it someday."

Caroline asked, "Meaning?"

"Fortune change. You may have som-ting today, and I tomorrow. I de next day, you no-ting."

Caroline wasn't entirely clear of her meaning, but she gathered the gist. She changed the subject. "But that Dix, he lacks flint of any kind."

Octavia chuckled. "Him's flint might just spark in way you don' yet have sight to see."

Caroline scoffed, "It's doubtful."

The wagon pulled up and out onto the riverbank. The horses exited without drama. The winds began to pick up. Ahead, where the sky had once been a clear blue, a yellow haze settled in.

DIX

Waterly, Texas (Unsettled land)

Dix's wagon sat, waiting across the river for the last few to traverse. Caroline's wagon was the last passenger wagon in line. The road had been rough. At one point, they'd passed off the range at a place called White Plains. They'd been compelled to pay seventy-five cents for each two-horse wagon, and one dollar for every vehicle that looked like a carriage for passing over three miles of a miserable and almost impassible road called the Walden Turnpike. He suspected this was a regular neighborhood co-partnership fraud practiced on strangers. They had been on the range for days and passed nothing of importance. The turnpike led to nothing but more trail. And he wondered how much of the wagon outfit pocketed from the fraud, if they were in on it.

Dix, Ford, and Henrietta alternated between reading and reminiscing on their journey. The brothers spoke fondly of their childhoods, telling Henrietta funny stories of mischief living with so many siblings. They kept the tales light, omitting any tragedies the family had endured. And there had been many. Henrietta delighted in watching her husband and brother-in-law laugh and tease. The two men had a deep connection. Brothers by happenstance; best friends by choice. She loved that for Ford.

She related a story to the men about a time with Caroline and Minnie. Dix had forgotten about Minnie, the refined and elegant lady that somehow came from the same mother and father as the crass and stubborn trouser-wearing, foul-mouthed Caroline. That *if maybe she were more like her sister.*

Henrietta defended her best friend, giving some insight as to some of Caroline's circumstances and tragedies, that she had reason to be blunt and angry.

Dix had interjected: "And crazy."

Henrietta frowned. Ford held her hand.

She continued, "Minnie and Chuck may have been born of the same mother and father, but Minnie didn't experience life with her momma and then have to mourn that loss as a child. Chuck did. Chuck worked hard even as a child to watch out for Minnie, worked hard to help Mr. Higgs. She is incredibly smart, loves books, loves gardening, and is very clever at it, I must say. She is a fiercely loyal daughter, sister, and friend. I realize you understand loss as a child. Buford has told me about the loss your family suffered, losing John and Elsa. For that I am truly sorry. But there's a kind of loss that Chuck has experienced, a tragedy like nothing you could ever imagine. None of us could. The things she witnessed were so brutal, evil, so violent and wicked." She covered her mouth and squeezed her eyes tight. Ford rubbed her back and Dix stared in confusion. She sniffed and straightened up. "I'll just leave it at if you or I were to have endured the things she did, we might seem crazy too."

Ford interjected lightheartedly, "You know, she didn't always wear men's britches. First time I met her she had on a dress."

Henrietta nodded with a smile. "Yes, the perfect politician's wife." She looked up to see Caroline and Octavia's wagon approaching the river. She held a hand up and waved in big, exaggerated sweeps. Caroline waved back.

"You know, she actually spent a great deal of her childhood teaching Octavia there to read and write." She continued to wave.

Dix watched as Caroline and Octavia's wagon entered the water, how the Geechee woman caressed Caroline's red hair. He watched as Caroline smiled at her best friend across the way, saw the love in her eyes, and felt a twinge of shame for how hard he'd been on the woman.

A sudden gust of wind blew and the wagon rattled. He looked up into the sky. He hadn't noticed the change. Their clear weather had at some point turned ominous. A storm was building.

ELZI

Fat Man's Squeeze in Waterly, Texas

Elzi heard the roar and then a whoop from the Indian in the distance, though he was certain there should be miles between them by this point. He feared he'd been walking in circles or that possibly the Indians were trailing him. He walked briskly, propelled by terror, though not certain of his direction. He had been walking for miles somewhat aimlessly when he finally came upon a trail, a wagon trail. The sight calmed his nerves and slowly the fear began to fade, replaced step by step with the anger and vengeance he needed to push him to his destination.

At some point, the sweltering summer heat had been swept away by gentle breezes. The skies had been clear and blue. The burnt earth of the plains turned to tall Johnson grass, yellow lemon paintbrush flowers, and black-eyed Susans—post oaks, cedars, elms, and cottonwoods all green and alive with squirrels and birds chirping their happy songs. He'd seen whitetail deer, fox, plenty of raccoons, and a pair of skunks he was happy to detour the trail for temporarily.

What were gentle breezes picked up and built into forceful gusts and then all at once settled, leaving the blue skies a dusty yellow and a stillness that was troublesome. A storm was coming and Elzi knew he needed to seek shelter. He picked up his pace and ran along the trail. Suddenly small bits of ice began to fall from the sky. At first he covered his head with his arms, trying to keep under the canopy of the trees. The small bits grew into marbles, pinging off of his forearms, Mother Nature's bullets. Then the bottom completely fell out and balls of ice bounced all around him, pinging off the ground and the trees. The sound was a rushing roar like a waterfall. He backed up to the trunk of a great oak and watched as the sky dumped its ice, beating the trees, the flowers, the grass. Then just as if Mother Nature had shouted *Enough!*, it ceased, leaving broken limbs, rogue leaves, and beaten flowers strewn about the hail that blanketed the ground. The yellow sky darkened, signaling that the calm was short lived. The wind gusted hard then stopped. Gusted again, stronger this time. A storm was building and Elzi knew it was about to get terrible.

He crunched his way across the hail, his steps quick and sure. He had to find shelter and fast. The clouds continued to darken and swirl above, Mother Nature stirring her pot. The trail led around a grouping of hills, rocky and thick with cedar trees and prickly pear. The wind gusted hard, resisting his steps now, pushing him this way and that. The sky above him spun slowly. Lightning struck followed by an immediate clap. Elzi kept moving, rounding the craggy hills, looking for anything to hide under. At the far end of the escarpment, he spotted a darkened area. He broke into a sprint. Rain dumped in slanted sheets that switched directions every few seconds. He ran hard, panicked, soaking. The world was a roar of falling water and angry winds. Nothing could be heard but the sound of driving rain whipped about by howls. Nothing could be seen but darkened areas through the blinding sheets of water.

He finally reached the shadowed area and found it was a small fault cut into the rocky escarpment. He squeezed through, raking past thorny bushes. He sidestepped, nervous and reconsidering his choice with every step. After five or six feet, the narrow slit turned and opened into a low keyhole. He crouched down and ducked into the opening, leaving the roaring storm behind.

The darkness of the cave was unnerving with the howling storm echoing within. Elzi could not see much aside from the small amount of light at the opening and imagined himself crouched in a coyote den among snakes and spiders. Water continued to pour off his rain-soaked body and he shivered, wet and exhausted.

In time, his eyes adjusted to the darkness. The little bit of light that crept through the crevice slowly revealed his surroundings. It was a stony alcove with mossy rock walls. A stone floor covered in silt, dry save the rain dripping from his body. The area was small and empty but for spider webs and leaves and dozens of granddaddy longlegs. With the storm ravaging the world outside, he resolved to get as comfortable as he could, curling up in the middle-most area of the cave. Exhaustion took the reins, and he fell into a deep sleep.

He dreamed of a land low and flat, nestled between hills and a winding river, with a light breeze that carries the scent of juniper. In the dream, he is small and being carried, watching the tall grass pass underfoot. His ear is tight against a warm and velvety-soft bosom. Behind it, a heart drums out sounds of love, deep and precious. He feels profoundly snug and safe. His feet do not dangle and bounce with each step but rather mirror those of another pair, tiny with pink bottoms pressed against his own. Elzi looks past the feet to see a baby's russet-brown face pressed hard against the naked rich umber-brown breast of a woman. The baby suckles and grunts greedily. He looks up to the face of the woman. Her dark eyes watch ahead as she walks. Her short wide nose centers prettily on her face and her head is wrapped in a vibrant golden fabric knotted at the temple. Beads of amber dangle from her ears and swing with each step.

The three, mother and babies, approach a creek. She crouches down and spreads a cloth over the grass and places the babies atop it. The other baby instantly protests with a wail as the breast is ripped from its mouth. Elzi looks on quietly. The woman walks to the creek, dips a handkerchief into its water, then wrings it out. She returns and leans in close, her smile one of pride and great joy. She wipes the baby's face with the cool cloth and begins to sing. Its cries quiet. She wipes Elzi's face and tiny hands, her onyx eyes taking him in.

She continues to hum and settles in on the blanket in between the two babies. She pulls a leather-bound book from her bag and begins to write in it, humming all the while. To his right, just behind her back, Elzi can see the head and hands of the other baby, its hands clasped one second and reaching aimlessly above the next. To his left, he sees the sweeping limbs of a great willow hanging low and swaying in the breeze. Straight above, leaves flap and rustle against the blue sky.

A woodpecker drums.

At this, the woman looks up and halts her humming. Elzi can sense tension in her. From the right, a tall and slender man approaches. An Indian. She quickly returns her book to the bag. The two exchange words, his tone condescending, hers indignant.

" . . . Voodoo hound imported from jungle of Africa . . . " the Indian says.

" . . . ignorant conna fool of de tribe . . . " she responds, her voice dripping with disdain and a hint of fear. She spits at the man's feet and grumbles, "Medicine man, ha."

The Indian squats down and eyes the two babies. He is old with a severely crooked nose, his eyes small and dark, beady. She quickly scoops up the other baby as the Indian hovers too close. The baby begins to cry. The Indian smirks and reaches across to Elzi. She places a hand across Elzi's chest, pressing him to the ground. Elzi sees his own tiny hands reach up toward the treetops. The Indian with the crooked nose flicks Elzi's chin and scoffs. He stands back up, stares at the three, his eyes full of malice and a hint of jealousy, and then walks away.

The woman pulls Elzi back to her chest. She scoops up his counterpart, cradling the two babies together, and rocks. No longer does her heart sing a song of comfort and love but that of fear. It races, and Elzi feels his own heartbeat match hers. He begins to cry the wails of an infant. The other baby joins him. She bounces them, shushes them, and over his own cries he hears her.

"Never let no man effect fear into your hearts. You are destined to be great protectors. One day may you watch over dis land. Grow into fierce warriors from ya father's blood, sly houngan leaders from the blood of ya mother." She bounces and shushes and sings until Elzi begins to slip into sleep. He closes his eyes and hears her voice, soft and ethereal.

"Sleep, sweet babies. And when you awake one day as men, see that none render evil f' evil unto any man, but ever follow dat which is good, both among ya-selves and to all men."

WALKER

The Catacombs of Hadacho Hills
Element Dale, Texas

Walker came out of hiding after the Indian of Black and Bones left his campsite. He'd allowed some time to pass, debating the safety of exiting the bushes. He'd not known fear of another human being, even of his father, like that before and it rankled him. He had been outright petrified squatting behind that bush and struggled with the shame of it. *How dangerous could one man be?* he thought to himself. Still, the buzzing of his nerves lingered, and so to caress his ego, he told himself that Indians are savage animals, known to rip the beating heart from a torso with the bare hand, and he himself hadn't even a gun. He had been wise to conceal himself, not gutless. He decided, also wise, to forego sleep that night and abandon the site. The possibility of the Indian returning to his campsite petrified him and he knew there was no way he'd be able to sleep anyway, so he packed up his belongings and continued heading west, all the while wishing he had a drink.

Walker walked and watched the sky switch from its natural

course of dusk melting into darkness to, instead, yellow and heavy, thick and still. Intuition pushed him to pick up his pace until he finally heard the whispering flow of water. He watched as a great hawk swooped down low and flew away. He thought back to words from his PeePaw Westberry: *Flyin' high means a clear sky. Flyin' low, prepare for the blow.* A hard gust of wind momentarily swept away the evening's sounds of chirping crickets. It died down and the coyote yips and the *gricket-gricket* of frogs returned. He could no longer make out the short bursts of squeaks, chuckles, squawks, or rattles of birds that had been so vocal before. The wind whipped again, bringing a burst of mixed cool and warm air into the thick stillness. In the distance, he could see storm clouds forming, ominous and threatening.

He reached the creek and followed alongside it. Across the way stood curious earthen mounds, man-made some time ago as vegetation blanketed each one. As he walked, he passed by a flat-topped mound, then a conical-shaped mound, and finally one with a dome-like top, the once-sacred grounds of an Indian race he'd known nothing of. Once past the mounds, the creek narrowed to a ribbon of water. An outcropping of stones offered up a natural bridge to hop across to the other side.

Silas Creek flowed alongside the mounds until it penetrated the deep and thick woods just outside of Element Dale. Walker found himself in a small clearing within the dense woodland just as the sky opened up and began dropping bits of ice that trickled through the tree cover. The anxiety from his almost encounter with the Indian had subsided from his hours of walking and he was overcome with weariness and outright physical and emotional exhaustion. He was hungry and wet. He'd been hotter than he'd ever been along the journey, dirtier than he'd ever been, aided the hiding of a dead body in a pit—he just knew it—almost got scalped, and now the sky was threatening to pummel him. If ever he regretted leaving the Black Mountains and his comforting hooch, it was now.

He found shelter under the canopy of an oak. He watched as the wind whipped the long wispy branches of a weeping willow that hung at the water's edge. Marbles of ice plunked and bounced along the ground and splashed in the creek for a few minutes until it was replaced by a dumping of rain. He lowered down against the tree's great trunk to his bottom and sat, watching, soaked and miserable. Then just as if the bucket held by the hands of heaven had emptied, the rain stopped and all became quiet save the drops of water trickling from the trees above onto the debris of leaves scattered about the ground.

He pulled a cigarette from his shirt pocket. It was soaked through and through. He flicked the cigarette aside and sighed. He leaned his head back and closed his eyes, water streaming down his face. Somehow, by either the grace of God or the hounds of Hell, he passed out in the soaked darkness. If an Indian was going to come steal his heart or swipe his scalp, *so fucking be it*.

CAROLINE

Waterly, Texas

Not long after the wagon brigade traversed the river, the ominous skies dropped pellets of ice. Caroline and Octavia huddled back under cover of the canvas and a man climbed up and seized the lines.

"We have to get to cover. It's about to get nasty."

The hail stopped just as suddenly as it had started, like a grain shoot closed off in one fail swoop.

"Well, now that wasn't all too bad," Caroline said with a victorious smile and anxiously smoothed her trousers.

The man replied, "No, ma'am, I suppose it weren't. But here we are in the calm and I don't like it not one bit." He whipped the reins. "Hya!" The nervous horses started at his whip and picked up into a run, knocking the women back in their seats.

"Is that really necessary?" shouted Caroline, but the man ignored her.

The horses dragged the wagon up beside a nearby escarpment along a craggy ridge. They pulled up as close to the mountainside as the terrain would allow. Suddenly the wind sucked the tail end of their wagon up into the air and it slammed down with a terrific crash. The women screamed out. The man threw Caroline the lines—"Hold these!"—and then leaped over the side. Another man joined him and began to hammer pins deep into the earth. In desperate haste, the two struggled to tie the wagon to the pins. The loaded wagon kept lifting off the ground, threatening the ropes that creaked and strained in protest. The horses squealed and stomped, and each bang of the wagon provoked a scream from the women. Caroline abandoned the reins and climbed back under cover. The man hollered out something to the ladies but the howling wind stole his voice. Looking around the edge of the wagon cover, Caroline and Octavia saw the whole earth behind them billowing to the sky. Water from the river rippled and then lifted and then started to spin. They could actually see the howling yellow wind as it swallowed up the water, then the earth of the riverbank, then the leaves from the surrounding trees. Its savage and terrifying tunnel pulled at the treetops that bent and moaned until some cracked and split away, unable to resist the evil summons of the twister.

The canvas of the wagon violently ruffled and popped, slapping against the wooden frame and the whole thing trembled and then shook with such fury Caroline was tempted to abandon it altogether. Octavia held her close like a child, cradling her head into her great bosom, rocking. Though Caroline could not hear a sound from Octavia over the ear-piercing winds and slaps and pops of the wagon, she could feel the vibration from Octavia's chest. The woman was either humming or praying. Too terrified to cry, Caroline squeezed her eyes shut and prayed harder than she'd ever prayed in her life, harder than she'd even prayed when she'd asked God to take her husband's soul and stop his haunting her, whether than meant casting him once and for all to the depths of Hell where he mostly certainly belonged or graciously receiving him through the gates of Heaven (she'd take that too—anything to be rid of him). She prayed for the safety of the brigade, that God would pluck the twister from the earth with his great hand and toss it into the wind to scatter apart. She prayed Henrietta was safe and adequately comforted by Ford. She prayed for the animals and the men, for their supplies.

"And God Almighty, I humbly ask you even bring peace to the frightened heart of Dixon Artope, though I imagine he oughtn't be in fear as he seems to righteously be within your cahoots. But should he be so weak as the lot of us to fear the wrath of Mother Nature, I pray you settle his worry."

The winds sounded to Caroline just like the approaching train in Gem City, and she'd allowed herself a moment of regret for agreeing to this wagon brigade instead of riding the train. If they'd taken the train, they'd have arrived in Element Dale weeks ago. If she'd really tried, really dug her heels in, she felt deep down she could have talked her daddy into allowing Octavia to remain behind just as she'd wanted. But she hadn't tried all that hard for she held a fear deep somewhere in the pit of her being that she couldn't do life without Octavia, without someone to watch over her, to keep her grounded to reality when what was tangible blurred with the ethereal haunts of trauma. Now because of her own weakness of mind, her inability to operate as a grown woman—and one of means nonetheless—Octavia was stuck here under the guise of shelter of mere fabric, trembling in terror and praying in fervor that Mother Nature's wrath forsake them all.

DIX

Fat Man's Squeeze

"Everybody out!"

Dix's shouts went unheard. The wind dragged the wagon backwards against the will of the horses who fought and bucked in terror. The rear of the wagon lifted and then whipped to the left, spinning 180 degrees and slamming into the side of the horses, pinning one to the other against the escarpment. Between the bursts of wind and the wild thrashes of the horses, the wagon quaked and rocked and hammered, its wheels lifting and violently crashing back down. The horses bucked and pitched, coming down upon one another in a tangled mess, overpowered by wild instincts to be rid of the wagon holding them captive to the oncoming twister.

Dix's heart pounded against his precious Bible hugged to his chest. He had clenched his eyes tight and prayed to his Lord and Savior, but the unbearable deafening threats of the wind, the violent shaking of the wagon, and the horses' likelihood to pummel them took hold and he abandoned the wagon, all the while screaming into the chasm of ruthless wind "Get out! Get out!" leaving Ford and Henrietta to their own fates.

Dix tucked the Bible into his shirt to protect it from the elements and ran opposite the twister following along the escarpment. The wind beat at his back and ripped the hat from his head. Debris flew all around and threatened to injure. Shrapnel of Mother Nature's war. Millions of tiny stings from grains of dirt assailed his neck and face. He squinted to keep his eyes clear and searched for any type of refuge he could find. Up ahead he could see the rest of the brigade, wagons and animals lifting and spinning like feathers in the wind. He turned to look back. His wagon remained in place though was resting on its side, the horses still tethered and stomping in place but no longer bucking. He leaned hard into the rock with each step, speaking his prayers loudly into the wind. He could not hear his own voice over the staggeringly blaring howls of wind but knew his God heard them. The wind pulled at him, his clothes and hair whipping violently, and he pressed his body into the rock and kept his progression until at last he came upon a split in the escarpment, God's parted sea of stone. He slipped into the opening, unfazed as he hurriedly raked past needles of prickly pear. Pieces of pencil cacti caught his shirt and broke off, hanging on like desert barnacles. He sidestepped, following the crevice deeper into the rock until it finally turned and revealed a keyhole opening low to the ground. He slid down into a crouch, his long and slender body now folded up into a bony crab, and backed a few feet into the opening until stone sheltered him.

Dix sat squatted just inside the entrance of the keyhole with his eyes clenched tight. Light bursts of wind hit his face. He hugged the Bible against his bare skin beneath his shirt. Loud and incessantly he prayed, oblivious to his surroundings, grateful for the cover. He thanked his God for this blessing of shelter. He pled for the safety of his brother and sister-in-law. And then just as quickly as gratitude for shelter came, sickening guilt washed it away. He had deserted them to the elements. "Forgive my cowardice, oh Lord. I do not deserve this shelter you have so provided. I have been overwrought with my own weakness of character and have abandoned my flesh and blood. Precious Jesus, please forgive me. Please watch over Buford, dear God. Please God." He rocked in his squatted stance, the burn of his thighs intensifying with each passing minute. His heart slammed against his chest with the adrenaline-pumping anticipation and terror that he'd never before experienced. He then began to thank God in earnest for watching over his brother, a premature expression of appreciation for his safekeeping. Dix leaned hard on the power of his God and knew, regardless of his own weakness and fear, that Buford Artope would in fact prevail under the protective hand of his almighty God.

He pulled out his Bible and held it at his forehead and shouted his words from the opening where he crouched: "As Paul once wrote to the church in Thessalonica, brethren, ye have no need that I write unto you. For yourselves know perfectly that the day of the Lord so cometh as a thief in the night. For when they shall say peace and safety, then sudden destruction cometh upon them and they shall not escape.

"But ye, brethren, are not in darkness, that that day should overtake you as a thief. Ye are all the children of light and the children of the day. We are not of the night, nor of darkness. Therefore let us not sleep as do others, but let us watch and be sober."

A loud crash outside the rock shelter startled him and he stumbled back, falling onto his butt. Pain pierced just under his right buttock at the thigh. He imagined more cacti scattered about the floor and scrambled back up toward the opening, brushing his trouser leg and taking a position on his knees, resting back on his feet. He resumed his prayer.

"For God hath not appointed us to wrath, but to obtain salvation by our lord Jesus Christ who died for us; that, whether we wake or sleep, we should live together with him. Wherefore comfort yourselves together, and edify one another, even as also ye do. And we beseech you, brethren, to know them which labor among you, and are over you in the Lord, and admonish you."

He felt a wave of lightheadedness and thought it best to lower his shouts, his efforts. "And to esteem them very highly in love for their work's sake. And be at peace among yourselves. Now we exhort you, brethren, warn them that are unruly, comfort the feebleminded, support the weak, be patient toward all men. See that none render evil for evil unto any man, but ever follow that which is good, both among yourselves and to all men."

His head swam and a thought energized him. Was he possibly, in this moment of disaster, encountering the Holy Spirit? The Lord was with him, pouring His Spirit into the body of Dix. He raised his hand high, and out of the opening he shouted, "Rejoice evermore! Pray without ceasing!"

A deep burn pinched hard behind his thigh. He reached back to rub the area, cautiously expecting to contact the spine of a cactus. He felt none. Shifting his weight to his left, he resumed his loud prayer, though the pinching now interfered with his conviction. "In everything give thanks, for this is the will of God in Christ Jesus concerning you!"

The pinching in his thigh now seared down to his knee and intensified to a throb. Dix sat his Bible on the ground and shifted onto this left where he could better inspect the right side with his hand. He reached back to find a wetness under his thigh. He lifted his hand up to the rock opening. His hand glistened from the bit of daylight revealing a deep crimson wetness. He was bleeding. He leaned over farther and palpated his buttock and thigh once again, unable to locate the thorny culprit he had obviously fallen back on. The sudden tightness and pain of his knee prompted him to straighten it out. In the light cast upon him, he could see his alarmingly swollen leg, tight and plump from the hip to the knee. His heart raced once again and his vision began to blur. He reached back again, frantically hoping to pluck the evil thorn he was reacting so adversely to from his body.

He racked his medical mind of poisonous thorny plants, but

concentration eluded him. A wave of nausea overcame him along with the sickening combination of sweat and chills. He lowered himself down onto his left elbow and then, with a great involuntary retch, the contents of his stomach spewed from his mouth splashing onto his arm and hand and ground. He coughed and gasped for air. The realization of being hidden away from the possibility of help struck him and he clumsily scrambled up onto his hands and knees. He crawled a few inches toward the opening, his right leg extended behind. Once through the keyhole, he grabbed onto the crevice wall, pulling himself up and onto his feet. He side-hopped, his chest scraping against the wet rock, until finally, the world swirling, he crumbled down. He fell as far as the narrow space allowed. Wedged low between the craggy crevice walls, Dix panted, feeling his tongue swell, his heart race, and the world—once a dusty threatening yellow —tunnel into deadly darkness.

ELZI

Fat Man's Squeeze

"Rejoice evermore! Pray without ceasing!"

Elzi shuttered awake to the sounds of a man's shouts echoing all around him. He was momentarily lost as to his whereabouts. He had slept hard and deep, dreamed he was an infant, dreamed of another baby, one that was his mirror image, and of a woman. His blood mother. He had woken bewildered, feeling displaced, and now watching this tall lanky White man on his hands and knees crawl toward the cave opening, he was even more confused.

He sat quiet and stock-still in the back of the cave, taking it all in. He could see the rain had stopped and the light from the opening had brightened. The wind no longer howled. The pressure in the cave no longer pushed and pulled inside his ears. He watched as the man struggled to heave himself onto his feet, clawing at the rock to gain purchase. The man stood weakly on his left leg, struggling to bear any weight on the right, then hopped inches at a time to the left, all the while mumbling words of prayer.

Elzi's initial reaction was to remain hidden. He'd not known the circumstances of this White man's affliction, nor did he think it wise to sneak up on him. Confounded, he tried to imagine how the man had entered the space of the cave unbeknownst to himself—and what had transpired to cause him such injury. He could go after him, help the man. And that could go one of two ways: one resulting in the man's deep appreciation, or one ending in Elzi regretting getting himself tangled up in the tumult of a White man's personal crisis.

He sat, debating. Then a faint puff of air, stinking and acrid, swirled in the cave. The sharp smell urged Elzi to his hands and knees. He began crawling toward the opening. Another caustic whiff hit him in the face. He scanned the cave. Just to his left he spotted the culprit, a pile of vomit. He scooted as far to the right side as possible, avoiding the foul puddle. A book sat up against the rock to the right, a Bible. He reached out to pick it up. Just as his hand approached, a spine-tingling high-frequency *ch-ch-ch-ch-ch* echoed and filled the confines of the small cave. Elzi sprang back from the rattler's telltale warning and scurried frantically to the opening, leaving the Bible to remain the hostage of the seething serpent of the devil himself. *If that White man want his Bible, he gone have to muster up the mettle to retrieve it his own self*, he thought.

As he stood up in the narrow crevice, the sun shone down on him. The air was clean. Birds chirped as if God Almighty hadn't just, minutes before, threatened to wipe the earth clean and start anew. Elzi sidestepped back out toward the opening. He came upon the man, lying on his side, his legs bent and wedged between the rocks, his upper body laid out on the ground. He laid there panting, drenched in sweat, paler than any White man Elzi had seen before.

Once his Pa Godwin had fallen poorly with lockjaw after an infection set in. He'd been working the steamship and cut his finger clear from his hand. He'd acted like it was nothing, and at the time, Elzi had thought him strong and noble. Within the week, John Godwin fell terribly ill, first with fever and chills, then seizures and spasms in his face, neck, and back. Elzi remembered his pa lying in the bed, uncontrollably arching his back, clenching his jaw, losing his bowels. Elzi couldn't put together how losing one's finger could inflict such havoc on the body. Pa Godwin pulled through, but Elzi never forgot how frightening it was, watching his pa, strong and vigorous, wilt into a writhing shell of a man.

This man looked much the same. Elzi braced himself against the rock, equally pushing his hands to the front and his back to the wall behind him. He worked his body, scooting up the wall a bit, allowing him to swing his legs over and clear the crumpled man without stepping on him. Just outside the crevice, the world stood in disarray. Trees, ripped from the earth, had been dropped back down on top of another. Debris scattered everywhere—wagon wheels, hats, clothes, pots. People milled about sorting through it all with looks of emotional depletion following what must have been sheer terror. Elzi could see men in the distance rounding up rogue animals, and children running and playing, the threat now gone. People hollered out names.

Shouts sometimes returned, "He's here!" or "I'm all good!"

One name called out with no shout volleyed back. "Dix! Dix! Dixon Artope, you 'round here?!"

Elzi heard the man on the ground behind him groan. He looked back. The crumpled man, white as a ghost, wheezing and drooling, held his hand up. It wavered back and forth and dropped back down.

Elzi squatted down to him. "You call ya-self Dix?" he asked.

The man attempted to raise his hand once more.

"Dix? Dat ya name?" Elzi turned to stand. Just as he was about to holler out to the people, he saw a man in the distance take notice in their direction and break into a mad dash.

"Dix, sir, looks like hep is coming. Hold tight."

As the man rapidly approached, his hat flew off and Elzi saw it wasn't a man at all, but a redheaded woman dressed in britches and a button-down shirt.

"Dix!" she shouted, barreling toward them like a freight train. She called out over her shoulder, "He's over here!" She ran so hard that once she made it and dropped to her knees, she all but slid into the man.

"Oh my God. What in the hell?" She picked up his head and sat it upon her lap, turning it this way and that, roughly inspecting. She turned and looked up to Elzi, her face confused, then looked back down to the man they called Dix. "What in the hell happened here?"

Dix panted like a dying dog.

She began drilling questions to Dix, to Elzi, to anyone, to herself. "Why is he half wedged in this rock squeeze? Dix, what happened? Your legs. Did the twister toss you here?"

Dix took a break from panting to answer. "A thorn," he wheezed.

"A thorn?" She looked around for some type of answer, evidence. "What the fuck?"

A White couple hurried from the debris to join the redheaded woman. The man squatted down with the redhead and the wounded man on the ground. He said, "Dix! What transpired here? Dear lord. You would have been safer to have just remained in the carriage with Henri and me." He paused and took in the sight, the downed man's pale sweating face, the stench of vomitus, the lower half of his body crumpled and pinned between the narrow walls of the stone crevice, his panting like a dog. "I don't understand what happened here."

The redhead replied, "I don't totally neither, but how 'bout we work out the details later and get him out of this fucking fat man's squeeze for now." She slid her arm up under the man's neck and began pulling him up off the ground. The two of them then hooked an arm under each of his and pulled in earnest.

"My leg!"

They lowered him back down.

"Seems his legs are stuck, Chuck," the man said.

Caroline stood and craned her body over the injured man. She wedged herself into the narrow cut of the escarpment. She grabbed at the bend of his right knee and pulled, lifting it to turn and straighten it out. Dix screamed out in pain. She slid her shoulders down lower and lifted the left.

"Okay," she huffed. "Let's try this again."

She resumed her position. The two of them lifted Dix from under his shoulders and dragged him out into the open. He laid there a quivering sweaty mess.

The other woman pointed and said, "Ford, it looks as if he's injured his right leg."

The redheaded woman they all called Chuck replied, "He said he got stuck by some kind of thorn."

"A thorn?" inquired Ford.

Elzi, standing a bit behind everyone interrupted. "Weren't no thorn. A rattler got 'em."

"Oh," replied Caroline. "Not a thorn, a rattlesnake."

"A rattlesnake!" exclaimed Ford. "Shit, Dix! What do we do?"

Dix moaned, "A snake?"

Caroline, searching for confirmation, turned to Elzi.

Elzi replied, "Yessum, a rattler got him in the cave." He pointed. "Up inside dere."

A plump Black woman approached the group from behind. "What gwine on here?" Elzi noticed her accent was laden with remnants of Africa, a creole quite distinct from his own.

Dix huffed out, "A thorn."

Ford, anxious and confused shouted, "Shit, Chuck. Which is it? A thorn or a snake?"

Caroline whipped back around to Elzi, her hands up. "Well?"

Elzi replied, "Rattler struck 'em right in his hindquatahs."

She turned back to Ford.

Not satisfied, he stared hard into her eyes, eagerly awaiting her reply. "What?" she shouted.

"I asked which is it, a thorn or a rattler."

Caroline, frantic and patience running thin, shouted back, "Your ears is just as good as mine, Ford. Shit! Look at his right leg!"

The group glanced down at Dix's right leg, swollen and threatening to split his trousers at the thigh.

Ford shouted at Dix, "What kind of thorn was it, brother? What do we need to do here?"

Dix's eyes closed as he laid there, short of breath.

Caroline turned back to Elzi. "You positive it was a rattler?"

"Sho is."

Elzi watched as Ford eyed the redhead for a moment, looked to the other woman momentarily, then to the Geechee woman they called Octavia. He sensed a silent agreement among the group.

Octavia said, "Miss Caroline, time to be clear now. Him needs to know. If'n it a rattler, well, we's in some trouble. If'n it a thorn, maybe he be ah-kay."

Caroline shot her a look of utter disgust and disappointment. "Octavia, I can understand maybe Ford here thinking to pay no mind to this man standing here telling us the particulars of Dix's injuries, but you of all people—to just dismiss his words."

Octavia tucked her chin and furrowed her brow, flashing only a second of confusion, before her face loosened with clarity. She nodded discreetly to the woman standing beside her. The woman—Ford's wife Elzi gathered—stepped forward and gently placed a hand on Caroline's shoulder. She quietly said, "Chuck, why don't you come with me for a moment. Take a breath. Ford and Octavia here will tend to Dix."

Elzi watched as Caroline shrugged the woman's hand from her shoulder. The redhead shot up, fuming mad and screamed at them all, "Listen to the goddamned man. For once in your goddamned lives, listen! He was bitten . . . on his ass . . . by a motherfucking rattlesnake . . . in a cave . . . just through that goddamned squeeze right there. And if we don't come up with a way right this minute to help him, he's going to motherfucking end his days right here in this goddamned dirt amongst all this goddamned trash!" She stood huffing and glowering.

Henrietta took a few steps back. Her face full of fear and concern.

Octavia kneeled down to Dix and took his face in her hands. "Mista Arra-tope, snake bit you, yeah?"

Dix remained quiet and trembling.

Elzi took a step towards Octavia and placed a hand on her shoulder. "Ma'am, he was indeed struck. Saw it wit' my own eyes. We need to get to helping him right away."

Octavia did not respond but simply shivered him off. Elzi pulled his hand from her shoulder, careful not to upset her.

Caroline said to him, "Pardon my rude comp'ny."

Elzi nodded.

He heard Ford speak to his wife. "Henri, Love, can you please fetch the brigade marshal, see if they can help us here?" Henrietta nodded, hiked up her skirt and rushed away. Ford looked back to Dix and spoke loudly and firmly. "Dix, I need you to look at me." He lightly slapped Dix's cheek. "Look at me, Dix. Brother. Brother, I need to know what to do here. Do you have some type of remedies in your belongings to aid us here? A solution for whatever this shock, this affliction is?"

Dix did not respond.

Ford looked back at Caroline. "I'm going to find his trunk, see about digging out his medicine chest. Has to be something there." He stood and sprinted away.

Elzi remained standing with Caroline and Octavia—and Dix on the ground. The two women faced away from one another, a tension in the air between them. Elzi broke the silence.

"Missus, I believe it best if you get to cutting that trouser leg away and tying off the leg above the strike. Might use ya belt to ligature it, stop the venom from creeping up at his heart."

"Good thinking," replied Caroline.

Octavia asked, "Good tinking what? Who you talk to?"

"To him!" she shouted, pointing back at Elzi.

Octavia turned and looked back behind her, back to Caroline, sucked her teeth, and cocked her hip.

Caroline, irritated, dropped to her knees, taking hold of Dix's trousers and pulling, a weak attempt to rip the fabric.

Octavia huffed and took a wide stance before lowering herself to the ground with a grunt. "Move chile." She reached into her bosom and pulled from the deep crease between her breasts a small pocketknife.

Caroline raised her eyebrows.

Octavia flipped open the knife, pinched up a bit of fabric, and began cutting the pants at the bend of the hip. She sat the knife aside and grabbed the cut fabric, ripping it apart. She tore around the leg, revealing angry purple-red flesh, hot and slick smooth with edema. Caroline scrambled down and pulled the boot from his foot and together the women pulled the trouser leg from Dix's grotesquely swollen extremity. They stared in awe at its incongruous size compared to the scrawny stick of a leg on the left.

Elzi suggested they turn him.

They rolled him onto his stomach. On the back of his right thigh, two puncture wounds bled from just beneath the cut trousers. Caroline pulled her belt from her waist and slipped it under his thigh.

Elzi stopped her. "Wait. A strap maybe ain't best. I's remembering now. It'll trap that poison right where you restrict the flow. Once it come off, a great flood of venom gone rush to his heart and threaten to stop its beat."

She paused and turned to him, panicked. "Well, won't it just flow there now?"

"Flow where?" asked Octavia.

"To his heart!" she replied. She asked Elzi, "Won't it flow there now if we don't stop it?"

Elzi answered, "It will, but at least it won't be a burst of poison all at once when you do finally take the belt off."

"Okay, then what do I do?"

Octavia growing more and more concerned asked cautiously, "Chile, is it Mista Colley?"

"What?" Caroline snapped back. "Mr. Colley what?"

Octavia responded with a gentle admonition. "Mind yer head, chile. Dis ain't the time fa dat."

Caroline stared back at her bitterly. Octavia met her stare, searching Caroline's eyes for those flashes of confusion and mania she'd seen too many times to count. She saw fear. She saw anxiety. She saw a bit of incredulity. But she saw nothing of mania, no signs of hysteria or paranoia. Just a woman kneeling over the fading body of her best friend's brother-in-law.

"Yessum," Octavia said.

Elzi thought back to the writings in Ora B.'s book. It had stories and tales, folklore and ancestral histories. It also had a section she titled *Grimoire*: a collection of recipes, potions, and remedies paired with evoking incantations, energetic touch, or spells—a sort of magi-therapeutic dimension of her practice. He had read the pages of this book over and over for years, though he hadn't really understood much of it. Today, he remembered the hekavu, the healing practice for injuries and insults from malevolent forces. Certainly the venom from an earthly serpent would fall into that category. He said, "You gots to get the snake."

"Get the—what the fuck?" Caroline replied.

Octavia looked up. "I did not say a ting to you."

Elzi replied, "The snake, ya gots to fetch it." He squeezed his eyes tight, visualizing Ora B.'s words before him. He recited, "To rid the body of poison, first ya must pierce the site and pour the milk of a goat over the wound. Then place a poultice of"—he strained his mind for the exact ingredients—"salt, snakeroot, alder bark, and peyote on the opening. Cover it wit' the skin of the snake that bit him, for to seal it in."

Caroline looked at him and shook her head. She held up her hand. "I'm not sure what kind of witch doctor you're posing to be"—she looked him up and down, noticing his uniform—"or what kind of mess you might be running from, but one, I'm not about to go after no fuckin' snake and somehow steal its skin; two, if we had milk anywhere in this brigade, it'd be flung halfway back to Melroy at this point; and three . . . peyote?"

Octavia scooted back. "Miss Caroline?" She looked all around, confused, concerned.

Elzi sighed. Hearing it repeated back to him brought about the same sense of embarrassment he'd felt in his younger years regarding his blood mother, when he'd been naïve enough to speak of her writings to Maymee and Pa Godwin. He'd learned over time to just keep it to himself. He glumly looked back at Caroline. He had only tried to help.

Octavia spoke. "Chile, how you know 'bout snakeskin?"

Caroline ignored Octavia and turned to Elzi. "I'm sorry," she said to him, embarrassed by the rude treatment from her companions. She hadn't guessed Octavia would be so insolent, snubbing a man outright regardless of his color or status. Her childhood nanny, known to be fickle in her mood, sometimes turned her nose up at the colored hands at the plantation, sometimes perplexing Mr. Higgs with her sudden changes in disposition toward him even.

Elzi subtly shook his head. "No matter, ma'am."

Octavia said, "Skin of the evil dat bite do remedy the poison dat kill."

Caroline, dumbfounded, replied, "Really? You're serious? You too?"

Octavia nodded.

Caroline said, "How we s'posed to find the snake anyhow? And if we do, then what? I ain't about to go toe-to-toe with a damn snake like such a fool."

Octavia shrugged then leaned down to Dix. "Mista Arra-tope, where bouts de snake? Mista Arra-tope."

Elzi spoke up to offer what consolation he had. "Ma'am, being bad off as the mister here is, I suspect that snake ain't got much more poison left in them fangs to give."

Caroline stared in disbelief. He was serious.

"And the snake, well, like I say, it's up through what you call the squeeze there, 'round a right bend and down up in a little cave. Or that's where we left it anyhow."

Elzi watched as Caroline sat and thought a moment. She looked around. In the distance, Ford and Henrietta flipped upturned trunks upright and opened each one, searching.

Caroline said, "Not sure what they think they're going to find. A bottle that says snake cure inscribed on its face?" She huffed, put her hands on her right knee, and hoisted herself up and onto her feet. She said, "Octavia, can you see about the milk and salt? I'll go find some mistflower."

Elzi corrected, "It say snakeroot, Missus."

"Yes," she agreed, "snakeroot, mistflower, white boneset—they're all one and the same. We'll have to forego the peyote and alder bark as I don't much see no fucking Indians or piney woods in these parts." She stomped off toward a grouping of trees, irritated and afraid all at once, leaving Elzi standing alone with a dying man at his feet, and Octavia wandering the debris for supplies, wondering what kind of aberration Caroline was experiencing this time.

CAROLINE

Fat Man's Squeeze

Caroline stomped through the trees searching the grounds for the plant the soldier had said she would need. It was still blooming time for mistflower, and for that, she thought them damned fortunate. She angrily whacked tall grasses and bushes from her path, all the while keeping her eyes peeled for white tufts atop purplish stems with jagged leaves. She was tired of constantly being watched and monitored and mumbled as much.

"Don't get me wrong. I'm grateful for Octavia, but she needs to mind her place too. Questioning me like I'm some kind a screwball when a man lay on the ground perishing. There is a time and place to be leery of strangers, particularly Black ones roaming the hills, looking like a runaway deserter, but this man is offering help and the whole fuckin' lot of them is turning up their noses at him. Georgian snobbery at its finest right there."

She spotted the flowers and sprinted to them, pulling the tall slender plant from the earth at its roots. She had studied mistflower—or snakeroot as so many called it—and knew it was poisonous, particularly if ingested. It had wiped out many a nursing animal from taking in the tainted milk of its momma. She wasn't certain how adding poison to a poison was beneficial, though she knew from experience that there was indeed a fine line between a medicine and a poison, and that line was dosage. Her deep curiosity and love of healing with plants allowed her to consider the recommended poultice. *And,* she thought selfishly, *if this works, I can add it to my healing cookbook.* She ripped up a patch of greenbrier, knowing she'd not be finding any alder bark, and sprinted back.

She huffed, breathless, dropping the plants on the ground, "Okay, there ain't gonna be no alder in these parts, but the roots of greenbrier have natural placatory properties. We might can substitute?"

Elzi shrugged.

"Now what?" she asked.

"The snake, ma'am. "

"Shit."

"Last I seen it, it be laying right up inside dere. Right up by Mista Dix's Bible."

She turned and looked toward the crevice then turned back to scan the strewn debris for something useful. She hopped up and ran toward the busted-up wagon by the river and spotted an ax for wood splitting. She grabbed it and returned.

The soldier, dressed in filthy blues, stood in anticipation. She wanted badly to hand the ax over to him, for him to take care of the dangerous work, a man's job, a hand's job, but Dix was nothing to this stranger. And she knew deep down, if she did ask him, he'd feel he'd have no choice but to carry out her request. She hated that the world was this way, that it groomed some people to believe their worth lay only in service to another people, an oppressive people.

"I'm going in."

"Careful, ma'am," said the soldier. "Snakes be the devil slitherin' on the ground, in cracks and crevices just waiting for to snap at you, poison or no poison."

She nodded and headed toward the crevice with the conviction of a warrior. While sidestepping through the squeeze, she considered the soldier's words—"poison or no poison"—and it brought back a disturbing memory, a warning from a dead and hanging Davis Colley: "Mother Nature will wield her poison." She shuttered and thought, *This is it. Davis fucking Colley finally speaks the truth.*

Elzi watched as Caroline tossed the ax out from the squeeze and then turned back. Moments later, she stepped out carrying a limp snake in one hand and the Bible in the other. Octavia, Ford, and Henrietta sat kneeled down, tending to Dix who laid quietly shivering. Elzi stood a few paces behind the group, watching from a safe distance.

She spoke out to him. "Now what?" She flung the snake and it slapped down on the ground beside the mistflower and greenbrier.

The group jumped back.

Ford said, "What the hell, Chuck?" Octavia had informed him of the plan, all that she could gather anyways, and he was concerned. Concerned for his brother and concerned for Caroline who clearly seemed to be cracking under pressure. "Chuck, I found his medicine chest, but I don't see anything directly for reactions to thorns—or snake bites." He raised a glass bottle into the air. "I did find this, though." She took it from him. *Morphine.*

"Well," she said. "Here's our peyote." She grinned at the soldier. He politely smiled back.

Ford turned and shot a look behind him at Henrietta, then back to Caroline. "Okay? Now what?"

Caroline looked up to the soldier.

Elzi replied, "Says you got to cut him open and cleanse with the milk of a goat."

"Makes sense," she said. "Milk is a natural neutralizer." She turned to Octavia. "You find any milk?"

Octavia handed over the milk and a bag of salt.

"Well I'll be damned. The miracles just never cease," replied Caroline. "Now, how 'bout that knife again?"

Octavia reluctantly handed it over.

Caroline called out, "Turn him on his side. We need to get a bit of this morphine in his mouth."

Ford and Octavia pulled Dix from his stomach and onto his left side. His head hung limp. Caroline leaned down and trickled the liquid into his mouth, holding his chin up. Dix grimaced and sputtered. She trickled in a bit more and held his mouth closed. He shook his head slightly but couldn't put up as much of a fight as she knew he wanted to. They rolled him back onto his stomach where Caroline poured the milk over the wound followed by a bit of the morphine. Then, without hesitation, she inserted Octavia's knife into his flesh and cut a slit from one puncture to the other.

Dix hollered out.

"Chuck, are you sure?" Ford, by this point, was pacing back and forth with Henrietta trailing behind.

Caroline poured the milk over the bloody area then turned to Elzi. "Now what?"

Ford stopped his pacing and shouted. "I certainly have no clue of your plans, Chuck. I was hoping you did."

She spat back, "I wasn't figuring you did, Ford."

Henrietta placed a hand to the back of his neck, drawing him into her face where she lovingly shushed him. He yanked away and resumed his anxious pacing.

Elzi replied, "You needing to grind up dem roots, I believe, and mix in the peyote—or what ya got there. Make it a paste. And then"—he hesitated—"I guess the skin." He looked to the heavy-bodied limp snake, headless and bloody. It was about four feet long and thick, a combination of various browns, and lined with black diamond-shaped blotches.

Caroline looked at Octavia and handed over the knife. Octavia took it and waited, holding the bloody thing out to the side as to not drip blood on her skirt. Caroline began ripping the roots from the plants. She turned to Henrietta.

"You think you can find me one good-sized flat stone and a smaller one to fit in my palm?"

Henrietta nodded and rushed away and was back within seconds.

Caroline turned to Octavia, "If you can't bring yourself to skin it, maybe you can talk Ford here into doing it."

Octavia flinched, flinging the knife in Ford's direction.

"Okay then," remarked Caroline. She addressed Ford, "I need about a four-by-four section. You think you can manage?"

She retrieved the stones from Henrietta and began grinding the roots. Dix lay sleeping now, no longer shivering, and Caroline wasn't sure if that was a good sign or not.

ELZI

Fat Man's Squeeze

The man they called Dix had fallen into a deep sleep, no longer crying out in pain or moaning or shivering. The redhead they called Chuck, the Black woman Octavia, the other White woman Henrietta, and Ford—Dix's brother, Elzi gathered—managed to lift the man and get him into the back of a wagon where he seemed to rest comfortably. Once settled, the group left him to be while they joined the rest of the brigade folks to gather up the debris that the twister had flung about. Some men repaired wagons. Women organized the supplies and belongings once more. And children milled about, sometimes helping, sometimes breaking into a game of tag. Elzi watched as three little boys all chased after one, squealing and laughing, and it reminded him of a painful but pivotal point in his childhood.

When Elzi was ten, his Maymee Godwin finally told him the truth about how he came to be in their family. No longer were they able to keep up the fairytale that a great blue heron carried him from Texas to Louisiana and dropped him at the banks of the bayou, that as a toddler, he played amongst the alligators and frogs until one day she and Pa Godwin came upon the beautiful baby boy, cradled in the knobby knees of the ancient cypress where he napped with dozens of purple martins and a swarm of emerald jewel-wing dragonflies hovering and zipping about him, warding off mosquitoes. And that it had been the happiest day of their lives.

That day he had come home, upset from being teased, being called a Letiche. He had always told the other children of his magical arrival via the great blue heron when asked why his ma and pa were White or why he was not. The once-naïve children grew older, crueler, and had taken to calling him Letiche, a half-alligator/half-human child of the swamps. They would chase him, threatening to pull down his trousers and reveal the bony scoots of his certain hidden tail.

He had questioned his parents with fierce adamancy: where had he really come from? who were his blood ma and pa? Sad for the fairytale to end, Edmee told her sweet hurting child the truth. Their neighbor, "vile and ignorant," named Rene Hayes had come upon a chance to trade with an Indian while traveling back to River City from New Orleans. Alongside the old lanky Indian were two mules weighted down with bags of various goods, with piles of ornate clothing and beads draped and hanging. One mule had a large trunk strapped to its back and inside it slept two babies: Elzi and Abe. Rene couldn't image how this Indian came upon any of the goods he peddled, or the babies for that matter—imagined he'd most assuredly "kilt some fancy Negro family"—but that was none of his concern.

Elzi, the least sickly of the two, was part of the deal. Rene made the trade and then promptly handed him over to a woman slave on the Hayes place to raise until old enough to be put to work.

"There were two a you," said Edmee to Elzi, "but we learned your brother was a sickly child. Rene left him with the Indian." She bowed her head and said, "It's likely he perished."

John Godwin had caught wind of the toddler trade and

mentioned it to his wife. Poor Edmee had been barren, always longing, and—unrelated—fiercely opposed to the practice of trafficking humans like common property. When Godwin approached Hayes about the boy, he was told he had always been trouble anyhow, "a sickly mutt not worth the mule I lost for 'em." John Godwin offered the man money for the child to take home to his wife.

Edmee hated this part, having to tell her son he'd been purchased, a commodity not unlike the livestock in their back fields. But it had been necessary. Elzi sat quietly after learning this truth. Delivering the revelation had broken Edmee's heart. But he'd not cried nor gotten mad. He'd not said much of anything for days and his silence frightened her until one day when he asked could he go see his blood ma and pa.

Rene Hayes had mentioned the boys having a relation to an Oliver Dupre out of New Orleans, a freed man who'd gotten word of the trade. Seemed the items draped across the mule's back, along with the children, had belonged to the man's sister. Year before last, she'd made her annual pilgrimage to Texas to gather essential goods for her apothecary and—much to Oliver's surprise—had not returned. He received a letter some months later. She'd fallen in love.

"Abandoned her roots f'dat medicine man," he'd said. He shook his head. "Nevah to return now, it seem." He hung his head in grief. He had bought a necklace off the Indian, her favorite, unable to afford much else. And what was he to do with a toddler anyway?

The Godwins met with Oliver not long after acquiring Elzi. It was important the boy have a real opportunity to take in his family. Mr. Dupre hadn't felt he could raise the child and said as much. He also believed the Godwins had no business trying to raise him either, "but what White folks take a mind to do ain't none a my business."

Once Edmee told Elzi where he had really come from and he'd asked to meet his blood ma and pa, the best the Godwins could do was a close relative, and that was Mr. Oliver Dupre.

Oliver handed over a leather-bound old journal to the ten-year-old, said it was all that remained of his sister's belongings. "I had to sell off evahthang else from her 'pothecary. Got to make ends meet. Can't see no sense in hanging on to all her gris-gris when she ain't nevah gonna come back and tend to it herself. And if you don't mind, I'd like to hang on to the necklace."

Edmee had nodded in earnest agreement. "Of course," she had said.

Elzi stayed silent during the visit. Edmee, sensing he yearned for more, asked of the man, "What was your sister like?"

Mr. Dupre, declining to sit even though the Godwins had insisted he should—"please don't stand on our account"—limped across the wooden floor. Elzi had wondered what was wrong with his leg but didn't dare ask.

His uncle replied, "She was a beautiful woman. A business lady. Momma passed down her mambo ways and Ora Beatrice took a right shine to it. I didn't much care for it. Voodoo don't do nothing but bring us more hate than we already gots to contend wit'. Nobody look too nice at folks like dat. Been chased, spit on, beat for being 'black barbarians' because of dat Voodoo."

Edmee's hand flew to cover her mouth as she shook her head. Mr. Dupre noticed and looked at John.

"I 'pologize. I mean no disrespect to you or yours." He cleared his throat. "But folks took a real likin' to Ora Beatrice. Come from all around for her to cure, cast, and conjure. She done help ladies carry, help spirits to find dey way home, help babies with dey teeth. She done right good, but it sho make some folks unsteady." He hobbled over to a small mantel and picked up a book. He turned and faced Elzi. "This here's her journal. She kept it till—well, I guess till she couldn't." He offered it to Elzi. "I don't rightly know when she lost it, how it came to be in the hands of the lady who brought it to me." He scuffed his foot and gave a little laugh. He shook his head, disbelieving his own thoughts, it seemed. Elzi quietly accepted the book.

"What is it?" asked John.

Oliver Dupre looked the boy right in the eyes and said, "Well, son, your momma's book come to me by ways that I can't quite wrap my thoughts around. A lady come this way a few years back knocking on my door. I answer. She standing there, a big bearded dog pacing and whimpering at her feet. She say she bought the book at dis here 'pothecary a few weeks before. Dis 'pothecary. Ain't no 'pothecary here no mo', not for years. Not since Ora Beatrice took off. So she ain't bought it at the 'pothecary. Not that Ora Beatrice would be selling her personal book no how. But the lady say she did, so maybe she did. I ain't one to argue. Anyways, said she called herself Geneva. Felt the need to tell me she call her dog June or som'in of the sort. I can't rightly see how she thinking I's curious for her dog's name, but I say yessum anyhow. I'm not rightly sure how she come about having my sister's book neither. She seem a kindly woman, and I ain't in no position to question. So I took it and she left. It's my sister's journal. Most of what you'll find is done in her hand, but I believe the lady might've took to using it too. They's some sketching and writing that don't belong to Ora Beatrice in there. Anyways, I believe the boy should have it."

Elzi had learned to read by the time he was four. Edmee had made sure of it, knowing life was hard enough for a Black boy as it were. She wanted him to have every advantage she could think of, and nothing outweighed the power of knowledge. Nothing supplied more access to knowledge than the ability to read. While she was certain to offer him books for his age, when the opportunity arose, he'd often sneak the journal from the trunk in Edmee's bedroom and thumb through the pages, imagining the woman that wrote it. Wondering who she was, what her voice sounded like, how she smelled.

When he turned fifteen, Edmee gave the book to Elzi to keep. He'd read it cover to cover, working through it almost every night since. He'd not understood much of it, the rituals, the lore of some small place his blood parents had made a home, but he still read it. It wasn't until the man named Dix had taken ill from the rattlesnake that he'd seen any benefit from having read its words over the years.

The redhead called Chuck mentioned they were headed west, to Element Dale. Element Dale—the name brought a feeling of home, of memory. The book had mentioned the land of his father's people, nestled in between the hills and the river. A dale where the water had powers, elements to heal. He was certain it was Element Dale and for the first time since beginning his trek to River City to get to Albin, he reconsidered his path.

"You're certainly welcome to come with us," Caroline offered, "being as you helped save our friend's life back there."

"No thank you, Missus. I'm to get to Louisiana. Have some business f' tending to."

She eyed him. "Some soldiering business?"

He looked away, uncomfortable under her stare. He thought about his circumstance and looked down at his boots and his light blue government-issued trousers. Getting to Albin *was* soldier business in a way. He had been on a mission when Albin deserted him, left him for dead, thieved any means he might have used for survival. Elzi's heart rate picked up and his breath quickened at the very thought. It pinched at his heart, a physical heartache.

He answered Caroline, "Yessum, soldiering business."

She replied, "Well, soldier, you've quite a ways to go then. We passed through Louisiana weeks ago." She paused a moment and added, "By wagon."

Elzi nodded his understanding but could not hide his disappointment. He felt truly torn. His pain and confusion about Albin's actions left him exhausted and defeated. Also, he was simply tired and not sure what to do. Technically, he was absent without leave from his military duty, AWOL. Things could go badly for him. He could be court-martialed. What shame his Maymee and Pa Godwin would endure. Probably they all think he's dead. And he had no real means to travel such a distance anyways. No horse, no wagon, no provisions.

He thought a moment about provisions. It seemed he'd been living on adrenaline and fury alone, walking for what felt like weeks fueled by—*by what?* he thought. His head spun, a sudden wave of disorientation. And then her voice brought him to.

"What's your name, sir?"

"Ma'am?" he asked softly.

She eyed him curiously. "I say, what's your name?"

He replied, "Elzi, ma'am. I'm called Elzi Dupre."

The redhead extended her hand. He looked down at it and back up to her face. She gave a quick nod. He reached down and took her hand. She gave it one hard shake. "Caroline Colley. Nice to have met you, Mr. Dupre." She nodded once more and then headed back to the wagon where the group loaded up the last bit of salvaged belongings.

He stepped back and turned to resume his journey east, though his resolve had dwindled. Just ahead the remains of the ordeal of saving the man called Dix littered the ground. Perched nearby, a black vulture hissed, ripping the guts from the snake. Elzi veered his path somewhat, but as he got closer, the bird looked up at him. Elzi stumbled, the sight bringing a weakness to his legs. The black bird's beady eyes followed him, looking him dead in the eyes, its broken beak slightly agape. It spread its ragged wings and hissed once more. A sudden surge of fear pulsed through Elzi's body and the thought of wandering another day alone to face the elements, the truth about Albin, his parents, his nightmares, this damn vulture—it all was just too much. He turned and sprinted back toward the west, away from facing ugly truths that lie in wait for him in the east. He sprinted toward the train of wagons and approached the last where a woman sat atop with her fire-red hair whipping in the wind.

She looked down and smiled. "Hop on, soldier."

ADVENT

. . . we then busied our souls in dreams—reading, writing, or conversing, until warned by the clock of the advent of the true Darkness.

—Edgar Allan Poe

JERYL LARSON

September 20, 2023
Element Dale, Texas

Today Lucillia Baldwin invited me inside. The rain was blowing up on the porch in sheets and we had no choice. Well, I suppose she could have just turned me away—she has before—but she did not.

"Well, don't just stand there like a turkey waitin' for someone smarter to call you in."

Oh, she has a way with words, that one. She waves me in, in her irritated gesture I've come to no longer wince at. The cabin is oddly tidy, nothing like the yard. Bookshelves line the wall to the right holding everything from Mark Twain to Donna Tartt. The area is basically all one space, small but clean and minimal. When you walk in, you're standing in an area between the living room and kitchen. The kitchen is on the left. It has lower cabinets and open shelving above. If you're standing in the front entrance, an old refrigerator sits just to the left of the front door, and across from it sits a small table with two chairs. The living room is to the right with a wall of bookshelves, a recliner, a sofa, and a coffee table. A potbelly stove sits in the far-right back corner, its large pipe exiting up through the low ceiling. I spot no photographs whatsoever, and if you turn and face the front door, just left of it hangs the only painting that adorns any wall, slightly askew: a landscape piece depicting the river with a wooden bridge spanning across it.

"This piece is nice. Is this local?" I ask her. I want to straighten it badly but refrain.

"That's the Barron River Bridge. You crossed it on your way here," she replies.

I do not recognize that bridge. "How long ago was that bridge replaced?" I ask assuming that it had been.

She thinks for a moment. "Years. I don't know. I wish they hadn't. Elzi built that bridge . . . in a roundabout way."

I wonder how a person "round about" builds anything. I walk and scan the wall of books while she pulls down two glasses from the shelf above the kitchen sink. She has a fantastic collection of books, really. I wonder how she's gotten them. I can't imagine her ordering them, what with no internet or computer. Well, I assume no internet or computer. I'm certain she doesn't use email so I can't imagine her filling an Amazon cart. Does someone drive her to town? Does Element Dale even have a proper bookstore?

"Little lady named Rosalie used to drive out from time to time. Her momma works at the library next town over, Waterly. She would occasionally take me to pick out a few. My favorite is when they'd have their book sale to clear space on the shelves. Pay five dollars and they give you a sack to fill as you please. I'd buy my favorites so that I can reread them as I fancy."

I ask, "What are you reading now?"

"Oh, something by Kayen Rice. *The Theory of Misery*," she says.

After scanning her collection, I notice that the entire bottom shelf is nothing but notebooks. I slide one out. The cover has January 1967 written across it. I open to a random page:

—that the Tomb of Ora B. Dupre—a powerful nineteenth century Voodoo priestess, whose remains were supposedly interred in the Silas

Creek Cemetery—marks the first star of Baron Comb's veve. This would place one Gate outside the city. Then there's one at the crossing of Westworth Avenue and Oak Street. The other stars in the veve mark tombs or monuments in the nearby streets.

The order in which the gates are opened is also of key significance. Approached incorrectly, the gates can allow dangerous spirits to enter the world of the living, dragging the unwary seeker—body and soul— back with them to the land of the dead. A traditional rhyme amongst—

Ms. Baldwin gently pulls the notebook from my hands. "I've got years of journals to pull from, all me just a-bitching and a-moaning about these simpleton motherfuckers. Years of observing this town. And then of course I wrote down every story Elzi and Mutty Sid ever shared with me. In fact, I've got volumes and volumes of stories."

"*Mut-ty?*"

"Yes, Mutty. Mutty Sid."

"Oh god." Someone named their poor child a mongrel dog. Ew.

She says, "He's who introduced Rosalie to me—the gal who used to run me to Waterly to get books sometimes."

"Mmm. I see. And how long have you been keeping journals?"

She says she supposed since she'd learned to write. "Damn-near forever."

"And these journals," I ask, "these are just your thoughts, or are they stories?"

She turns away and scans the upper shelves of her books as if deep in thought. Nonchalantly she replies, "Oh . . . thoughts, stories, poems. This and that."

WALKER

Element Dale, Texas

Birds whistled and chirped, happy and relieved in the trees above where Walker woke. The sun hadn't yet come into view, but the air was crisp and the skies clear. Remnants of last night's storm littered the ground and drops of water pattered down onto the fallen leaves with each light breeze. The whispering creek ran a little louder, a little fuller. Walker stood, soaked to the bone, and stretched. A cup of hot coffee on this cool morning came into his mind. He looked around, taking in where he had spent his night. His bag rested up against a pile of stones—actually, a pile by design, he noticed. Another pile, just a foot or so tall, had been erected nearby. And another. His eyes followed along the green paths between the piles until they became erect flat stones of slate and sandstone. He picked up his bag and walked over to one.

Etched into the surface of the gravestone, it read: EDWARD HARTLEY—*born Dec 5, 1818, killed Mar 2, 1857.* He approached another: LITTLE BESSIE EDDINGTON—*born Jan 2, 1865, became an angel July 4, 1875, aged 10 years.* At the far end stood a fairly new-looking tomb. He made his way to it. It stood some five feet in height, a massive block of a type of cast limestone concrete. On its face read two inscriptions: ELMER NELSON—*born Sept 16, 1869, was killed by lightning while plowing corn July 7, 1884.* Walker shuttered. He'd plowed corn his entire life. Hadn't once thought of dying by strike. ANNA OLEN—*Feb 1, 1816 to Dec 10, 1884, R.I.P.* He continued walking, noticing how the grave markers varied from rudimentary piles of stones, some etched, some not, wooden crosses, erect tablet stones, a few tall obelisks, and of course the one vault tomb.

He continued walking through the graveyard, following a natural path that led him out of the cemetery and to a trail. The trail winded through a thicket of pecans and oaks until it finally opened up, revealing a muddy road, rutted from the wheels of wagons. He walked just beside the road in the grass for what seemed only a mile or so until he came upon a boy on a horse. He looked to Walker to be about ten or eleven years old. Walker nodded. The boy returned the nod, staring a bit. Walker imagined he looked rougher than he'd ever looked and wished for his cabin. He'd enjoyed the thrill of dancing with the revenuers, keeping out one step ahead, but in the end he'd lost most everything that brought him any comfort. His bed. Morning coffee. A swig of shine anytime he fancied.

He turned back to the boy and hollered, "Where 'bouts is this?"

The boy turned around on his horse to face him. He held up a hand to block the morning sun from his eyes and hollered back, "Elemdale, sir!"

Walker nodded and the boy turned and continued on.

Walker walked south alongside the road where it curved to the west and led him to a wide wooden bridge that crossed the river. Just past the bridge stood a wooden sign with *Welcome to Element Dale* carved into it, fancy-like with the first letters of each word large and curling. A sense of relief came over him and he allowed a smile to stretch across his face for the first time in days. He had no clue where he was going or what he was going to do in this town, but he'd finally made it.

He walked along the main road through town and took it all in. The man back in Fort Worth told him the town was young, yet he'd still pictured a little more than what he saw, which was only a few houses, a general store, a butcher, a church—and there, about as out of place as anything could be, towered a great building some many stories high and spanning enough space for three or four businesses. Walker continued past, eyeing the grandness and its arcade portico that faced the main street. People bustled about its grounds, working atop an edifice of scaffolding, hammering and sawing. Two men climbed twin ladders, dragging a banner up the rungs. Walker paused to watch as they stretched it across the top of the second-floor entrance. The banner read *The Baldwin Hotel. Grand Reopening Soon!* From the many first- and second-floor windows, men stripped wood from those that were once boarded up. Masons stacked and mortared bricks. He rounded the corner, following the great arched base level, to see a young couple, seemingly newly arrived, unloading a wagon into the hotel's service entrance. He watched as the man and woman struggled with a large trunk.

"Here!" he called. "Let me." He sprinted across the street, dropped his bindle, and took the place of the woman. "Pardon me," he nodded. She gratefully gave up her end of the heavy trunk.

"Thank you, kindly," the man said. "Seems we got more work than help on our hands."

The two men carried the cumbersome trunk. Walker had never seen anything like it—the entrance descended, down an underground path, out of sight of visitors. They sat the trunk down in the dank, dark area.

"I'll get someone to help me from here. I do thank you, sir." His voice slightly echoed in the space. The man extended his hand. "Lawton Phillips."

Walker wiped his hand on his pant leg and accepted the gesture. "Walker Westberry." They shook and returned to the wagon, back out into the light of day.

Walker inquired, "You working here?"

"You could say that," replied Lawton. He pulled a handkerchief from his breast pocket and wiped his forehead. "My wife and I—though I apologize as I'm uncertain as to where she's run off to—are the new proprietors, tasked with the renovations and reopening." He looked up, his hand shielding his eyes from the glare of the sun. "And I fear the prospect that we may have bitten off a bit more than we can chew."

Walker nodded. The two men stood gazing up at the towering structure. From the front, it appeared to take up an entire city block. From where the men stood now, around its northwest side, Walker could see the architecture was designed to fool the eye, give the appearance of a grandiosity greater than what materialized.

Walker said, "I suspect things will conclude as they should." He looked around and took in the meager surrounding buildings. "Seems you's expecting folks to make their way here." He couldn't hide the doubt in his voice.

"Indeed. That is the plan."

Walker asked, "Something special come with a room?"

Lawton's eyebrows furrowed. "Special, sir?"

"Special. As in I ain't seen no real reason folks might incline to make this their destination as it were, being as"—he extended his arm out toward the main road with the few various businesses—"this is all of what's to entice them."

Lawton nodded. "Ah, yes. The hotel itself *is* the destination. We plan to create such an attraction out of the hotel itself that it will put Element Dale on the map. A place that draws the wealthy and self-regarding."

"And what might that draw be? From the hotel."

Lawton grinned. "You said Westberry; is that right?"

Walker nodded, now wondering if he should have given a false name. A slew of other considerations followed: what lengths would the revenuers go to, to find him; what should he tell people of himself; what work might come of this town; what was to come of his new life. The quickness of anxiety spread about him, something he wasn't accustomed to feeling. Adrenaline rushes, yes. But pure worrisome anxiety, this was a first.

Lawton continued, "And what, sir, drew you?"

The question caught him. What had drawn him? Nothing had. It was the push from the mountain, not the pull from wherever he now stood. He cleared his throat.

"I am a beverage craftsman."

Lawton nodded, curious.

"Uh, that is to say"—Walker stumbled on his words for a moment —"to say—to say my specialty is—is . . . Coca-Cola."

Lawton's eyebrows raised.

"Inventor." Walker sniffed.

Lawton did not reply but allowed the silence to burden Walker until he felt compelled to continue. "Well, I been in the crafting business my whole life. My granddaddy showed me all he know'd. Then I came about the idea of Coca-Cola back in Georgia, but then my notion was snatched, leaving me destitute and someone else rich, you see."

Lawton's eyes narrowed. "So you know Pemberton?"

Walker scratched his neck. He'd been sure not to mention Dr Pepper, being as he figured local Texans would know better. Now it seemed the choice to mention any branded beverage was a poor one. He took a stab at it anyway.

"I do."

Lawton nodded. "I'm not detecting the Georgian drawl."

Walker ignored the comment, set on backing his lie. "But if the man really wanted to be rich, he'd devise a way to sell to the individual and not the shop."

"Oh?" Lawton questioned.

"Bottle the beverage in a way that a man can carry it away. Treat it like a luxury you can take home and not have to belly up to the counter at the drugstore. Keep the bellying up to the saloons."

Lawton replied, "Not a bad idea." He thought a moment. "And Pemberton declined, you say?"

"He declined. But not before he pushed me out, collecting my ideas for all his own."

Lawton frowned. "And this would be Charles you speak of, yes?"

"Uh . . . yeah. Charles," Walker nodded.

"Shame about John."

Walker continued to nod, the conversation trapping him, suspicion thickening the air. Claiming to hail from Georgia had clearly been a foolish choice, and Lawton's now exaggerated Georgian drawl said as much.

Lawton asked, "And what, pray tell, happened to your face?"

Walker touched his face. To say he had been attacked by an owl, he could not. He'd not only invented Coca-Cola but also was the recipient of a rare owl attack? It was all a bit outlandish, he could see. He was eager to wrap up this conversation. And his appearance, that of a drowned rat, suddenly made him self-conscious. Until he settled on a sound backstory, he figured it best he kept talk of himself to a minimum.

"A brush with nature," he replied.

The two men stood, secretly sizing one another up until Mrs. Phillips returned with a welcomed interruption. "Thank you, kindly, sir. We've found ourselves short on manpower, it seems. And so your help was all too timely. To think"—she scoffed—"me . . . . carrying cargo." She laughed, slightly uncomfortable, taking in the sight of Walker, dirty and damp.

He watched her eyes and could see she found him handsome. Women often did. Uniquely handsome with his cotton-blonde hair, sun-kissed skin, and icy blue eyes. But he was filthy and shabbily dressed and wet and could sense this gave her pause.

"I'd be happy to help any way I can," he offered. "New to town, however, and believe I might should first be getting my bearings."

"You've a place to stay?" she asked.

"No, ma'am. Not as of yet," he replied.

She nodded then gave Lawton a quick glance. Lawton extended his hand.

"Well, Mr. Westberry, it was mighty fine to meet you."

Walker shook his hand and then tipped his hat to Claire.

"Mighty fine, indeed," he replied.

He could see her blush slightly. He nodded to Lawton, fetched his bindle, and then continued on, uncertain as to where he should go. The buildings were but a few and ended not too far from the hotel on the main thoroughfare. He walked past the supply mercantile and took a right. Just ahead, the boy on the horse who he'd seen once before was dismounting in front of a large two-story house. He approached, calling out to the boy.

"Yello again, young man."

The boy grinned upon seeing him once more. A gate stood between the road and the property, though no fence flanked it. Just a freestanding pedestrian gate with two signs affixed to it. The top read *Nelson Boarding House* and the bottom, *Nelson Shipping and Post*. Walker called out to the boy once more.

"This a place to stay?"

"Yessir," replied the boy. He pointed up to the front door. "Momma'll hep ya."

Just then a woman, worn and haggard, stepped out onto the front porch. She hollered out, "Thirty-five cents if ya got it."

Walker nodded and opened the gate to enter. He could have very well just stepped around it, but the gate compelled him to pass through. He stepped up on the porch. The woman had already gone inside, but the boy held the door open for him. Walker tipped his hat at the boy. "Sir." The boy grinned, letting go of the door as soon as Walker cleared it. The spring pulled it to, slamming it hard.

"Goddammit, Samuel!" hollered the woman, who was now

standing behind a small counter to the left. "How many nights?" she asked Walker, a cigarette dangling from her lips.

He thought a moment, then dug through his savings. He slapped a few dollars down on the counter. "Let's start with a week."

CAROLINE

Element Dale, Texas

Three wagons carrying Buford and Henrietta Artope, a sickly Dixon Artope, Caroline Colley, Octavia Kassoula, Elzi Dupre, and what provisions survived the tornado broke away from the brigade just past the town of Waterly. It had been a long journey, and an eventful one at that, and Caroline was none too shy to let out of whoop of joy when they crossed the bridge and spotted the sign.

"Welcome to Element Dale, Dix!" she hollered out. Dix laid in the back of her wagon, the group deciding Caroline would be the best person to handle any type of medical predicament should one arise. "You hear that?" she continued. "We made it." She turned to a sweaty and sickly Dix, stretched out as best he could in the back of her wagon, Octavia now driving the supply wagon since the split in Waterly. "We'll get you situated in no time."

Dix forced a smile. It had been touch and go and at times Caroline was certain he'd not survive. She allowed him sleep whenever possible. The times where pain and nausea overcame him, she did her best to talk him through it or even distract him. She shouted out stories from the driver's position to the back of the wagon where he laid under the torn canvas. Stories about anything that came to mind. Stories about her and her sister, Minnie, as little girls. Stories about getting whooped by Octavia for a practical joke she'd played on her: removing every canned good from the root cellar and replacing them with her jarred bug collection. Stories about her imaginary friend, Mable, and how she'd missed her, that she hadn't seen her in quite some time since—she wanted to say since she started getting her visits from Davis, but she couldn't bring herself to say as much. *How crazy would I sound?* she wondered. *A woman missing her childhood imaginary friend who'd been booted out by visits from her dead husband.* Caroline had gone on and on with her stories, shouting out into the clouds it seemed, into a void. However, when she paused at the idea of Davis, the moment of silence must have roused Dix because she heard him softly inquire "Since?"

She shook off any thoughts of Davis, glad to know that it'd been weeks since she'd last seen him. She replied firmly, "Since I grew up, I s'pose. You feeling okay? We should be there in no time."

"I'll make it," he replied weakly.

"Well, that's all we can ask of ya." She began delivering a commentary of the sights as they passed. "Town's got a nice little bridge over the river. Not much of a river, but a river nonetheless. And a right nice welcome sign. Then I see here a house or two. They got a little butcher shop. Oh, and of course a church. I know just as soon as we get settled, we can talk their flock into clucking on over and laying some hands on you, Dix."

She waited for a snide comeback but was met with nothing but silence.

"No takers?" She gave it a moment. "All right, then."

Dix finally replied, "Maybe so."

Caroline gave a little half laugh. "Maybe so. In all seriousness, soon as we get you settled, I certainly don't mind helping you in any way you need. I don't imagine there's gonna be any doc 'round here, being as you *are* the doc now. So you just tell me how best I can care for your leg, and I promise to take direction. No fussing outta me this time."

Dix said, "Caroline, I certainly do appreciate all you've done. Truly. I may have died out there. I don't know how on earth what you did saved me, but I thank you for it."

"It wasn't me, Dix."

"True." He replied. "The hand of God does indeed guide in the strangest of ways."

"God?" she retorted. "Ha! Maybe the hand of the man laying back there with ya. That's who you really need to be thanking."

Her remark led only to silence.

She thought a moment and then said, "I believe that one day, in our lifetime even, people will see people for their hearts and minds. The flesh will be of no concern. And every man will help the other and thank the other as equals." She paused then said again to herself, "One day."

"Ho-ly shit," she said. "You guys have got to see this."

"Everything okay, ma'am?" asked Elzi. He'd been seated next to Dix. He'd leaned up against the corner and slept deeply most of the way.

"Take a look for yourself," she replied.

Dix pulled back a bit of the canvas that had torn from the frame during the storm. Ahead, just to the right stood a massive building with people all around it. A great banner hung just above its main entrance. *The Baldwin Hotel—Grand Reopening Soon!* it read.

Caroline asked in awe, "What on earth do you suppose an almost town like this is doing with a hotel like *that*?" She took a deep breath and let it out. Something about the outlandish existence of the building sitting smack dab in the middle of a blip of a town lifted her. It epitomized new beginnings and big dreams. Something she was quite on board with. She was finally rid of Melroy, of its hauntings, and for the first time in a long time she could breathe.

The wagons pulled up to the main entrance. A voice hollered out from a window above. Caroline looked up to see Claire Phillips giving a grand wave. "Welcome to Elemdale!" she hollered down with a broad smile. "We're so happy y'all finally made it!"

Caroline waved back. She had mixed feelings about Claire and Lawton. She understood their position back at the train station a few weeks earlier. Octavia wasn't anyone to them personally. Even so, she'd secretly judged them, and quite harshly. They should have stood their ground with the rest of the group. Change would never come to this country so long as people like them weren't willing to be inconvenienced by rebutting the prejudiced acts against the oppressed.

A man with cotton-white hair and the most striking eyes Caroline had ever seen came out from around the side of the building and motioned for the wagons to pull around. As they did so, Caroline could see that the drive turned back into the hotel, descended, and disappeared into the darkness.

"We'll a-get you unloaded here. I reckon the ladies would like to take a look around," the blue-eyed man said.

Ford replied, "Actually, sir, we have my brother who needs help before we tend to any unloading. Let's get him settled in first. He's quite ill."

Lawton Phillips appeared from the darkness of the descending side entrance. "Hello all! So happy to see we've made it safe and sound!" He clapped his hands together and rubbed them vigorously. "Let's get y'all unloaded, shall we."

The blue-eyed man replied, "They say they needing hep with a sickly man first." He followed up, "sir."

Lawton furrowed his brow, "Oh no." He quickly scanned the wagons. "Buford, don't tell me. Your brother's fallen ill?"

Ford replied, "Snake bite."

Lawton and the blue-eyed, white-haired man flinched with faces of disbelief.

"Snake bite? How on earth?" Lawton asked.

Ford replied, "It's a yarn for another time." He hopped down from the wagon, stretching his back and groaning. "For now, if you've got space ready for us, I'd like to go ahead and get Dix settled in. Caroline here will look after him."

He turned to Caroline and appended, "With the good doctor's guidance, of course."

Caroline, now standing in the driver's seat, made a small sarcastic curtsy and replied, "Of course."

The handsome man approached her wagon and held out a hand. "Walker Westberry. Hep ya down?"

She took his hand and jumped down. He was much taller than she. Standing face to face, she immediately blushed. "I—I—I've got some salve for that."

Confused, he asked, "For?"

"Your face."

He reached up and touched the scratch that spanned from his forehead straight down to the bottom of his cheek. "Ah, ain't nothing."

She nodded, still standing just inches from him. She thought him extremely attractive, but something made her uncomfortable. Plenty of men had approached her, attractive and unsightly alike, but never had one made her feel unsteady. She could not pinpoint just why this man did.

She said, "Dix is in back here." She broke away and rounded the wagon. "Mr. Dupre's been fine comp'ny, watching over him." She hollered back to Lawton. "Maybe we could put him up for a night or two, just until"—she found Dix sitting up, trying to hoist his splinted leg from the bedroll where it rested. She turned and scanned the immediate area then turned back to the wagon. "Where'd he go?"

"Where'd who go?" grunted Dix.

She sighed. "Don't get cute on me now."

Walker, Ford, and Lawton came around to the back of the wagon, their presence naturally pushing Caroline to the side. She looked around the streets. No sign of the soldier. She then walked back around to the front. He could have been taking in the place from the main street view. She could not find him anywhere. Slightly deflated, she walked back to the wagons. Henrietta had gone inside and Octavia waited on the sidewalk.

"Where you been, Miss Caroline?"

Caroline shook her head. "I can't believe he just took off. Well, I sort of can. I don't imagine the Phillipses would have been too interested in putting him up, but still, not even a goodbye, fuck off, nothing."

"Miss Caroline?"

Caroline continued scanning the street and buildings across the way, seeking him out.

Octavia said, "Look a me, chile." She took Caroline's face into her hands and gently turned her head until they stood eye to eye. Concern blanketed Octavia's face and just then Caroline knew something wasn't right. She tried to crane her head back to the street, but Octavia held her face tightly. "Look a me, Caroline. We made it. We finally here. Melroy, Mista Colley, it all in de past, behind us now. No need to bring it along wit' you. You safe. You hear?"

Caroline nodded against Octavia's grip.

"Good." She placed a hand atop Caroline's head and gave it a little press. "Now let us see 'bout our tings."

As the two unloaded the wagon, Caroline asked, "Your ride go okay from Waterly?"

"Fine. Fine," Octavia replied. She pulled out the bedroll Dix had been using and subtly shook her head at the blood.

Caroline said, "You know, Octavia, I was certain he wasn't gonna make it. And if he didn't—" she stopped, unable to speak for the knot tightening in her throat.

Octavia stopped what she was doing. "Yes, chile?" She could see great anguish in Caroline's face.

Caroline took a deep breath and shook her head, slinging any threat of tears away. "And if he didn't, that'd made what Davis had been telling me all along true. That death will soon pay a visit. And he'll bring Mother Nature along to—"

Octavia cut her off. "But it not true, Miss Caroline. It not true.

Mista Dixon, he fine. He might have no good leg from now on, but he fine enough. He not dead no how." She handed over Dix's carpet bag. "Take dis to he. Gwine need it fa certain."

Caroline held the bag at her chest. She asked, "What do you make of that Mr. Westberry?"

Octavia continued pulling bags from the wagon.

Caroline said, "I can't explain it, but he gives me the willies."

Octavia halfheartedly replied, "Trust no mistake. When bush shake, tear out. Here, take dis too." She plopped the bedroll atop the bag Caroline was holding and headed inside. She hollered out over her shoulder, "Come now."

DIX

Element Dale, Texas

Tattered and weak with his leg throbbing, Dix woke to the sounds of bottles clinking in the room that would be his home for the next six months. The residents of Element Dale had been left to their own devices when it came to dealing with illness and injury, having no doctor or druggist. Serious events sometimes drew help from the neighboring town of Waterly, but rarely was that doctor available for anything shy of the threat of death, and for a hefty compensation to boot. But that was soon to change. The Phillipses had offered Dr. Dixon Artope a space on the lower level of the hotel to serve as his clinic, office, and sleeping quarters rent free for six months while the hotel's grand reopening was underway. In exchange for a contract as the hotel's concierge medical practitioner, a draw for both guests and townspeople alike, he'd have a place to live and a place to establish himself as doctor to the townspeople until he acquired one of his own.

Caroline stood at the far end of the room, unloading his medical trunk and lining bottles of tinctures and elixirs along a shelf mounted on the wall. She hummed as she worked, quite off key, Dix thought. She seems content enough, a nice break from her typical swearing and bullheaded nature. He watched the woman, her hair beautiful and fire red like the leaves of the sweet gum tree in autumn. She turned and noticed him awake.

"Well, having your own practice doesn't seem like it's everything it's cracked up to be if you're the only patient, huh?"

He gave a halfhearted smirk. "And it is said about the sweet gum, in all its beauty, the only good sweet gum tree is a dead one."

Caroline rebuked without hesitation, "And what would Mother Nature's autumn extravaganza be without the Georgian sweet gum? Boring."

"Sure, if one considers the litter of prickly goblin balls it dumps at will an antidote to boring."

She replied, "If you refer to the tree's fruits that our brilliant mother of nature employs to concoct medicines and salves to cure a variety of ailments and treat wounds, why yes. Speaking of, how's your ass cheek holding up." She covered her mouth to hide a giggle.

Dix, now sitting up rather askew, pulled himself back as to lean upon the headboard but then settled on his left side and elbow. "It's holding up." He paused. "And I've you to thank, I suppose."

She waved him off. She held up a bottle of elixir. "Not sure how you plan to arrange all these. They'll have to do here for now."

"I'm sure it'll be fine," he grunted, trying to find a position of comfort. "They all survive the twister?"

"Indeed." She held up his copy of Joseph Maclise's *Surgical Anatomy*. "This has been a doozie."

"Oh yeah?" he inquired. "Some fascinating illustrations, yes?"

"Not bad for a picture book, I guess. Though somewhat limited."

"Limited?" Dix asked incredulously.

"Well yeah. I mean, I was hoping to get a little insight into what I's dealing with, with your snake bite there. Not too much mentioned on the buttock and thigh area. Now, had that serpent got hold of your manhood, seems only then would there be any real guidance. Pages and pages and pages about the ole jingling johnny."

Dix frowned. "Truly. It is these moments that the name Chuck suits you far greater than Caroline."

She paused then huffed out a laugh. "You're not wrong." She asked, "You sleep okay?"

"Afraid to say it sometimes, but yes, like the dead."

"Good." She asked, "And the little girl's not bothering ya?"

"Little girl?"

"Yes. The Phillipses' girl, I presume. She seems to be a nocturnal babe, prefers practicing her caroling up and down the halls come bedtime."

"I don't recall the Phillipses having a child at the station, but either way, no. I believe the consistent doses of morphine you've administered have made my days and nights rather fuzzy . . . and my pain tolerable. For that, I am most grateful."

Caroline replied, "You're welcome. Though I haven't touched your morphine."

Dix's head slightly tilted.

"I mean, not since right after the rattlesnake got ya. I wasn't about to cut you open without it."

Dix winced and reached back, gently placing a hand on his dressed wound.

"And once you get up and at 'em, you're gonna want to get you some more. Used it all."

Dix's voice rose. "All?"

"Well yeah. I needed some for your leg and some to just knock you out. You can get more, right?"

"I'll have to," he replied. "And I've had none since, you say?"

Caroline flashed a wide grin. She walked over and picked up the dirty Bible from the bedside table and sat at the edge of the bed. She placed the book on his lap. "Nope. I've used the remedies Octavia and I created for our book. I'd say I've been quite pleased." She slapped the Bible. "And Ford's been real nice to come read to you. Seems you haven't missed a day of your catch-as-catch-can dissemination of the word of God."

Dix flushed and snatched the Bible, annoyed at her newfound knowledge of his quirk.

"And you can thank me for that too." She nodded toward the Bible. "What are the odds? A snake and a Bible at the heart of a squeeze." She stood up and returned to the trunk and pulled out the remaining bottles of medicine, placing them on the shelf. "At some point, I'll need to get those stitches out. But I'll let you be the judge of when, being the doctor and all." She turned back to him and gave a wink.

The woman had a way of getting under his skin. There was no doubt about that. Even so, deep down, Dix was grateful she had been there. There at the wagons. There these last days and hours he'd seemed to have lost. And there now. She'd saved his life. Saved his Bible. Saved his leg. For these things, he would force himself to forever be in her debt, as difficult as he knew that would be.

Dix spent the next few days with more clarity. The fuzzy nature of Caroline's natural painkilling remedy had passed. He guided her to care for his wound while face down and, at times, humiliated. She'd listened, sometimes argued, but ultimately gotten the job done. And done well. Little by little she revealed what Dix was starting to recognize as a brilliant mind, even if riddled with strange "intuitions" and sharp defenses. The two had plenty of time together and he'd come to finally let his guard down and asked about her method of treatment while on the brigade, how she'd known what to do and, more importantly, where on earth she concocted such a remedy.

Complete exhaustion overcame Caroline's face at this question. He could see she'd been asked this before, that it was a touchy subject that brought about her natural defensive propensities.

"I don't know how else to say it. *I* didn't know what to do." She drew out the "I" in her statement with great emphasis. "Octavia and I have worked hard on our remedies book over the years. And I suppose my intimate acquaintance with most plant life was surely a big advantage out there. But never did we work on no remedy for a rattlesnake bite to the butt."

"Okay?" Dix nodded and scratched his chin.

"Okay is right," she shot back. "You all were there—well, you get a pass I guess, being as you was about passed out from pain and poison all at once. But we all were there, and I know things have changed and all after the war, but really they haven't."

Dix furrowed his brows, lost and starting to regret his inquiry.

She continued, "We got a man, a soldier no less, sticking his neck out for us and all we see is his skin. That man saved your life, Dix. And I know you couldn't have known what was going on, but it's the goddamned truth."

Dix winced at her choice of words. She lacked such reverence for the Lord and it annoyed him. He thought for a moment and replied gently, "Henri mentioned you were married."

"What's that a damn thing to do with this, Dix?" she barked.

"And that he passed."

Caroline sat down, her eyes fixed on her knees, her hands wringing in her lap.

"And that you"—he paused, choosing his words carefully —"struggle with his absence."

Her eyes met his. "It ain't his absence I struggle with, Dr. Artope."

He knew her meaning. The rigid martinet that made him the disciplined man and doctor he'd become wriggled within, wanting so badly to prod her, coerce her to say it out loud, that she hallucinates, that her mind is unreliable. He did not. For once, he gave greater weight to the fragility of emotion than the certainty of fact and truth and science—and let it go.

She stood to leave, and he apologized for pushing her, for inserting himself into her personal business. When she approached the door, she stopped and turned back to him.

"Thing is, it's hard to know what's true sometimes. My husband warned me. Warned me about you even. Well, I didn't know he was talking about you at the time, but he was, I guess. True to his nature when he was alive, he exaggerated a tad. That's the politician in him. You *were* poisoned. He told me this much would be true. But he also told me you wouldn't survive it." She looked down at her feet and Dix could see she was fighting off some type of deep pain. He wasn't quite sure what to say to her. She looked back up, tears in her eyes. "You must think I'm insane."

He thought momentarily of playfully tossing out "Finally, something we both can agree on" but thought better of it. He did think she was a bit off her rocker. Despite that, he was starting to see Caroline Colley in a different light. He was starting to see that under the harsh and bullheaded exterior was a woman with quick wit and ambition and boundless knowledge with the heart of a doctor. He'd never say as much, but he believed it true. He also believed that her mind was oftentimes polluted by a painful history that left her disarranged.

He said, "I don't think you're insane. I think you're just . . . haunted by your trauma, is all."

Like always, whatever he'd said somehow rubbed her wrong. But everything did, he'd come to learn. He saw in her face that she had something to say, words to rebut, but she said nothing. She held her tongue and then gave a half smile and left him there. An improvement, no doubt, he thought.

Where she'd been standing, just to the left of the door, hung a frame. She had framed and hung his certificate from the Southern Physio-Eclectic School of Medicine. *Whereas Dixon Artope has pursued the required course of study and has presented satisfactory evidence of a sufficient degree of knowledge to entitle him to the Degree of Doctor of Medicine.* It was signed by Dr. Eddington Locke, now jobless and a laughingstock in the medical community. The certificate was a slap in the face. He sighed. He would not have a framed license from the Regular Board of Medical Examiners proclaiming him duly licensed to practice medicine. No board would ever allow him to sit, no matter his knowledge or skills. The school had cursed him, branded him a fraud.

"Damned school," he mumbled under his breath and flung the blanket from his lap. He grabbed his Bible, closed his eyes, and opened it at random. His finger slid down the page until an urge stopped him. He opened his eyes and read the words his finger indicated: *He that walketh uprightly walketh surely: but he that perverteth, his ways shall be known.*

"Well hell." He slammed the book shut.

ELZI

Element Dale, Texas

Elzi walked through the town taking in the progress. The massive hotel had people crawling all over it, hammering, mortaring, sawing. He thought the building odd, out of place in the otherwise lowly town. Along the main street were a few businesses, a church, but mostly the streets were dirt, and outside of the main area, the streets vanished into fields or wooded areas and a few homesteads.

He rounded the corner past the supply mercantile to see a yellow two-story house. He thought it beautiful with its long porch that spanned the front and charming dormers on the second floor. A lone gate stood between the street and the yard, the house's sentry as there was no fence flanking it. Continuing past, he followed the road until it faded and sprouted into grass. He high-stepped through the tall grass uncaring as to his destination. He had walked for so long, for so far, had been through so much. The last days and weeks had been a blur. Like a dream. He thought back to the desert land, the heat and thirst, the dying men and animals. The desperation of it all. A flash of memory hit him, forcing his heart to skip. Flies buzzing and bouncing around Jasper as he sat, leaned up against that mesquite bush. He shook off the vision, of the knowing that he had left him there. An image of Albin walking in the distance replaced it. Elzi's heart skipped once more and then quickened. He pictured Albin at camp sitting beside him at the fire, holding Ora's book, working the pencil, tracing his letters. Elzi's heart pounded as he considered his plan. He'd been so angry, so certain, determined to get back to Louisiana. He'd been on a path. And now what the hell was he doing here? What had possessed him to hop on a wagon heading the opposite direction? He needed a horse.

Defeat and confusion filled him. He had deserted his post and lost his best friend. He had lost the book, the only tie to his natural roots. A fallen limb blocked his path and he kicked it, somehow missing. He stumbled, losing his balance momentarily, and that fueled his frustration. He quickened his pace. The terrain soon became an entanglement of briars and bushes and trees. He forced himself through, working out his frustrations. Within a few minutes, the thicket spat him out at the edge of a creek. He turned left and followed the creek, thinking and fuming as he walked. Where he was going, he had no idea. Finally he dropped to the ground, his chest heaving with exhaustion, his head spinning, and he laid back flat in the grass.

The sky was clear and blue, the air crisp. Not a cloud in sight. He watched as the amber leaves of the trees above gently rustled in the breeze and then broke loose, flipping and spinning their way to the ground. He laid there and listened to his own breath. Then when the heat of fury subsided, worry filled the spaces in his heart where the anger had been. *What will Maymee and Pa think? Their chosen son, a deserter. Not a Deviser but a Deserter.*

Elzi rolled onto his side and sat back up. He looked up and down the creek canopied by arching russet- and amber-leaved trees. The place was tranquil, filled with whispers of nature. He nestled in the buffalograss, its soft, thin sprigs a vibrant green. He turned to take in the space around him, noticing the anger and worry retreating. He crawled forward and dipped his hands into the water and splashed his face, leaving his skin cool. He leaned over and splashed his face again, this time catching a glimpse of something above in the reflection. He looked up to the sky and spotted a bird and watched as it soared, coming to land in a nearby oak. An owl. He thought it odd—an owl out in that hour of light. He splashed his face once more and then moved back into sitting, then resting back on his elbows, his head tilted back and eyes closed. Water dripped down his face, tickling as it pooled in his ears. He took a deep breath in through his nose and gently released it from his mouth, collecting himself. He opened his eyes.

To his left a great weeping willow stood, its long, feathered branches sweeping the ground. Behind him to his right, the grass wended through oaks, cedars, and hackberries. His heart slowed, calmed, and familiarity warmed him, as if he'd been here before. Déjà vu, Albin's ma used to call it. His eyes followed the grassy trail to a pile of stones. A few feet from it sat another pile. And another. He heard a sound. Rhythmic shuffle-stomps mingled with the fluctuating gusts of wind. Footsteps. The sound grew louder, and for a moment, he imagined a tall thin Indian with a crooked nose approaching him where he sat. A twig snapped and he scrambled up to his feet. It was the redheaded woman, the one they called Chuck.

"Elzi, right?" she asked. Her smile was broad and confident and Elzi thought her eyes were beautiful, the color of cognac.

He replied, "Yessum."

She nodded and looked around. "Beautiful 'round here."

"Yessum."

She turned and cocked her thumb toward the rock piles. "You fond of cemeteries?"

Elzi raised his eyebrows then leaned back slightly, taking a better look at his surroundings. He spotted a cross or two and an erect tablet stone, a grave marker. He nodded studiedly and said, "Huh. Well, I s'pose I ain't got nothing ginst 'em."

"Say, you got a place to stay?" she asked.

He hesitated.

She continued, "Because I imagine I can find you something. We're to stay in the hotel for just a few—"

"No, ma'am. I be just fine." He turned and squatted back down at the creek and scooped up another handful of water, splashing his face.

She said, "No need for all the yes ma'ams and no ma'ams. Chuck is just fine."

He continued splashing his face with the cool water.

She said, "We intend to stay. Or I do, anyhow. Can't rightly speak for no one other than myself."

Water dripped from Elzi's face and he watched it gently rain back down into the creek.

Caroline continued, "But myself, I'm certainly glad to be here. Anywhere but Melroy to be honest."

The water began to settle, its ripples calming.

She said, "Melroy wasn't nothing but a pain in my ass, tell you the truth. I'm certainly glad to have left them troubles behind."

Elzi mumbled, "Seems like mine just getting started up." He could feel her watching him, and he knew he should turn and stand, face the woman, but he really just wanted to escape, to disappear.

"Say," she said, "would you like to come to the hotel for supper tonight? You got anything to eat?"

As a knee-jerk response, he politely declined; although when he thought about it, he wasn't actually hungry. He watched a falling leaf land in the water just before him and spin on the water's surface. As a matter of fact, he hadn't thought about being hungry since—he could not remember the last time he'd been hungry. Or thirsty for that matter. *Well, yes I can*, he thought. *It was in the Plains.*

"No, but thank ya much," he replied.

He reached to grab the leaf, now spinning ever so slowly, and something caught his eye—or didn't, rather. He pulled his arm back and then reached it out to the leaf once more. His heart quickened a bit. He knitted his brow and tilted his head. He reached out once more, this time waving his arm over the water, oblivious to Caroline's words coming at him from behind. Leaning forward, cautiously and slowly, he peered down. The leaf floated on the surface in his periphery. He saw the canopy of russet, green, and amber waving in the water's reflection. He saw the sky. And he saw the face of the redhead, now leaning out over the water. He did not see his own.

He jumped back, scrambling from the water's edge.

Caroline jumped back too. "Whoa, you okay? Is it a snake?"

His chest grew tight and his ears whined. Her voice was there but muffled under the pulsing hum. His head spun, his vision narrowing.

"Elzi?" she asked again.

His body began to tremble and he, for the first time, never even considered holding back the tears. And they came like a storm. He looked up to Caroline and could see deep concern. Her mouth moved, and even as she squatted down to get closer, he could not make out her words. In the sky above her, a bird soared. He turned back to the water and watched its reflection, watched the bird grow closer. He leaned over once more. He saw the sky, the treetops, and now the bird. No Elzi Dupre.

The bird swooped down. Caroline ducked to avoid it.

"Shit!" she hollered out.

It landed on the ground just a few feet from them both.

"Well, would you look at that," she said. She turned to Elzi. He was trembling, eyes locked on the bird. "Elzi? You okay?" she asked. "You look like you seen a ghost, my friend." She paused and mumbled under her breath, "And don't I know that look."

"It—it—it be a owl," he said.

"Indeed it is," she replied. "Not too sure what she's doing out this time of day, but here she is, no less."

Caroline smiled at him, and his wrenched chest loosened slightly. The two turned back to the petite bird standing just a few feet from them. It watched them intently. Its round amber eyes blinked, regarding each of them.

"Look at her little tufts. She's beautiful." Her tone changed from one of awe to concern. "Think she's sick?" she asked.

Elzi shook his head, still in a fog, still confused. He wiped his tears.

She said, "Owls ain't like robins. I get lots of robins flock to me when I'm turning over my garden. Waitin' on a worm," she said. "They come to expect it and ain't afraid a bit. But owls—"

Elzi reached his trembling hand out toward the bird standing barely over seven inches. It didn't move, didn't flinch. Its eyes blinked so fast one might miss it.

"Elzi, if it's just sitting there, it might be sick," she warned.

He slowly extended his first finger and made contact, gently touching the top of its head just between the two tufts. He stroked its gray-brown feathers. Its bark-like presentation, deceiving to the eyes, meant to blend with the trees, was smooth and soft. Wonder and awe, a sense of connection washed over him and forced out any remaining anxiety. He slowly turned back to the water and leaned over to peer, careful not to frighten the tiny bird. In the water's reflection, he should have been looking back into his own eyes. But none existed. No deep umber-brown eyes, no nose, no lips. He did not see the tears he felt drying on his cheeks. He did not see his ears or his dense black hair, his coin necklace. No hat. No uniform. No nothing. Simply sky and trees waving above in the breeze. He sighed and turned back around. The bird and the woman stood firm, watching one another then watching Elzi. He pulled his knees back to stand and the owl took flight.

"Why I never," Caroline said, her voice full of allure and amazement. Her eyes sparkled and Elzi could tell she felt inspired, that nature was this woman's high.

He nodded, incapable of turning up words, suspended in a fog.

She said, "You a medic with the Army? 'Cause what you did for my friend back at the wagons—"

He replied with a gentle shake of the head and said, "No, ma'am. I ain't no medic. I's a Tenth Calvary buffalo soldier."

"Well, you saved his life."

He ignored her compliment. "I's in the outfit that was trying to get a handle on the Indian raids. Except it went terrible bad. Many of the mens, they died out there." He stepped back and leaned over the water once more. For confirmation. "They all died 'cept my best friend. He got out of there. Back at camp, they says he was discharged. Thinks he headed back home ova by River City." His cheeks grew hot. Thinking about Albin stealing from the dying and dead, from him, his fellow Deviser, invoked the sting of returning tears. He could see pity in Caroline's eyes. "So I'll be headed there as well. Soon as I get my bearings and a horse, I'll be headed back home too." Hattie Mae's face entered his mind and the sting softened to a warmth as the cruel truth, in the form of a rogue tear, trickled down his cheek.

WALKER

Walker Westberry had always had a unique draw on people, making them feel both intrigued and unnerved all at once, unsteady in their conviction. It was a feature of his character that had both hindered and served him well, garnering his way in most situations, occasionally shutting him out in others. People would have a sense of this character trait, an inkling within, but often could not pinpoint its exact nature. When he'd been asked about the scratch down his face, he'd shrugged it off, a flip comment about a brush with nature. And he'd settled on a backstory, one he figured people could get on board with. With it, he had convinced the Phillipses and the rest of the arrivals from Georgia, all except the redhead. She'd always seemed to eye him a little too long. Once he'd overheard her ask about him to the Geechee woman they brought along. The woman had sucked her teeth and said, "Trouble follers sin as sho as fever follers a chill." For the first time in a long time, he had been the one unnerved, and he made a mental note of the redhead and the Geechee, to keep a close eye on the two.

The Phillipses had taken note of his generous help with the wounded doctor, and of his self-reported business background, and proclaimed he possessed great work ethic and ingenuity. They offered him a room in exchange for help around the hotel. He'd paid up for the first week at the Nelson place, so he declined, instead requesting to receive cash for any work. To his delight, they'd readily agreed.

Working around the hotel allowed him to earn money while keeping close to the Georgia crew, and it eventually allowed him to be present for any planning. He learned the Phillipses were a couple out of Georgia. The wife was the daughter of a wealthy hotelier. He had purchased the forgotten and forlorn Baldwin and sent his daughter and son-in-law to manage the revitalization and reopening of it. The hotelier seemed to have a firm belief that the town and its economy was on the rise very soon with the railroad bolstering this ascension and was determined to get ahead of it. To get it back up and running, bigger and better than ever, before the coming holidays.

He learned that the other couple, Ford and Henrietta, were family to the snake-bit doctor—and newly married. That Ford was transferred to Texas with the railroad commission. That his wife was a schoolteacher looking to start up a proper school in Element Dale. And that she dreamed of becoming a mother soon.

He learned that Dix and Caroline, the snake-bit doctor and the redhead, were not a couple as he had initially assumed. In fact, they seemed to struggle at times to conceal some type of disdain for one another. He could see why. The redhead—her looks were deceiving. A beautiful woman, sexy somehow even wearing britches and a button-down. But the minute she opened her mouth, the beauty and allure waned. She was, much of the time, he thought, a proper asshole and wore her history on her sleeve, whatever that was. He saw her as a woman that could use a real man to put her in her place. And Dix, he did not believe, possessed any such ability.

He found Dix, Dr. Artope that is, odd with his matter-of-fact monologues and screwy quirks. A tad on the squirrely side. He came across about as exciting as a stick-in-the-mud, and yet Walker still liked him and was happy to help him out since he had a hard time getting around.

The town itself hadn't much to offer. He'd heard all the grand plans, the vision—fantasy rather—of people traveling to Element Dale in droves to stay at the hotel, but he didn't feel the same optimism as the others. He learned many of the townsfolk didn't either. The Nelsons, Clifton and Paulette, who ran the boarding house and post office, saw The Baldwin as both a joke and a threat. They allayed such notions of threat with the comfort that the haunts of the hotel would send guests their way after a night or two. Paulette, in particular, believed there to be two ghosts that resided at the formidable edifice. Walker laughed this off. He did not buy into ghosts or superstitions or any type of local folklore.

Back on the mountain, sometimes he and his family and a few locals would sit around a fire and pass the shine around. Inevitably someone would start up with the stories. The legend of the "Light at Farmer's Turnout" and the "Devil's Tramping Ground" were the most told. He knew them by heart and could easily picture the train conductor, headless and carrying a lamp, walking the tracks at night searching for his head—the storyteller would always finish with *They found Joe's body. They found Joe's head! They buried 'em both, but he ain't dead! On a dismal night on the old rail lines, you can see his lantern flicker and shine!* Or he'd picture the devil himself, pacing and walking a circle, his feet beating the grass down to the dirt while he schemed his next evil deeds on earth. Yes, tales were fun, but Walker considered anyone who believed them a touch on the simple side. And it seemed Elemdale was full of believers.

If he wasn't working around the hotel, he liked to spend time at the creek. The town wasn't exceptionally busy aside from the work being done on the hotel, but it was still more than he was accustomed to. The Nelson House always seemed to have a lot of traffic in and out. Mountain life certainly offered its fair share of solitude if one so required, and he'd not yet adjusted to what busyness there was in town. Silas Creek ran east and west and connected two cemeteries—

an observation Walker found odd. There seemed to be more real estate for the dead than the living in Elemdale. The townsfolk called the one he saw east of the Barron River, the one he saw as he entered town for the first time, the Catacombs of Hadacho Hills. It sat just west of the great Indian mounds. Silas Creek Cemetery, the one out west of town, nestled in the woods past where the main road fizzled out, making the town a literal dead end.

Walker liked to short-cut his way through the Silas Creek Cemetery to get to the creek, and he'd follow along its wending path sometimes and find himself at the Catacombs. His frequent visits allowed him a certain acquaintance with the departed. He put two and two together on a few of the gravestones. It seemed his landlords lost their oldest child not too long back. He shuttered every time his mind took him to the imagined scene: a boy plowing his way through the corn and then, *bam*, lightning strikes him dead. He tried not to think of what the family must have come up upon, his condition, but his mind went there anyways to a burnt and smoking corpse gripping the plow. The Nelsons hadn't mentioned a word of any such tragedy, but he'd heard Samuel mention Elmer's name and Paulette immediately shut the boy down.

"Five years, Samuel! You know this!" She'd frantically thrown open a window and announced, "And don't nobody close this here! Y'all understand!"

He'd had to ask Samuel later, in private, to explain. It seemed she believed that once the deceased was buried, speaking their name in the first five years following pulled them from their resting place. The spirit would attempt to return home. A window was then left open to avoid the spirit being trapped and lingering to inhabit the dwelling as a disgruntled haint. The hope was that the spirit would make a visit and then quickly move on and return to its resting place.

Walker had met most everyone at some point during his initial few weeks living in Elemdale. Though there was one man that seemed to elude him. A few times when passing through Silas Creek Cemetery, he'd come across a man also passing through, but each time he was on the farthest side. From afar and through the trees, Walker wasn't able to make out too much about the man other than he carried a stick with him, had a heavy, lumbering gait, and kept his head down. After the fourth time glimpsing him, he decided to follow.

He hadn't known there to be anything past the cemetery other than the creek, but this man seemed to have something drawing him through and out the other side. Walker exited the far end of the cemetery and into the thick trees, following along the creek to the south. He eventually found a narrow walking trail that wended through the thicket and spit him out just at the bottom of a craggy hill where it seemed to just dead end. He couldn't make out any trail leading up the hill anywhere. To the left or right, the ground remained undisturbed. He walked alongside the hill, making his way around. Nothing stood out to him, nothing out of the ordinary. Simply raw land with mesquites, cedars, cottonwood, and sycamore trees overgrown with ivy shooting up from thick Johnson grass and reeds. Stumped, deciding there must have been a trail offshoot somewhere along the way he'd overlooked, he turned to make his way back. Just before arriving back to the outskirts of the cemetery, he spotted the big man.

"Hey there!" he shouted.

The man stopped and turned back. His skin was as dark as hickory and the whites of his eyes were all that shown under his hat. Walker raised his hand but the man simply turned back and continued walking.

"Hey!" he shouted again. "I's talking a you!"

The man, bulky and tall, continued on.

Walker picked up the pace to an easy jog and caught up with the man at the cemetery entrance. As he approached him from behind, he hollered up ahead, but the man continued walking, his head down. Walker reached up and grabbed the man's arm from behind.

"I said I'm fucking talking a you."

Walker could feel the man's muscle through his shirt, firm and large. The man slowly turned and faced him. Walker swallowed. The man towered a good foot over him. His shoulders were broad and hulking. His eyes met Walker's only for a moment before he shifted them down to the stick in his hand. The stick was unusual, not a walking stick but spindly and forked like a Y. Walker was uncertain what to say next. His mission simply was to set the precedent that he was not to be ignored, but the size of this man standing before him was nothing shy of intimidating. Walker raised his chin and set his jaw.

"You couldn't hear me talking a you?"

The man stood still, eyes locked on the ground before him.

Walker said, "Boy, you best look at me when I speak."

With his head lowered, the man lifted his eyes. Walker noted the man's eyes did not convey anger nor challenge of any sort. If Walker had to bet on it, he'd say they were eyes filled with something akin to sorrow, like his spirit was in the midst of great languish. Walker raised his chin even higher and curled up his lip.

"What's your name, boy?"

The man was no boy. Probably in his fifties, Walker thought. Walker noticed lines etched to the sides of his eyes, crow's feet.

The man did not respond. Nor did he look away.

Walker waited a moment then huffed. "What? You struck dumb or something?"

The man held his gaze for a split second longer then averted his eyes back down to his feet, his head still hanging low.

Birds chirped and tweeted and called from all around where the two men stood. Walker, unknowing of what to do or how to respond to such indifference or apathy, or whatever it was, turned and spat just to the side of the man's feet. He pointed up and said, "You fucking mind yourself, you hear me." He held his finger at the man's chest for a moment longer, nodding his head, staring him down. When he got no reaction, he dropped his hand and walked past, leaving the giant man behind him. He mumbled under his breath, "thick-witted fucking coon." But he dared not look back.

Back at the Nelson House, Walker and Clifton rocked in chairs on the front porch and passed a bottle of whiskey while Paulette cooked supper. Walker rolled a cigarette while Clifton puffed away on his pipe. Walker inquired as to the big Black man with the stick.

Clifton answered, "Name's Sterling. No idea if'n he's got a last name or not. Probably not." He called out to his wife inside the house. "Paulette, you think Sterling got him a surname?"

She barked back from the kitchen, "Hell if I know, Clifton. Just always known him as Sterling."

Walker thought on it a moment. "He got a gimp leg or som'in?"

Clifton puckered his lips and tilted his head slightly. "Gimp leg?"

"Well, he carries a stick."

"Oh. That ain't no walking stick. No sirree, that there's a witchin' stick."

Walker nodded his head slowly, but Clifton could tell he wasn't following.

"For locating water. A witchin' stick. You ain't never heard a one?"

Walker shook his head.

"Yep, that man there's what they call a water witch, and his stick is his dee-vine rod. Points out the underground water."

"You fucking pulling my leg?" asked Walker.

"If I'm lying I'm dying," Clifton replied. He yelled out to his wife, "Ain't that the truth, Paulette?"

She yelled back, "What truth is that, hon?"

"That ole Sterling's a water witch and his stick heps him locate the underground rivers!"

She replied, "Yep. His witchin' stick. Dug our well for us 'bout twenty years back I'd say. Used his stick magic. I don't question it. Don't rightly understand it neither. But I got plenty a water. That's good word enough for me."

"Well ain't that some shit," Walker said.

Clifton replied, "Yes sirree. And he been known to find peculiar water."

"Peculiar?"

"Peculiar." Clifton took a swig and offered the bottle over.

Walker took a swig and wiped his mouth on his shirt sleeve. He asked, "Peculiar as in how?"

"As in some say his water gots powers and such."

Walker lifted a brow. "Powers, you say?"

Clifton replied, "Powers."

"Of what sorts?"

"They say of the healing sort," replied Clifton. "Matter fact, healed Paulette's old lady." He leaned in close and lowered his voice to a whisper. "That old bitch used to be a lunatic. And when I says lunatic, I mean she was plum fucking 'round the bend. Gave her the water ole Sterling brought by. Bam. Cleared that shit right up. Sane as you and me."

Walker chuckled and passed the bottle back to Clifton. He lit his cigarette, took a deep drag, leaned his head back and exhaled a plume of smoke. He said, "Clif, I ain't no fool. And I can spot when someone's telling me a thumper."

Clifton replied, "Hey, if I'm lying I'm dying. And that's the bottom fact." He glanced back at the door then turned back to Walker. "Before the water, I'd have to go a-chasing her down in the night. She'd get a mind to running about the place stark naked and carrying on about this and that. One night the neighbor, Mr. Turner, showed up on the front porch pounding on our door. I find him holding her by the arm. Woo-wee, she stunk to high heaven. Covered in shit. Said his donkeys took to fussing in the night. He grabbed his gun expecting to find a sneak thief creeping around. Instead, he finds Paulette's old lady naked as a jaybird and covered in shit from head to toe. I couldn't deal with it. Woke Paulette and she tended to the mess." He leaned in closer. "Come sunup, Mr. Turner was back pounding on our front door mad as an old wet hen. Says he went to feed and ever one a his donkeys was painted in shit—and demanding I go clean 'em up." He shook his head. "Fucking lunatic woman, I tell ya."

Walker wrinkled up his nose. "Why on earth?"

Clifton replied, "I told ya, son. Fucking lunatic. Going on 'bout she was covered in ants, that the donkeys was covered in ants. I thought we was gonna have to tie her down at one point. She'd a mind to paint the whole fucking house in shit, trying to ward off the ants."

Walker couldn't help but scan the floors and wall behind him. His skin crawled just thinking about ants everywhere.

Clifton said, "They weren't no damn ants, Walker."

Walker nodded slowly and took another drag.

Clifton continued, "Anyhow, Paulette come to giving her some of that peculiar water on the regular and she straightened right up. Ain't had to clean up a shitty wall or shitty donkey since." He took a swig and passed the bottle back to Walker.

Walker lifted it and said, "I'll drink to that." He took a swig and handed the bottle back to Clifton. Walker said, "I ain't seen no old lady around since I been here."

"Yalp. Rest her soul. She didn't take too good to our boy"—he dropped his head—"well, when our boy got struck, it was her that found him. The sight of him, it unsettled her. She refused to eat or drink for days. No water. No nothing." He shook his head. "Lunacy come back with a vengeance. Had to put her down."

Walker stopped rocking. "Put her down?"

Clifton replied, "It was that or leave her to suffer the tortures of the damned at one a those incurables hospitals." He shook his head. "We don't talk about it."

"I see." Walker sat still a moment, his mind carrying him through all sorts of scenarios. He said, "If you don't mind me asking, when I come to town, I did pass by your son's resting place at the graveyard out east of town, the one with the Indian hills."

"The Catacombs of Hadacho Hills," Clifton said.

"Sure," replied Walker. "Why not bury him at the place behind here, the boneyard at Silas Creek? Ain't it a lot closer?" He could sense Clifton struggling and thought he probably shouldn't have asked. Losing a child can't be easy.

Clifton cleared his throat and leaned in. "Ya see, I did want him buried there. That-a-way I can just walk on back through the woods and be at his . . . resting place in no time. But Paulette there, well, she ain't about having the body of her boy resting alongside heathens."

"Heathens?"

"Heathens. I know for a fact Sterling's got some folks buried there. Nothing's marked. And some say that's where his wife and son were laid, that is if it's a fact they were laid and not sold off. Being buried in the same ground as a Black man or no Indian don't make me no mind. If you think about it, whether you're buried ten feet apart or ten miles apart, if you're buried in Texas, you're sharing the same dirt. But Paulette, she don't see it that-a-way, so I says, okay, bury the boy wherever suits you best. I suggested here out back, making us a family cemetery, but then she goes on talking about haints too close to home and—well, Walker, once you get married—assuming you ain't—"

Walker shook his head.

"—well once you do, it's best to just go along with a woman. Keeps the brow beatin' to a minimum, if you catch my drift."

Walker nodded. He knew exactly what Clifton meant yet disagreed wholeheartedly. He decided on shifting the topic back to Sterling.

"So that big jig, I figured he's a simple or something. Couldn't conjure up a thought if he tried."

Clifton, thrown for a bit, said, "Big jig? Oh! He ain't dumb. Just cain't speak. Ain't got no tongue."

"Get the fuck out," Walker laughed. Their chairs were now rocking in sync.

"Hey, if I'm lying I'm dying," Clifton replied. His demeanor perked back up. "Ask Paulette." He yelled over his shoulder, "Ain't that the truth, Paulette?"

She hollered back from inside, "Now what truth is that, hon?"

"That ole Sterling got his tongue cut out!"

"Yep. Ain't had no tongue since we know'd him anyhow."

Walker asked Clifton, "How'd he lose his tongue?"

Just then little Samuel rounded the house and hopped up on the porch where the two men sat. "Savages!" he shouted. "They ain't wanting no kinky hair so they nabbed his tongue 'stead of his scalp!" The boy lunged at the men and pretended to rip the scalp from his own head.

Clifton shook his head. "Sam, go on mind your business."

The boy, now hopping on one foot in circles, patted his mouth, "wah-wah-wah-wah-wah-wah," mimicking the Indians of his imagination. Clifton extended his leg and shoved the boy in the butt with the toe of his boot.

"Hey!" Sam shouted.

Clifton nodded his head. "I said git."

Sam's body fell into a slump and he stomped off. "That's some bullshit," the boy said.

"Hey now," replied Clifton. "Ain't having none of that." He turned back to Walker. "We don't rightly know what happened. But that's the tattle of it all, that at some point the Indians cut it right out of his head."

Walker thought back to his time traveling from North Carolina to Texas, to the Indian of Black and Bones, to the great mounds east of town. He asked, "They still Indians 'round these parts?"

Clifton laughed, "Ah nah. Most 'em run off. Nothing to worry with here." He leaned back in his rocker and crossed his legs at the ankles. "Just the occasional house raid and lady rape."

"Is that a bluff or you meaning it for real play?" Walker asked.

Clifton took a long puff from his pipe. "You cain't never trust a gone Indian is gone for good." He let out a great plume of smoke and grinned at Walker, his front right tooth but a rotten shard. "No sirree."

Walker rocked and drifted into deep thought, rubbing the pierced coin that now hung around his neck. When he first lifted the coin from the soldier in the swimming hole, he'd figured on selling it. He'd tied it around his neck at some point and had become accustomed to rubbing it between his fingers when anxious or deep in thought. He'd come to think of it as a token of his resettlement, a good luck charm that had warded off the revenuers from pursuing him—and that Indian painted like a skeleton—as he had continued his travels. He hadn't thought about that Indian until little Samuel brought up scalping. The Indian of Black and Bones was his first ever sighting, and just hearkening up that vision brought him chills. His body shuddered and he gave his head a great shake as if slinging the sight from his mind.

Clifton said, "Walker, you got you a cold chill there? Season's barely here."

Walker pushed up from the rocker and replied, "Som'in like that. Thank you much for the nip." He handed the bottle over to Clifton. "I'm fading. Think I'll call it a night."

Clifton said, "If you go up now, you gonna miss supper."

Walker stood for a moment and shook his head. "Nah, it's all right. My tired is a-hanging out. I'll catch up with you come breakfast."

Clifton gave a nod and lifted the whiskey bottle. "Suit yerself."

CAROLINE

Caroline stabbed the spade into the earth, twisted it, and pulled from it a plug of dirt. She tossed it to the side and sat back on her feet. A gentle breeze cooled the sweat on her brow. She tilted her head back and took a deep breath. All was quiet where she sat surrounded by freshly plowed earth. She was in her happy place. She grabbed a handful of seeds and sprinkled them into the void. As she worked, she let her mind run freely.

She had all sorts of thoughts about Elzi, this so-called soldier. Something niggled at her. Something was . . . off. She'd witnessed him acting a little unhinged back at Silas Creek. Typically, she wasn't too tolerant of a grown man crying, but something seemed so very sincere about him, and gentle. Had it been someone else, she might have been throwing out insults. But this man's tears seemed true, warranted. She didn't know what exactly provoked them, other than she supposed a rough go out in the plains—and truth be told, life in general within the bounds of an oppressed race—but she knew deep down that any tears that fell from him were rightful. She also had a strong suspicion that he wasn't exactly meant to be out on his own, that undoubtedly he was AWOL, a runaway from that Tenth

Calvary he'd mentioned. Again, she thought, she didn't much care. She liked him right from the start, felt him to be good to his core. She had a way of sensing these things. Something had had him spooked back at the creek. She'd witnessed him all but crack, on the verge of completely losing it. She herself knew that feeling. Regardless of what provoked it, the panic in his face, the sheer fright, she knew it all too well. It was as if he'd seen a ghost, and that feeling too she knew.

The Phillipses had offered her room and board in exchange for overseeing the revitalization of the grounds and landscaping at the hotel, an unlikely job for a woman, and because of that, she was all the more eager to accept. She'd taken liberties to start a vegetable garden in back of the property, even though it wasn't rightly part of the deal. Just a small one where she could get away from people and drop a few of her seeds from her herb and vegetable garden back at the plantation. She missed her garden deeply, and her father. Digging her hands in the dirt allowed her a sense of home; so she found herself in the dirt seven days a week, making excellent progress despite refusing any help from the hired hands. Octavia spent a good amount of time helping her when she wasn't tending to the hotel kitchen. On days when Caroline would get lost out there for hours planting and watering, she'd find herself instinctively starting to tell stories to Mable, though to her dismay, it seemed Mable hadn't come along, that she was just telling stories into the void. When she'd left Georgia behind, she'd also left Mable. The thought of never seeing her childhood imaginary friend was only slightly saddening, as it also brought to mind that she hadn't seen Davis either. Losing Mable was well worth not running into her husband hanging from a noose at every turn, and for that she was grateful.

Even though she purposely sought solitude in the garden and sometimes down at the creek, she still felt a bit disjointed from the group, like something was still not quite right. People still watched her closely, particularly Octavia. She'd felt fine. She'd not had any episodes, no hauntings from her husband. But she could always feel Octavia keeping tabs on her. And sometimes Dix too. She thought

Henrietta had probably mentioned to Dix some of her troubles, her internal ails of the mind, as he too seemed to study her at times. Which for all she cared, Dix Artope could worry about his own cerebral quirks. Henrietta did check in from time to time with a little nonchalant "How ya feeling?" It had been nice to be able to report honestly for once that she felt just fine. Leaving Melroy was the right thing to do.

She smiled and plunged her spade into the dirt. She felt relief. She was okay. Elemdale was okay. She wasn't exactly sure what her life would look like in this town, but things just felt right for once.

"You gonna spend ever' waking moment digging in the dirt?"

Caroline smiled and sat back on her feet. Henrietta stood before her, her dress flowing in the breeze.

Henrietta continued, "I thought you could only harvest in the fall. You're planting?"

Caroline replied, "Yes, I'm planting broccoli, collards, onions, beets, pintos. They like it when the days are warm and the nights cool. There's quite a bit you can put in the ground this time of year. The soil's not quite the same as back home, but I'm willing to give it a go."

Henrietta said, "Well, when you get a minute, Octavia's got supper ready. There's a big crowd at the hotel today helping out."

"That Westberry there?" asked Caroline.

Henrietta replied, "He is."

Caroline nodded.

Henrietta grinned. "You got a thing for him, don't ya?"

Caroline hoisted herself off the ground and dusted off her pants. "I most assuredly do not have a *thing* for him."

"Uh-huh," Henrietta replied. "I hear ya."

Caroline could see the grin on Henrietta's face, that she didn't believe her. While Caroline did ask about him from time to time, it wasn't because she had any romantic interest. She just felt the need to know—what? She wasn't entirely sure.

Caroline said, "I wonder, you seen Elzi around town? I'd be nice if he'd join us for a meal sometime."

"Elzi?" Henrietta asked.

"Yeah. I'm sure he could use a good hot meal. I'm not rightly sure where he's been staying. I think at the creek. Poor thing."

Henrietta tilted her head slightly. "I guess I'm not following, hon."

"Ah," replied Caroline. "The soldier." She bent down and gathered up her tools and seeds. "You know, I'm not so sure he's not in a bad way. He's sure been through a lot."

Henrietta nodded, studying Caroline closely.

Caroline continued, "And I come up on him down at the creek. You should have seen him. Not at all the calm man from back at the squeeze." She began walking back up to the hotel. "Not at all. Matter fact, he was a right mess. All out of sorts."

She realized she was walking alone and stopped. She turned back to find Henrietta still standing in the garden where Caroline had been planting. Caroline called out, "You coming or what?"

Henrietta nodded, hitched up her dress, and trotted to catch up. Hesitantly, Henrietta asked, "Chuck? You feeling good?"

Caroline replied, "Great. Hungry, now that I think about it."

The two walked in silence the rest of the way. Caroline could sense something in Henrietta. That feeling she got when people were concerned for her. She thought back to the creek, to Elzi. Had *she* been what startled him? Maybe he'd been in deep thought. She knew better than to walk up on someone. And she knew, him being a Black man, she probably shouldn't put him in such a position. He'd been through a lot. Last thing he needed was some White woman approaching him alone out somewhere. She thought back to the rattlesnake, how her friends had ignored him. The injustice of existing in skin seen as less than by others—or worse, unworthy of recognition at all.

She said, "You know, Henri, we really all owe that man a great deal of gratitude."

"What man?" asked Henrietta.

"Elzi. The soldier."

Henrietta said, "Chuck, you're really starting to worry me."

Caroline replied, "And you're really starting to get my hackles up."

Henrietta stopped walking. "*I am?*"

"*You* are." Caroline said, "I know you're better than this, Henri. That man saved Dix's life. Black, white, brown, yellow, no matter his skin, he saved him. And to withhold gratitude because he's Black, I can see Ford maybe. But you? Come on."

Henrietta replied, "Now wait a minute. I haven't withheld any gratitude from anyone who deserved it."

Caroline pointed at her and said, "And *there* it fucking is."

Henrietta stomped. "Chuck, what the hell are you talking about?"

Caroline spun around and waved her off, leaving Henrietta standing alone and dumbfounded.

At dinner, Caroline ate, but she fumed while doing so. She looked around at the people chatting it up and laughing and thought about Elzi, alone somewhere, probably hungry. She was short with anyone who attempted to engage, and as per usual, people took her hint and carried on without her. She watched Henrietta and Ford. He'd smiled gently at Caroline, did not engage as he normally would, so she figured Henrietta must have talked to him about their little quarrel in the garden. Which made little sense, him smiling. It had been a smile of pity. She hated the smile of pity. She finished her bowl and stood from the table. She thought about announcing she was going to turn in early but then changed her mind and left without word. She didn't owe any of these people an explanation.

As she laid in bed, her thoughts raced from one to the next and, with them, her emotions. The rattlesnake flashed in her mind, its rattles echoing all around the cave walls. She'd been terrified but somehow just forced herself to swing the ax. Fear had tempted her to close her eyes when she swung, but she knew better. A feeling of pride came, but only for a moment before a vision of Davis hanging from a noose entered her mind. Her heart hammered and she squeezed shut her eyes and shook her head to rid him. She opened her eyes and looked around the room. He was not there. He had only been in her mind this time. A moment of relief came. She took a deep breath and her thoughts settled back on Elzi at Silas Creek. She had seen him quite frightened. But if it was her that had startled him, his reaction was a bit much, certainly nothing to come to tears over. She replayed the scene in her mind over and over. Him scrambling on the ground, him touching the owl. Then she remembered, actually, she hadn't startled him. When she first walked up, the two had had a pleasant conversation. She had invited him to supper even. A flash of him panting and crying came to mind. Of him jumping back. She had asked him if he'd seen a snake—that's right. She hadn't walked up on him and startled him. He'd seen something.

She struggled to remember it all. Closing her eyes, she took a deep breath. The beautiful rustling canopy of trees came to mind. The gentle breeze. The smell of earth and water. His dirty blue uniform. She watched herself in the vision standing behind him as he crouched down and splashed the water on his face. She could hear the water, its continuous *drip drip drip* as he leaned over the water to —what? He was reaching. For what?

She clenched her eyes. A bird interrupted the sound of the breeze. She remembered a soft *cr-r-oo-oo-oo-oo*. In the water's reflection, she'd seen the bird flying above. A vision of the bird entered her mind. She saw the sky, the bird flying over her head, then her red hair hanging down toward the water as she leaned over Elzi. She paused and reviewed the scene once more. The trees—she could see them in the reflection and hear them rustling in the breeze. She could hear the drips of water dropping from his face. She could see the leaf spinning atop the water, his hand reaching for it, the bird overhead, her face, her hair.

Her heart stopped. Her hands quickly flew up and covered her mouth. She opened her eyes to look around the room. She suddenly had that feeling, that feeling she got when Davis was around. Her eyes darted from corner to corner, to the door, to the window. Davis was not there, yet the feeling was as strong as when he was. A tear escaped from her eye as the truth annihilated any relief she'd found from escaping Melroy. The water had mirrored all the surrounding life—the trees, the sky, the bird, her—but had not reflected that of the buffalo soldier in blue. And now she knew what it was Elzi had seen. What it was he had not seen.

She laid in bed fighting back the urge to rush to Octavia. She was here to be better, to escape the haunts back in Melroy. Octavia would certainly find a way to report back to her father that Elemdale was no better for her. She closed her eyes and began breathing slowly and deeply, in for five counts and out for eight. She did this while making every effort to focus on the sound of her own breath, to let any more thoughts that entered her mind pass by like a parade. She counted and breathed and counted and breathed until she forgot she was counting and breathing and simply slept.

Caroline hadn't known she'd fallen asleep until she was awakened by a child laughing outside her door. The room was dark. She heard the giggle again and the pitter patter of feet. She rose from her bed and walked to the window. The moon was up high, and it was sometime in the middle of the night. The child pitter-pattered past her room once more. Annoyed, she walked to the door and flung it open, ready to give a good scolding. She glimpsed the child in the darkness. A girl. She had made it to the end of the hall and disappeared around the corner. Caroline closed the door and headed back to bed. As she was climbing in, she heard a small knock and a giggle and the child ran once more down the hall. When she opened the door, the little girl was at the far end of the hall, the moonlight casting light on her dress as she spun and twirled.

Caroline holler-whispered down the corridor, "You best get to bed. You don't want me waking up your momma and daddy."

The girl stopped and let go of her dress. Caroline couldn't make out her face, but she imagined her smile fell. The girl stood slumped.

Caroline said, "Go on now. Git. It's late. I don't want to hear you out here anymore. People's got to get up and work. Now go to bed."

The girl gave a little stomp. No doubt she was frowning, Caroline thought. Then she turned and disappeared around the corner once more.

Caroline walked back into her room and closed the door behind her. "Little shit," she murmured.

DIX

Dix Artope no longer took his morning run. For a time, the physical pain and accompanied disappointment had him down and he failed to move in any way resembling his daily gymnastics. He'd all but given up on Physical Culture. He had traveled all that way for a new start, only to be physically attacked by a slithering Satan, and it had him shook. He laid in bed and mentally teetered back and forth as to what, if any, meaning this had. Was God sending a message that he shouldn't have left Melroy, that he was running away? Was it his punishment for doing so? Or was He giving him the push to not turn back? Maybe it was to be a central focus to unite the crew, mainly he and Caroline. Or maybe it was sheer deviltry trying to stop him from doing good for the people of Element Dale. Genesis 3:1 came to mind: *Now the serpent was more cunning than any beast of the field which the Lord God had made.*

His leg had once been a sickly marbling of black, green, purple, pink, and yellow from hip to toe and pulsed with searing pain as if every nerve was an inferno fit to burst. The first few days had been so unbearable that he'd prayed for death. By day eight, he could finally stand with help. The wound itself could have been worse. He could have lost the leg altogether had it not been for the care of Caroline. He had his leg, thank Jesus, but now he dealt with the afflicting nerve pain and a crater-like indention just below his buttock which, combined, made walking difficult and agonizing. Despite it, he pushed on and did so with the help of others—something he was not accustomed to—and his cane.

The cane was a gift from Walker Westberry, the curious man who'd greeted the crew upon arrival and helped move Dix from the wagon and into the hotel. As Dix understood it, Walker had himself only just arrived to Element Dale by way of Georgia, though he could not detect that distinct Georgian lilt, the foregoing of the R sound. Not that it really mattered, but Dix did sense a bit of falsity in his story. Walker was around the hotel daily, helping out in various ways. And a few times he'd stop in and visited with Dix, eventually presenting the cane.

"My pa had a sorry leg. It was pert-near useless. Used two a them canes to get around," he said.

Dix thanked him kindly for the cane, though it brought about an uncomfortable pondering. Would he need this cane forever? Either way, he accepted it with gratitude and saw it as a gift from God by way of Walker Westberry. He asked him the nature of his father's aliment, but Walker just waved the question away and replied simply, "He rurnt it working on the mountain."

"The mountain?" Dix asked. He watched Walker turn over the question for a moment.

Walker replied with a vague "Yeah, Blue Ridge" and then changed the subject.

He'd supposed Walker could have hailed from the Blue Ridge Mountains of Georgia, but it certainly didn't sound like it to him.

The day Walker had presented the cane, he'd also presented a bottle of whiskey. Dix had declined, obviously, and made every attempt to not allow his personal disdain to cross his face.

"No, thank you" was all he said and attempted a polite smile.

Walker nodded and threw out a justification on his behalf. "Prolly aren't not drink when you're taking simples anyhow."

"True. True," Dix replied.

When Dix was finally well enough, the two men walked from Dix's quarters in the hotel to the grounds out behind it. Dix had explained his proclivity to daily calisthenics to Walker and he guessed Walker felt obliged to further him along, though he hadn't asked him to. It was a slow walk, but Dix was making progress nonetheless.

Walker said, "I know you ain't much for the likker, but—"

Dix cut him off. "I am not."

"Right." Walker paused and Dix could feel him turning over his next words as they walked. "I know it's not for you. But back when I worked with—with—back when I was in Georgia, I had the idea to bottle up the beverage and—"

"You're referring to Coca-Cola, yes?" Dix inquired.

"Uh, yes," Walker replied. "Anyhow, being as I'm—how you say it —highly conversant with the beverage business, I was thinking of running my idea by you."

"If you're thinking of getting into the spirits industry, I'd think again, Walker. I imagine it's nothing like developing and selling Coca-Cola. Not that I wholeheartedly support that beverage either, but at least you weren't partaking in ministering to the utter ruin of your fellow beings."

"Utter ruin?" asked Walker. He chuckled at Dix's smug retort.

"Utter ruin," Dix repeated. "I find the consumption of ardent spirits progressively deranges the will while it sickens the body and puts one's family under siege with its drink-induced domestic violence. And that's to say nothing of the headaches, crapulous debility, and nauseous qualms that follows it all."

Walker gave another chuckle. "Well, I cain't say I know anything about the, as you say, ardent spirits business, but I'll take your word for it, Doctor." And then an idea occurred to Walker. He said, "I was more thinking of water."

"Water?"

"Water. As a type of simples."

Dix stopped walking and gave the back of his leg a rub. Walker stopped alongside him. "You holding up, Doc?"

Dix sighed. "Just fine. Walker, there are obvious benefits to one consuming water. Fresh and pure water is what the body needs most. But it's not—what did you call it?"

"Simples."

Dix shook his head. "It's not to be confused with the likes of studied and measured professional medicine."

"Because?" Walker asked.

"Well"—Dix thought carefully to not come across as arrogant as he knew he sometimes could. He knew Walker only meant well and gathered his education was most likely not of the academic nature. "Well, Mr. Westberry, because even though the body requires water to survive, one mustn't confuse that fundamentally natural resource with the healing properties of pharmaceutics."

"But what if there was water that did heal? That did more than just quench the thirst?"

Dix gave a little laugh. "Then I suppose whoever held that water would be a rich man and could build a mansion next door to the owner of the fountain of youth."

Walker nodded and grinned his crooked smile. "I hear ya, Doc."

The two walked past the garden. In the far back corner, they could see Caroline down on all fours. Dix pointed out, "Caroline there seems to think that plants can replace advanced modern medicine and pharmaceutical science. As much as it'd be nice to believe that God planted remedies for the sick to pluck at will, it just doesn't work that way."

Walker said, "She flusterates you at times, I see."

"She flusterates everyone at times," Dix agreed.

Walker asked, "What's her story? Lady come all this way with no husband. First I thought it was you."

"Oh. God no," Dix retorted.

Walker laughed. "I mean, she's a looker. Even in them britches."

Dix laughed and nodded. "She is rather curious."

"Where's her husband? Though now that I ask, I can fully imagine a man rightly booting her ass right out the door! That mouth a hers."

The two laughed together. Dix found he liked Walker. Which he also found odd as they were so incredibly different.

Dix pushed up his glasses and replied, "Caroline has had quite the distress in her life for someone of such young years. Circumstances have been manacling for her and she's struggled to . . . cope."

"You a-trying to nicely say she's a loony?"

Dix found this word harsh, and a bit of defensiveness surfaced. He never thought he'd be defending Caroline Colley, but how could he not? The crass and stubborn woman *had* saved his life.

"I am saying no such thing. I am saying she is a woman who has undergone a great deal of personal turmoil in her life that she struggles to . . . mentally manage."

Walker looked at Dix and shot him another crooked grin. "Meaning she's a loony. I hear what ya ain't saying."

Dix turned to head back to the hotel. His leg was beginning to burn with exhaustion. As he walked, he could sense Walker hanging back. He wondered if he'd been too stern. Walker couldn't possibly know all that Caroline had been through, nor the immense gratitude Dix held for her. He felt a bit of shame. For if Mr. Westberry hadn't sensed his gratitude for Caroline Colley, it could only be because he hadn't expressed it.

He hollered over his shoulder, "Mr. Westberry, are you intending to join me or are you headed back to the inn?"

Walker said, "There's water here that's really som'in, Doc, and I think you should take a look at it."

Dix hollered back, "How 'bout on our next walk, huh?"

"Sure, Doc."

Dix maintained a concentrated study on his steps, leaning on the cane and forcing his right to advance equidistant the left, until he approached the back entrance to the hotel where Octavia met him with a large glass of water. He drank the water in one go and handed back the glass, thanking her and then continuing on around the west side of the hotel until he came to his quarters. A sign now hung at the door of his entrance: *Dr. Dixon Artope*. He allowed a slight smile and tilted his head up to the clouds and gave quiet thanks to his god in heaven whom he felt certain was still testing him. He needed to hold fast to his faith and be diligently mindful of all whom he encountered, of all potential messages. The glass of water sparked his thoughts on Walker's request. "Water as medicine," he scoffed. "Asinine."

"Mind if I come in?"

Dix turned to find Caroline just behind him. She had a polite smile on her face, which he'd come to learn meant she was struggling with something and trying to hide it.

"Of course." He stepped aside and held out his arm, gesturing for her to enter.

"The place is coming along real nice, Dix," she said.

He replied, "Many thanks to you," as he nodded toward his wall of elixirs. She'd painstakingly organized them all in a manner that was both functional and esthetically pleasing.

She gestured to his leg. "You're getting along much better, I see."

"Yes," he replied. "With the help of my trusty cane here."

"Ah, that Mr. Westberry crafted for you."

He said, "Indeed." He noticed her smile slightly faded when referring to Walker Westberry.

"Caroline, what can I help you with?"

She dug into the pocket of her trousers and pulled out a handful of seeds. She fingered them in her palm while speaking, avoiding eye contact. "I was figuring that maybe we could display some of my seeds here alongside your elixirs as personal remedies for the home."

Dix furrowed his brow. "I'm afraid I'm not quite following, Caroline."

"Course you're not," she shot back.

Dix took a half step back and Caroline cleared her throat. "I mean," she continued, "let me be more compelling. I was thinking about divvying up some of my seeds, and maybe oils, enclosing them neatly with a small explanation of ways to use them for personal remedy needs. I'm near close to completing my remedies book." She looked up and stared him straight in the eyes. He could see her begin to light up. "And people could buy the book, and then if they don't already have some of the ingredients at home, they could come up here and purchase seeds, start their own home healing gardens."

"Or they could just sit down and have an actual doctor see them about whatever they are seeking to remedy," Dix added.

She wrinkled up her nose and thought. Dix could tell she was measuring her words for a change, that this must mean a lot to her.

"True," she said. "If it were more urgent, yes. But it couldn't hurt for families to have an option more . . . natural for their needs."

"But natural isn't always the proper solution, Caroline. There is modern medicine for good reason. We can't expect people to turn to nature when times are serious."

"Like when someone gets struck by a rattler?" She cocked her head.

Dix's hackles began to rise. She was getting that tone, that pushiness that he'd tried so very hard to overlook. "Like when someone gets struck and is in great need of the assistance of actual pharmaceuticals such as morphine."

"It wasn't the morphine that saved you, Dix. That just kept the pain down while I—"

He cut her off. "And I will be forever in your debt, Caroline, for what you did for me out there, what you've done since."

She had been staring him down, poised to protest. But she did not. Dix could see her demeanor shift and he was now looking at the top of her red head as she stared down at her feet. She stood quietly and Dix could feel some sort of tension thickening the air. Not the tension of quarrel, but the tension of anxiety.

"Caroline?"

She looked up. Giant tears welled in her big brown eyes and Dix felt the urge to just tell her yes, that she could sell whatever she wanted in his clinic, as long as she kept her hysterics to herself. He thought of reaching out to her, offering a hand of comfort, maybe on her shoulder, when a tear spilled from her eye, and he knew this was about something more than seeds and a plant cookbook.

"Would you like to sit, Caroline?"

In the confines of his spanking-new practice where all his drugs lined the shelves, his certificate hung on the wall, and his beloved books sat atop his desk, he saw his first patient. He listened patiently as she unburdened herself. He listened as she cried. He listened as she yelled. He learned of her visions of her husband, how she'd seen him time and time again swinging from a noose in various places, mostly at the foot of her bed back in Melroy. He'd known about Davis Colley, the tragedy of a politician gone mad, the rumors surrounding the circumstances that brought him to hang, the rumors about the hanging itself. He watched Caroline tremble as she spoke of her late husband. Then he saw the trembling calm and a smile return when she mentioned Mable, her childhood imaginary friend. He assured her that childhood friends, both real and imagined, were never something to worry with. Though he marked down in his notes the fact that she'd interacted with this Mable even in her adult years, up until the move to Element Dale.

Element Dale was Thomas Higgs' last-ditch attempt at remedying his daughter's mental anguish. The rumors and familiar places, sounds, and smells around Melroy, he believed after much thought, triggered her painful memories of Davis. And a move, since no other medical remedy had been successful, was the last option Mr. Higgs could think of for her . . . lest he consider the lunatic asylum.

"And has that helped, Caroline? Does not seeing the familiar surroundings you once shared with your late husband—has that stopped the hallucinations?" Dix asked. He watched as she sat atop his treatment table thinking, one foot tucked up under her, the other dangling, her ankle twitching, her rolling a seed back and forth between her fingers. She looked up to speak and paused. He could see her set her jaw, the muscles tighten as her neck grew corded with tension. She opened her mouth to speak and then closed it. She shifted on the table.

"It's okay if you've still have them, Caroline. I'm not here to judge," he said.

He noticed her forehead glistening. The poor woman still saw her husband. He could see it all over her. He picked up his pad and wrote *neurasthenia, mild hysteria.*

With great caution in her voice she said, "It's not Davis that I see."

"Then Mable, is it?" he assumed.

She shook her head.

Dix furrowed his brow.

She took a deep breath, closed her eyes, and with her thoughts clear in her mind, she began to tell Dix Artope about the buffalo soldier that saved his life, that before leaving Melroy, Davis had predicted Dix's death. Davis had said Mother Nature would poison and kill one of them. She'd thought all along he'd meant her. He'd meant Dix, it seemed.

Dix reassured her that Mother Nature had in fact not killed him.

"But she sure as hell took a good stab at it," Caroline retorted.

Dix gave a polite smile. "But she hadn't," he calmly reassured.

Caroline told him about Elzi at the squeeze, in the wagon, at Silas Creek with the owl, how the man had no reflection. Dix considered that somehow he'd just missed seeing this man back in the brigade, but Caroline said with great conviction that he rode alongside Dix in the wagon from the squeeze in the mountainside all the way to Element Dale. Dix had been near death for that ride. It was possible he'd never woken to witness the man's presence, though he was sure he had. Either way, he could see real conviction in Caroline's face. She clearly saw this man, just as she had Mable, and as she had Davis. However, he noted, seeing this buffalo soldier caused her little personal distress. Nothing in the way that seeing Davis had. He could see she was fond of this particular person but struggled with the idea of it being another hallucination.

He completed his notes and then looked up. "Caroline, I see no danger in seeing this—this . . . Elzi. I imagine your mental state is still somewhat fatigued from your time in Melroy. Please consider this an adjustment period. If you start to feel frightful or confused, by all means, let us revisit this topic. But if not"—he lowered his pen and eyed her over his glasses—"if not, might I suggest you focus on the subsistence of certainty, and we shall keep the matter in my custody."

She nodded and turned to wipe her face on the shoulder of her shirt. She hopped off the table and proceeded to the door. He thanked her for coming to him, for her courage. She nodded once more and left.

He mulled over his notes. He assessed that she, without a doubt, suffered from feminine hysteria. If he didn't keep a close watch on her, on who she shared her cerebral infirmity with, she'd no doubt find herself committed. Then he remembered where they were, in this town of little resource, of little education and profession, a town yet barely a town at all. There was no one here to make such calls. No one other than himself. This town was the fresh new start Caroline had been after. That he'd been after. He was the doctor in town, the voice of educated direction, the only resource, the only true answer for all whom might fall ill in Element Dale. Dix Artope felt something he hadn't since being accepted into medical school: pride. It warmed him, invigorated and vitalized him, resurrected his ambition. People would call him Doctor here. People would heed his advice. People would respect his principle, his word, his lead. No one would whisper behind his back. Not anymore. Not here. For there is nothing for them to whisper about. Life begins here. Life starts here anew. *Thanks be to He*, he thought.

ELZI

Elzi had felt a sense of peace and familiarity in the cemetery at Silas Creek. He had even felt drawn to it. And now he suspected the reason. He was dead. All this time he hadn't known, had been oblivious to the state of his very existence. And rightfully so. He didn't feel dead. *Whatever that feel like*, he thought. A woman did speak to him after all. He thought about Miss Caroline, how it could be. Maybe she was dead too? But her fellow travelers, she was clearly a part of them, a living part. Yet somehow she could see and hear Elzi. They could not. He thought back to the rattlesnake, the wagon ride. He'd watched her bicker and protest, shame her friends for their unwillingness to acknowledge him. He thought back to their faces of confusion and concern at her scolding. He'd watched her gardening for days on end back behind the hotel, mostly alone. Occasionally Octavia would garden alongside her. Her friend, Henrietta, she'd sometimes check on her, but she never touched the dirt, a proper lady. Not Miss Caroline. She seemed a touch on the crazy side, but he couldn't deny his relief in knowing that he had someone who acknowledged his existence, even if she was a bit cracked.

Then the specifics of his existence, his whereabouts plagued him.

He clearly was neither in Heaven nor Hell. He is dead and—what? Where is he to go? What is he to do? He walked along the grassy path between gravestones, stopping for any that had inscriptions. Some had no words, simply rudimentary drawings etched into them. He missed Hattie. He missed his parents. If he were being honest with himself, he missed Albin. Regret crept in as he thought back to the Plains, to camp, to the Calvary. He had had no business going with the group after the Comanches. He only wanted to get away from the constant chiding, the pestering from the officers, their constant indignities.

He pondered the idea of punishment, of karma, of setting out to go to war with the Indians. He was not of Comanche descent, but he was half Hadacho. Was his participation in hunting Comanches with the Tenth Calvary considered treachery by his Indian ancestors? He thought back to Ora B.'s book. He remembered talk of the Sea of Night. Was this the Sea of Night of his father's people she wrote about? It couldn't be. This felt more like purgatory, not a place one strived to enter. Why was he still here?

Suddenly a horrible thought came to him. He looked down at his dusty boots, his light blue trousers. He extended his hands out in front of him and turned them over. Was this his body, or was his body in the desert? If it was true that he was dead, when did he actually die? *Where* did he actually die?

Elzi plopped down and sat at a pile of stones and scanned the boneyard, looking at all the various gravestones. It occurred to him he was a dead man sitting amongst the dead. But where were *they*? How is it they moved on and here he sat, a nobody seen by no one but a half-crazed White lady. He sat, his head in his hands, his elbows resting upon his knees. He stared down at the ground between his legs, his necklace dangling. He took the coin and yanked it. The necklace snapped from his neck. Once again tears welled in his eyes and rippled his vision.

I'm soft as a dead man, he thought.

He wiped his eyes on the sleeve of his shirt and took a deep breath. He turned the coin over and over between his fingers as he sat, wishing to sort out his predicament but having not the slightest clue as to how. If Albin were there, they'd figure it out. The Devisers would sort the situation, devise a plan. But The Devisers were no more. Anger crept back in and he reared back and flung the necklace.

"A Deviser no mo'," he grumbled.

Within seconds, regret replaced anger and he hopped up to his feet.

"Shoot!"

Elzi hurried in the direction of the necklace, but it seemed to have disappeared. He inched about the gravestones, his eyes trained on the grass, searching for the coin. A flash caught his eye. It had settled in a pile of stones, its string curled in a crevice like a tiny snake. He reached down to pick it up and noticed markings, etchings. One of the stones had a small drawing. He looked closer. It was a bird with giant round eyes. An owl, he thought. The bird perched atop a symbol of sorts. A small circle, layered upon it, an X, and surrounding the circle and X, arrows directing the eye around and around. He traced the etching of the symbol with his finger. He'd seen this before, the Yowa cross. Ora had sketched it in her book and written about it.

Under his breath he recited, "A voyage of souls. Where two roads meet. Offer your gift to the Iwa. A grail you will seek."

A whisper. "The Harvest Moon is coming."

Elzi shot up to his feet and spun around. His eyes darted to the trees behind him, up toward the creek, from the gravestones and woods beyond. "Who dere?" he shouted.

"But you must remain," the whisper continued.

He turned this way and that. "Show ya-self!" He waited, his heart pounding. "Miss Caroline, you dere?" he asked.

"You are the Watchman, Elzi," the voice whispered.

He continued to scan the cemetery, the woods, but there was no one. The whisper repeated, this time the words echoing, coming in layers. "The Harvest Moon is coming, but you must remain—is coming. You are the Watchman—Harvest Moon—Elzi—must remain —you are the Watchman, Elzi." It was the voice of the orb.

He shouted out, "The Watchman of what?" He waited. "Of what?" he demanded again. "I don't understand." He waited.

A breeze rushed through the trees then calmed. The voice did not answer. A shadow slid across the ground and along the stones. Wings whipped the air above. He looked up. High in the sky, the black bird soared.

The voice whispered, this time with a sense of urgency, "Watch the gates, Elzi. But know, it is Blackbird that watches you. Don't let him enter."

"I don't understand," he pleaded.

Elzi turned and turned where he stood, his eyes seeking out the voice, scanning the woods, the trees, the sky. Deep down he knew he would not find it. He knew the voice was from the intangible, possibly only in his mind. Even so, he recognized it. He did. It was the voice from his dreams, from one of the illuminated orbs, from the woman who held his infant body at the creek, this very creek, he realized. The voice, he was certain, was that of Ora B. Dupre, the voice of his blood mother.

"You are the Watchman, dear heart."

"I don't understand," he pleaded.

The wind whipped once more and then calmed. A cool front settling in. He waited. The ethereal whisper was gone. Elzi stood in the cemetery alone but not alone, he knew. He was a soul not quite dead, not quite living. Stuck between worlds. With the beady eyes of Blackbird watching from above.

WALKER

Walker was settling well into his new life in Element Dale, and he very much enjoyed his time working on and around The Baldwin Hotel. He'd never been inside anything so grand before, so modern. In Fort Worth, he'd seen the Texas Spring Palace but could not venture inside as it was not yet open to the public. The Baldwin wasn't technically open to the public either, but it definitely had its fair share of traffic.

The renovation and revitalization efforts raced against time as the goal of the Phillipses was to host the kickoff of the Harvest Festival on the hotel's grand entrance steps and then immediately open its doors to the public, inviting them in for tours. Walker expected the public would be in absolute awe of the beautiful lobby and ballroom, its grand staircase, the stylish rooms, the mezzanine and, best of all, the rooftop ballroom they dubbed The Nest, located at the pinnacle of the forty-foot tower. Walker had watched as engineers came and went, built their massive boiler systems in the basement, ran conduits and pipes throughout every room, every floor, connecting the water from the well out back to the boiler and to a tank system which fed to the pipelines throughout the hotel. It was extravagant and complex.

When Walker inquired about the purpose for the basement boilers and lines everywhere, Lawton started to reply, but Claire enthusiastically cut him off: "The entire hotel is to be illuminated by electricity, and guests shall be able to turn the lights in their rooms on and off at will."

Walker at first laughed. *What a notion*, he thought. But when he saw the shit-eating grin on Lawton's face, he knew Claire had been serious.

Walker asked, "What do you mean lights?"

"Glass bulbs," Claire answered. "Each a source of light to be powered with electricity generated from the boilers."

Lawton added, "And the lifts are to be completed this coming weekend."

"Lifts?" asked Walker.

Claire said, "To carry our guests up to their rooms. And to The Nest, of course."

The Phillipses promised him the opening would be nothing shy of spectacular, more than the imagination could even fathom. They hired photographers and invited journalists from around the country. The Baldwin was to be an absolute exhibition of luxury and the entire country would soon know its name. It would put Element Dale on the map.

Walker nodded and quietly listened as the couple went on and on about how everyone who is anyone would soon vie to stay at The Baldwin. The hotel was grand, impressive—innovative, really. Lightyears ahead of any local modernity. Even so, other than experiencing steam-generated electricity and indoor plumbing for a night or two, once someone had taken in the beautiful Spanish-Colonial architecture and danced in the ballroom and had a handful of meals, there wasn't much else for the town to offer. He knew that the railroad expansion would pass nearby in the future and that commerce was likely to follow, but that seemed like it was years in the making, that this grand reopening might be a touch premature.

Walker had agreed to work as the hotel's hostler, employed to look after any horses belonging to guests. Until the opening, he was simply a general handyman, there to assist any contractor with any needs he might have. He also helped out Dr. Artope anytime he needed. But he wanted more. He was used to being his own man, creating, crafting, negotiating, running a business. Being the Georgian crew's lackey and gopher guy wasn't going to cut it.

Dix Artope opened his medical office, located on the west side ground level of The Baldwin, to the public with little fanfare. The group had wanted to celebrate its opening, his officially becoming a private practicing physician, but Dix would have nothing of it. Walker took notice of Dix's humble nature when it came to celebrating his practice. Self-effacement looked good to Walker, but money looked better. He could see that Dix had a passion for healing but no penchant for profit. Walker had halfheartedly pitched the idea of selling healing water alongside his medicinal elixirs and the doctor hadn't given it a second thought. But he still believed that somehow they should be able to figure a way to use Dr. Artope's credentials and Walker's knowledge of the peculiar waters to their favor, for profit. The quandary stuck with him day and night as he turned over the possibilities in his mind.

And then it hit him. The well-digger. Sterling. If he could get Sterling to ensure the hotel's water well tapped into the same source as the peculiar water that healed Paulette Nelson's old lady of her lunacy, then he could pitch to Lawton and Claire the idea of healing pools. Back on the mountain, his hoboing uncle had bragged once about sneaking into a bathhouse below Lover's Leap outside of Asheville. He'd said the bathhouse had eight four-foot-deep, marble-lined tubs and that rich folks went there and stayed upwards of three weeks sometimes just soaking, eating healthy foods, getting hands-on body treatments by medical gymnasts—all because they'd suffered various unseen ailments. Walker had, at the time, thought his uncle full of shit and said so. But the more he hung around the Phillipses, the more he learned just how entitled and extravagant the world could be, that rich folk paid plenty to feel elevated and allowed a certain prestige not available to others, treatments unmatched by the average medical remedy. How to spin it so that he played a vital role in the equation was the catch.

He muttered, "And how the hell I'm ever a-gonna convince that mute to help is beyond me."

One of his jobs to complete before the festival and grand reopening ceremony took place was to address the unsightly single brownstone obelisk that stood phallic and awkward where the hotel's exclusive courtyard was to be. The obelisk was installed some years back, when The Baldwin was The Barron Inn. Baker and Eleanor Eddington, the then owners, had, along with the townspeople, erected the memorial in honor of Elliot Ashworth, the original property owner.

The Baldwin Hotel began as a one-room cabin built in 1840 by Ashworth, one of the co-founders of Element Dale. Ashworth was an original Texas Ranger who fought during the state's battle for independence from Mexico. He received a plot of land as reward for his service to the Republic of Texas. He built a basement under his cabin to serve as an Indian raid shelter and jail when needed. Ashworth died tragically while holding outlaws Benny and Etta Benson. The Bensons were wanted for robbing the Union Pacific train of 70,000 dollars' worth of gold coins. While on the run, the two robbed and murdered across Texas. They stopped off in Element Dale where former Ranger Ashworth, who served as the town sheriff, postman, jailer, and local preacher, spotted them. When he did not show for Sunday service, locals grew concerned. They found him in the underground jail. He had been brutally murdered: robbed, scalped, and stabbed over thirty times. Rumor had it his dog was a victim of the heinous attack as well, found dead beside him, its throat cut so deeply it was all but guillotined.

At first the town panicked, believing Indians would be sneaking into their homes during the night, and so they remained sheltered for days. Later, after the people believed it safe, thinking the Indians had moved on, they returned to the cabin for a thorough inspection. On his desk, they found a small stack of letters. Among them was a telegram from Ashworth to the Texas Rangers, written to inform them of the arrest and imprisonment of two of the most wanted outlaws of the day. Law enforcement later caught up with Benny and Etta Benson where they shot and killed them in a shootout. The townsfolk buried Ashworth behind the cabin, now the hotel, next to his dog.

And now he needed to be moved, relocated to the cemetery.

"Where the dead belong," Claire added after Lawton made his request. She wrinkled up her nose and dusted her hands as if the very words soiled her.

Walker nodded, agreeing to the task, but cursed the couple in his mind. He thought back to his time in Gem City, Georgia, to the supposed cesspool he'd dug in exchange for a night's room and board. He knew, with every fiber of his being, that he'd not dug a cesspool but rather the grave for some poor soul, never to be seen again, placed most discreetly under a lovely bench with flanking flowerpots. Along with moonshiner, handyman, and hotel hostler, he could now add glorified gravedigger to his skill set.

Thirteen hours passed from the time Walker stabbed the earth with his shovel for the first time until he finally gave up.

"He ain't here, Lawton," he said, dripping sweat and heaving with exhaustion. The two men stood in the twilight side by side scanning the destruction. The earth before them had been turned over as if a team of giant feral moles had come and uprooted the land for the deepest grubs they could find. Massive holes flanked by massive mounds of dirt.

Lawton shook his head. "Well, what the hell are we going to do?"

Walker leaned on his shovel. His back ached. His hands cramped and stung with blisters. Dirt streaked his white hair. "Tell you what. You go on in. I'll take care of it. He's around here."

Lawton continued to shake his head with a look of defeat and disbelief on his face.

"Go on," Walker said. "I got it. He'll be resting in peace up at the Silas Creek boneyard come sunup, guarantee ya."

"I hate to think of you out here, all night digging," Lawton said.

"Think nut'in of it. It's what I'm here for." He nodded to Lawton. "Come sunup."

Lawton nodded back, hesitant to leave, but not so worried for Walker's sake to grab a shovel and pitch in, Walker noted. Lawton reached out and gave him a hefty pat on the back, nodded once more, and headed back up to the hotel. Walker stood, still leaning heavy on his shovel, taking in the sight of all the dirt. In the distance above the trees, a lilac afterglow bathed the sky high above the fading light of a brilliant early fall sunset. Full darkness was soon to come. He took a deep breath, wiped his brow, and began shoveling once more.

Within six hours, he'd come to a stopping point. Within seven, he'd dumped the obelisk over onto a sled harnessed behind a horse and dragged it out of the courtyard and into the thoroughfare. The town slept. All was quiet save the grinding scrapes the sled made as Walker's horse dragged it toward the cemetery.

When he finally laid his dirty head down at the Nelson House, the sun was just rising. He closed his eyes and drifted off, his mind completely blank, and slept like the dead.

CAROLINE

Morning rays of pink and orange warmed Caroline's face. She opened her eyes and stretched. She looked around her room, its style simple and clean. The walls alive with beautiful roses of cream and yellow against a pale green backdrop. She smiled, delighted. It had been weeks and weeks since she'd last awakened to the horrible sound of Davis hanging above her bed. Relief and gratitude filled her, and she flung the blanket from her body and sprang out of bed. Coming to Element Dale had been the key. She could finally move on.

She dressed and made her way down to the kitchen. The smell of Octavia's cooking filled the air. A grand breakfast for them all.

She pulled up a chair in the dining room next to Dix. "Good morning, Doctor." She grabbed a napkin and draped it across her lap.

Dix reached for the coffee and poured her a cup. "Good morning to you."

Henrietta, relieved to see her friend chipper again, said, "Chuck, you have been looking so . . . blooming and full of vigor lately. Is your gardening treating you well?"

Before she could answer, Dix jumped in. "The outdoors does

supply one a wholesome level of fresh air and Vitamin D. And sleep really helps the body in ways we can't even imagine, particularly uninterrupted sleep."

Caroline nodded, squirreling her bite of toast into her cheek. "I can't say that my sleep has been uninterrupted, though my garden"—she looked to Claire and amended her words—"working in the hotel's garden always brings me comfort and a sense of well-being."

Claire said, "Caroline, how do you keep it so . . . healthy? Anything I've ever attempted was either burned up by the sun or eaten by pests."

Caroline replied, "Oh that's easy. First you got to place your plants where they make sense, where there's shade if they need or sun if not. And then I'll tell you my secret for pests: sprinkle you some dried, crushed-up chrysanthemum heads all around. And dead fish."

Claire's hand shot up to cover her mouth.

"That'll do the trick. Just cut up some fish and bury the bits at the base of your plants. Natural fertilizer."

Claire removed her hand and then feigned delight in having learned such a thing. A futile gesture, Caroline thought, as if Claire Phillips would be caught dead on her hands and knees in the dirt. Caroline said, "Say, Claire"—she looked around the dining room—"is that family of yours or Lawton's that is staying here? Are they coming to breakfast?"

Claire furrowed her brows and slightly tilted her head. "Pardon me?"

"The family staying over. I'm assuming they are personal guests of yours and Lawton?"

Claire turned and looked to her husband. The two exchanged a confused look and then turned back to Caroline.

Caroline crammed a piece of bacon in her mouth and continued as she chewed. "Not that I'm complaining. My sleep has been excellent most nights. But I guess last night the guests were back?"

The room grew quiet. People looked from one to another searching for an answer.

Finally Henrietta spoke. "Chuck, what family is it you are referring to?"

"I guess whatever family it is with the little girl. I don't know who they are. That's why I ask." She finished chewing and swallowed, allowing herself a beat or two to check her tone. She could hear the irritation in her own voice. "They're really no bother. Well, the girl can be. She's a little night owl. Likes to do her acrobats and twirling up and down the halls at hours inappropriate for anyone, much less a child." She paused and glanced at Claire, fearful of offending. But Claire had no look of being offended on her face. Only a look of total perplexity.

Octavia, standing behind Ford, leaned over and set a big bowl of steaming grits on the table. Caroline locked eyes with her, and suddenly she knew. She quickly changed the subject.

"Less than one month until the grand reopening. You all have worked hard to help get this hotel ready and I, for one, cannot wait to see the final touches, the guests file in, and the look on all their faces when they do." She smiled and shoved another piece of bacon into her mouth. The others smiled as well, but the awkward uneasiness continued to dampen the room. She held her coffee cup up in the air and said, "To The Baldwin."

The others returned in kind, "To The Baldwin."

As they were clinking their glasses of juice and coffee, a dirty but oddly elated Walker Westberry walked in.

"What are we a-celebrating?"

Lawton stood. "Walker, my fine fellow, please pull up a seat."

Walker held up a hand. "No need. I don't intend to intrude on your breakfast. And I ain't much fit to be sitting in a crowd no how." He gestured at his clothes, filthy with soil.

Caroline turned in her seat to see what Walker was referring to. "What on earth?" she exclaimed.

"More like what in earth," Walker returned. He stood in the doorway smiling, but also looking like he hadn't slept or bathed in ages and grimaced from time to time as if any movement brought him great pain.

Caroline said, "You look like you've been dragged behind a plow mule."

"Feel like it too," he chuckled. He raised his head as if to speak over her and directly to Lawton. "Say, when you finish up in here, mind coming out back? You too, Doc." He did not wait for an answer but turned and slowly hobbled away.

Lawton set his coffee down and stood. Caroline could see a bit of concern in his face. "What is it?" she asked.

He gestured with a quick head jerk to Dix. "It's nothing," he said. He addressed the table, "Please, enjoy breakfast."

Dix scooted his chair back and leaned forward, bracing himself against the table as he pushed to stand. He grabbed his cane and followed Lawton to the door.

Ford said, "Dix, might I help you with something?"

Dix shook his head. "I'm uncertain as to what I might need help with, Ford. Have your coffee. I'll return momentarily."

The two men left, leaving the others sitting curious and quiet at the table. Caroline finally broke the silence. She threw down her napkin, pushed her chair out, and shot up. "Well, I ain't gonna just sit here staring at the likes of you guys."

Ford said, "Chuck, maybe just let them handle whatever is it that's needing handling."

"Something's up," Caroline replied. She took one last drink of her coffee, slammed the cup back down, and left.

When she stepped out onto the back veranda overlooking the future courtyard, she couldn't believe her eyes. Yesterday the area looked as she figured it had for the past years, save her garden addition. This morning, it seemed every inch of earth had been turned over and moved, like some type of excavation site. A single layer of brick outlined the entire area, separating the hotel's courtyard from the bordering streets. Her garden sat in the far back northwest corner, just as she'd left it, except now it also had a single row of bricks separating it from the rest of the courtyard. The lone obelisk that stood in the far northeast corner was gone, and in its place was a massive circular hole approximately four-feet deep and lined with the same bricks that created the courtyard borders.

Lawton and Dix stood in awe, neither speaking a word. Walker stood proud, clearly waiting for someone to acknowledge his efforts. Caroline took it upon herself to start the conversation.

"What in the hell is all this?"

The three men turned to her. Walker's smile instantly fell.

Dix added, "Yes, Walker, what is it we're looking at here? This is your doing?"

"Well, I was digging here, looking for—"

Caroline could see Lawton and Walker lock eyes for a moment.

He continued, "I was cleaning up a bit back here, and like me and Doc here was talking before, we really got something here with the water."

Lawton furrowed his brows. "The water?"

Caroline heard Dix let out a small sigh under his breath.

Walker continued, "The water, yes. Seems Elemdale's got peculiar water, water that's like medicine. Cured Paulette's momma right up."

Caroline asked, "Paulette?"

"Lady that runs the inn. Anyhow, her old lady done gone plum nuts. Drank the peculiar water. Fixed her right up. You can ask Paulette and Clifton about it. Said not all the water's peculiar, but some is. Just got to find it."

Dix said "Walker, I'm not following. And we've talked about this."

Walker interrupted, "Yes, I believe we have, Doc. But I also believe we didn't bring our talk to its rightful completion." He looked at Lawton. "The water heals folks. And I was thinking maybe me and the doc here could bottle some up and sell it to his patients right outta his office there."

Caroline narrowed her eyes and stared Dix down. "Well, Doc, pretty certain water is about as natural as seeds." She crossed her arms. "I'm guessing your modern-science pharmaceutical bullshit only steps aside if and when it's a man that stands to gain?"

Dix said, "Stands to—what?" He turned to Walker. "Walker, if I wasn't clear before, please, let me be now. I can't sell simply water to people needing medicinal assistance. It doesn't comport with my Hippocratic oath. I'm sorry if I wasn't clear earlier."

Walker's smile returned. "No worries, Doc. I understand you ain't fully wrapped your mind around what I'm suggesting. Which is why I figured we could bring in ole Lawton here." He gave Lawton a hefty whack on the back.

Lawton coughed. "I'm afraid I too am not following, Walker. What does all this have to do with the courtyard?" He leaned in close and said, "And I'm assuming our project yesterday was a success?"

Walker said, "Oh yeah. A success. Don't you worry with that."

Caroline asked, "Worry with what? What project? Lawton, you know about all this? And what on earth is it? Walker, what's with the giant hole?"

Walker held up his hand to Caroline, a bit too close to her face for her liking. She swatted his hand away. He smirked and said, "Now, now. Don't go getting your feathers ruffled, little lady. I might could get my point out there if you'd mind your mouth for two seconds."

"I'll mind whatever I damn well choose," she scoffed.

Lawton interrupted. "Walker, please. What is this? I don't believe this is what I asked of you."

"It is not," Walker agreed. "But you'll thank me, I promise." He turned to the courtyard and held his hands out before him, his hands forming a frame from which to view the land. "Picture this. The row of brick outlining the yard there, build 'em up about six feet or so. Then cain't no one gawk from the street. Guests have the courtyard to themselves, a private sanctuary, if you will." He shifted his frame to the northwest corner. "This here garden, let it be. Chuck here can continue to dig in her dirt all she want. But maybe put a special effort into her plants that's remedies too." He floated his frame slowly across the area. "The yard here, I see it having purty grasses and flowers, some walking paths that lead to a bench here and there to sit. Maybe a table or two tucked away in some trees and bushes. Give 'em some privacy. One thing the mountain gots that Elemdale don't seem to is privacy afforded by nature."

"The mountain?" asked Caroline. "What mountain in Georgia you grow up on?"

Walker cleared his throat. He floated his hand frame over to the far northeast corner where the massive circular void was. He cracked a smile from ear to ear. "And here—you'll have to really think on it to see it—but here will be a healing pool." He dropped his frame and turned back to face Lawton, Dix, and Caroline. "They's a bathhouse back home that I once took to. One rich folks come to. It had eight four-foot-deep pools like that but lined in marble and enclosed for privacy. People's naked inside, au naturel, you see. People went there and stayed upwards of three weeks sometimes, for what you call convalescence, just soaking in the water, eating healthy foods, getting body treatments by medical gymnasts."

Caroline eyed Walker. She said, "Wait. Where was this? I don't know of any such place in Georgia."

Walker frowned back at her. "Not the point."

Caroline could see Dix shaking his head. She took it as a sign and ran with it. "Walker, I don't know what you got going here, but we didn't come all this way to set up a hotel to swindle the folks of Elemdale."

Walker raised his voice, "Ain't no one talking a you, woman. And ain't no one talking nothing about no swindling neither."

Caroline's jaw dropped. She took a step forward, ready to light into this arrogant, filthy man she knew deep down was a con. Dix gently touched her shoulder. She turned and saw his face. He subtly shook his head no. His eyes spoke to her, said that all was okay, that she needn't worry.

Lawton said, "Walker, go on."

"Go on?" Caroline said incredulously.

Lawton shot her a look. "Yes," he said sternly, "please go on."

Walker grinned at Caroline while he spoke and his words crawled all over her. "Yes, Lawton, the water, I guess, was peculiar in that it had elements in it that were natural medicines. The place there called the water a blessing in affliction. People from all over the country come there just to sit in those big marble holes hoping to fix their gout and stiff joints. I heard people talking 'bout clearing their blood of any poisons, their minds of any hysterical affliction." He eyed Caroline with those words.

Lawton asked, "And I guess you paid a sum to enter the baths?"

"A hefty sum," he lied.

The group stood silent, taking in the upheaved courtyard and Walker's proposal. Caroline herself felt torn. She did believe in the power of natural healing, of the remedies plants provided. If she were honest, she couldn't ignore the fact that water had its own way of reviving the body just as plants did. She thought about how she felt every time she took a dip in the river. She thought about the one time she'd been to the Atlantic, how just being in the ocean's presence soothed her, the sound of the waves calming her nerves. How she'd experienced invigoration when submerged in the water. How her skin felt after a swim, so soft and smooth. Just thinking about the water seemed to bring about a calmness, but then when she considered the source of the subject, she bristled. The idea of Walker Westberry peddling water as some sort of elixir didn't sit well with her.

"Peculiar Water, that's what we could call it." Walker nodded his head. Satisfaction spread across his face as he continued. "Westberry's Peculiar Water or"—he turned back to the yard and held his arms out in grand fashion—"West Water, Curative Waters of Elemdale." He turned back to the group. Lawton, eyebrows raised, nodded his head. Dix scratched his chin, deep in thought. Caroline looked from man to man, disappointed as she saw the acceptance creeping in.

Caroline corrected, "It's Element Dale. Pretty sure if you think you're gonna sell a thing, you might want to at least name it correctly." Walker ignored her.

Dix asked, "Walker, how can you be certain the well the hotel's got here possesses the water you speak of? We can't just say any water is curative. Though I don't know that I yet feel comfortable with that word curative at all as it pertains to water. But on any account, how can we be certain this well here has the elements you say the Nelsons' well has?

Walker thought a moment and replied, "You just sleep on it for now, get your head around the idea of water as a business venture. I got the plan and just the man to tend to the well question. Alls I need is a place to showcase the good thing we got going on here." He looked at Dix and said, "And a doctor who'll vouch."

"We?" asked Caroline. "I don't see how this is a *we* thing. I mean, you're proposing to use the hotel's well, Dix's clinic, and slap your name on it?"

"Both a which weren't gonna see no benefit without my innovation, my idea. So yeah, my name. And *we*."

She gave a sarcastic laugh. "It's only an idea, a pipe dream. And a ridiculous one at that!"

Walker ignored her, speaking directly to the men. "Sleep on it. I'll get back to you tomorrow with a solid plan. Remember, my idea made someone else a rich man in the beverage business. I'm thinking it's time I made all of us rich men."

Caroline retorted, "Coca-Cola? Seriously? You expect us to believe—"

Lawton held up his hand to interrupt her. He said, "We'll think on it. We've not got much time, though, before our grand event. So whatever we decide, we've got to act fast." He turned to Dix and said, "Please give it some real thought. I could see this being a good thing for the hotel, for your clinic, for Element Dale. Another possible draw from the surrounding cities, states even." He clapped his hands as if to signal the ending of their meeting. "I'll put together a few service offerings we could present to guests staying at the hotel—or even just visitors stopping by. A tour with benefits. I don't know. I'll think on it. Dix, you think on it too. Walker, I need a solid plan for construction on this courtyard by tomorrow as well as some type of word that we can comfortably advertise our water here as something curative or healing in some way. I would like confidently stand behind any type of service or product The Baldwin is associated with."

Walker said, "Got it." He turned to Dix. "Say, your brother's a land surveyor, ain't that right?"

Dix replied, "He is indeed. For the railroad."

Walker grinned and turned back to Lawton. He snapped his fingers and pointed at him. "On it." He turned to Caroline and winked. Rather than pointing at her as he did with Lawton, he pulled a trigger to his imaginary gun and gave a glottal click with his tongue.

Caroline rolled her eyes. "Ass."

DIX

As he'd done for the past many years, Dix woke early, before first light. Per usual, he sat at the edge of his bed and fired up the lamp for his session of Bible roulette, words from the Lord to contemplate while performing his morning gymnastics. This morning, he was guided to the fifth chapter of John: *After this there was a feast of the Jews; and Jesus went up to Jerusalem. Now there is at Jerusalem by the sheep market a pool, which is called in the Hebrew tongue Bethesda, having five porches. In these lay a great multitude of impotent folk—of blind, halt, withered—waiting for the moving of the water. For an angel went down at a certain season into the pool and troubled the water; whosoever then first, after the troubling of the water, stepped in was made whole of whatsoever disease he had. And a certain man was there, which had an infirmity thirty and eight years. When Jesus saw him lie and knew that he had been now a long time in that case, he saith unto him, Wilt thou be made whole? The impotent man answered him, Sir, I have no man, when the water is troubled, to put me into the pool, but while I am coming, another steppeth down before me. Jesus saith unto him, Rise, take up thy bed, and walk. And immediately the man was made whole and took up his bed and walked; and on the same day was the sabbath.*

He closed the book and sat. He did not immediately rise to stretch and move; rather he remained still, conflicted in his heart. God's timing was always true, this he knew. His words, however, weren't always the easiest to unravel. Was he to believe this a sign? That peculiar water could bring those to Element Dale, for him to do good, to use his God-given gift of healing unto? Or did the water represent false hope, false idolatry even? That those seeking healing from the water were never going to find healing but for placing their faith in Jesus Christ? He thought about the words God had revealed to him some days before his decision to leave Melroy: *No one can serve two masters, for either he will hate the one and love the other, or he will be devoted to the one and despise the other. You cannot serve God and money.* What if Walker was on to something and the water made them all rich? He sat the book aside and stood. He needed to go for a walk and really think. He dressed, grabbed his cane, and left The Baldwin.

He stepped out into the cool, crisp air. There was a slight breeze. All was quiet save a few birds that chirped, just waking for the day. He walked along the main street, heading west from the hotel. Passing the mercantile he continued on, now subconsciously following a trail created by ruts in the street, by something having been dragged. The words he'd read lingered in his mind. Still unsure as to their meaning, he whispered as he walked, "Lord Jesus, please show me the way. It is your will I seek."

He continued along the street, the dead end ahead approaching. Most times, his Bible roulette seemed as random as one would think. But then other times, the words his Lord guided his finger to were, no doubt in Dix's mind, a direct message from God. Today was one of those days. The message spoke to the topic of using the peculiar water, he just knew it. The problem was he couldn't work out if it was a sign for or against it. *If only I had a sign,* he thought. Immediately shame crept in, for the Lord had just given him a sign and he was apparently too dense to understand it. He stabbed his cane into the ground and then flung it into the woods before him. "I'm not worthy!" he grunted.

Frustrated, he slowly kneeled, his damaged leg trembling under his weight. He lowered his head and pulled off his glasses. He placed his hands upon the dirt and closed his eyes and with everything in his being, he listened. Crouched at the end of the road, he listened intently for the voice of God. He needed to hear, for he believed the words on the page were only a clue. Dix Artope needed confirmation, a concrete sign from God. Reading between the lines had never been something his personality would abide. He required the concrete black on the page, not the blank canvas of the white to be interpreted at will. A tear came to his eye and dripped onto the ground between his knees as he thought about how his medical career had been spoiled and marred before even getting started back in Georgia. And then Element Dale, he thought, was God's way of preserving his dedication, the blood, sweat, and tears he'd put toward the medical literacy of healing his fellow man. Element Dale had been his second chance. And now what if he botched that too? What if the water was but a test from God? "Show me what I am to do!" he hissed. Then he listened, his eyes squeezed tight.

He sat, squatted there at the end of the road, energy and anxiety swirling within as if he could at any minute spring forth into a sprint. He waited. A cool breeze rustled his hair, but no voice from God came. He let out a sigh and placed his glasses back upon his face. In an attempt to stand, he pulled his left leg up and placed his foot on the ground. He rocked forward forcefully and pushed from his thigh, but he could not heave his own weight and fell back, catching himself. He steadied himself and then rocked forward again, looking for momentum to carry him forward and lift. Instead, someone swiftly lifted him from under his arms and onto his feet as if light as a feather.

He stared into the chest of a massive man. He straightened his glasses and stumbled back a step, startled. The man reached and grabbed his arm once more, steadying him on his feet. He offered Dix's cane. Dix looked up to find he was standing before the man Walker had mentioned. There was no doubt in his mind that this hulk of a man before him, having not made a peep, was Sterling, the well-digger.

"Why thank you, kind sir. I apologize for my start. I hadn't known I was in the company of another."

The man tipped his hat, giving only a hint of a smile. He carried a stick of his own, an odd wiry forked stick. He stood a good two heads above Dix and looked to weigh nearing 300 pounds. He turned to leave, heading back toward the woods.

"Are you Sterling?" Dix asked.

The man's lumbering gait halted and he turned back to Dix. The whites in his eyes flashed under his hat and he nodded.

Dix placed his cane in his left hand and quickly shuffled his way toward Sterling. He extended his right hand, "I'm Dixon Artope."

The man looked down for a moment, Dix's hand left suspended, and then finally took it into his own. His hand was warm and meaty and completely encased Dix's. He squeezed Dix's hand and gave it a solid shake. Dix took in the man's breadth, his wide shoulders, his stout stature. He was a beast of a man, solid. But when Dix looked into his eyes, he saw nothing resembling anything raw or hostile as Walker had implied. If anything, he saw a man weary, even a little melancholic. He looked to be older than Dix and the others, upwards of late fifties. His dark skin was lined with age, worry, and hard labor, Dix thought.

The man let go and turned away once more. Dix reached out to grab his arm but then thought better of it. Instead he held his hand in the air and called out. "Sir," he said. "You are the well-digger, yes?"

Sterling turned and held his stick up, giving a single nod.

"I knew it," replied Dix. His face lit up with excitement and a broad smile. He continued closer to Sterling, shifting his weight swiftly to the cane with each laborious step. "Where is it you're headed, sir?"

Sterling nodded toward the woods.

Dix raised his brows. "There?" He paused. "All righty, then. Mind if I join you?"

Sterling glanced down at Dix's cane and back up. Dix sensed hesitation in him and awaited a decline, but to his surprise, Sterling gave him a nod.

The two men strolled through the trees along a worn trail, and Dix carried on nervously. He had never ventured beyond the roads of town until this point, and he had no clue where they might be going. The man never spoke a word, never even made a sound. He simply lumbered steadily toward his intended destination. Dix found himself rambling, unknowing of their destination, and Sterling's input came to be unnecessary to fill any such moments of pause, for there were none. When they'd first entered the woods, a bit of anxiety fluttered in Dix's stomach—a twinge of fear even—and to ward off the nerves, he began his incessant monologue. At the time, he'd noticed the pink and orange rays of light barely peeking through the trees and it occurred to him that no one in town was probably even awake yet, that no one in town knew of his whereabouts. Therefore, no one in town would know where to find him, should the need arise.

He pushed the thought aside, pushed through his cautionary nerves, and asked, "I'm to understand that there is water, that you know of, that has some peculiar properties. Is that so, Sterling?"

Sterling continued to walk, his eyes straight ahead. He nodded.

"That's a yes?"

He nodded once more.

"Yes. Okay," Dix said.

He struggled to keep up. Dix's legs were long, longer than most with his six-foot-three-inch frame. But Sterling's steps, while slow, covered much greater distances. Dix felt like a wounded hobbit trying to keep up with a giant, and his damaged leg burned with fatigue. He took up a handful of his right pant leg and assisted his leg forward, heaving it along, panting with exhaustion. Just as he was about to ask that they take a break, it occurred to him he still had no idea where they were headed. He looked around and realized they were passing by the courtyard obelisk, the monument of Elliot Ashworth. Rather than erected upright at the foot of any burial spot, it laid haphazard on the ground as if simply discarded.

He stopped, his face contorted as he contemplated what he was seeing. He scanned the area. Various grave markings—some erect tablets with the names of loved ones etched, some simple piles of stone, some rudimentary wooden crosses—surrounded him. As he looked from grave to grave, his chest tightened, leaving his breaths shallow and quick. His heart raced and his head swam. The ground before him flashed from flattened earth to an open grave cradling the pallid and sunken corpse of Mrs. Mary Lamott.

Dix shuttered and stumbled back, tripping and falling to the ground. Sterling stopped and turned back to find Dix seated on the ground, leaning back onto his elbows and panting. Dix's chest heaved and his head beaded with the sweat of guilt. Sterling scanned the cemetery slowly. Having seen nothing unusual, he went to Dix and held out a hand. Dix wiped his brow on his shirt sleeve and then grasped his hand. Sterling pulled him up and onto his feet and then took a few steps back, giving Dix some space. Dix dusted off his trousers then his hands. He wiped his brow again and straightened his glasses.

"Excuse my fumble there," he said as he took in the cemetery around him. "I must have tripped. This cane here . . . " His heart rate slowed and his chest loosened as the ground before him appeared as it should—Mary Lamott but a mere memory, no longer before him. He gave an unsettled laugh. "Now what was it I was saying?"

Sterling watched as Dix took a few labored steps, and Dix noticed the man's concern. "I'm fine, sir. Don't mind me. It's just the leg." He slapped the back of his right thigh a few times playfully. "It's not fully recovered from a quarrel with nature." He grabbed a handful of his trousers and assisted his right leg forward. "Yep.

Mother Nature, one. Doctor Dix Artope, zero." Dix heard himself once again rambling on nervously and he became annoyed.

"The water, Sterling. That's really my intent here. I am hoping to gain some understanding about the water that some say heals. My acquaintance, Mr. Westberry"—at the mention of Walker, Dix noticed the man shaking his head in disgust—"he tells me of the Nelson family. That you provided certain water to heal an elderly mother of her mania. Is there truth in what I'm told?"

Sterling stopped shaking his head.

"So it is not true?"

Sterling gave a single nod.

"It is true?"

Sterling nodded once more.

Dix said, "Yes. Okay. I see."

The searing pain in Dix's leg was now a dull, heavy hum and he had to forcefully drag the leg forward with each step. The leg was done for. He'd gone too far, pushed it beyond its means. He stopped.

"Sterling, sir," he panted with a hand held high. "Please, can we stop for a moment and just converse? No further. Please."

Sterling, a few yards ahead, stopped and turned to face Dix. Dix stood leaning heavy on his cane with both hands now. They were no longer in the cemetery but had gone completely through and out the other side. Dix wished badly that he'd not come. He couldn't imagine how he was ever going to make the return walk back.

Up ahead, Sterling stood, his long arm outstretched, pointing to the north. Dix followed his gesture and could see nothing of interest.

"I'm sorry, sir. I'm not understanding."

Sterling dropped his head and began to approach Dix, this time his pace quicker. Dix felt a moment of panic as the man grew closer, and within seconds, Sterling had him under the arm and he was light on his feet, being assisted in the direction Sterling had pointed.

"Where is it you're—ah."

Sterling walked Dix to a fallen tree and pointed, directing him to sit.

"I see. Thank you." Dix sat, never more grateful for rest than this moment. "I really should not have ventured out this far," he said. "Not a wise choice, I'm now coming to see. But I must remember to think of my leg as my thorn. Just as Paul the Apostle so pointedly wrote: *And lest I should be exalted above measure through the abundance of the revelations, there was given to me a thorn in the flesh, the messenger of Satan to buffet me, lest I should be exalted above measure. For this thing I besought the Lord thrice, that it might depart from me. And he said unto me, My grace is sufficient for thee: for my strength is made perfect in weakness. Most gladly therefore will I rather glory in my infirmities, that the power of Christ may rest upon me."*

He leaned his cane against the tree and wiped his brow and when he looked up, Sterling had already disappeared into the woods. Dix could hear his steps, a steady heavy crunch of leaves underfoot, but he could not make out his whereabouts. Dix looked around. He sat among sycamore trees overgrown with ivy. Thick Johnson grass and reeds surrounded him. Close by he could see the worn trail continue. His eyes followed it until he could make out a craggy hill through the trees. He heard the trickle of water from a nearby creek. Silas Creek, he assumed. He'd heard Caroline speak of it. Walker too. But his crippled leg had not allowed him to take in much of Element Dale past the hotel and immediate roads. Walker had even once offered to assist him onto a horse. He could have ventured, taken in more of the area, but he had declined. For what reason, he was uncertain. Pride maybe. Fear possibly. In any event, he could certainly use a horse about now.

The sky that was once just waking up was now fully burning to life, the sun in plain view. Animals scurried from time to time somewhere in the woods around him, but Dix never spotted one. Birds sang overhead. Leaves rustled. Water trickled. The air smelled of earth and moisture. Dix tilted his head back and took in the sounds and smells, the fresh air, the brisk breeze. The beauty of it all—it was the perfect reflection of the art and creation of God Almighty.

Dix jumped as a heavy hand grabbed his shoulder. He spun around to find Sterling. Dix gasped, "Jesus. You scared me." Sterling held a large glass jar of water under his arm. He handed it over to Dix and nodded. Dix took the water and held it up, turning the jar, inspecting. "Is this—"

Sterling nodded.

Dix took a drink. Then another. Then finished it all.

The three men sat at the desk of Dr. Dixon Artope.

Walker said, "Told ya. And it'll bring the rich from far and wide if they think we got the fountain of youth here."

Dix corrected, "It's not exactly a fountain of youth."

Walker replied, "Well, I cain't say I see how's it'll hurt anyone to say as much. I mean, so what. It helps your body. When your body feels good and your mind feels good, maybe you feel like a spring chicken again. If that ain't a fountain of youth, I don't know what is."

Lawton nodded along, quietly agreeing with Walker.

Dix said, "It's a stretch, and I don't believe in false advertisement. But we can definitely promote its benefits, ethically."

Walker stood, "Doc, you yourself say you don't even know how you made it back. You're proof right there, living and breathing before our very eyes."

"I had a much-needed rest and a drink of much-needed water. I didn't earn back my youth with a sip of magic water, Walker."

"No, but you said it yourself, you couldn't take a step more. Old simple there had to carry ya. Then you have yourself of drink of the peculiar water and, *bam*, here you are. And you say that mute ain't carried you back, that you walked yourself. So."

Lawton said, "Doctor, he's not altogether wrong. A touch crass, yes. But wrong? I don't believe it's such a stretch."

The three sat silent. Dix looked around his office, at his books, his pharmaceuticals, his framed certificate. He couldn't deny the burst of energy he felt, the lift in his spirits. He'd gone for a walk for some kind of confirmation from God. What more did he need? He looked from man to man. Walker sat leaning forward, a grinning Cheshire cat ready to pounce. Lawton sat erect, nodding with confidence. Dix extended his hand. Lawton took it.

Walker slapped his atop them both and hollered out, "Fuck yeah! Now let's get rich, boys."

—
ELZI
—

Elzi watched the townspeople and migrant workers day after day from the cloistered solitude of his newfound afterlife. The hotel, a brilliant ant colony in the middle of its flat and lackluster surroundings, came alive with crews coming and going in streams. Workers rejuvenated and improved the site under the reign of Claire Phillips, the hotel's queen. A strong division of labor, some worked inside, some repaired the exterior, and a great crew of a few dozen tackled the last-minute overhaul of the courtyard. He watched as bricks, stacked atop one after another, rose to create a great barrier from the surrounding streets and loads of beautiful plants and bushes having arrived by wagon embellished the grounds. Piped ditches connected a marble-lined pool to the hotel's boiler system. Finally, workers erected a beautiful room around the soaking pool, offering an oasis of privacy for guests inside.

Oftentimes he observed the cotton-topped man they called Walker venture back and forth from the hotel to the site out west by the creek, searching, cursing, storming back to town. Miss Caroline didn't like Walker and found great suspicion in every move he made, every word he said. Elzi had come to really like Miss Caroline, his only friend in his new existence. So he watched over her intently. He took in her words, her opinions. He sat with her as she gardened, carrying on with him about anything that crossed her mind. She cared not that people sometimes caught her in the throes of a great story and shooed them away, declining any help offered, ignoring the concerned looks of her best friend Henri and her former nanny Octavia, or the judgment of pretty much everyone else.

He had also noticed Sterling from time to time coming and going, often without acknowledgment. A man in plain sight, ignored like a ghost too. Miss Caroline said he's known around town as the well-digger, that he has a hidden well somewhere, its water swirling with healing elements that Walker claims to now possess rights to and intends to wrangle in the hotel and the doctor to peddle to patrons, to patients, to hotel guests as the ultimate elixir for life. Elzi had witnessed Walker many times follow Sterling into the woods, badger him, scold him even. Walker's chest held a depraved heart—Elzi just knew it—and it made him worry for Miss Caroline, for she didn't seem to know her place among iniquitous men. So he stuck close by, a watchful eye. The Watchman. Above all else, he was lonely and lost, a ghost wandering the dale between the river and the hills, watching life happen all around him.

He knew Miss Caroline liked him too. She sought him out, asked him all about his life from before, smiled her brilliant smile at him every time they spoke, made him laugh even, something he thought he'd never do again. They shared a strange bond, and he wasn't sure if it was simply because she was now all he had or if their friendship was true. What he did know is their relationship was unlikely, and if the public could see them carrying on, it could have even been dangerous for him. But that danger was nonexistent, just as he was to all but Miss Caroline. An upside to life as an apparition, he supposed.

So far he found his new existence to have two of these upsides: the ability to befriend the beautiful and brazen redhead, and the freedom to become a fly on the wall of any room he pleased. Other than that, he fought mightily to keep his spirits up. He missed his life back in Louisiana. He missed Maymee and Pa. He missed Hattie Mae. He missed Albin. And he hated himself for missing Albin. How could he miss the damned deserter? Elzi clenched his jaw to renew his anger. Not a Deviser. A Deserter. Albin the Deserter. Albin the left-him-for-dead-in-the-desert trader.

Caroline found him at the Silas Creek Cemetery one fall afternoon, seated on the ground before a pile of stones. "Who do you suppose was buried there?" she asked. He shot up upon hearing her voice. And she tried to wave off his chivalrous and revered nature as she'd done many times. "No need to jump, Elz. It's just me."

"Yes, Miss Caroline."

"Chuck," she corrected. "For the hundredth time, Elzi, call me Chuck. Only folks that call me Caroline are Octavia—which I gave up on her in my teens—doctors, and political vultures vying to win my daddy's vote . . . and money."

Elzi amended, "Chuck."

She smiled. "I been thinking about you, Elzi. And I think that you still should go back to River City. Go find your friend."

Elzi wanted to shoot back, *that deserter ain't no friend of mine!* But he did not. He did not want his only connection to the living world to see the hatred he clung to. Instead he lied. He calmed himself and politely declined.

"He won't be able to see me no how."

"How do you know? I can see you. Maybe he could too. You won't know unless you try."

He thought about what he might say if he could say anything at all to Albin. *Why'd you leave me? Was I already dead? Did I die later, alone?* Then the worst thought that'd ever passed through his mind occurred to him. *What if Albin . . . did it?* Grief and confusion and anger threatened to surface. He took a deep breath and collected himself, focusing instead on the words coming from Caroline.

"I could be your medium, Elz!" she offered.

He considered this. Pictured him speaking to Caroline and her repeating his words to his parents, to Hattie. He thought a moment longer then asked her, "Why you s'pose you can see me?"

He watched as she turned it over in her mind. She too seemed to grow a bit anxious, even a tad angry. She set her jaw and said, "I don't know. Could be I'm as crazy as they all say and you ain't even real."

"I'm real, ma'am." He hung his head. "Sometimes I ain't wanting to be, but I am."

She asked gently, "Why do you suppose you're still . . . around?"

Elzi stood shaking his head, searching for an answer as to what he did to deserve being locked in this world between worlds. "I cain't know f' certain." He thought back to Ora's book and felt a sadness for having lost it—no, for having it stolen from him. He remembered the writings in the pages about life and death and resurrection, the Harvest Moon, the Gates, and a place called the Sea of Night and wondered if this was the Sea of Night. If he was stuck in the Sea. But he couldn't be, for the Sea of Night was a splendid destination Ora wrote about where the souls of the Hadacho ancestors carried out their eternal existence. He really needed the book. Deep in his heart, Elzi knew the book held the answers.

"I could say I'm homesick, make a trip to see my daddy come spring. You could just go with me. We can stop off at—you say it's River City where your folks are?"

Elzi nodded.

"What have you got to lose? Have you even been on a train before?"

"I cain't be asking ya to do that Miss Caro—Chuck."

She put her hand on her hip and smiled. "No one said you're asking me to do nothing." She reminded him of the help he gave in saving Dix's life and that he should let her return the favor, that he had no place he had to be anyhow.

Elzi knew she was trying to be funny, but the notion of having no place to be for eternity did not settle well. After some thought, he agreed. It was all he knew to do, given his circumstances. Ora B.'s book had the answers, the key to whatever hell he was stuck in. Of this, he was certain. And Albin had the book.

He took Caroline up on her offer. They'd make the journey come spring, though he couldn't imagine how things would even go. This redheaded White woman dressed like a man just showing up on Maymee and Pa's doorstep to say, hey there, I've got your son here with me. You can't see him 'cause he's dead, but he says hi. And then what of Albin? Would Albin, if he has his book, even give it over to her? And why would he? Rather than tending to his needs, Albin had rifled through the belongings of his dying best friend and taken all that mattered: his canteen and his only ties to his birth family. Or maybe he'd already been dead. A worse thought entered his mind.

Maybe—possibly—no. Elzi shook the thought from his mind, but it crept back in. He pictured a weary, sunstruck Albin, withering in the heat, choking out Jasper, then Luke, then Elzi. Gathering up their rations, canteens, and any valuables one by one. He shook this thought away. He couldn't have. No way. Surely not. Truth be told, Elzi had no idea exactly when or how he came to be dead. The more he thought about it, the more he settled on a theory that he could stomach, that had to be that Albin did not steal from him during a time of greatest need; rather he'd gathered his best friend's belongings, his best friend who lay dead at the base of a meager mesquite bush. He took those precious belongings with him to preserve what he knew to be Elzi's most important possession. A mix of relief and sadness washed over him. Finally. The thoughts of betrayal he'd been hauling around had been so painful, so heavy. But now that cold, dark space warmed as the love he'd once felt crept back in. He smiled.

"Well?" Caroline asked.

He came to. He'd been so deep in thought, lost back in the Staked Plains, he'd forgotten where he was. Caroline stood staring him down, grinning. A touch of mischief sparkled in her eyes. He didn't need to avenge his death or seek revenge from Albin. He just needed the book. Still needing to understand his current predicament, he knew the answers could be found between the pages of Ora B. Dupre's book.

"Okay," he answered.

Caroline gave a single clap. "Right! And once winter has come and gone, we can set out for Georgia by way of Louisiana. We can get you taken care of. And you can come see where I grew up. Oh, Elzi, you'd love it on the planta—" She stopped mid-sentence.

Elzi could sense her discomfort. "It's fine, Miss Caroline. Guess I found my third good reason to be . . . like this. Cain't no one put me to work nowhere I ain't wanting to work."

She replied with a gentle smile.

"Besides, I ain't never seen Georgia. And I got nothing but time. Albin and me, we used to talk about going ova by up north after our days were up. Say our goodbyes to the Calvary and head to New York City. Well, Albin used to say as much. I figured on just heading back ova home."

Caroline added, "To Hattie Mae."

Elzi nodded. "To Hattie Mae."

Caroline said, "I can tell her whatever you like, Elzi. I'd do that for you. Actually, I'd be honored to meet her."

Elzi closed his eyes and let his head drop. Grief suddenly erased the small excitement of an adventure. He'd never hold Hattie Mae again.

"We got a deal?" Caroline said.

Elzi opened his eyes. Caroline had a hand extended, waiting. He looked into her eyes, full of sincerity, affection, and confidence. He reached out and took her hand.

"We got a deal."

The two shook on it. Then it struck Elzi. Shaking Caroline's hand was the first time he'd felt another person in months. The last touch he could remember was at the mesquite bush. The shoulders of Jasper and Albin. Albin—he missed Albin so much. He missed home. But home was beginning to feel foreign, a place from the past. Thoughts of River City seemed to be turning into just thoughts of another place of long ago. The longer he'd been in Element Dale, the more drawn he'd felt, to Caroline, and particularly to the cemetery. It had become the only place of any comfort at all. And the thought of that unnerved him, that the feeling of connection was building at a boneyard. *Because this where I should be, six feet under*, he thought.

"I can feel you," Caroline said.

Elzi looked down to their grasped hands. "I can feel you too."

The two let go. Standing facing one another, she reached up to grasp his shoulder, but her hand passed through him. She wrinkled up her nose and they stood staring at one another, perplexed.

Elzi started to reach out for her shoulder but then hesitated. She nodded, so he continued cautiously and placed his hand atop her shoulder, cupping it.

Caroline's face lit up. "I can feel that!" she said.

WALKER

"You can feel what?"

Caroline jumped. "Whew, you scared the shit outta me, Walker."

Walker took a swig from his flask and scanned the woods. "What are you doing hanging out 'round the cemetery? You some kind of secret weirdo?" Caroline bristled and rolled her eyes. Walker continued closer, leaving little space between the two of them, and Caroline took a step back. He held out his flask. "For the lady?" he offered.

He could see her eyes darting back and forth between him and something to her left. Scanning the area, he confirmed it was just them two. *Loony broad*, he thought. He eased forward and coyly said, "Ain't no need bein' shy." He reached toward her gently. "You know, this the first I seen hair this color before." He fingered a rouge lock of vibrant copper and leaned in. She reflexively batted his hand away. He dropped his flask, grabbed her wrist, and pulled her in close. "It's been a while since I felt the affection of a woman, even if she is bat-shit and wears britches. And I'll bet you're as spicy as you look." She yanked her hand and Walker instinctively grabbed her behind the neck. "You's a feisty one, ain't ya," he said, his breath sickly sweet with whiskey.

Caroline whispered through gritted teeth, "Get the fuck off a me."

He could see her nostrils flare and her jaw flex. He held her tight, squeezing her neck. Their faces so close that rouge red lock of hair shuttered with his every exhale.

"Ain't doing no such thing," he replied with a sinister grin. He yanked her even closer, gripping her neck hard, his sour breath hot on her skin. Against her squirm, he forced his hand into her pants, and then his fingers inside her, and watched her brown eyes grow wide. Suddenly, a burst of pain exploded at the back of his head. The world grew dark, and Walker felt himself floating down, down, down.

When Walker opened his eyes, the world soft and blue blurred above him. He blinked hard and the blur slowly formed into shapes. He blinked once more and the shapes sharpened, revealing embossed beading and intricate vine motifs. He rubbed his eyes hard, hoping to clear his vision. When he opened them, Dix was leaning over him.

"Welcome back."

Walker's head pounded. Confused he asked, "What?"

"Looks like you took a tumble." Dix leaned in further and pulled each of Walker's eyes open and inspected. He held up a finger and instructed Walker to track it. Then he held up Walker's flask. "I know I've talked to you about the menaces of alcohol, but you might consider taking it a bit more seriously. You're lucky Caroline here found you. You may have bled out in the woods. Hit your head something nasty on a headstone, she said. You were in the cemetery?" Dix stepped back out of view.

Walker stared up at the blue tin ceiling and tried hard to think back. The cemetery? What had he been doing there? He thought about the Ashworth obelisk and wondered if anyone had seen it, seen how he'd just dumped it, seen that there was no disturbed ground for which it should have been erected upon.

"I's tending to som'in," he muttered.

Caroline leaned in over him, that lock of fire-red hair dangling down. Her wide bourbon eyes sparked the remembrance of sudden, searing pain and finally the world blotting out.

She narrowed her eyes as she spoke. "Yep, knocked your noggin hard out there." Her voice was oddly upbeat, light even, but her eyes swirled with venom. It unsettled Walker, vulnerable under her leer.

Dix leaned back into view. Adjusting his glasses he said, "You just rest here in my office. You're sutured up with a bit of catgut, so your wound is taken care of. You've no fracture, but I do believe you've sustained a bone contusion and possibly concussed the brain. So I want to keep an eye on you for a bit. And when I feel certain you're safe to leave, I'll send for someone to assist you back to the inn." Dix gave him a pat on the chest and disappeared from view.

Walker pulled himself up onto an elbow and watched Dix close the door behind him. It was now just he and Caroline. She stood with her arms crossed at her chest. She reached down and picked up the flask, turning it up. When she was done, she swiped her shirt sleeve across her mouth and slammed the flask down on the table beside Walker. He jolted at the sound, his head a thrum of pain.

She said, "Decided to take you up on that drink after all." Scowling, she turned and walked out, leaving Walker alone to unravel the details with only the clues of a headache and an empty flask.

CAROLINE

Caroline stepped out of Dix's office. The sun was setting in the distance. It surprised her to find Elzi waiting, leaned up against the brick. The afternoon had been eventful, to say the least. She and Elzi headed east down the road. The two walked without a destination in mind. Just simply looking to digest the last notable hours. Both were in a bit of a haze. Caroline couldn't believe what had happened, that Walker had come at her like that. More so, she couldn't believe that Sterling, out of nowhere, came to her rescue. His steps were as silent as his voice, and he managed to come and go often with little heed from others, a giant who crept along and the world all somehow unawares of his existence.

She felt deep gratitude, and she said as much to Elzi. "Did you know Sterling was coming up?"

Elzi admitted he had seen him but wasn't sure exactly where he'd come from. He wasn't there one minute and the next he was. He also admitted that he had tried to step in himself, but each attempt to grab hold of Walker's hand failed. "My hand just passed through him, Miss Caroline." He held out his hands and looked at her with great confusion, his face crestfallen.

"No matter, Elzi. Sterling was there. And I'm just fine." She smiled, hoping to ease his obvious remorse. The two continued walking, clearing the hotel, passing the butcher's shop and the church. She asked, "What do you know of Sterling anyways?"

Elzi did not right away answer but thought a moment. Caroline liked how Elzi always seemed to think before he spoke. A real altruist with his words. Well, in every sense really, she thought. She figured she too could stand to mind her mouth a bit. Back during her husband's campaigning days, before the unspeakable thing had happened, she'd exchanged words with the wife of Davis's political opposition—the cow suffering too tight a corset and turned-up nose, she thought. That woman had looked Caroline over then said, "You certainly don't speak the way you'd expect of a beautiful person. How exhausted you must be, dahlin'. Being beautiful, it comes with such preconceptions." Caroline hadn't been able to bite her tongue and took the bait. She had replied, "And it must be awful, dahlin', waddling 'round like a wood tick, living off the blood of the unscrupulous ill-repute." The woman's jaw had dropped. Caroline turned to find an audience far larger than just the wife, and her feeling of righteousness sank into guilt, for Davis would certainly find out. He would not have been pleased to hear such smut come from his wife's mouth. And she had, for the most part, proven the woman's insult true. Caroline's beauty was but a ruse, for she had the manners of a lowbred when taunted.

"I ain't knowing too much, Miss Caroline—Chuck," Elzi amended. "I know I sees him a-coming and going back at the boneyard. He ain't stopping to pay no respects, I tell ya that. Just passing through. I sees Mr. Westberry making to follow him a time or two. But ole Sterling, he somehow manages to forsake him, leaving him dopey and scratching his chin." Elzi gave a little laugh.

"You ever hear him say anything?" she asked.

"Not a peep."

"Wonder why?"

"I cain't be f' certain. I hear'd some stories. The Nelsons, they come to thinking he ain't got no tongue in his head. Say Indians plucked it at its root. Some say he gots a tongue and that actually he was struck dumb after his wife and boy was sold off and that he ain't never spoke a word since."

Caroline suddenly became self-conscious for belonging to a race that just a handful of years ago had been responsible for such acts of defilement against Black families.

Elzi carried on. "I am pretty sure he gots him a place back there somewheres. Maybe he stays on down the creek a bit. I know I ain't seen him a house in town nowheres."

Caroline nodded as they walked along. She turned back to see the sun completely tucked behind the trees now, leaving behind a wash of pinks and purples and oranges in the sky. She said, "It's going to be dark soon. I'm thinking we should head back." The two had walked just to the edge of town where but a scattering of homesteads flanked the main road. They turned to head back. Caroline said, "What do you think of the peculiar water?"

Elzi gave a chuckle.

She watched as he walked along beside her, his hands tucked away in his pockets, his gaze to his boots. The evening was cool and silent. The breeze had stopped and the only sound to be heard was that of her heels striking the dirt. One set of footfalls. She turned and glanced back. Only one set of prints in the road. She was walking and carrying on with a—*what?* she thought. *A ghost? A specter? A lost soul?*

She admired his calm manner, no doubt always forming his thoughts, running his words through his mind before haphazardly blurting them out. This man that had been there with her on the wagon trail and guided her to save Dix's life, this man that had been with her just about every day while she gardened, that had been with her and tried to save her from Walker. *An angel, that's what he is,* she decided. Her guardian angel.

She went on before he could answer, "Walker says the water will bring them all a good living. Says the water is healing. What do you think of that?"

"Well, Mr. Westberry been looking out for Mr. Westberry. So he gone do and say as he please to get him what he needs, you can bet on that."

"So it's bullshit," she added.

Elzi thought a moment. He said, "I ain't said that."

"Well, then which is it?"

Elzi stopped and faced Caroline. The two were now back in front of the hotel's main entrance. A man carried a wooden ladder and hand lamp, heading down the main road to light the gas streetlamps. He tipped his hat at Caroline and she and Elzi paused their conversation until he'd long passed.

Elzi replied, "I had this book. Almost my whole life I been having this book. Ora B. wrote it. It's like a hash of her thoughts, her history, some recipes, spells."

"Spells?" Caroline scoffed. But she could see Elzi's face fall slightly so she urged him to go on.

"This book gots all kind a answers about stuff I don't even know about. But I do 'member writings about her making her way from New Orleans to a place in Texas to come find some strangler vine and healing salts from the water, and I cain't be f' certain, but I's thinking this here is right where she come."

Caroline asked, "Strangler vine and healing salts?"

He nodded. "Yessum. Say she come on the regular to gather what she need for her 'pothecary back home. Come down during Harvest Festival and met my father—"

Caroline heard him cut himself short. "Your father?" she asked.

"I don't really know, Miss Caroline. But anyways, she met up with a Indian medicine man, a conna, and she stayed on, didn't never go back to New Orleans. And I think she was writing about the water here."

Caroline nodded, trying to take in what Elzi was telling her. She could see in his eyes that he was sincere in his words, that he was trying to offer her anything he could to help her, but she could also see a bit of sadness. "So this book, you think it talks about the peculiar water? Does it say where it is? Is it all the water around here?" she asked.

"I don't rightly know."

"Well, can't we just read it and find out?"

Elzi shook his head. He looked up into the night sky and let out a great sigh. "I don't have it no mo', Miss Caroline."

"Well, where is it?"

Elzi replied, "Albin Banks."

"Albin? Your friend Albin?" she asked.

She saw him hesitate and then nod. There was more he wasn't saying.

She said, "Well there ya go, Elzi. All the more reason to take that little trip come spring. Swing by and say what you need saying to your folks and Hattie Mae and when we stop to see Albin, I can just get your book for ya."

Elzi's smile did not match her own. The more she thought about it, the more she loved the idea of this little adventure. But she could sense his concern, his hesitation, and she itched to settle his worries. The two rounded the northwest corner of the hotel and entered the courtyard through a brand-new pedestrian gate. She looked around. All the progress, the beautiful walking paths, rose bushes, the bath house nearing completion, her garden. Before she stepped into the back entrance of the hotel, she turned to face Elzi.

"You know, never mind that mess with Walker earlier today. I don't even care about that." She waved off an imaginary burden. "This is the first time in years that I've felt—well, free. And happy, Elz." She gestured to the courtyard. "The garden is thriving." She turned back to the towering hotel and looked up. "This hotel is going to be something else. Something good. I just know it." She faced Elzi and with a glimmer of joyful tears in her eyes she said, "I think I'm going to love this town, love having a life here. Friends." She wiped a fallen tear. "I miss Daddy something fierce. I do. But I can't tell you how happy I am to be free of—of—of Davis Colley and all the judgment I get from something I can't even control. I can't control what he does. Not then. Not now. But it seems he's finally moved on. And I don't rightly know what to think about you, truth be told, but what I do know is I'll be forever grateful for having met you. For your selfless help with Dix, for your watchful eye. Mostly I'm just so grateful to have you as a friend, Elzi."

Elzi's smile spread wide, a mix of affection and pride. He pulled off his hat and said, "This the first time I felt happy since—well, I guess since . . ." He looked down at his boots.

Caroline knew he was struggling to say the words and she wanted to jump in, change the subject, ease his burden. She did not. For the first time, she held her tongue and allowed the discomfort to come and go. Elzi was a strong man who didn't need her protection from his own feelings and she needed to heed that fact.

He continued, " . . . well, since I done kicked the bucket somewheres along the way."

The two stood smiling, a sense of relief overcoming them as they both understood this was deep, a friendship in the making.

He said, "So I guess I think I may like it here too. In Elemdale. I like having a friend here. I guess I'm happy too, as best I *can* be. It just sure seems like they must be a reason I'm here at all."

She said, "Like there's something you're meant to do."

"Like they's something I'm meant to do," he agreed.

The two nodded, an unspoken agreement, an arrangement of sorts. Elzi would be Caroline's watchful eye and confidante. Someone who wouldn't judge, try to control, or change her. Caroline would be Elzi's proxy, his surrogate for messages and deeds among the living. Caroline reached out her hand, a gesture of surety, and Elzi took it. The two shook, shoring up their pact and, with it, their friendship.

HARVEST MOON

I hear the night train singing in the distance
Maybe the angels are coming soon
With the harvest moon if the river's rising
Look to the dark horizon
For the harvest moon.
—Bedlam

DIX

The Harvest Moon

The completion of the revival project and grand reopening of The Baldwin Hotel couldn't have come at a better time. Dix learned that the town—before it was even a town—since the early 1800s, and inhabited by the Hadacho Indians, had celebrated the fall harvest with a festival that lasted for three days and culminated on the night of the Harvest Moon, a night when the moon had reached its peak illumination. People since then have come from all over to celebrate, to receive gifts from the locals and to give back. These festivals drew kinfolk and allies near and far for the several-day celebration of Hadacho life: feasting, tobacco-smoking, black-tea-drinking, dancing, trading, negotiating, courtship, and just genuine gayety. Over the years, the White man pushed the Indians out, stealing not only their land but their festival tradition and sacred burial mounds from which to celebrate. This year, the town would move the opening ceremony site from the sacred mounds along Silas Creek to the front steps of The Baldwin Hotel. And it would have a new gift to offer the public: peculiar water.

Dix was ready. He'd given his practice one last once-over before stepping out and joining the budding crowd. His office was pristine, his tonics and pharmaceuticals perfectly organized. The shelving of books, including Caroline's newly published *Recipes of Health for the Home Healer* displayed nicely on the far wall, the first thing people would see as they toured his small clinic.

The sun set quickly, the moon ushering it aside to take center stage for the evening. Streetlamps blazed early, and a handful of people were charged with carrying torches to illuminate the crowd. Every festival boasted the town's central figure, that being one the locals of times past called the Baron of the Catacombs (or Baron Combs for short). Often depicted as a skeleton with Hadacho paintings on his face, a patch of waist-length hair sprouting from his crown, and wearing a cape of deer hide, the Baron was a powerful symbol of death and rebirth, guarding the crossroads at gates which formed portals to other worlds. He wore a massive headdress of feathers and beads and carried with him an owl, said to be his wife reincarnate, perched on his left shoulder. A beautifully taxidermized owl, Dix noted.

Dix weaved through the crowd. It seemed people must have come from all walks of life, people from the woodworks: the rich, the destitute, the old and young, the thriving and the freaks. Dix saw mothers and babies, businessmen and investors, farmers, tradesmen, photographers, journalists, children running and playing. Women in lavish dresses, women in unseemly attire. Whole families of pygmy stature and harelipped faces. Performers of all sorts. Chief Black Cloud, a Native American performer, rolled through the crowd atop a ball juggling bells, his tinkling performance heard over the chatter and laughter. Madame Lemoine, the gypsy fortuneteller, offered taro reading. A traveling salesman hawked Opera Puff cigarettes that "don't stick to one's lips."

Smells of tobacco, smoked pork, and fried hand pies of peach and blackberry filled the air. Dix visited the various peddlers of furniture, pottery, collectables, artwork, and tools. Some offered tastes of their local culinary goods: fried cornmeal flapjacks, fluffy biscuits, fried catfish. There were of course a smattering of peddlers pushing alcohol for whom Dix referred to as dipsomaniacs. They offered beer, whiskey, and a muscadine wine. And it was at the muscadine wine table where Dix spotted Caroline heavily engaged in conversation, laughing and gesturing grandly, a sure sign she was tipsy.

The crowd laughed and danced to folk music, ate and drank, and made purchases from the vendors. A guitar solo strummed from one direction, a fiddler from another. The silvery sound of a flute floated through the crowd. He walked and took it all in. People from time to time stopped to greet him, somehow already recognizing him to be the town's official physician and druggist. He shook hands, patted backs, listened to the occasional story of great physical ails, and even scheduled a few appointments for the upcoming week. Children ran and skipped and squealed and played, sometimes underfoot, sometimes hanging from the trees above. And then the drums and the chanting: "Seven nights, seven moons, seven gates, seven tombs." A group of children holding hands skipped in a circle around the man dressed as Baron Combs with his perched owl-wife. The Baron held his hands high and gazed up toward the moon. Others joined in and chanted to the beat of a drum, pounded upon by another man dressed in Hadacho garb and intricately adorned.

Dix took a moment to rest his leg and leaned up against a great pecan across the street from The Baldwin. He loved what he saw. The people, the gayety, the community. He loved watching his brother shake hands and introduce his bride, watching as she met with families and discussed her vision of a schoolhouse. He loved seeing the people carrying on as if there wasn't a care in the world. He loved his new town. He felt like someone respected, revered, even if it was by folks that chanted once a year to the moon.

Walker approached him at the tree. "You 'bout ready to kick this thing off?"

Dix nodded. "I believe I am."

Walker grinned. "Doc, I hope you are, 'cause we a-gonna be

busier than you can imagine. And richer, you can bet your ass on that one." Walker soft-punched Dix in the shoulder and headed back across the street, disappearing into the throng.

In the next moment, Caroline appeared beside him. She was holding a cup of muscadine wine and smiling the way she sometimes does before giving him a hard time.

"Maybe one sip to celebrate the biggest damn day, Dix?" She held out her cup and he took measured efforts to wave her offer away with no signs of harsh judgment. "Oh Dix, I don't imagine one drink'll kill ya."

"Well, it is basically diluted poison, Caroline. A slow drip of misery and unwellness."

She laughed. "If anyone can handle some poison, it's you." She held up her glass. "To the only man I know who can defy the prophesy of the dead and shun the strike of a rattlesnake. To you, Doctor Dixon Artope." She took a drink and Dix nodded.

He didn't approve of her drinking, but she had impressed him with her flattery, acknowledging his perseverance against all odds. He'd been through a lot. His education had been brutal and then his efforts tainted in the eyes of the medical community. He'd escaped the vitriol of his future fellows only to suffer the literal venom of the devil's right hand on his way out. It had been a rough road. Even so, as he looked across the street and saw his sign hanging outside his practice entrance, he swelled with pride. He'd overcome so much. And now all of his hard work, his worry, his suffering, and of course his commitment to God was about to pay off.

ELZI

The Harvest Moon

It took some time, but Elzi finally learned to exist contently on the outskirts of the living. Once over the initial shock of his new state of being, and after acclimating to the almost palpable draw to return daily to either of the two cemeteries, it had not been so very bad. The painful thought that his best friend betrayed him had mostly passed, and the anger with it. What remained were feelings of sadness and confusion, for he did not truly know what had become of Albin, nor what had become of his own natural body. As was the case with many in those days, there had been a great deal of loss.

He thought about Albin and his experiences of loss and mourned on his behalf. First there was the loss of Byron during childhood, his literal other half gruesomely ripped from his life, and now Elzi, his very best friend, lost somewhere in the abyss. Elzi had spent so much time angry at Albin that he'd not considered how Albin must have agonized out in the desert, to discover himself the lone survivor of the group—Elzi had to view it this way. He could not bear to think that he'd been alive the last Albin laid eyes on him. He couldn't bear to picture Albin leaving him for dead. He'd even thought maybe Albin had somehow done him a favor by ending his suffering. But he just could not remember, couldn't quite picture the circumstances of it all, and that troubled him.

He missed his maymee and pa, and Hattie of course, but for the most part, he'd learned to push those griefs aside. He summed his life up in two simple narratives: He was dead; and he lingered. That was it. As he saw it, there was nothing to be done about that. Nor could he see any purpose to it. The lingering dead cannot do anything for the living but watch. And that's what he'd done for months now, just watched. Watched life go on, moving forward in time as his time stood still. A stagnant existence.

As he stood and watched the festival goers, he noticed he did feel the slightest sense of belonging. He'd gotten to know the people, albeit on a very one-sided basis, as a spectator. Being dead had afforded him the grace to go and see things that he'd never been able to, had he been alive. He watched people in their homes. People at their jobs. People in the fields. People in the river. People making love, fighting, stealing, lying, suffering alone, complaining, celebrating, burying their dead, birthing their babies, causing the suffering of others. He had watched intently as Reverend Forrest placed his mouth over the barrel of his rifle and blew his brains all over the First Baptist Church of Element Dale. The discovery left the town shook, ignorant to the relentless guilt that had forced his hand, the guilt of touching his own two little girls night in and night out and then looking his wife and those quiet children in the faces at the breakfast table each morning—and the congregation each Sunday. Elzi had witnessed the horror the father brought into their room at night while they should have been sleeping. He watched as the preacher used the Word to justify his actions and silence the girls. Elzi had worried himself sick, unknowing what to do, what he could do.

One night, Elzi entered the holy man's bedroom as he lay sleeping next to his wife. He'd leaned over the edge of the bed, hands outreached, nervously poised to take hold of his neck and squeeze the children's suffering from his very throat. He badly wanted to stop the horrors the preacher had inflicted on the confused and conflicted girls who sought sleep in the room next door. But his hands would not meet the flesh of this man. Each attack swept right through him, leaving the pastor momentarily chilled and reaching for the blanket, but nonetheless still breathing. Elzi could not contact another, a living being, in the spirit of anger. This he had come to learn. So instead, he walked into the room of the little girls who'd now cried themselves to sleep, and he touched their hot cheeks and sang quietly into their tiny ears the song his Maymee Godwin once sang to him when his heart burned with grief for his lost heritage and sleep eluded him.

Dreamland opens here,
Sweep the dream path clear.
Listen, chile, now listen well,
What the tortoise have to tell,
What the tortoise have to tell.

Dreamland opens here,
Sweep the dream path clear.
Listen, chile, dear little chile,
To the song of the crocodile,
To the song of the crocodile.

Dreamland opens here,
Sweep the dream path clear.
Listen, chile, now close your eyes,
In the canebrake the wildcat cries,
In the canebrake the wildcat cries.

Elzi saw it all. He saw humankind, skins of all colors, the rich and poor, the believers and the skeptics, the old and young—he saw all their secrets, their lies, their dirty deeds. He saw man say and do things he'd never imagined before. And he saw the souls of the unrighteous dragged away by a vicious creature he'd come to refer to as Wrath.

Wrath was a feathered hound with horns and wings. He was black as night, snarling and teeth dripping, and always accompanied by the watchful Blackbird. That Sunday night, long after Reverend Forrest's sermon, long after Sunday lunch, and long after Caroline had whispered in his ear, the pastor pulled the trigger and, within seconds, Wrath had his teeth sunk deep into his soul. The hound slung him violently, delivering the kill shake—needless for a man already dead—before dragging him away. Elzi later described to Caroline, "Wrath is the devil as a snarling hound. He roams about seeking someone to devour. Last night, he devoured the rev'rend. So town's gonna need a new one."

Yes, Elzi saw it all, except for Miss Caroline. *Chuck*. He could not watch her without her knowing. She was always aware, though oftentimes forced to ignore his presence. He could not explain why, what it was about her that she was the only person who could see him. Whatever the reason, he was truly grateful. She was his one true tie to the world.

He watched as she learned to navigate their unlikely friendship, him being a Black man of Indian blood *and* dead. He watched her attempts to sway friends' and family's perceptions of her sanity. They'd talked about this many times, she and Elzi. She'd told him about her troubles, her haunting visits from her late husband, and how she couldn't quite reconcile believing Elzi could be real but then denying Davis's existence. To two had finally concluded that some things in this world were just unexplainable and that she should rejoice for having finally shed that burden, that Davis seemed to have been left behind and, along with him, his foretelling of death. Dix hadn't died from the poisonous snake bite. Nobody had died. They were all happy—and mostly healthy.

Elzi thought about this foretelling, the words of Davis Colley being a harbinger of sorts. He wondered if Davis was like him, subject to this strange existence, tethered to no one yet unable to move on, to be fully dead. Maybe, somehow, Davis's foretelling explained Elzi's passing, that it was *his* death the words were meant for. He'd offered this explanation to Caroline, partly joking to allow some levity on the subject, but partly secretly hopeful for some type of explanation for his own circumstance.

Caroline had put in a lot of thought before answering, a skill he was proud to see her actively work on.

"No," she said. "I'm certain he said poison. For sure. And you weren't poisoned, Elzi." She'd tilted her head slightly. "Or actually, what did happen?" she'd asked quietly with great caution so as to not sound crass or unthoughtful.

Elzi thought back to the Staked Plains. He was reminded of his incredible thirst, the heat, the men all around him dying. He'd responded, "I don't rightly know f' certain. I don't remember dying. I only remember dreaming."

Their conversation had brought about disturbing images. The Indian of Black and Bones flashed before his eyes. The vulture and its evil eyes, its broken beak. The head lying against his leg. The orbs. The voices. Albin walking away from him.

"I can't decipher what was dream and what was real. What happened before or after . . ." He paused.

Caroline asked, "Before or after?"

"I guess before or after I died. I just don't remember dying."

Caroline lifted her chin and responded with such confidence. "Well, maybe that's best. Maybe it wouldn't have been much of a pleasant memory anyhow."

"No, I guess it prolly wouldn't a been."

This talk had forced him to think about that awful time. The days leading up to whenever he had come to die definitely had been what he'd call hell on earth. He'd have been just fine to have died before those days and skipped all the horror. But that was then. This was now, and he was fine, as fine as one lingering dead man could be.

"I s'pose I just died from bad luck and ill-fated decisions."

"One of the many mysteries of fate," Caroline had replied.

One of the many mysteries of fate, he now thought.

A voice boomed over the crowd, rousing Elzi from his thoughts. A man hollering through a great cone announced the grand kickoff of the night and urged the people to come forward. The crowd pressed forward, and Elzi at first started to move out of the way but then allowed himself to stand in place, the people passing through him. He was beginning to get used to his unphysical being. He turned his attention to the stage. Dix and Walker were getting ready to present the water and then, following that, The Baldwin's doors would welcome tours.

A table was situated at the top of the hotel's steps in front of a great illustration. A five-foot rendering of a single bottle of water. On the belly of the bottle was a label featuring the words Curative Water scrolled in blue across a coin. And on the face of that coin was the symbol of the ankh. Elzi's mouth dropped.

"The key to life," he whispered.

The announcer boasted, "Feast your eyes on the water that promises to change your life. This water, pumped only from the sacred and peculiar wells of Element Dale, holds the key to health and healing. Element Dale presents to you Mr. Walker Westberry and Dr. Dixon Artope and their supernal Curative Water!"

The crowd clapped and cheered as Walker and Dix took center stage. Walker said a few words and then stepped aside to allow Dix to impart his credentialed wisdom. Elzi heard words like gout, sciatica, blood poisons, physical debility, mental exhaustion, liver complaint. He watched as Dix reluctantly listed off a deluge of ailments they claimed Curative Water could combat. However, the words were not the focus of Elzi's attention. It was the illustration of the bottle. The coin on its label.

A voice whispered in his ear, "It can even bring back the dead."

Elzi turned to see Caroline. She was holding a cup of wine and sporting a tipsy grin. But the moment she saw the look on Elzi's face, her smile fell.

"Elz?"

As Dix went on, the crowd gasped and cheered and Elzi stood stunned in the middle of it all, rife with disbelief. The coin on the label—it was Albin's coin. Elzi made his way to the stage, passing through the crowd, his wake a brisk breeze on an otherwise still evening. He walked up the steps of the hotel. The two men smiled and clapped along with their admiring crowd. Although Dix sported a smile of pride, Elzi was certain Walker's was of sordid satisfaction.

Elzi now stood alongside the two men, the crowd and they oblivious to him. He got close, eying the giant rendering, then eyeing and circling the two men. He approached Walker. Then he extended his hand, right to Walker's throat.

CAROLINE

The Harvest Moon

"Elzi, no!" shouted Caroline from the crowd. The crowd continued to applaud and the band played on. "Elzi!" Caroline pushed her way through, parting the crowd, disturbing person after person, her wake refilling with momentarily bothered onlookers as she passed.

Walker shouted, "And not only can you purchase health in a bottle here and now tonight, but any man, woman, or—well, anyone that purchases a six-pack earns themself a free soak in the hotel's healing pool out back!"

The crowd roared and whistled. At this, Claire Phillips stepped up, her hand held high to garner a bit of attention. The crowd quieted.

She smiled and nodded to Walker, then addressed the crowd. "Yes, you'll find an exquisite and state-of-the-art bathhouse in The Baldwin's exclusive courtyard for guests only. Should you find you wish to enrich your body with this Curative Water both inside and out, and you can present proof of purchase of the requisite six bottles, the staff at The Baldwin would gladly arrange for a visit." She gave a little curtsy and stepped back.

Walker shouted out, "What she said!" The crowd laughed, boosting his confidence and widening his smile.

Caroline continued to push her way toward the stage but the congested crowd held her back. She rose on her tiptoes, trying to find a way out, an escape. She could see heads for what seemed like city blocks. A man, sporting a red-and-white striped suit with a black top hat, towered a good four feet above the crowd on stilts. Instruments banged and tooted and strummed. Shouts to try this food and that food rang out. A photographer's camera burst, capturing the moment. Children squealed. People slammed into her, knocking her this way and then that. Her heart pounded and her ears buzzed. Dizziness crept in, the crowd spinning around her. The world shifted and, for a moment, she was somewhere else, in another time. She looked up to see Davis standing on the stage, a noose around his neck, a bag over his head. Her stomach dropped and she thought she might vomit. The crowd shifted and a man slammed into her. She dropped her cup, the wine a splattering of purple onto the back of a dress in front of her. She closed her eyes and took a deep breath, counting backward from five. She bent down to pick up the cup. When she stood back up, the stage before her was once again the hotel, not Melroy's town square.

On that stage, she saw Elzi, his hand just inches from Walker's throat.

Dix clapped and shouted over the crowd, "And here are your lovely hosts for this year's festival: Lawton and Claire Phillips! Give them a round of applause!"

The crowd roared.

In that moment, Elzi's hand swiped through Walker's neck. Walker shivered, then turned and followed Dix off the stage, leaving Elzi stunned where he stood. Lawton then passed straight through Elzi, taking his place at the podium. Caroline saw Elzi turn to face the crowd with a look of panic and fear and rage. She too scanned the crowd. All around her she saw faces of sheer delight and wonder. They were clapping and whistling. She looked back to Elzi where he stood, his face now full of confusion with hints of anger and a touch of sadness.

She shook her head and mouthed as gently as she could, "Elzi, no."

ELZI

The Harvest Moon

Elzi could hear Lawton addressing the crowd but could not focus on his words. His ears rang and his heart pounded. He stood, frozen in time, not knowing what steps to take next. He locked eyes with Caroline who stood down below, her arm outreached, summoning him to come down off of the stage. He looked back up and scanned the crowd. In the distance, he saw the crowd part, cut by the great center figure, the Indian with the owl. Elzi watched as he posed with a young boy for a photograph, a great burst of light followed by smoke.

Then he saw it. Another figure, the Indian of Black and Bones. The two locked onto one another. The Indian's face fierce, vehemently fixed on Elzi, a raggedy black vulture perched upon his shoulder. If Elzi's heart could beat, it would have stopped in that moment.

"Elzi!" shout-whispered Caroline. "Come down!"

Elzi made his way to her.

"What's going on? Why are you trying to strangle Walker? I told you, I'm over it. Besides, I can take care of myself."

Elzi shook his head, a shroud of confusion, disbelief, and panic covering him. "That ain't it."

Caroline said, "Then what?"

"The coin." He rose up on his toes, craning his neck and scanning the crowd.

Caroline affirmed, "Yes, on the water."

"No." Elzi furiously shook his head and Caroline could see the same mix of anger and fear she'd witnessed from him back at Silas Creek the day the water denied him his reflection. Elzi continued, pointing up to the podium, "Around Walker's neck. That's Albin's coin." He reached into his shirt and pulled out his own necklace and held it for her to see. A pierced, threaded, and crudely stamped coin.

"Okay?" she inquired.

"Albin gave this coin to me the day we became . . . "

"Yes?"

Elzi blushed. He'd never told anyone about The Devisers. The two were boys when they'd first dreamed up the name of their two-man club. As a gesture to make it official, one day Albin presented Elzi with a coin. A charm, he called it, something to act as the counterpart to his own coin.

"When Albin's twin brother left this world, he left behind his coin. Mr. Banks passed Byron's coin on to Albin. Albin done worn his coin since—since he was fourteen. He gave me one, and I been wearing mine since I's fifteen." *Since we became The Devisers*, he thought.

The crowd's applause picked up and then the two of them turned to see Walker shaking hands with the county commissioner. Walker stood proud and satisfied. He'd managed to win over the town, win over Dix even. But he was up to something, Elzi and Caroline both knew it. They'd always known it really. They just couldn't put their fingers to it. Now Walker wore the coin of Albin Banks around his neck. And he'd used its likeness on the label of the water.

"How could Walker have possibly gotten Albin's coin?" she asked.
Elzi shook his head. "I cain't possibly know."

CAROLINE

The Harvest Moon

Caroline assured Elzi that she'd help him get to the bottom of this, though silently she wondered how they'd ever know such a thing. She couldn't imagine any scenario in which Albin would hand over the precious keepsake memorializing both the history and voyage of his father from slavery to freedom, and the life of his fraternal counterpart. And then there was the possibility that it wasn't the same coin at all. This prospect, however, she wasn't yet ready to offer to Elzi.

She told Elzi that she'd never been more clearheaded than she was at that moment—the muscadine wine a reasoned omission, she thought—and that before she left this earth, or maybe just this worldly realm, she'd help Elzi find out how Walker Westberry, supposedly from Georgia, ended up with the coin of his best friend, supposedly somewhere either in the Staked Plains or back in Louisiana . . . or—given the current knowledge of the coin—dead. She'd already offered to help him travel to River City to find Albin and ultimately his book. But the coin hanging from Walker's neck, that changed things, added a level of mystery and therefore urgency one would expect from a sleuthhound.

She had grown to love Elzi, to see him as the kind soul that he was. She'd once felt her visions of the dead a curse. Possibly her curse was more of a gift, a gift to this soldier and son and friend trapped in a world between the living and the dead. She had only seen Davis once more, just moments before actually, but she still felt strong, and she felt a deep abiding purpose for finally having something to direct her energy toward besides numbing out and avoiding life, spending hours in a garden or turning up a bottle. It was good to feel necessary, needed. After all, Elzi had no way, in his current state, of tending to any of these things.

But she could. And she would.

She would help him find his book and she would help him get back his friend's coin, whatever that took.

ELZI

The Harvest Moon

The crowd around them settled, the people now craning their necks, arms outreached for their serving. Women draped in all white made their way through, handing out samples of the water. People took their offering, handling it with caution. Some gave the tiny cup a quick sniff before tasting. Some tossed it back as if preparing to suffer a shot of whiskey. Others sipped with reverence, their holy communion. However each consumed their sample, the result was the same: an undeniable lifting of the spirit.

The world spun around Elzi. His heart confused and inflamed in a throng of smiling, uplifted, and laughing festival goers. The sun had set, and the streetlamps and handheld torches illuminated the merry crowd, sending dancing shadows onto the street. An announcement droned on in the periphery of his awareness, but his current turmoil suspended him in fog. He could think of nothing but the coin. Caroline's voice shouted muffled calls to him, but he could not answer nor focus his eyes nor tear his attention from his thoughts. The pierced coin around Walker's neck sent an urge through his body as powerful as the draw he felt to the cemetery. He wanted badly to just rip it from the man's neck.

The drums ramped up, the crowd clapping in time with the beats, sending percussive jolts through his chest. People bounced in sync, all eyes upon the hotel. Then the countdown began.

"Ten!" shouted Lawton Phillips from the podium.

"Nine!"

Clarity of sound returned to Elzi's ears.

This time some of the onlookers joined in. "Eight! Seven!"

Elzi scanned the teeming crowd.

"Six!"

People pushed forward, passing through his body, bumping into Caroline.

"Five! Four!"

He looked down to see Caroline smiling up at him, even as people shoved and knocked her about. She gave him a gentle nod, an unspoken assurance that all would be okay.

"Three!"

That even in the midst of a mob, the two of them had each other.

A flash of memories flickered through his mind: the Indian of Black and Bones; then his Maymee Godwin reading a book to him on the front stoop of their home; the crossroads where he handed three redfish over to Albin and Byron; Hattie Mae leaning in, her lips plump and soft.

"Two!"

The sound of the rattlesnake in the cave.

"One!"

A great boom from the hotel silenced the crowd. Caroline and Elzi turned to face the podium. All eyes were on Lawton and Claire who stood with arms spread wide and high.

"Behold!" cried Lawton.

In that moment, the hotel burst to life, every window emitting electrified light. A woman in the crowd screamed and then fainted and Lawton yelled out, "Welcome to The Baldwin Hotel!" The crowd roared. He shouted over them, "The residents of this beautiful town have been so gracious and patient as we've hammered and sawed and dug to get her up and running better than ever. We are forever grateful for you, Element Dale. Now, please, if you'll file in orderly, we offer you a tour of the finest hotel in all of Texas!" The crowd cheered with excitement and pressed forward.

Caroline and Elzi snaked their way through the crowd, detouring around the corner. Elzi scanned the streets, a bit on edge. The Indian of Black and Bones was nowhere in sight. He'd seen him. Or he thought he had. Maybe he too was a character in tonight's festival, a townsperson showing respect for the Hadachos that had once inhabited this land. Maybe Elzi himself had troubled visions as Caroline did. Maybe the Indian was just a daymare, something his dying mind had conjured up in the hell that was the Staked Plains and held on to as a cruel reminder that he was, in fact, dead.

As the two walked, Elzi's mind calmed, allowing him to sense Caroline's desire to join in the festivities. "You go on, Miss Caroline."

"Not a chance," she replied. "You got real shook up back there, Elz. That necklace—"

He held up his hand. "Oh, that necklace ain't mean nothing. Prolly all kinds of folks got necklaces of all sorts."

Caroline nodded along as he spoke. He figured she was probably grateful he'd come to this conclusion. But he was certain that behind her eyes and her reassuring smile, he could sense she wasn't believing his words at all. So he tried once more.

"Really." He took the coin from his neck and rubbed it between his fingers. "Dis here ain't nothing special. Plenty of 'em, I'm sure. I just got . . . well, it just got my goat for a minute is all." He smiled, trying his best to convey a sense of calm. "Now, you go on. Go on to your folks. I's gone head on back."

She stood for a moment, saying nothing. Crickets sang from the shadows. He knew she was giving him space to say anything else he might wish to say, that she was holding her tongue. Instead, he held his words. He wanted Caroline to enjoy her night, her friends, her new town, her new community. One where but a few knew of her traumatic past, her current curse, and loved her anyways.

She reached toward his face. He took her hand and placed it on his cheek. She cupped it gently.

Elzi said, "I feel that."

"I feel it too," she replied.

Elzi watched as Caroline disappeared around the corner. The hotel was a sight. Beautiful really. He'd never in his life seen such a magnificent display of ingenuity. It was a sign of the world changing, evolving before his eyes. He was struck with the sudden urge to talk to Hattie, to tell her about the majestic electric illumination of the hotel. That was the thing about being in love. You wanted to share every good thing with your person, every beautiful flower, every funny moment, every new friend made. Maybe he could write to Hattie Mae. Maybe even his maymee and pa. He hadn't considered that before. Maybe he could write to Albin, ask him the truth about the desert. But then what would his reason be for not coming home? What would he tell them had come of him? He would run this by Miss Caroline next time he saw her.

Elzi walked in the direction of the creek, along the eastern edge of Silas Creek Cemetery. He noticed the obelisk that once stood in the hotel's courtyard memorializing the founder of this town strewn haphazardly in the leaves. He shook his head in disgust and let out a huff. "Wretched man," he mumbled to himself. He knew it had to have been Walker's doing. He made a mental note to speak to Miss Caroline about the obelisk. It was deplorable how Mr. Ashworth's stone had been tossed aside. He looked around for where the old Ranger's remains may have been buried. He saw no evidence of any such thing. "We gone have to do som'in about dis here," he said to himself.

He continued along the creek until reaching the other cemetery east of town, to the Catacombs of Hadacho Hills. He strolled under a full moon, the Harvest Moon. Crickets chirped, and he counted them out for fifteen seconds, then added forty to the count. *Seventy-three degrees*, he thought. A trick his Pa Godwin had taught him.

The breeze disturbed the treetops, bringing the occasional powerful gust. He passed by the stone of Bessie Eddington, the tomb of the Nelson boy and his grandmother, and then came upon the great mounds. He approached a rudimentary marker of piled stones. He squatted, lowering himself into sitting, scooting back to rest upon a tree. As he pondered the events of the evening, a gentle *coo-coo, coo-coo* echoed from the branches above. At its sound, Elzi's heart filled with love, with peace, damping his pitiless thoughts of Walker.

He sat for what seemed like hours, listening to the natural world and thinking about the coin, thinking about Ora's book, thinking about how it all seemed to somehow tether him to this purgatory. He had reassured Miss Caroline that his initial reaction to seeing the coin was a mistake, that there were probably many coins like Albin's. But that had been a lie. Mr. Banks' coin arrived in America in the clutches of his fist. It had only the round woven fan of grass on its face. But it was Mr. Banks who'd stamped the ankh onto its other side after Byron died. "To ensure life after death," he had said. Later, Albin had gotten him to make one for his best friend, for his fellow Deviser.

Elzi, deep in thought and rubbing the coin between his fingers, soon drifted off to sleep. As the breeze blew in his face in this natural world, he flew through the night in another, soaring like the Goliath herons he used to see flying along the marsh. He looked to his right and left as he flew, his great pale chestnut wings beating the sky. He felt free, light. He soared above the trees heading straight up into the stars and into a blackness. He circled the stars, tilting hard to the left and then the right. Free as a bird.

In the blackness, two orbs pulsed. "You Watchman, my son," a deep voice said. And then the other, soft and ethereal, "My love, do not fear."

And Elzi did not. He felt no fear. Only peace.

The soft-spoken orb suddenly flashed and then let out a screech that broke the night.

Elzi's eyes flew opened. He was not soaring through some darkness but sitting, still among the dead and buried, leaned up against the tree, not sure what to do above the dirt, uncertain if he was truly ready to be under it. The breeze rustled the trees, and the crickets chirped. Then the sound of footsteps caught his attention.

He turned to glimpse someone walking away. Startled, he leaned up. He had thought he was alone.

It was the Indian, the Baron of the Catacombs. The man in dress from the festival. Then Elzi looked down to discover a tiny owl perched atop his thigh. Her great golden eyes locked onto his.

The breeze blew once more, clearing the clouds. The moonlight illuminated the world around as bright as white daylight.

Elzi leaned even farther forward just in time to catch one last glimpse of the Baron. His great headdress hung from his hand revealing a bald head, save the long patch of hair at his crown. Elzi noticed the stuffed owl missing from his shoulder. He wondered what the man could have been doing in the cemetery. He looked around, but the surroundings revealed no clues. Nothing disturbed. Nothing left behind.

The man turned, his painted face shimmering in the moonlight. His expression one of affection, of love. He said in the deep voice of the orb from the darkness, "My son, the Gap is yours." He lifted his arm, gesturing all around. "Keep close eye on this world. You the Watchman."

The small owl hopped up into the palm of Elzi's hand. He gently stroked her with a single finger as he'd done before. The bird leaned in and, in return, Elzi lifted her gently to his face. The bird placed its head against his cheek, and in that moment, his heart swarmed with a love like nothing he'd ever felt in his life.

Her talons momentarily dug into his hand and then the bird burst into flight. It flew a giant circle above and then its wings flapped silently. It circled once more, slowing as it descended and landed onto the shoulder of the Baron, who stepped out of the light of the Harvest Moon and into the trees.

A soft voice echoed from the darkness, "Elzi, ya've heard my words. Now ya must read them."

Elzi sat in silence, waiting, his body humming with anticipation.

No more words came.

A breeze rustled the trees, its leaves spinning and tumbling to the ground. He sat back against the tree, his heart feeling full, his mind racing with excitement. He was the Watchman. *The Gap*, the Indian had said. This world, this land of the not quite living and not fully dead was the Gap. It had a name. And her words—they were clear. To go home, he must read her words. He smiled, laughter bellowing from the depths of his body.

"Yes!" he hollered out.

He jumped up and clapped a single loud clap and nodded his head, grinning from ear to ear, not knowing what to do with himself. Joy overcame him and he jumped. Then he spun and slapped his thigh and began dancing in the moonlight to the beat of a song he and Albin used to love as boys. After a moment, he calmed, slowly spinning where he stood, head tilted back and eyes focused on the Harvest Moon above.

"Yes," he said once more, this time a bit quieter. "I'm da Watchman of the Gap."

He relished the notion of such a charge, a title. *Watchman*, he thought. Not that he understood just yet what that meant. But he soon would. All he had to do was what he was told. He needed to read the words. *Read the words*, he thought. The words of the orb.

Where he stood, the commemorative pile of stones rested at his feet. He crouched down and gently ran his finger across the etching, across the bird and the Yowa cross. He smiled once again. Words he had read before, words from Ora B.'s journal flashed in his mind: *A voyage of souls; where two roads meet; offer your gift to the Iwa; a grail you will seek.* Even though he wasn't quite certain what that exactly meant, he knew she meant those words for him.

He would watch over this world, over the Gap. He would find the book. And while he was at it, he would get back Albin's coin.

The delicate voice of the orb echoed in his mind once more: *Elzi, ya've heard my words. Now ya must read them.*

To which he replied, "Yes, Momma."

JERYL LARSON: EPILOGUE

September 29, 2023
The Harvest Moon
Element Dale, Texas

Lu hollers out, "Run on out and grab some wood, why don't ya? I didn't get enough brought in, it seems."

I am absolutely not dressed for this. Not for this random cold front, not for this task. In fact you will never find me outfitted for manual labor. Nonetheless, I dash out into the cold over to the wall of stacked wood. I pull an armful off and turn to head back to the cabin, walking past the stump and ax. Then it strikes me. (Not the ax, silly. A thought.) I return with the wood.

"Lucillia, when we first met—or rather when you invited me out, in your letter you said you'd be out on the porch with your two beloveds. I'd assumed that was your husband and then possibly a dog or something. You've made it quite clear that you'd never been married, never had any children. Can't blame ya there, sister. I've seen some goats and chickens running around. Who chops this wood for you?"

She drops her hand from her hip as if it were too heavy to handle. "Well, who the hell do you think?"

I pause, not really knowing how to respond. "Mmm-Lucillia, I don't think. That's absolutely why I'm asking. Does someone come out to help you? Like maybe someone Rosalie brings?"

She returns her hand back upon her hip. "Nope."

"*You* chop this wood?" I ask.

"Jeryl, a lesson for ya: If you cut your own firewood, it'll warm you twice'd."

In-fucking-credible.

She waves me off, annoyed, with that gesture of hers: *stop asking stupid questions*. She yanks two logs from my arms and turns and shoves them into the potbelly.

I brush the wood bits from my sleeves, and we sit waiting for the new logs to catch fire. As we wait, I hold my hands out, ready for the warmth. Her cabin is drafty, not so airtight. When I'd first started coming out and we would have moments of quiet like this, I felt the awkward need to fill the space with small talk, or even leave. I was, after all, there on assignment, not to just hang about. Over the weeks, with me getting less affected by her scoffs and occasional outright scolding about my questions or how I dressed or how I held my face, I feel we've moved passed the strict editor-subject relationship to now friendly acquaintances and possibly even trusted future colleagues.

The flames take hold and the wood begins to pop and crackle. I lean back in my chair. "So Lucillia, do tell, who were the two beloveds?"

She reaches over and picks up her glass of whiskey then cuts her eyes at me. "Sometimes I don't know about you, Jeryl." She turns up her glass and empties it in one fast gulp. She wipes her mouth with the back of her hand. And then she says the oddest thing. "Jeryl, I like you and all, but you can be just as dense as the rest of 'em. I've been sharing my two beloveds with you since the day we met. I see you're finally warming up to the Texas Tea, but if you don't start paying attention to what me and old Elzi here have got to say, then I cain't hep ya."

She holds out her glass and clinks it in the air, as if to cheers someone—not me—nearby. Then she smiles her wry smile and narrows her eyes. "Elzi's decided he's okay with us telling his stories—writing 'em, that is. Question is where to begin. From the start seems logical I s'pose, but any good writer knows that's not as fun for the reader, just as reciting the ABCs ain't nearly as fun as a game of Scrabble. So I shall present my town as the mystery it's always been to me. All mixed up."

And this, Dear Reader, is how Lucillia Baldwin, me, and apparently the deceased Elzi Dupre came to collaborate on *Southern Lore*. You may or may not understand the Elzi part. I myself am quite befuddled. That inner conflict actually ignited my first disagreement with Lucillia: me proposing we market the book as fiction (I mean, obviously), she demanding it be categorized as a biography. We settled on historical fiction, though I desperately try to avoid the topic at all costs to keep her razor-sharp tongue at bay.

I believe that much like the telephone game, whereas a story gets passed from ear to ear and the details morph with the spell of imagination, what I've found in those volumes and volumes of journals is worth its creative weight in gold and will provide hours of entertainment for its players—ahem, I mean readers. I'm asking you to suspend disbelief when it comes to Lu insisting we collaborate with the late Elzi Dupre. I know it makes little sense. But does it really have to? I just need a book. And I'm willing to suffer Lucillia Baldwin's insults and spitfire nature to get it.

And so the story begins, on this Harvest Moon I am now realizing. Kismet? Maybe.

But before you dive on into the pages, babydoll, first a warning: We've preserved the antiquated and offensive language of the time, along with peculiarities of spelling and punctuation. I argued this point with Lucillia, but she would only come back with, well, if Elzi and I had to live through it, the least you could do is let me write it. I can relate, I suppose. Some of these words are the words of folks who lived long ago, before some knew any better, or before some knew but held tight to their roots, as rotten as they may have been. Having left you with this assertion, let us begin, darlin'.

Warmest regards.

A REVENANT FOR TRUTH

Southern Lore—Tales of Elemdale: Book Two

By Bebo Franklin

TIME HANGS HEAVY

Caroline unfolded the newspaper clipping she'd pulled from her copy of *A Strange Disappearance* by Anna Katharine Green and read it again for the first time in years.

MELROY OBSERVER, OCTOBER 13, 1875
THE MOST GRUESOME CRIME TO EVER BLOT MELROY COUNTY'S HISTORY

AT 1:01 PM, politician and husband Davis Eldridge Colley was officially declared dead. Officials placed his body in an open coffin in the jailhouse where it was viewed by thousands as the last person to legally hang in Melroy County.

AFTER BEING FOUND guilty before a jury of his peers, Judge Warner ordered Davis to die by hanging. One spectator commented on Davis's appearance at trial: "Guess the sleepless nights—and fear of the rope—left him looking pretty ragged."

THOUSANDS GATHERED IN Melroy's town square to watch as the man they all thought to be the answer to their economic problems stepped up onto the gallows. The event drew people from all over the South, including journalists, photographers, a variety of vendors—all looking to profit from the act of justice. A man selling postcards for the event reportedly stated: "Murder is, doubtless, a very shocking offence; nevertheless, as what is done is not to be undone, let us make our money out of it."

DAVIS'S ONLY REMAINING family member, wife Caroline Higgs-Colley, declined to comment. Her father, Thomas Higgs, spoke in her stead: "As that trap door opened, the soul of Davis Colley was swept into hell. May we all mourn the circumstances for what they are, move on from this spectacle, and get back to the lives God intended for us."

A FEW MONTHS following her initial arrival to Elemdale, Caroline's father—rest his soul—had been generous enough to send the remainder of her belongings with her sister, Minnie. Of all the boxes she unpacked, it was the ones containing her precious books that had most delighted her. That is until she saw *A Strange Disappearance*. Her heart had immediately dropped when she pulled it from the crate, for she knew what lie hidden between its pages: inked memories, evidence of a brutal truth folded and tucked away.

Now, some twenty-odd years later, she was opening the book again. She held the newly clipped article alongside that of her late husband's—another brutal memory to be stamped in print for all of eternity.

ELEMENT DALE TRIBUNE, APRIL 1, 1906
Twist in April Fool's Prank—A Bizarre Burial

UNDERTAKER CLEMENS ARRIVED early this morning, per usual, at Silas Creek Cemetery. Having spent the evening before preparing the earth for the interment service planned for later this afternoon, he was shocked to find his freshly dug grave occupied. In the hours between 11 p.m. and 6 a.m., the body of Dr. Dixon Artope of Element Dale was dumped in the grave meant for another. It is unknown as to the cause of the doctor's death at this time.

A FEW LOCAL teens are being detained for questioning by Sheriff Hartley. The exact details remain murky at this time; however, sources say the teens claim to have dragged the man to the cemetery as an April Fool's prank but believed Artope to be simply passed out at the time, not dead. A peculiar story, but the group remains adamant that they found the doctor, believed him to be passed out after a drunken brawl with his business partner, and thought it would be funny for him to wake in a grave.

WHILE THE DETAINEES are not available for comments at this time, one parent reportedly stated: "These boys ain't killers. Stupid maybe. But not killers. I can't imagine such a prank would ever have ended in a real tragedy like this. We just hope the sheriff is able to get to the bottom of this whole mess so our boys can come on home."

A MORBID AND MYSTERIOUS end to a distasteful prank. One that likely our town will never forget. Rest in peace to our beloved Dr. Dixon Artope. Services are being held at the First Baptist Church this Saturday, April 7, 1906.

MORE TO COME as investigations continue.

"Drunk my ass," scoffed Caroline. She folded up the article and slipped it into the book along with the *Melroy Observer* clipping. "You know damn good and well ain't no way Dix was drinking. Couldn't make that man drink if God Almighty come down and handed him the bottle himself."

Elzi nodded in agreement.

She slammed the book closed and tossed it near her feet where she sat. It landed on the wooden planks of the porch with a great slap.

Elzi flinched.

"Sorry," she said.

The two sat on the front porch of Caroline's modest home overlooking the Barron River. She had inherited half of what her father left behind—that being cash and the remnants of his torched plantation—and invested in as much real estate as she could, now being the largest landowner in the county. The other half went to her sister, Minnie, the now bereft widow of Dr. Dixon Artope.

"And that weasel Westberry, he ain't gonna get off so easy as he seems to think."

Elzi said, "You f' sho' thinking Mr. Westberry kilt him?"

She sat and thought for a moment. As much as she detested Walker, she couldn't actually see him murdering Dix, no matter how at odds the two men had become. But she couldn't see those boys having a hand in it either. It didn't make a lot of sense. None of it did. And leaving it up to Sheriff Hartley was a clear conflict of interest, being as his boy was one of the teens involved in the tasteless prank.

Octavia rounded the corner carrying a basket of leeks. She shuffled, shifting her weight side to side in her toilsome stiff-legged gait. Her back definitely felt the heavy hand of time and it showed. Caroline jumped up from her seat and hopped down from the porch onto the ground. She reached to relieve Octavia of her load, but her old Geechee nanny, true to form, waved her off.

"Chile, till my body too broke to tote my own bas-kit, I tote my own bas-kit."

"Okay, okay." Caroline held up her hands. "Love you anyhow," she said with a grin.

Octavia sucked her teeth. "Hush up."

Caroline placed her foot up on the first of four steps and held out her elbow. Octavia eyed it a moment, hooked her arm into Caroline's, and then heaved herself up. Caroline looked straight ahead and smiled.

"Hush up, chile," Octavia scolded.

"Not sayin' a word."

Elzi stared down at the floor, a grin on his face. The two women walked past him. Caroline scooped up the book then opened the door for Octavia. When the door closed behind them, a whisperous voice called from around the corner.

"Is she gone?"

Elzi looked up to see Dix craning his neck around the edge of the house.

"She gone. And if'n she weren't gone, Doctah Artope, she cain't see you no how. Miss Octavia cain't see what Miss Chuck see."

Dix stepped out from hiding. He was filthy, covered in dirt from head to toe. He still wore his lab coat. His glasses sat askew on his face.

"I see you done found your spectacles, sir."

Dix hesitated. He reached up, pushing his glasses back up onto the bridge of his nose. They were bent. He said, "I did. They were tucked away in my lab coat pocket here."

Elzi nodded. "Dat's good."

Dix nodded back in agreement.

The two men remained silent in the evening's spring breeze. An awkward tension filled the air. Elzi looked the man over. He had aged so much over the last few years, faster than time should have allowed, his hair graying, his posture rounded and forward. He stood at the far end of the house, still in the grass, next to the porch. Elzi stood and turned to face him.

He said, "Sir, you care for to sit?" He gestured to the chair beside him where Caroline had just been. Dix eyed the chair, then eyed Elzi. Elzi could see he was unsure, unsteady, confused. He knew the feeling intimately. He gently said, "Come on up, Doctah."

Dix hesitated a moment and then walked around to the front steps. He stepped up cautiously. Elzi could see he was half expecting to need to bolt, lest Octavia come back out.

"You all good," he assured him.

Dix crossed the porch and sat down. Elzi nodded then sat down next to him. The two men looked out over the river, quietly watching the sun go down behind the trees in the distance. After some time, Elzi could sense Dix looking at him. He let him. And Dix sat beside him, the buffalo soldier in blue, and took him all in.

Elzi took a deep breath and said, "Sun somehows look differ'nt now, huh?"

Dix turned and faced the sunset. Tears streamed down his face, the water cutting tiny rivers into his dirt-covered cheeks.

In a soft voice Elzi said, "It'll pass."

"Huh?"

"The pain and shock, it'll pass."

Dix cleared his throat. "Oh...yes. No, I was just thinking about Chuck. All these years, I never believed her." Another tear dropped. He shook his head and stared down at his feet. "She came to me. About you. I never believed her."

"Dat's understandable."

"Understandable maybe. But not acceptable."

Elzi turned and faced him. "Look here at me. Miss Chuck just fine. She always gone be fine. She tough. Tougher'n any man, woman, or rattlesnake, I tell you dat."

Dix let out a little laugh.

"But Doctah, when she tell you you gots only seven days to figure dis out, she mean it. Seven days for you to find out who done you in. Dem's the rules. Seven days. If not, you got to wait till the next harvest moon. Dat ain't till end of September. It be a real long time, Dr. Artope, to spend here in the Gap."

Dix nodded his head slowly at first, but the more Elzi talked, the more frantically he nodded.

"Took me a bit to work it all out, but dem's the hard facts. Seven days or the harvest moon. So take a moment to grieve the situation you find ya-self in, but then get your head right, 'cause you gots a murder to solve.

[Thank you for reading *The Harbinger of Elemdale* and the opening premise of *A Revenant for Truth*, the second book in the *Southern Lore: Tales of Elemdale* series. If you'd like to be notified of *A Revenant*'s release or even follow along with the work-in-progress, please visit BeboFranklin.com and join my reader community. I'd love to have you.]

A FEW HISTORICAL NOTES AND REFERENCES

***The Buffalo Soldier Tragedy of 1877* by Paul H. Carlson**
Thousands of African American soldiers fought in the Civil War, and from their efforts, inspiration was born. The United States Congress created six new and permanent Black regiments: four infantry plus what became the Ninth and Tenth Calvaries, what we've come to know as the buffalo soldiers. These troops guarded mail routes, chased outlaws and cattle thieves, protected Indian Territory from White incursion, and engaged in other civilian-related activities. The buffalo soldiers are remembered most, however, for the role they played in Texas and the Southwest during the soldier-Indian wars of the post-Civil War period. Along with countless hours on the internet, this book provided a great amount of detail, enabling me to create Elzi's experience in the Llano Estacado.

***Barracoon: The Story of the Last "Black Cargo"* by Zora Neale Hurston**
When first creating Elemdale, I started my story in the 1990s with a mixed-race boy, Frankie, who was abandoned by his parents to be raised by his White racist grandparents, also fanatics of the Civil War. His character struggled with identity and acceptance and the realities of racism. However, as a middle-aged White woman, I had little personal knowledge of any such struggle from a personal vantage point. I could only listen to friends, read as much as I could, and use my imagination. I built a character sketch for Frankie which included a family tree. And that tree's roots sprawled all the way to Africa.

Later, I created my beloved Octavia, a Gullah-Geechee freed woman from Sapelo Island, Georgia; and then Mr. Banks, the father of Albin

Banks. He is how the coin enters the story. *Barracoon* provided some background for me when creating him. The book tells the story of a freed man, who once was not. And it tells it from his point of view, his central truth, something often historically omitted. The man's name was Cudjo Lewis (his African name Oluale Kossula), and he was the last-known surviving African of the last American slave ship —the *Cotilda*. This book helped form the perspective for some of my characters and nurtured my understanding of a world I can't possibly ever know firsthand. I hope my efforts are not lost.

God, Dr. Buzzard, and the Bolito Man by Cornelia Walker Bailey with Christena Bledsoe

Octavia resides in the fictitious town of Melroy, Georgia, before moving to Elemdale with Caroline Colley. When I created her character sketch, I delved into the movements of the enslaved people, during and after emancipation. I learned that once our government passed the law of emancipation, many enslaved people in Georgia fled out to the Sea Islands and created their own economy, their own free world in a place that was environmentally as close to home in Africa as it was going to get. Of the islands off the Georgia coast, the people were called Gullah and Geechee. I learned of the Gullah-Geechee culture, tales, and dialect from this book, along with countless hours of online research, which allowed Octavia to come to life.

Davidson, James M., "Rituals Captured in Context and Time: Charm Use in North Dallas Freedman's Town (1869–1907), Dallas, Texas," *Historical Archaeology,* *Vol. 38, No. 2 (2004), pp. 22-54*

For research on the pierced coin. The ankh symbol on the front of the coin—sometimes referred to as the key of life or the key of the Nile—is representative of eternal life in Ancient Egypt. Created by Africans long ago, the ankh is said to be the first—or original—cross.

The Texas Spring Palace in Fort Worth, TX
When Walker steps off the train in Fort Worth, Texas, he comes upon the Texas Spring Palace. The Texas Spring Palace was, in fact, built but never truly enjoyed. Designed as a state exhibition meant to show reverence to the natural resources, history, and heritage of Texas, Walker is witness to its pre-adornment phase of construction. An excerpt from an article by architect Max Levy describes the plans for its exterior: "But as the ornamentation is applied, the building's curious character comes to life. The process requires more time than the construction did, and three times as many workers. Instead of shingles, stone, clapboards, and brick, the entire surface of the building is covered inch by inch with a harvest of raw materials representing every region of the state. From farming counties come sixteen railroad cars of wheat, seven cars of millet, two cars of cane, four cars of broomcorn, rye, and sorghum, two cars of cotton and wool, ten acres of cornstalks, and eight acres of alfalfa and Johnson grass. From the state's prairies, hills, and coast come four cars of mosses, oleanders, and shrubbery, four cars of cacti, four cars of cedar, four cars of coal and other minerals, one car of seashells, and one car of pelts and hides. And finally, from the ranching counties come an unspecified quantity of cattle horns, skulls, and one taxidermized steer. Even the roofing is specially altered: In place of gravel, shelled corn and oats are embedded in the tar."

The exposition in Fort Worth was designed to attract settlers and investors to Texas. Built in 1889 and lasting only two seasons, the fair's main structure was destroyed in a massive fire the following year and never rebuilt. Walker finds himself in Fort Worth some years before this actually, but I took the creative liberty and used the palace's likeness to give him something to admire upon his arrival to Texas to show him just how grand and over the top us Texans can be.

The Baldwin Hotel, Element Dale, Texas
The Baldwin Hotel is fictitious, just as is the town of Element Dale.

It was created, however, with my hometown hotel in mind: The Baker Hotel of Mineral Wells, Texas. The hotel was built in the mid-1920s as a world-renowned destination spa resort for the rich and famous. The war (and the town's military base) brought about an economic boom for the town until about the '50s. Then things started to get rocky. From there, the hotel had its ups and downs, shutting down and reopening numerous times, until finally closing its doors in the '70s. In the late '90s, a group of investors began efforts to renovate the hotel, and to this day (2023), it's still undergoing reconstruction.

The hotel, in my lifetime, has always stood awkward and gaudy, in the town's center, seen from miles and miles away—an out-of-place and decaying relic. Yet it has always been alluring, evoking curiosity and hope (and a few ghost stories). Maybe one day, I'll get to see her up and at 'em again. Until then, I thank her for the inspiration.

Currey, Craig J., "The Army and Moonshiners in the Mountainous South During Reconstruction," Fort Leavenworth, Kansas, 1994
Writing Walker Westberry's character has turned out to be the most fun for me. Learning about moonshining was even more fun. I think I've tasted actual moonshine maybe two or three times in my life. I'm more of a bourbon gal. But the lengths these folks went to to conduct their business, which they wholeheartedly believed in, was nothing shy of fascinating. As was the lengths the government went to to get their financial cut. I stumbled across this thesis paper written by a Master of Military Art and Science student and learned far more than I'd ever imagined about the history of moonshiners. Between this and the months I did devouring all I could online, I hope I did the craft justice.

Religion, Beliefs, and Spiritual Practice
I decided long ago that I know a little about a lot of religions, beliefs, and spiritual practices; but I'm no expert in any area at all. Which is

where my creative brain came in real handy. Throughout this series, you will find references to Christianity, Voodoo, various Native American beliefs, atheism, Satanism, you name it. Discussion and debate about religious beliefs, for me personally, are about as welcome as an outhouse breeze. I don't do it. For one, I don't feel it's proper manners to impose your beliefs onto another; but also, it just so very often leads down a road that's hard to come back from. However, those roads in novels make for juicy subtext; so you'll find it sprinkled here, there, and ever-damn-where in this series.

I pulled a lot from the Bible (easy enough); but my characters interpret those versus as they please. They use them for spiritual assurance. They use them for psychological ammunition. Same with the practice of Voodoo. The Fisherman and I took a trip to New Orleans and I tried to soak up as much as possible about the practice. I bought some books, researched online, took some educational tours. I did not sit with a medium psychic or card reader. Total fail on my part. Regarding the Native American references, I read a few books and did tons of online research. My favorite reference was the novel *The Wolf and the Buffalo* by Elmer Kelton. It flipped back and forth between the perspective of the Indian and that of the buffalo soldier. It's not often you get either one. Most narratives are told from the mind of the White man. So I soaked this up.

Rather than sort out all the "rules of religion" that Elzi has to follow, my characters Ora B. Dupre and Irving Whitewing brought their respective practices together to form what they refer to as Voodacho. It's basically me borrowing elements of Voodoo and marrying them with some of the Indian beliefs and then mixing them up with my own special sauce. I get to make the rules. So if you're a religion buff, you might find your eye twitching on occasion. Just be willing to suspend disbelief. It's fiction, yeah? Enjoy it.

ABOUT THE AUTHOR

Bebo Franklin is a small-town gal, born and raised in Texas. She graduated from Southern New Hampshire University where she studied fiction writing in the English and Creative Writing Program. Under her given name, she's published three nonfiction titles. She lives in Texas with her husband, two children, two dogs, and lots of books. To learn more, visit BeboFranklin.com.

DEAR READER

Thank you, sincerely, for reading my debut novel. It's been an absolute joy to dream up, and I'm thrilled you've taken the time to read it. And if you are inclined to leave a review and/or rating for this book, I'd be forever grateful!

Book reviews/rating do three things:

- You get to leave your two cents
- Potential readers are armed with valuable information (to buy or not to buy)
- And it helps the book stay alive

You can leave reviews for *The Harbinger of Elemdale* at various retailers and book sites, and any social media shout-outs are always appreciated.

Find all review links at BeboFranklin.com/LinkTree

If you'd like to keep in touch, please sign up for **SOUTHERN LORE—THE NEWSLETTER** at BeboFranklin.com.

If you'd like exclusive early access to the next book, find me at ReamStories.com/BeboFranklin.

Again, from the depths of my Southern soul, thank ya much.

Stay Sinister My Friend, Bebo Franklin